I0561639

THE WORKS OF

CHARLES PAUL DE KOCK

⚜

The Barber of Paris

⚜

TRANSLATED INTO ENGLISH BY

EDITH MARY NORRIS

The C. T. Brainard
Publishing Co.
Boston   New York

LOUIS E. CROSSCUP & CO.
Printers
Boston, Mass., U. S. A.

CONTENTS
VOLUME I

CONTENTS

LIST OF ILLUSTRATIONS

Barber

CHAPTER I

The Barber's House

Upon a certain evening in the month of December, of the year one thousand six hundred and thirty-two, a man walked at a rapid pace down the Rue Saint-Honoré and directed his steps towards the Rue Bourdonnais.

The individual appeared to be forty years old or thereabouts; he was tall as to his figure and sufficiently good-looking as to his face; the expression of the latter, however, was rather austere and at times even melancholy; and in his black eyes might sometimes be noted an ironical light, which belied the suspicion of a smile.

This ungenial personage, on the occasion of which we are writing, was wrapped, one might almost say disguised, and he looked like one who would lend his personality to disguise; he was wrapped, then, in a long brown cloak which only came down just below his knees, and he wore, drawn low down over his eyes, a broad-brimmed hat, which, contrary to the fashion of the day, was ungarnished by a single feather, but which effectually protected his face from the rain which was now beginning to fall very heavily.

The Paris of that time was very different from the Paris of today. The condition of the beautiful capital was then deplorable; many of the streets were unpaved, many of them were only partly paved; heaps of rubbish and filth accumulated here and there before the houses, obstructing the course of the water and stopping the openings of the drains. These waters being without outlet, overflowed on all sides, forming puddles and filthy holes which exhaled miasmatic and fœtid odors. Then one might have alluded with truth to —

Paris, city of noise, of mud and of smoke.

The streets were unlighted. People carried lanterns, it is true; but everybody did not have these, nor were lanterns any defence against the robbers who existed in very large numbers, committing a thousand excesses, a thousand disorders, even in broad daylight, being only too well authorized in crime by the example of the pages and lackeys whose habit it was to amuse themselves each night by insulting the passers-by, abducting the girls, mocking at the watch, beating the sergeants, breaking in the doors of shops, and annoying the peace of the inhabitants in a multiplicity of ways, excesses against which parliament had in vain promulgated statutes, which were incessantly renewed, and just as incessantly violated with impunity.

The stealing of purses, and even of cloaks, was then a thing so common that the witnesses of the robbery contented themselves with laughing at the expense of the victim, without ever running after the thief. Murders were committed in broad daylight on the squares and on the walks, the criminals insulting their victims as they departed.

There were two kinds of thieves, — cutpurses and tire-laines. The first nimbly cut the strings of the purse, which it was then the habit to carry hung at the belt; the second, approaching from behind, rudely tore the passer's cloak from his shoulders.

Vainly from time to time they executed some of these criminals. These examples seemed to redouble the audacity of the vagabonds, the insolence of the pages and lackeys. Justice waxed feeble, while custom allowed each one to execute it for himself. Duels were nearly as common as robberies; it was considered a great honor to have the power to boast of having sent many people into the other world. Indubitably this was not the golden age, nor the good old times so vaunted by some poets, so regretted by those gloomy minds which admire only hoops and farthingales.

We do not pretend to write history, but we have thought it necessary to recall to the reader the state of Paris at the time in which our barber lived. Undoubtedly he has already divined, by the title alone, that the story is not of our time; for now we have in Paris many artistes in hairdressing, many coiffeurs, and many wigmakers, but we have no longer any barbers.

The individual whose portrait we have just drawn, having reached a corner of the Rue des Bourdonnais, stopped before a pretty house on which was written in big letters, "Touquet, Barber and Bathkeeper." At that time the luxury of signs was not known, and the streets of Paris did not offer to the consideration of loiterers a character from Greek or Roman history at the front of each grocer's or haberdasher's shop. The portrait of Mary Stuart did not invite one to go in and buy an ell of calico; nor did Absalom, hung by the nape, indicate to one that he was passing a hair-dresser's parlors. We have made great progress in such matters.

The man who had stopped before the barber's house would have had, no doubt, much trouble in reading what was written on the front of the shop, which was shut; for the night was dark, and, as we have already said, there were no street lamps to aid those who ventured to be out in the evening in the capital. However, he seized the knocker of the smaller door, which served as an entrance, and gave a double knock without hesitating, and as one who was not afraid of making a mistake; in fact, it was the barber himself. In a few moments heavy steps were heard, and a light shone against the lattice-work above the door, which opened, and an old woman appeared, holding a candle in her hand. She nodded, saying, —

"Good God, my dear master! you have had

horrible weather. You must be very wet. I have been praying to my patron saint that nothing should happen to you. Oh, if one only had a secret for preserving one's self from the rain! I'm very sure there are some people who can command the elements."

The barber made no answer, but passed toward a passage which led to a lower room in which there was a big fire. On entering the apartment he began by removing his cloak and hat, from which latter escaped a mass of black hair which fell in ringlets on his collar; he unfastened a large dagger from his belt, it being then the custom not to venture out without being armed. Touquet hung the dagger over the mantelpiece, then threw himself into a wicker armchair and placed himself before the fire.

While her master rested, the old servant came and went about the room; she placed the table beside the barber's armchair, drew from a buffet a pewter cup, some plates, a cover. She placed on the table tankards containing wine or brandy, and some dishes of meat which she had prepared for the supper.

"Has anyone been here during my absence?" said the barber, after a moment.

"Yes, monsieur; first, some pages, to know the news and adventures of the neighborhood, to talk evil about everybody, and to mock at the poor women who were weak enough to listen to them.

Oh, the young men of today are wicked. How they boasted of their conquests! Some bachelors came to be shaved, then the little dandy who's delighted to wear powder, protesting that soon everybody will wear it. Perhaps they'll powder the hair likewise; still, that may preserve it from something worse. Ah, I forgot; and that big, noisy and insolent lout who, because he has a satin doublet and a velvet mantle, a hat adorned with a fine plume, and beautiful silver points, believes that he has the right to play the master over everything."

"Ah, you're speaking about Monbart?"

"Yes, of that same. He made a great shouting when he found you were not here. He said that since monsieur is rich he neglects his business."

"Why should he meddle with it?"

"That's just what I thought, monsieur. M. le Chevalier Chaudoreille also came. He fought a duel yesterday in the little Pré-aux-Clercs and killed his adversary, and he had still another duel for this evening. Blessed Holy Virgin! that men should kill each other like that, and often for some mere trifle."

"Let them fight as much as they please; it's of little importance; it's not my business. Did anybody else come?"

"Oh, the gentleman who is so droll that he makes me laugh, and whom I have sometimes

seen play in the farces which everybody runs to
see at his theatre in the Hôtel de Bourgogne, —
M. Henry Legrand."

" Why don't you say Turlupin ? "

" Well, Turlupin, since that's the name they
give him at the theatre, and by which he's also
known in the city. He does not make one melancholy. He came with that other who plays
with him, and acts, they say, the old men, and
delivers the prologues which precede the pieces."

" That's Gautier-Garguille ? "

" Yes, monsieur, that's his name. He wanted
to be shaved, bathed and have his hair dressed ;
but as you were not here, one of them played the
barber and shaved his comrade ; then the other
took the comb and soapball and rendered him
the same service. I wished at first to prevent
them, but they wouldn't listen to me ; if they
didn't make me sit in the shop and talk downright
nonsense about scent and soap. Some people who
in passing had recognized Turlupin and his companion stopped before the shop ; presently the
crowd grew dense, and when they wanted to leave
they could not find a way through ; but you know
Turlupin is never embarrassed, and, having uselessly begged the curious to let them pass, he went
into the back shop and brought a bucketful of
water, which he emptied entirely upon the crowd.
Then you can imagine, monsieur, the excitement,
the shouts of everybody. Turlupin and Gautier-

Garguille profited by the confusion to make their escape."

"And Blanche," said the barber, who appeared to listen impatiently to old Marguerite's story,— "I hope that she was not downstairs when these merry-andrews attracted such a crowd about my house."

"No, monsieur, no ; you know very well that Mademoiselle Blanche seldom comes down to the shop, and never when there is anybody there. Today, as you were away, she did not leave her room, as you had advised her."

"That's well ; that's very well," said the barber.

Then he drew near the fire, supporting one of his elbows on the table, and appeared to fall again into reflection without listening to the chatter of his servant, which continued as if her master were paying the greatest attention to her.

"Mademoiselle Blanche is a charming girl ; oh, yes, she is a charming child, — pretty, very pretty. I defy all your court ladies to have more beautiful eyes, or a fresher mouth, or whiter teeth ; and such beautiful hair, black as jet and falling below her knees. And with all that, so sweet, so frank, without the least idea of coquetry. Ah, she is candor, innocence, itself. Of course, she's not yet sixteen years old ; but there are many young girls at that age who already listen to lovers. What a pity if such a treasure as that should fall into the claws of a demon! But we shall save her from that. Yes, yes; I'm sure of it. I shall do all that's necessary for that, for it's not enough to watch over a young girl; the devil is so malicious, and all these bachelors, these students, these pages, are so enterprising, without counting the young noblemen, who make no scruple of abducting young girls and women, and for all compensation give a stroke of the sword, or cause to be whipped by their lackeys those who complain of their treatment. Good Saint Marguerite! what a time we live in! One must allow one's self to be outraged, offended, robbed even, — yes, robbed, — for if you should have taken your man in the act, if you demand justice, they will ask you if you yourself were a witness to it. If you say no, they will dismiss the guilty person, and if you say yes, they will first find out if you have the means of paying the expenses of the law, in which case you may have the pleasure of seeing the thief flogged before your door, and that will cost you a heap. But if it is someone with a title who has offended you, it's necessary for you to be silent about it, unless you wish to finish your days at the Bastile or at the Châtelet."

Marguerite was silent for some minutes, awaiting a response from her master. Receiving none, she presumed that he tacitly approved of all she was saying, and resumed her discourse.

"Finally, they pretend that it's always been

thus. They hang the little ones, the bigger ones save themselves, and the biggest mock at everyone. One's ill advised to go to law now that the advocates and the attorneys drag a lawsuit along for five or six years, receiving money from all hands, so as to maintain their wives and their daughters in luxury, playing the Jew to ruin their poor clients. As to the sergeants, they run all over to find criminals; but if they arrest some thieves, they let them go very quickly, for fear that the latter will give them some money. Poor city! Don't we hear a frightful noise every night? And still we're in the best neighborhood. And that does not prevent them from committing vandalisms, robberies, murders. There are shouts, a clash of arms; what is the use of provosts, sheriffs, sergeants, archers, if the police do so badly? It's not the merchants I pity; they'll give themselves to the devil for a sou; they sell their goods for four times more than they cost; to draw customers, they allow every passer-by to go into their shops, leaving them at leisure to chat with their women, to take them by the chin, to talk soft nonsense, to make love to their face, — all that to sell a collar, some rouge, a dozen of needles. It's a shame to see everything that goes on amongst us. If I go to market to get my provisions, I'm surrounded by thieves who amuse themselves by stealing from the buyers and the sellers; they rummage in the creels and baskets, then they sing

in my ears indecent and obscene songs. Good
Saint Marguerite! where are we in all this? The
scholars, more debauched than ever, insulting, pil-
laging, doing a thousand wickednesses; the young
men of family who haunt the gambling-dens, the
drinking-houses, always armed with daggers or
swords. Ah, my dear master, Satan has taken
possession of our poor city and will make us his
prey."

Marguerite stopped anew and listened. The
barber still kept the deepest silence, but he was
not asleep. Several times he had passed his right
hand over his forehead and pushed back his curls.
For those who love to talk, it is much the same
whether they are listened to or believe themselves
to be listened to. The old servant was enjoying
herself; she did not often find so good an opportunity to talk, and she began again after a short
pause : —

"Thanks to Heaven, I am in a good house,
and I can say with pride that, during the eight
years that I have lived with monsieur, nothing
has passed contrary to decency and good manners.
I remember very well that when they said to me,
eight years ago, 'Marguerite, M. Touquet, the
barber-bathkeeper of the Rue des Bourdonnais, is
looking for a servant for his house,' I considered
it twice. I beg your pardon, monsieur; for bath-
keepers' houses and lodging-houses don't have a
very good reputation. But they said to me, 'M.

Touquet is in easy circumstances now; he doesn't take lodgers; he is contented to exercise his call-ing in the morning, and for the rest he hardly ever sees anybody at his house, where he is care-fully educating a little girl whom he's adopted.' My faith! that decided me, and I've not had cause to repent my decision. If there come in the morn-ing to the shop a crowd of men of all profes-sions, not one of them penetrates to the interior of the house. Monsieur does his business honor-ably, I am proud to say; and that which I admire above all is the interest which he bears for the orphan he has taken under his care, for I believe that monsieur has told me that she is an orphan. Yes, monsieur has told me so. She surely merits all that anyone can do for her, that dear Blanche; but I believe I have not told monsieur by what means I preserve her from the snares that wait for innocence. Oh, it's a secret, it's a marvellous secret, which I shall confide to monsieur. The neighbor opposite the silk merchant told me how to make it; it is a little skin of vellum, on which some words are written; then one signs it, and it becomes a talisman to prevent all misfortunes. Queen Catherine de Médicis had a similar one which she wore always; the talisman which I have given to Mademoiselle Blanche, very far from at-tracting evil spirits, should make them fly from a place and prevent the effect of all sorceries which anyone could employ to triumph over her virtue.

Oh, the precious talisman, monsieur! Alas! if
I had had one eight years ago! — But you don't
sup, monsieur; haven't you any appetite?"

Touquet rose abruptly and went to look at a
wooden timepiece which stood at the end of the
room.

"Nine o'clock," said the barber impatiently;
"nine o'clock, and he has not come."

"Why, are you waiting for someone, monsieur?" said the old servant in surprise.

"Yes; I'm waiting for a friend. Put another
drinking-cup on the table; he will sup with me."

"I very much doubt whether he will come,"
said Marguerite, while executing her master's orders; "it's late and the weather is frightful; one
must be very bold to risk himself in the streets at
this hour."

At this moment somebody knocked violently
at the door of the passageway, and the barber,
smiling to himself, cried, —

"It is he!"

CHAPTER II

The Great Nobleman and the Barber

On hearing the knock old Marguerite started affrightedly and looked at her master, as she faltered,—

"Must we open the door at this time of night, monsieur?"

"Of course, haven't I told you already that I was waiting for a friend?" replied the barber, putting some more wood on the fire, "go to the door at once."

The old servant was very fearful; she stood and hesitated; but a single look from her master decided her; she took a lamp and directed her steps towards the corridor which opened into the passageway of the house. Marguerite was sixty-eight years old; work and the weight of years had long since bent her body and deprived her limbs of their natural agility; she could only walk slowly, and the high heels of her large slippers made a uniform flapping noise which the poor old handmaid could not prevent and of which she was, indeed, unconscious.

The good woman had shuffled as far as the middle of the passageway, when another knock, louder than the first one, shook all the windows of the house.

"Ah, mon Dieu!" said Marguerite; "he's in a great hurry. Which of my master's friends would allow himself to knock in that manner? There are some panes broken, I'm sure. Can it be Chaudoreille? Oh, no; he only gives a very soft little knock. Turlupin? Of course not; I should hear him sing in the street. Besides, he's not my master's friend. Ah, I'm very curious to know who it can be."

Despite her curiosity Marguerite did not advance more quickly. However, she arrived at the door, and, having mentally recommended herself to her dear patron saint, she decided to open it.

A man wrapped in a large cloak which he held against his face, his head covered with a hat ornamented on the edge with white feathers, and drawn well down over his eyes, so that no one could see them, appeared at the end of the passageway, and asked in a loud voice if this was Barber Touquet's house.

"Yes, monsieur," said Marguerite, trying, but in vain, to discover the features of the person before her. "Yes, this is it; and it's you, no doubt, for whom my master's waiting."

"In that case conduct me to him," said the stranger.

Marguerite closed the door and bade the unknown follow her. While guiding him along the

passageway and the long corridor which they had
to traverse, she turned often and held her lamp
to the stranger, under the pretence of lighting
him, but in fact to try to see something by which
she could recognize the person whom she had
introduced into the house. Her efforts were in
vain. The stranger walked with his head down,
holding his cloak against his face. Marguerite was
reduced to examining his boots, which were white,
with turned-over mushroom-shaped tops, and gar-
nished with spurs. This seemed to indicate a refined dress; but many men then wore similar
ones, and this part of his dress could not help
Marguerite in her conjectures. They reached the
lower room, and the stranger entered with a light
step, while the servant said to her master, —

"Here's the person who knocked. I do not
know if it is the friend you were waiting for; I
was not able to see him."

The barber did not allow Marguerite time to
finish her phrase. He ran toward the stranger and
made him come to the fire, saying to him, —

"Thou hast arrived at last, then. I feared that
the night, that the bad weather — But place thy-
self here; we will sup together."

"Good," said the servant to herself; "in order
for him to sup it will be necessary for him to re-
move his mantle, and I shall at last be able to see
his face. I don't know why, but I have the greatest curiosity to know this man. If it is one of my

master's friends, it must be that he has come here very rarely. I did not recognize his voice; his height is ordinary, — rather tall than short; he should be young. Yes, he's not a scholar; however, I bet he's a pretty fellow; by his walk I judge him to be a military man. We shall see if I'm mistaken."

The old maid did not take her eyes from the stranger, who had thrown himself on a chair, and made no sign that he wished to relieve himself of his cloak and hat, both of which were drenched with rain.

"If monsieur desires it," said Marguerite, approaching the stranger's chair, "I will relieve him of his cloak, which is all wet; and I can dry it while he is supping."

"It is unnecessary," said the barber, putting himself precipitately between the old woman and the stranger, who had not stirred; "we have no need of your services. Leave us, and go to rest; I will shut the street door myself when my friend leaves."

Marguerite seemed petrified on receiving this order. She looked at her master, and was about to allow herself to indulge in some observations; but the barber fixed his eyes upon her, and Master Touquet's eyes had at times an expression which compelled obedience.

"Leave us," said he again to his servant; "and above all, do not come down again."

Marguerite was silent. She took her lamp, bowed to her master and turned to leave the room, throwing a last glance on the man of the mantle, who remained motionless before the fire and whose features she could not see. She was obliged to go to bed without being able to base her conjectures on facts, without knowing if she had rightly divined the age, the condition, the face of the unknown. What a punishment for the old maid! But her master pointed with his finger to the door of the room, and Marguerite went at once.

As soon as the old servant had departed, and when the sound of her steps was no longer heard, the stranger burst into a shout of laughter and threw his hat and his cloak far from him. Then one perceived a man of thirty-six years or thereabouts; his features were fine, noble and spirituel. His brown mustache was lightly outlined above his mouth, which in smiling disclosed very beautiful teeth. His expressive eyes, in turn tender, proud and passionate, denoted one who was in the habit of expressing all his sentiments; but the disgust, the weariness, which were depicted also on the pale and worn features of the stranger seemed to indicate that, having once indulged his passion, it was only with an effort that he could bring himself to experience it again.

His costume was rich and tasteful; the color of his doublet was a light blue; silver and silk were blended on the velvet which formed the foundation; superb lace bordered the collar which fell on his shoulders; a large white belt surrounded his figure, and a sword ornamented with precious stones glittered at his side.

Since the departure of his servant the barber had changed his tone toward the stranger. Respect, humility, had replaced the familiarity which Touquet had affected in Marguerite's presence.

"Deign to excuse me, monsieur le marquis," said he, bowing profoundly to his guest, "if I permitted myself to be too familiar, with my thee-ing and thou-ing; but it was only according to your orders, the better to deceive my servant and prevent her from having any suspicions as to your rank."

"That's all right, my dear Touquet," said the marquis, displaying himself before the fire; "I assure you I had the greatest trouble to maintain my gravity before the poor woman, who did not know by what ruse she could see my face, which would not have been a very great matter, for it is hardly presumable that she would have known me."

"No, monseigneur, she does not know you; I think so at least, for M. le Marquis de Villebelle has made so much talk about himself with his gallantry, his conquests, his feats of arms. His name has become so famous, his adventures have made so much noise, that the lowest classes of society know him, — the bugbear of fathers, of tutors, of husbands, of lovers even; for monseigneur knows no rival. Your name is spoken with terror by all the men, and makes all the women sigh, some with hope and the others in remembrance; besides, as monsieur le marquis sought pleasure wherever he found beauty, since he sometimes stooped to the humble middle classes, and has deigned to honor with his regards some pretty shop girl or simple villager, it would not be impossible that my old Marguerite might have served with some house where monsieur le marquis had left souvenirs. It was, therefore, much better that she should not see monseigneur when he came to my house incognito."

"Yes, certainly; I wish to remain unknown; it is necessary now that I should put more mystery into my love affairs. Be seated, Touquet; I have many things to tell you."

"Monseigneur—"

"Be seated; I wish it. Here I lay aside my rank and my grandeur; in you I see the first confidant of my loves, the clever servant of my passions, the audacious rascal for whom gold excited the imagination, and who knew no obstacle when a purse filled with pistoles was the recompense of his services. You are still the same, I am certain."

"Ah, monsieur, age makes us more reasonable. Seventeen years have passed since I had the honor of serving you for the first time; but since that time my head is steadier; I have learned to reflect."

" Do you wish to become an honest man ? But it is not more than ten years ago that you were serving me ; you were still a knave then. Does your conversion date from that epoch ? "

" Monsieur le marquis is incessantly joking. He calls those services knaveries which I rendered to him because I was so strongly attached to him."

" Call it what you will, it matters little to me. It's not necessary with me, Master Touquet, to play the hypocrite, and man of scruples. In fact, are you disposed to be useful to me? Is your genius extinguished, and will gold no longer resuscitate it ? "

" To serve you, monsieur le marquis, I shall be always the same ; you need not doubt my zeal or my devotion."

" All in good time. That is all that I ask of you ; be a saint with other people if that pleases you, but see that I always find you the same to me as you were formerly."

Touquet did not answer, but he turned his head and his features seemed to grow sad. However, he soon recovered himself and turned smilingly toward his guest, who was tapping the wall of the chimney with his feet, and who remained for some time silent, as if he had forgotten that he was still at the barber's. The latter waited with impatience for the marquis to resume his discourse. At the end of five minutes the noble seigneur broke the silence.

"My dear Touquet, when I recall the events of my life to my memory, I am truly astonished that I am still in the world. Why, during all this time, has not the dagger of a jealous husband or father fallen upon my head? How many men have sworn to ruin me! And the women, — if all those I have betrayed had executed their projects of vengeance! Thanks to Heaven, we are not in Italy or in Spain; and, while we have among the French some vindictive spirits, who hold rancor toward one who has betrayed them, the total is small. Inconstancy is not an unforgivable crime among these ladies, who deign sometimes to put themselves in our places and say they would not have done differently to us."

"Certainly, monseigneur, your life, at least since I have had the honor to be attached to you, has been a continued series of very spicy adventures, and some very dangerous ones. Abductions, seductions, duels, attacks with force, made openly, — nothing stopped you when you had resolved upon anything. Could you find any obstacles? Rich, noble, generous, fortune and nature have done everything for you, monsieur le marquis. You have profited by it; you have enjoyed life; many men have envied you your good fortune."

"My good fortune! Do you truly imagine that I have been happy?"

"And what should have prevented your being so, monseigneur?"

"Nothing; and that is perhaps why weariness and disgust have often attacked me in the midst of the pleasures, the voluptuousness, I have tasted. Sometimes, without doubt, I have felt happiness, but it has been so short and has fled so rapidly. The appearance of beauty has inflamed my senses and made my heart palpitate. The charming sex, which I idolize, has always exercised an absolute empire over me. At the sight of a pretty woman I love, or at least believe I love; but no sooner are my desires satisfied than my love expires, and I am obliged to seek a new object to reanimate my benumbed senses."

"Happily, this capital contains any quantity of pretty faces; the city and the court afford you sufficient to vary your pleasures."

"Sentiment and memory are alike exhausted. I fear that, having once had force to take fire, my poor heart has become like those imperfect gun flints on which the hammer strikes without effect. I am tired of the intrigues of the court, which are even easier than the others. Where do you think I could find something more spicy? There everything is done with etiquette, and everyone is so polished. We know life too well to get angry at the least infidelity; one leaves or one takes with the most profound obeisances, and this wearies one to death; courtiers have nothing new to offer one. What should I accomplish in Marion de Lorme's circle? I should see always the same faces. When

the Cardinal had made her fashionable, I didn't
find the woman so witty that one would wish to
have anything to do with her. How different
with this young and beautiful Ninon ! People will
long speak of her; her name will go down the
centuries. But she has too much wit and too little
love, for me. My heart, cold before its time, needs
to come in contact with a passionate heart in order
to rewarm itself. In the city one does not fare
much better with the women. The little bour-
geoises have become coquettes. Still, if they only
knew how to be cruel; but a name, a figure, a rich
cloak, seems to turn their heads. The merchants
know how to rob us, and the grisettes entice us;
and in the midst of all that the husbands are so
kind, so complacent; they fear us as they would
fire; our titles render them mute; of honor they
are hopeless. If this continues, it will be necessary to make love à la turque; we should only
have then to throw the handkerchief."

"Then, monsieur le marquis, one always has
the resource of wisdom; and, since I have not had
the honor of serving you for ten years, without
doubt you have acquired that."

" My faith, yes; for it's not necessary to speak
of common adventures, which are not worth the
trouble of reciting. I have been in the army; I
have been in battle; that afforded me much pleasure, and I would willingly have stayed there much
longer; but peace is made, I have returned, I have

visited my lands, and have laughed with some little peasants who were sufficiently pleasing, but so
awkward, so simple. By the way, I forgot to tell
you; I married."

"Married! What, monseigneur! you?"

"Undoubtedly; my marriage was very necessary; my rank, my place at the court — and then
I was overloaded with debt. That didn't make
me uneasy; but they had arranged this marriage;
the Cardinal, the Queen herself, desired it. I married the daughter of the Count of Laroche. My
wife was very good, of very sweet character; she
didn't trouble herself about my intrigues; she had
what was necessary to me. I loved her — very
honestly, as one can love his wife; but she died
two years ago and left me no heir, which is in-
tensely disagreeable. I had an idea that I should
love children very much."

"Then you are a widower, monsieur?"

"Yes; and I find myself the possessor of a considerable fortune, very well considered at court, in
favor with the Cardinal, and even able to obtain,
should I desire it, the most important employment."

"I conceive, then, that monsieur le marquis
wishes more secrecy in his love affairs."

"Ah, my poor Touquet, I don't believe that
ambition will ever have much charm for me, but
nobody knows; and there are some convenances
at the court which one must not break; besides,

secrecy lends a charm to the most simple act. But why have you not enrolled yourself under Hymen's flag? I find that you are more thoughtful, less cheerful, less lively, than formerly."

"No, monsieur le marquis; I am still a bachelor."

"Oh, well, I believe you are better so. In your position a wife would restrain you, — you who are so clever, so discreet, in conducting an intrigue. Women are so curious; she would want to know everything, which would be troublesome for you. Besides, you have never been very gallant; you care for nothing but gold. It is your god, your idol; a well-filled purse makes you inventive, capable of working marvels. It's true that you play with it a quarter of an hour afterwards and at dice or cards soon increase the fruit of the efforts of your genius."

"Ah, monseigneur!"

"Yes, you are as big a gambler as you are a knave; I remember it very well. Perhaps in ten years you have become wiser; I almost believe so, for you appear in very easy circumstances, and this house does not indicate poverty; this servant, this supper served for you — The deuce! I must taste your wine."

"Ah, monseigneur, it is not worth offering to you."

"I always like best that which is not offered to me."

While he was saying these words the marquis filled one of the cups with wine and swallowed it at a draught.

" Really, it's not so very bad."

"Ah, monseigneur, if it were on your table —"

"Then I should find it detestable ; but what will you have ? Variety is the spice of life. And you have become rich, then ? "

" No, not rich, but well enough off to buy this house."

" What ! the house belongs to you ? "

" Yes, monsieur le marquis."

" Deuce take it, Master Touquet, it must be that you have made some big hauls in order to become a proprietor."

The barber's face contracted ; his black eyebrows frowned and almost met ; he slowly rolled his eyes around him, and murmured with an effort, —

" Monsieur le marquis, I swear to you — "

" O mon Dieu ! I do not ask you to swear, my poor Touquet," said the marquis, laughing. " You are as uneasy as if you had become a lieutenant in crime. Do you think that I came here to inquire as to the manner in which you made your fortune ? But by all the devils, I do not believe that you earned this house in your barber shop."

" Monseigneur, I assure you that my economies — "

"Yes, that's all very well; let's leave all that and speak of the subject which brought me here, for, of course, I came to you for something, and I'll be damned if I remember what it was."

The barber appeared to breathe more freely; his face assumed its habitual expression, and he raised his eyes to the marquis, who seemed to throw aside his insolence to explain the motive of his nocturnal visit.

"When I saw you this morning on the Pont-Neuf, I was following a young girl, a pretty little puss; without being a perfect beauty, she was graceful and interesting in appearance, with sparkling and very intelligent eyes. I do not believe that we should have much trouble in making a conquest of her. However, she walked faster, and would not answer any of my compliments. I carefully wrapped myself in my cloak, not wishing to be recognized by our amiable profligates, who would have made sport of me for running after a grisette. The little girl stopped to listen for a moment to Tabarin's songs, and it was while she was before the quack that I saw you and recognized you immediately; you have one of those faces that nobody forgets."

"I had also recognized you, monseigneur, in spite of the cloak in which you were enveloped; for ten years have not changed your features, monsieur le marquis, and one could not easily mistake that noble figure which captivates all the belles."

"You flatter me, rascal; which means that I have aged. But let's go on. As soon as you had given me your address, I returned to the side of the little one."

"If monsieur le marquis had explained to me this morning what he was after, I would have spared him the trouble of following this young girl."

"No, I had a good opportunity of examining her further; besides, I had nothing else to do. She took the road to the city, which she entered by the Rue de la Calandre, I still talking to her; she only smiled, without answering me, but her look was not severe. At last she stopped before a perfumer's shop; I wished to go in with her, but she opposed me, saying in a very singular tone, 'Monsieur le Marquis de Villebelle is too well known for him to go into this shop with me; I should lose my reputation, and I beg monsieur le marquis not to compromise me.' Well now, my dear, Touquet, can you imagine this grisette who pretends that I should cause her to lose her reputation? As for me, I confess that I was so much surprised by finding myself known to the young girl and hearing her speak thus, that I remained like a fool in the middle of the street; meanwhile my beautiful conquest had entered, and disappeared by the back of the shop."

"As I told you, monseigneur, you are known in all classes of society; even a young girl of

twelve years is as much afraid of you as she would
be of Count Ory of gallant memory."

" Better and better! Women are always curious to know these men who have been pictured to
them as so dangerous. Poor parents! When they
tell them to fly from me, it makes them run after
me. Here, Touquet; here's some gold. You will
see this young girl, then; since she knows who I
am, you cannot easily promise her that I will be
faithful. No matter; promise her anyhow. In
three days let me find her at my little house in
the Faubourg Saint-Antoine; you know it."

" Yes, monseigneur; I remember it; it is the
one that you formerly possessed."

" Yes; but I have made it a delightful retreat.
You shall see it; pictures, mirrors, marble, alabaster, are there mingled with silk, velvet and the
most precious stuffs. I have spent more than fifty
thousand francs upon it. Oh, it is divine! I have
had some charming suppers there with Montglas,
Chavagnac, Villempré, Monteille, and some other
profligates of the court."

" Was it not there, monsieur le marquis, that I
led that young girl whose abduction made such
an uproar? That was, I believe, our first affair of
this kind; you were then a little more than nineteen years of age; and the little girl — "

" Why the devil do you recall that?" said the
marquis, making an angry movement, and pressing in his hand the purse he was about to take

from his belt, and on which the barber had already laid avaricious eyes.

"Pardon, monsieur le marquis," said Touquet; "but I did not think I should displease you in recalling the adventure which commenced your reputation. The young person was beautiful and good, and the father, one of King Henry's old archers, did not understand joking. His arquebus was aimed at you, the ball went through your hat; but your sword stopped the old man, and he fell at your feet, while I bore off in my arms his insensible daughter."

"Be silent, wretch," cried the marquis, suddenly rising, and looking angrily at the barber, who received his glances with perfect indifference.

The conversation was again interrupted; the marquis walked rapidly up and down the room, and appeared buried in his reflections; soon, however, broken words escaped him, but they were not addressed to Touquet. The marquis seemed violently agitated as he said in a low voice, —

"Poor Estrelle! what has become of you? She loved me — she believed me to be a simple student. I loved her also; yes, never since that time have I experienced a feeling which I can compare with the love with which she inspired me. I was young — ah, Heaven is my witness that I did not wish to fight with her father. Thanks to Heaven, his wound was very trifling and was soon cured; but Estrelle, when she learned my name and that

event, cursed me. Yes, I believe I can hear her
still. Then she escaped from that house where I
had hidden her. I love her still. Since that time
I have never heard of her; and you, Touquet, —
have you never met her since?"

"Never, monseigneur; I have neither seen her
nor heard her speak."

"Poor Estrelle!" said the marquis after a moment; and the barber added in a low tone, —

"She would now be thirty-four years of age, or
very near that."

This remark appeared to lessen somewhat the
marquis' regret.

"In fact," said he, again approaching the fire,
"she would be nearly that age if she were living,
and would not appear the same to me as the one
I formerly knew. How time passes! Come, let's
forget all that; after all, it is much the same as any
other adventure, — a chapter in the history of my
life."

"And did the marquis say that the young girl
lived in the Rue de la Calandre in the city?"

"The young girl? What young girl?"

"The one monseigneur followed this morning."

"Yes, to be sure; I had forgotten. You will
easily recognize her: her figure unconstrained, her
walk brisk; twenty years or thereabouts, I presume; nut-brown hair, black eyes, beautiful teeth,
her skin a little brown. I do not think she's
French. Something lively in her countenance;

nothing that indicates timidity or simplicity. This is all the information which I can give you."

" It is sufficient, monseigneur; in two days I hope that the young person will be at your little house."

" That's very good. — Wait; this is for your expenses, and I promise you as much more if you are successful."

While saying these words the marquis threw on the table the purse filled with gold, which he still held in his hand, and a smile escaped the lips of the barber. His guest resumed his cloak and replaced his hat on his head.

" It is late," said the marquis, wrapping himself in his mantle, "and I must go home. The day after tomorrow, toward ten o'clock, I will return to learn the result of your proceedings."

" Shall I find anybody at your little house? "

" Yes, Marcel, one of my people, a devoted servant who lives there constantly. I will warn him."

" That is enough, monseigneur, and I hope that you will be pleased with me on this occasion."

" I leave it all to your zeal; in fact, the little one is very pleasing, and ought to amuse me for some time. Come, my dear Touquet, let us follow our destiny. Gallantry, voluptuousness, pleasure, — that is my life; that is the road which I follow where my passions lead me. I should not know how to follow any other walk now; like a blind man who trusts in Providence, I do not know if this road will lead me to happiness ; but I cannot turn aside from it."

The marquis turned his steps toward the door, and Touquet proposed to his distinguished guest that he should guide him to his dwelling.

"Thank you," said the marquis, "it is unnecessary ; I have my sword, and I fear nothing."

While uttering these words the marquis had plunged into the street and disappeared from the barber's sight. The latter closed the door and returned to the little room. Arrived there, he hastened to take the purse which lay on the table ; he counted the pieces which it contained, nor could he raise his eyes from the sight of the gold. But soon a dull, melancholy sound was heard ; it was Saint-Eustache's clock striking two. The barber turned pale ; his hair seemed to stand up on his head ; he threw about him gloomy glances, as if he feared to perceive some frightful object ; then he placed the purse in his bosom, took a lamp and went toward the door at the end of the room, murmuring in a sad voice, —

"Two o'clock ! Let's go to bed. Ah, if I could only sleep ! "

CHAPTER III

Blanche. A History of Sorcerers

THE welcome day had succeeded to the long
and rainy night; the merchants had opened their
shops, the watchmen were taking their much-
needed rest after their fatiguing nocturnal duties,
while the more hardy robbers of the darkness had
given place to the sneaking pickpockets and
thieves who exercised their calling in broad daylight in the most populous quarters. The servant
maids were up and about, briskly performing
their morning tasks; husbands left the nuptial
couch, for then it was usual for one to sleep with
his wife, at least among middle-class people, to
betake themselves to their daily avocations; wives
and mothers were attending to the needs of their
households and their children; lovers who had
dreamt of their sweethearts went to endeavor to
realize some of their dreams; and the young girls
who always thought of their sweethearts whether
they were sleeping or waking, went, thinking of
them still, to their daily work. In that time, as
in this, love was the dream of youth, the distraction of the middle-aged, and the memory of the
old.

The barber was always the first to rise in the house. He had no servants, although his means would well have allowed it; but when anyone asked him why he did not take a boy to help him and to watch in the shop, Touquet answered, —

"I do not need anyone; I can conduct my business alone, and I'm not fond of feeding idlers who are good for nothing but to spy on their master's actions and go and talk about them in the neighborhood."

The barber knew that Marguerite, though a little curious and somewhat of a gossip, was incapable of disobeying him in anything; she went out to buy the necessary provisions for the house, then she went upstairs again to the young girl of whom we have heard her speak, and with whom we shall soon have a better acquaintance. Marguerite went down only when her master was absent, which was rarely. Finally, the barber could not dispense with a maid since he had taken the little Blanche to grow up under his roof.

Touquet himself opened his shop; he looked up and down the street, but it was yet too early for customers to come. The barber was dreamy, preoccupied; he was thinking of the commission which had been given him by the marquis; then he returned indoors, saying, —

"Chaudoreille is late this morning; however, it's his day to be shaved."

Marguerite appeared at the entrance to the

room; and, after looking about her on all sides, perhaps to assure herself that the stranger of the night before was not still there, she greeted her master respectfully, and said to him, —

"Monsieur, Mademoiselle Blanche is up and wishes to know if she may come and say good-morning to you."

The barber still threw a glance into the street; then he passed into his back shop, saying to his servant, —

"Blanche may come."

Marguerite had hardly made a sign to someone in the passage when a young girl, light as a deer and fresh as a rose, sprang into the little room where Touquet was waiting, and ran toward him with the most lovely smile, saying to him, —

"Good-morning, my good friend!"

Then she offered Touquet her candid forehead, and the barber approached her and brushed it lightly with his lips. One would have said that a painful feeling restrained him, and that he feared to wither that tender flower.

Marguerite's portrait had not flattered Blanche. The young girl was as pretty as she appeared innocent and ingenuous. Her dark hair, smoothed in bands on her forehead, fell in ringlets on her right shoulder. Powder, which the court ladies had then begun to use, had not spoiled Blanche's beautiful tresses. Her skin accorded perfectly with her name. Her mouth was fresh and tender;

and her blue eyes, shaded by long lashes, had an
innocent and sweet expression, as rare then as now.

What a pity that her pretty body should be
imprisoned in a long corset, the bones of which
seemed forcibly to compress its charms! But it
was then the fashion. Today we have better taste;
we wish that the figure should be in its place; we
wish, above all, to be able to embrace it without
being hindered by farthingales, basquines, paniers
or hoops. Happily, the ladies are of our opinion,
and everybody gains thereby.

Despite her long figure, straight corset, frilled
sleeves, and her high-heeled shoes, Blanche was
no less pretty. Beauty adorns everything that it
wears, and innocence lends a more bewitching and
genuine charm to beauty. Blanche had, then,
every quality which could please. However, the
barber did not appear to remark the attractions of
the young girl; one would have said that he feared
to look at her, as he had feared to touch his lips
to her forehead.

"Did you have a good night?" asked Blanche
of him.

"Very good, I thank you."

"Marguerite was afraid that you went to bed
very late because you had one of your friends to
supper with you."

"I don't know why Marguerite should make
such a remark, nor what necessity there was that
she should tell you I had anyone here last night."

While uttering these words Touquet looked severely at Marguerite, who dusted and wiped the furniture without daring to look at her master.

"But, my dear," answered Blanche, "is there anything bad in one's supping with one of his friends?"

"Undoubtedly not."

"What harm, then, has Marguerite done in telling me that?"

"A servant should not incessantly tell tales about everything her master does. It should be very indifferent to you, Blanche, whether anyone comes to see me in the evening or not."

"Oh, mercy, yes, since you won't let me come down, though that would amuse me much better than staying in my room."

"A young girl should not talk to everybody, and many people come here of whom I know very little."

"Yes, in the morning; but in the evening you only receive your friends."

"I receive very few visitors in the evening except Chaudoreille, whom you know."

"Oh, yes; and he makes me laugh every time I see him, for he will give me lessons in music, and I believe at the present time I know much more about it than he does. You will never let me leave my room."

"Blanche, isn't it apparent to you that that is not convenient?"

"But when you are alone I should like much
better to keep you company and chat to you, than
to listen to Marguerite's stories, which often make
me very timorous and prevent me from going to
sleep."

"You know that I'm not very chatty; after a
day's work I'm tired and I like to rest."

"And Marguerite said that you didn't go to
bed until very late, that you kept the light burning a long time, and that she doesn't know if you
sleep one hour every night."

The old servant coughed, but unsuccessfully, to
make Blanche stop talking; but the latter, not
thinking that she had done anything wrong in repeating all that, paid no attention to her and continued to speak. Marguerite, in order to avoid
her master's look, wiped and dusted with new
ardor; but this time the voice of the barber made
itself heard, and it was she whom he addressed.

"Marguerite, I said to you when you came
into my house that I detested curious, indiscreet
people, — servants who spy on their master. Do
you remember it?"

"Yes, yes, monsieur," said the old servant, continuing to rub the top of the table.

"How do you know, then, whether I sleep late,
whether I keep the light burning a long time,
whether I am awake at night? — you who should
be in your room at nine o'clock every evening and
go to bed immediately."

" Monsieur, I beg your pardon ; but at times, when the wind blows or the thunder growls, it's impossible for me to sleep ; then, monsieur, I get up to pray to my patron saint, or cross my shovel and tongs, or to place a branch of boxwood on my bed. You know boxwood conjures the storm ; and if they had taken some of it formerly to the Arsenal, on the Billi Tower, it would not have been entirely destroyed by lightning in the year 1537 or '38 — I don't know which exactly."

" Hang it ! leave your boxwood and the Billi Tower alone ; answer the question I asked you."

" That's what I'm doing, monsieur ; it's always the wind or the storm which makes me wakeful, and as my window faces yours (when I say faces, it's a story above), then I see your light sometimes, and it seems to me that monsieur is walking about in his room. I'm not very certain of it, for there are curtains, and the shade deceives one sometimes."

" As I wish to prevent you from having the trouble of making sure that I am asleep, this evening you will change your room, and you will sleep in that which is above my apartments."

" What, monsieur ! in that room where nobody ever goes ? I do not believe that it has been inhabited since I came here, and I fear — "

" That's enough ; see that you obey ; and take care not to spy again on my actions, or I shall be forced to send you away from the house."

"Mercy! how ashamed I am at having made you scold Marguerite!" said Blanche, again approaching the barber. "If she said that, my friend, it was because of the interest she takes in your health. You know well that she is very much attached to you; but since it makes you angry, I promise you it shall not occur again. Come, that's the last of it; you won't say any more to her about it — will you?"

Blanche's voice was so sweet, so touching, that Touquet lost his air of severity and very nearly smiled as he answered, —

"Yes, that's the last of it; let us there leave it. As to you, Blanche, continue to be good, docile."

"And you will let me go out a little — will you not? You will allow me to go to walk in the Pré-aux-Clercs or on the Place Royale?"

"We shall see; we shall see a little later. To amuse yourself, vary your employments."

"That's what I do, my dear; I often leave my needle to spin some thread; or, better still, I take my tapestry work. Oh, you shall see; I'm making something very pretty."

"I know your talent — your taste. You have a sitar; you can amuse yourself by playing on it. Chaudoreille has given you some lessons."

"Yes; now I can play as well as he can, for I believe he's not very practised on it, although he says he's a great musician. But all that hardly ever amuses me; I should like much better to sit at the window which looks on the street, but you won't let me open it."

"No, Blanche; too many people are passing in this neighborhood; you would be seen, ogled, insulted, by the bachelors, the pages, who take pleasure in annoying people."

"Well, I won't open my window. However, if you were willing I could put a mask on my face; then they could not see me."

"They would notice you none the less; besides, Blanche, only the court ladies are permitted to wear masks. I repeat to you, avoid the glances of these impertinent louts who run the streets, ogling at all the windows. You are not yet sixteen years old. In some years I shall leave Paris; I shall sell this house, and I shall retire into the country; there you can enjoy more liberty, and there you will taste pleasures which are worth more than any this city could offer you. — But someone is coming into the shop; go, Blanche, upstairs to your room."

The young girl kissed the barber and quickly regained the passage, from which a staircase led to her chamber. She sighed lightly as she entered it, and said to herself, while glancing around her, —

"Always here! Always to see the same things! No one to speak to except Marguerite! She is very good, she loves me very much; but sometimes her stories are very wearisome to me. Well, then, if I must —" and Blanche took up a piece

of tapestry which she was making and sang, while
working, one of the three airs which her music
master had taught her. Soon the door of the room
opened; Marguerite had followed the young girl,
but did not arrive as soon as she, because her legs
had not the vivacity of sixteen years. The old
nurse pouted, for Blanche was the cause of her
having to change her room, which was no small
matter to Marguerite. Blanche perceived it; she
ran in front of the old woman, made her sit down,
and took her hands, while saying to her with a
calming smile, —

"Are you vexed with me, nurse? You must
have seen that I said all that without thinking
that there was anything wrong in it."

Who could resist Blanche's smile? The old
woman was much more sensitive to such sweet
manners because people rarely used them with
her; and that is why sometimes an old man loses
his reason when a pretty girl casts a tender glance
at him, because for a long time he has not been
in the habit of receiving such glances.

"Who could remain angry with you?" said
Marguerite, pressing Blanche's hand; "but for all
that, it's very disagreeable to change rooms — to
move at my age."

"I will help you, dear nurse; I will carry everything."

"Oh, it's not that; it's on the same landing;
it's not far to carry things. But the room I've

lived in for eight years, ever since I came here, was, thanks to my prayers and precautions, protected from the visits of all evil spirits. There I could defy all attempts of sorcerers and magicians; and all that I did there I shall have to do over again in the new room where I am to sleep."

" Do you believe, then, Marguerite, that sorcerers will come to visit you if you don't take all your precautions?"

"And why not, mademoiselle? Don't those people get in wherever they can penetrate? There are a great number of them in Paris. They carry away the corpses off the gibbets of Montfaucon; they commit a thousand horrors to make their sorceries successful. It is now nearly fifty years ago (it was my mother who told me that story) that a lackey, ruined by play, sold himself to the devil for ten crowns. The demon transformed himself into a serpent and took possession of the lackey, introducing himself into the latter's body by the mouth; and from that time on the unlucky man made horrible grimaces, because the devil was in his body. Some years later a watchman was carried off by a sorcerer."

" Ah, dear nurse, you are going to tell me some more of those stories which will make me timorous at night."

" I don't tell you these to make you tremble, but to prove to you that it's necessary to be on one's guard against magicians, and not to be like

those incredulous people who doubt everything
when we have so many examples of the power of
magic. I'll not do more than cite to you the Maré-
chale d'Ancre and Urbain Grandier, who lodged
some devils in the bodies of some pious Ursulines
at Loudun; that is too frightful. But I will only
tell you what happened to a magician called César
Perditor; that dates seventeen years back, or thereabouts. You see, my dear child, that's not very
ancient."

"But, dear nurse, aren't you going to begin your
moving?" said Blanche, who did not seem very
eager to hear Marguerite's story.

"We've plenty of time," answered the old servant as she drew her chair close to Blanche's, delighted to relate a story about sorcerers, although
that would make her tremble also. Marguerite
commenced immediately : —

"This César was, said they, very well versed in
his magic art, and produced at his will both hail
and thunder. He had a familiar spirit, and a dog
that carried his letters and brought back the answers to him. At a quarter of a league distant from
this city, on the Gentilly side, he lived in a cave,
in which he caused the devil and all his infernal
court to appear. Ah, my poor child; they say that
at a great distance from the cave a frightful noise
might be heard every night. He made love phil-
ters, and wax images, by means of which he caused
the persons they represented to languish and die.

"One day — no, it must have been one night — an old man came to the cave, who appeared to be suffering and in great distress. A great lord, a libertine, a worthless fellow, had stolen away his daughter, his only child; the old man in his despair, unable to obtain justice, went to the magician to procure the means of revenging himself upon the man who had outraged him."

"Nurse, it seems to me your master is calling you," said Blanche, interrupting Marguerite.

"No, no; he did not call me. Except at meal times, what need has M. Touquet of me? But as we were saying, the old man went to seek a magician, and the latter promised him help; in fact, they heard more noise than usual in the cave that night, — so much that the lieutenant of police sent some people there, and César was taken and led to the Bastile, where soon after the devil strangled him."

"And the old man, nurse?"

"He never returned to his dwelling; without doubt the devil carried him away also, or else the great nobleman, having learned that he had gone to the magician's house. But nobody knows anything further about it. Still, that will prove to you, my dear, how dangerous it is to have anything to do with those people."

"Dear nurse, this little talisman which you gave me, that I wear, — is not that the work of a sorcerer?"

"Certainly not, darling; on the contrary, it is
to preserve you from their snares that I gave it
to you. It is under the protection of my patron
saint; with that, my dear Blanche, you could go
about, run anywhere; your innocence would not
be in the slightest danger."

"Why, then, does my good friend never permit me to leave my room?"

"Ah, my dear Blanche, it is because M. Touquet does not believe in talismans; and it is very
unfortunate for him."

"But you, Marguerite, who are afraid of everything, — why don't you carry a similar talisman?"

"Ah, my child, the quality of yours consists
principally in preserving your virtue, and at my
age one has no need of a talisman to preserve
that."

"My virtue! Do magicians take virtue from
young girls?"

"Not only magicians, but fascinating gallants,
— finally, all the worthless fellows of whom M.
Touquet was talking to you this morning."

"And what would these people do with my virtue?"

"My dear child, that is to say, they would seek
to turn your head, to give you a taste for coquetry,
dissipation, baubles, vanity and deceit; then you
would be no longer my good, sweet Blanche."

"Ah, I understand; but, dear nurse, without
a talisman I fully believe that I should never have

those tastes. I would do nothing that should cause trouble to those who had taken care of me from my infancy, who have done so much for me since I lost my father."

" That's all very well, my child, but with a talisman you see I am much easier ; and if M. Touquet believed about it as I do, he would give you a little more liberty. Not that I blame him for fearing for you the attempts of worthless fellows ; you are growing every day so pretty."

" Dear nurse, do worthless fellows trouble pretty girls, then ? "

" Alas, yes, my dearie. I have seen them often do so ; and, unfortunately, the pretty girls listen willingly to the good-for-nothing fellows."

" They listen willingly to them, nurse? Is it because they speak better than other men ? "

" No, not better, but they know so well how to dissemble ; their speech is golden, their eyes deceptive, their manners — Ah, how glad I am that you have a talisman ! "

" But, nurse, since I do not leave my room —"

" That's true, my dear ; but you will not always keep your room, and under my watchful care it seems to me that one could very well allow you to take a little walk from time to time. M. Touquet is severe — very severe — to make me change my lodging because I noticed that he did not sleep at night. Is it my fault — mine — that he does not sleep ? "

" He prevents me from opening my window."

" Ah, that is because it opens on the street; and if he knew you looked so often through the lattice — But no one can possibly see you; the panes are so small, so close together."

" Oh, yes; it is like a grating."

" A father could not be more strict."

" Ah, Marguerite, he stands to me in the place of mine."

" Yes, yes; I know it well; however, he is no relation — is he?"

" No, Marguerite; I believe not."

" According to what I heard in the neighborhood, before I came into his service, you are the daughter of a poor gentleman who came to Paris to follow a lawsuit about ten years ago."

" Yes, dear nurse; I was then five years and some months of age. It seems to me, however, that I still remember my father; he was very good, and he often kissed me."

" And your mother, — do you remember her?"

" Alas, no; but I believe I can still remember the time when my father and I arrived here; we had been a long time in a carriage, and came from far off."

" And M. Touquet lodged you, for then he kept lodgings; and after that?"

" I was very tired; they gave me something to eat and put me to bed in this room, and I have always occupied it since."

" And after that ? "

" I did not see my father again. The next day
M. Touquet told me he was dead."

"Yes; it was very unfortunate, they say. There
were then, as there are very often still, fights in
the night between pages and lackeys and honest
men, who were often attacked by these cursed
scoundrels while entering their own houses. That
night they committed a thousand disorders in the
streets of Paris; several persons were assassinated;
and your poor father, who had gone out, was,
while returning, drawn into a brawl, and perished
trying to defend himself. That is all that I have
learned; do you know anything further ? "

"No, Marguerite; besides, you know very well
that my protector does not wish me to talk about
that."

"Yes, because he fears that it will give you
pain."

" He has deigned to keep me near him, to educate me as his daughter and give me some accom-
plishments; and I have for him the most lively
gratitude."

"Oh, yes; he has done very well by you. He
loves you, although he is not caressing, nor does
he say much; and I am very sure that he has the
greatest interest in you. It seems that he does
not intend himself to marry, although he is still
young. He is in easy circumstances, — more so
than he wishes it to appear."

"Do you believe that, Marguerite?"

"Ah, hush! If he knew that I had said that, and that I had sometimes seen him counting gold, he would send me away for it."

"You have seen him counting gold?"

"I did not say that to you, mademoiselle. No, no; I have seen nothing. Ah, mon Dieu! what a gossip I am! I had much better go and attend to my moving."

"I will go with you, dear nurse."

"Come then, if you like, Blanche."

Blanche followed Marguerite as she went up, and hastened to carry the furniture and clothing of the old servant to the opposite room. In vain Marguerite cried to her, —

"Slowly, mademoiselle; don't carry anything until I have sprinkled it with holy water."

Blanche, to spare Marguerite fatigue, had very soon finished the moving.

"You will be better here," said Blanche; "this room is more convenient, larger."

"I shall find it pretty sad," said Marguerite, casting fearful glances around her. "That large alcove, those dark hangings, those recesses — Oh, mademoiselle, do see, if you please, if there is anything in that big closet."

Blanche ran to open the closet, and, after having looked through it, brought to Marguerite a little book, thick with dust.

"That's all I've found, dear nurse," said she,

presenting the book to the old woman, who put on her spectacles and said, —

" Let's see a bit what it is."

Marguerite succeeded, with no little trouble, in reading, "Conjuring-book of the Sorcerer Odoard, the Famous Tier of Tags."

" Ah, mon Dieu ! " said Marguerite, letting the book fall; " I am lost if that sorcerer has slept in this room.   Miséricorde ! a tier of — "

" What does that mean, — a tier of tags ? "

" That is to say — that is to say, mademoiselle, a very wicked man, who doesn't love his kind; a man who casts spells to make folks unlucky."

" Are there any of those sorcerers now ? "

" Alas, yes, my dear child ; they are always casting spells, for I have met during my life several persons who have been bewitched by them.   Let us burn that ; let's burn that quick."

Marguerite hurried to throw the book of sorceries on to the hearth, where she lit a fire ; then she began to pray to her patron saint, and Blanche went down to her work.

CHAPTER IV

The Chevalier Chaudoreille

BLANCHE and Marguerite had no sooner taken their departure from the back room and returned to their customary avocations, than Touquet hastened to meet a man who had come into the shop, saying to him, in a friendly tone,—

"Come in, come in, my dear Chaudoreille, you've made me wait a deuce of a time and today I have something really important to say to you."

The personage who had just come into Maître Touquet's house was a man of a very striking and peculiar appearance, about thirty-five years of age, though he appeared at least forty-five, so worn was his face and so hollow his cheeks. His yellow skin was only relieved by two little scarlet spots formed on the prominence of his cheek bones, which by their brightness and their gloss betrayed their origin. His eyes were small but bright; and M. Chaudoreille rolled them continually, never, by any chance, fixing them on the person to whom he was speaking. His short snub nose contrasted with his large mouth, which was surmounted by an immense red mustache, the color of his hair; while beneath his lower lip a tuft of beard terminated in a point on his chin.

The height of the chevalier was barely five feet, and the leanness of his body was accentuated by the threadbare close jacket which enveloped it; the buttons of his doublet were missing in many places, and some ill-executed darns seemed ready to gape into holes; his breeches, being much too large, made his thighs appear of enormous size, and made the legs which issued from them appear still more lanky, for his boots, with flaring tops which drooped to his ankles, could not hide the absence of calves. These boots, of a dark yellow, had heels two inches high, and were habitually adorned with spurs; the doublet and smallclothes were of a faded rose color, and accompanied by a little cloak of the same tint, which barely covered his figure; in addition to these, he wore a very high ruff, a small hat surmounted by an old red plume, worn slanted over one eye, an old belt of green silk, a sword which was very much longer than anyone else carried, and of which the handle came up to his breast. The above is a very faithful portrait of the one who called himself the Chevalier de Chaudoreille, if we add that his slight Gascon accent denoted his origin; that he marched with his head high, his nose in the air, his hand on his hip, his legs stiff, as though ready to put himself on his guard; and that he appeared disposed to defy all passers-by.

On entering the shop Chaudoreille threw himself on a bench, like one overcome by fatigue, and placed his hat near him, crying, —

"Let us rest. By George! I well deserve to. Oh! what a night! Good God! what a night!"

"And what the devil did you do last night to make you so tired?"

"Oh, nothing more than usual for me, it's true: flogged three or four big rascals who wished to stop the chair of a countess, wounded two pages who were insulting a young girl, gave a big stroke with my sword to a student who was going to introduce himself into a house by the window, delivered over to the watch four robbers who were about to plunder a poor gentleman. That's nearly all that I did last night."

"Hang it!" said Touquet, smiling ironically, "do you know, Chaudoreille, that you yourself are worth three patrols of the watch? It seems to me that the King or Monsieur le Cardinal should recompense such fine conduct and nominate you to some important place in the police of this city, in place of leaving a man so brave, so useful, to ramble about the streets all day, and haunt the gambling-hells in order to try to borrow a crown."

"Yes," said Chaudoreille, without appearing to notice the latter part of the barber's phrase, "I know that I am very brave, and that my sword has often been very useful to the State — that is to say, to the oppressed. I work without pay;

I yield to every movement of my heart; it's in the blood. Zounds! honor before everything; and in this century we do not jest. I am what somebody at court calls a 'rake of honor': an offensive twinkle of the eye, a rather cold bow, a cloak which rubs against mine, presto! my sword is in my hand; I am conscious of nothing but that; I would fight with a child of five years if he treated me with disrespect."

" I know that we live in the age when one fights for a mere trifle, but I never heard it said that your duels had caused much stir."

" What the devil, my dear Touquet! the dead cannot speak; and those who have an affair with me never return. You have heard tell of the famous Balagni, nicknamed the 'Brave,' who was killed in a duel about fifteen years ago. Well, my friend, I am his pupil and his successor."

" It's unfortunate for you that you didn't come into the world two centuries earlier; tourneys are beginning to be out of fashion, and chevaliers who right all wrongs, giant killers, one no longer sees except on the stage at plays."

" It's very certain that if I had lived in the time of the Crusades I should have brought from Palestine a thousand Saracens' ears, but my dear Rolande was there. This redoubtable sword, which came to me from a distant cousin, was the one carried by Rolande the Furious; it has sent a devil of a lot of men into the other world."

"I'm always afraid that you will fall over it; it seems to me too big for you."

"It has, however, been curtailed an inch since I have had it, and that by reason of its having been used so much. I fear that if I should continue in the same style, it will become a little dagger."

"Stop talking about your prowess, Chaudoreille; I have to speak to you of matters more interesting than that."

"If you will shave me first; I have great need of it. My beard grows twice as quickly at night when I do not sup in the evening."

"It looks as if you had dieted for some days, then."

While the barber prepared everything that was necessary for shaving Chaudoreille, the latter detached his sword. After having looked all over the shop in search of a place in which it seemed convenient to put it, he decided to keep it on his knees; he relieved himself of his cloak, then he took off the faded ruff which surrounded his neck, and abandoned his odd, lean little figure to the cares of Touquet, who came forward bearing a basin and a soapball. The barber began by taking and throwing into a corner of the shop the sword which Chaudoreille was holding on his knees. The chevalier made a movement of despair, crying, —

"What are you doing, unhappy man? You will break Rolande, the sword which Charlemagne's nephew carried."

"If it's such a good blade it won't break. How do you think I can shave you holding that great halberd on your knee?"

"It's necessary to handle it with care at least. Zounds! you are nearly as quick as I am."

"Do you want me to cut your mustaches?"

"No, no,—never. A chevalier without mustaches! What are you thinking of? Do you want people to take me for a young girl?"

"I don't think anyone could so deceive himself."

"That's all right; I especially pride myself on my mustaches, and the imperial that gives a masculine air. Ah, King Francis the First knew very well what he was doing when he wore that little pointed beard on his chin. Don't you think that I bear some resemblance to that monarch?"

"You resemble him so much, in fact, that I defy anyone, no matter who it might be, to perceive it. But let's get to my business: I wish to employ you. Your time is free?"

"Free? Yes; that is to say, for you there is nothing that I won't leave. I've only two or three amorous appointments and five or six affairs of honor; but those can be put off."

"There's some money to be earned."

"I'm a man who would put myself in the fire to make myself useful."

"The business is not positively my own."

"Yes, I understand,—a delicate mission. You

know that I've already served you in many such cases."

"I hope that you'll be more adroit this time; for the manner in which you conducted yourself in the last matters in which I employed you should have prevented me from asking you to serve me again."

"Oh, my dear Touquet, don't be unjust; it seems to me that I managed them passably well. First, you desired me to carry a letter to a young lady without letting her parents know of it."

"Yes; and you positively gave the note to her mother."

"What the devil! how should I know it was her mother? That woman had rouge, flowers, laces, a corset which made her waist about as thick as my purse; I believed her to be the young lady. With their hoops, basquines and immense head-dresses, it will soon be impossible to distinguish the sexes."

"Another time I told you to feign a quarrel with one of your friends, so as to draw a crowd together in the street in order to stop the chair of a young woman to whom someone wished to speak; but after two or three blows had passed you ran away."

"Ah, my friend, but that does not detract from my bravery. I knew that the quarrel was only pretended; despite that, at the third blow I felt the blood mount to my face, and I ran away for fear of getting angry."

"This time I hope you will conduct yourself better."

"Speak, if you have need of my valor."

"No, thank God, I shan't have to put your valor to the proof; the matter is very simple and will not cost you a great effort of genius."

"So much the worse; I swear by Rolande that I feel disposed to brave every terror. — Take care, my friend; your razor almost touched my nose; you will end by taking off a piece, and that would destroy the charm of my physiognomy."

"Fear nothing, most valorous Chaudoreille; I will respect your face; it would be a pity to spoil it."

"Yes, most assuredly; it would cause tears to more than one great lady who deigns to look with favor upon your humble servant."

"Those great ladies would do well if they gave you another doublet, for yours has well earned its retirement."

"My dear fellow, love doesn't pause for such trifles; I please with or without a doublet; the figure is everything, and I'm more than a match for many a chevalier covered with tinsel and gewgaws; besides, if I wished to have some lace or cuffs or trinkets, I should not have to give more than a smile for them. Ah, by Jove! — Take care there, my brave Touquet. See! your neighbor's dog is going to take my ruff. Ah, the rogue! he's holding it in his chops."

"You must take it away from him."

"That's very easy for you to say. That cursed dog bites everybody."

Chaudoreille got up, half shaved, and ran and took his sword, which he drew from the scabbard; but during this time the dog had left the shop, carrying off the ruff, and the boastful chevalier pursued him into the street, crying, —

"My ruff! Zounds, my ruff! Stop thief!"

The shouts of Chaudoreille made the dog run more quickly, and the passers-by looked on with astonishment at the half-dressed man, with one cheek shaven and the other covered with soap, who ran, sword in hand, crying, "Stop thief!" The idlers gathered—for there were idlers as early as 1632—and followed Chaudoreille, that they might see the end of the adventure. The children stoned the dog, which redoubled its speed, passed through an alleyway and disappeared from Chaudoreille's sight. The latter, who could do no more, stopped at length, heaving a big sigh. His anger was redoubled when he saw everybody looking and laughing at him; he swore then, but so low that nobody could hear him; and, making the best of his way through the crowd which surrounded him, he sadly regained the barber's house.

"You must be a fool, to run through the street like that," said Touquet, who had grown impatient during Chaudoreille's race; "you deserve that I shouldn't finish shaving you."

"Oh, zounds! that is very easy for you to say; I have been robbed — a magnificent ruff."

"You can put on another."

"I haven't another."

"With a smile you could have as many as you wish."

"Yes, yes; but I'm not by way of smiling just now."

"Come, calm yourself. If our affair is successful, as I've no doubt it will be, I'll give you some crowns with which you can buy other collars; for ruffs are no longer in fashion."

This assurance alleviated somewhat Chaudoreille's grief, and he reseated himself, that the barber might finish shaving him.

"You will go today into the city," resumed the barber, while finishing the chevalier's toilet, — "into the Rue de la Calandre; you will go into a perfumer's shop which is about half-way down the street."

"Yes, yes, I know; that is where I supply myself."

"Better and better! It will be easier for you to obtain an entrance. You should know, then, the young girl whom I will describe to you: twenty years old, of medium height, unrestrained figure, brown hair and intelligent black eyes."

"Listen; I don't believe that I know her, seeing that it's two or three years since I bought any perfumery, because scents make me nervous."

"If you could dispense with lying to me, Chaudoreille, at every turn, you would give me great pleasure."

"What do I understand by that? I lie? By jingo! I swear to you, by Rolande — "

"Hold your tongue and listen. A great nobleman is in love with the young girl whose portrait I have just given you. This great nobleman is the Marquis de Villebelle."

"By Jove! What, the Marquis de Villebelle! He's a jolly fellow, who makes everybody talk about him. I'm delighted to work for a man of that stamp; he's as brave as he is generous. That's a profligate after my own heart. I shall be glad to give him proofs of my zeal and my genius."

"You'll have to begin by holding your tongue; remember, the least indiscretion will cost you dear. I should not have told you the name of the one who is concerned in this matter if the young girl had not known; but as she might herself tell you, it is better that you should learn it from me. Remember, you are still in my employ, and not in that of the marquis. I could myself have discharged the commission which he gave me, but I am beginning to have a reputation for probity and wisdom; it is generally thought that, turning from the errors of my youth, I no longer mix in intrigues, and I don't wish to disturb the good opinion they now have of me in this neighborhood."

"Ah, rascal, you're as mischievous as a monkey; you think of nothing but increasing your business, and your cold, severe air deceives some people. You're right, by jingo! One must dissemble; it's the essence of intrigue, and I shall try to throw off the appearance of being a libertine and a profligate in order that I may be more successful in wheedling the little innocent."

The barber shrugged his shoulders impatiently, and again approached the blade of his razor to Chaudoreille's nose. The latter's face became still paler, except the spots on his cheeks, where the color seemed immovable.

" Curse it!" cried Touquet, while holding the end of Chaudoreille's nose between his fingers, to prevent him from moving, while he plied the razor; "can't you ever keep still and refrain from trembling beneath my razor blade? You deserve to be slashed all over your face. — Come, get up; it's finished."

" Many thanks," said Chaudoreille, breathing more freely; "I am shaved like a cherubim. Oh, you have a hand as dexterous as it's nimble. That makes seventy-seven shaves that I owe you for."

"That's all right; we'll reckon that later."

"I know that you'll recall it to me; you're not like the barber who shaved one of my friends on credit, and who made a notch in him every time, to mark the shave, he said."

" Before the people come in, let us agree on what we have to do."

"Speak on; I am listening while I am washing myself."

"You will go, then, to the perfumer's shop, and while buying something —"

"Oh, yes; a collar or a ruff."

"No matter, — no matter what."

"I find that ruffs suit me better."

"Hold your tongue, cursed chatterer; there's nobody here to notice your face. You will enter into conversation with the young girl I have depicted; you will say to her that M. le Marquis is in love with her to the point of distraction."

"Yes; I shall say to her that he will stab himself before her eyes if she won't meet him."

"It's not a question of killing himself, idiot. That's a fine way to seduce a grisette!"

"I never seduced them any other way."

"Talk about presents, jewelry; they respond to that much quicker."

"Each one to his own method; as for me, I never make love that way; for the rest, I'll say everything that you wish; I'll make the marquis as generous and magnificent as a native of Gascony."

"Finally, you will demand a rendezvous, in the name of the marquis, for tomorrow evening."

"Where shall it be?"

"Wherever you like, but preferentially in an unfrequented quarter."

"Very well; and after?"

"Oh, the rest is my affair."

"A moment: if the little one doesn't grant an interview?"

"What are you thinking of? A shop girl who knows that she is pleasing to the noble Seigneur de Villebelle — I am certain that she's on tenterhooks already because no messenger has reached her. You must beware of committing any blunder which will render you unsuccessful."

"Be easy; I'm not a clown, I flatter myself, and I wish by this affair to put myself in the good graces of the marquis."

"Yet again, it is not for him, but for me, that you are doing the business; if you should allow a single word of this adventure to escape in the town, if you should have the misfortune to mention the marquis, remember that then the blade of my razor won't leave that face whole about which you seem to make such a fuss."

The barber's eyes evinced his firm determination of keeping his promise; Chaudoreille hastened to get his sword and attach it to his side while murmuring, —

"Yes, undoubtedly I make much of my face; it is very worthy of the trouble, and has given me many happy moments. This devil of a Touquet is always joking, but between friends one should not get angry. We are both aware of our mutual bravery, and it's superfluous for us to give proofs of it. I swear to you by Rolande that I will use

the greatest discretion, that I may be relied on.
Our acquaintance doesn't date from today ; for
nearly fifteen years we have been united in friendship. We are two jolly fellows who have played
our pranks. How many intrigues have we conducted by our skill, without counting our personal prowess! You, built like a Hercules, an
antique figure, noble carriage, — you would have
adored big women — that is to say, tall women ;
I, smaller but well made, with a more modern
physiognomy, — I prefer them more graceful and
slender. But love never troubled you much ; you
prefer money. Ah, money and play, — those have
been your pleasures. As for me, I'm fond of gam-
ing also ; I play a very strong game of piquet.
But gallantry employs a great part of my time. I
can't help it ; I love the women. But that's not
astonishing ; I am their spoilt child ; they have
strewn the path of my life with flowers, without
counting all those that still remain for me to cull.
I dedicated to them my heart and my sword. But
love and valor do not always lead to fortune ; you
have gathered wealth quicker than I, and I compliment you upon it. While I have been following
after some Venus, you have conducted without my
aid some intricate intrigues ; for this house did
not belong to you formerly, and now you are the
proprietor of it ; it did not fall to you from the
clouds."

"What are you meddling with ?" said the bar-

ber angrily. " What does it matter to you how I
acquired this house ?   When I've employed you
haven't I paid you, and often a good deal better
than you deserve ? I've already told you, Chaudoreille, that if you wish that we remain friends,
and if you desire through me to earn money
from time to time, you had better not begin your
foolish questions, nor seek to learn that which
I do not judge fit to confide to you ; otherwise I
shall show you my door and you will never enter
it again."

" Oh, not so fast. By jingo ! he's a little Vesu-
vius, — this dear Touquet. If I gave way to my
natural temper we should see some fine things ;
however, that's ended ; silence on that subject.
Now I am dressed ; I lack nothing but my ruff ;
how can I go out without that ? "

" You went out very well a minute ago, half
dressed."

" But a minute ago I was sword in hand, and
in those moments I see nothing but my victim.
It's all right ; I will pull my cloak up a little
higher. Ah, I was forgetting an essential. That
I may buy something in the little one's shop it's
necessary that I should have some money, and my
pockets are empty this morning."

" Wait ; take these ten crowns, on account of
what I shall give you if you fulfil my instructions
correctly."

" That's well understood," said Chaudoreille,

taking the money and drawing from his belt an
old silk purse, which had formerly been red, in
which he placed, one by one, with an air of respect, the ten pieces which the barber had given
him.

"It's still too early," said Touquet, "for you
to go to the perfumer's; those dames do not open
their shops as early as we do ours; while waiting
till the time comes for you to execute your commission couldn't you go up and see Blanche, and
give her a music lesson? That will amuse her,
and I notice that she does not find much to distract her in her room, where she sees no one but
Marguerite."

At the name of Blanche, Chaudoreille raised his
eyes to Heaven, and heaved a sigh which he stifled
immediately, crying, —

"By the way, how is she, the pretty child? I
was going to ask you about her, for it is a century
since I have seen her."

"She's very well, but she's tired of being in the
house and wishes to go out."

"What the devil! why don't you send me more
often to keep her company? I can amuse her, my
beautiful Blanche, and I can play something for
her."

"I'm not sure that you can amuse her much.
Blanche said to me that you always sang the same
things, and that she now knew as much as you do
of the sitar."

"These young girls are full of conceit. I confess that she's made rapid progress, and that is not astonishing; I have a way of teaching which would make a donkey capable of singing songs; besides, the little one is intelligent, but I flatter myself that I can still teach her something more."

"Chaudoreille, I have given you a great proof of my confidence in permitting you to see Blanche; you must swear to me that you will never speak of her beauty."

"Be easy; when by chance anyone asks me if I know the young girl who is under your care, I answer — since we are on the subject — that I have seen her three or four times, and that she is neither one thing nor the other, — one of those faces which people say nothing about."

"That's well; if anyone imagined that this house held one of the prettiest women in Paris, I should nevermore have a moment's peace; I should be incessantly tormented by a crowd of gallants, of profligates, of libertines; I should see this house become the rendezvous of all the worthless fellows of the neighborhood. I couldn't go away for a moment without one of them trying to introduce himself to Blanche, and Marguerite's watchfulness would be as insufficient as my own to frustrate all the enterprises of these gallants. It is to avoid all this annoyance that I withdraw Blanche from the notice of curious people."

"Oh, as far as that goes, you do very well;

I quite approve your conduct; you must not let them see her, nor allow her to go out for a moment. If you wish, I can say everywhere that she's horrible,—blind of one eye, lame, and hump-backed."

"No, no; one must never overdo one's precautions and fall into a contrary excess."

"It would be so sorrowful if some miserable adventurer should carry this beautiful flower away from us."

"How? carry her away from us?"

"I should say carry her away from you; it is only by favor that I see her. She is, in truth, a jewel; she has the candor, the innocence of childhood. Ah, zounds! how happy you are, Touquet, for you are guarding this treasure for yourself, I'll wager."

"For myself?" said the barber, knitting his brows; then he was silent for a moment, while Chaudoreille, placed before a little mirror, occupied himself in studying some smiles and glances of the eye. "I have already told you that I do not like questions," responded Touquet at last; "but I see that you will be incorrigible until your shoulders have felt the weight of my arm."

"Always joking. You are really a most ironical man."

"Come, go up to Blanche's room; you can stay three-quarters of an hour. You must leave by the passageway; I don't wish the people who will be

here to see you come from the interior of the
house. You will go where I told you, and you
will come and give me an account of the result of
your enterprise."

" At your dinner hour ? "

" No, this evening, at dusk."

" As you please, as you will. Ah, mon Dieu !
I am thinking how I can go up to my young pupil without a ruff."

" Will that prevent you from singing ? "

" No, but decency — this naked neck. Lend me
a collar, — anything."

" Hang it ! is it necessary to make so much fuss ?
Do you think that Blanche will pay much attention
to your face ? "

" My face ! my face ! It would seem, to hear
you, that I am an Albino."

" Here's somebody coming ; get out."

The barber pushed Chaudoreille into the passage, where the latter remained for a quarter of an
hour, seeking by what manner he could hold his
cloak, and deciding at last to go up to his pupil.

CHAPTER V

The Music Lesson

BLANCHE was seated at work near her window, the small, dim panes of which scarcely permitted her to distinguish anything in the street.

However, from time to time she glanced downward in that direction to distract her thoughts; not that she was at all sad, or that she had anything to trouble her, but a young girl who is nearly sixteen years of age experiences in the depths of her innocent heart certain void, vague desires which she cannot easily account for. She sighs, she becomes dreamy; a mere nothing renders her uneasy; the least noise, the sound of an unknown voice, makes her heart beat more quickly; she looks oftener in the mirror; she pays more attention to her toilet, though, as yet, there is nobody in particular whom she wishes to charm. But a secret instinct implants in her the desire to please, a sure symptom that she begins to feel the need of loving; and, for that reason, she falls into reveries and sighs without knowing why — so it was, at least, in the time of which we are speaking. As to the young girls of our own time, they dream, also, but they sigh less.

The character of the barber, the cold, serious manner which he wore before Blanche, did not invite confidence, and imposed a restraint on the young girl, whose ingenuous heart seemed to seek a friend. She respected Touquet and obeyed him ; she regarded him as her benefactor, but she could not chat freely with him, for the barber's laconic answers always appeared to indicate little desire to engage in a long conversation. To make up for this, Marguerite was very chatty, and would willingly have passed the entire day in gossip ; but the sole subjects of her conversation were sorcerers, magicians and robbers, and these were not at all amusing to Blanche, who preferred, to Marguerite's appalling stories, a tender love-song or a story of chivalry, the heroes of which were very strong on love ; and one of that ilk had no less prowess as a paladin because he was faithful to his lady for twenty years.

Blanche was dreaming, then, when somebody rapped softly at her door ; and immediately Chaudoreille's odd little head appeared between the door and the wall, and he said in mellifluous accents, —

" May one come in, interesting scholar ? "

Blanche raised her eyes and burst into a fit of laughter on perceiving Chaudoreille's face, this being the effect his appearance ordinarily produced on the young girl.

" Come in, come in, my dear master," said she,

rising to curtsey to Chaudoreille, who then introduced himself entirely into the room, bowing to
Blanche three times, so low that each time his
sword fell before him, and on rising he was obliged
to put Rolande into his scabbard again.

"I am so much in the habit of drawing him,"
said Chaudoreille, "that he can't rest quietly in his
sheath for two hours at a time. — Come, be quiet,
Rolande; you know well, my dear companion,
that the night never passes without my giving you
some occupation."

"Why, Monsieur Chaudoreille, do you fight
every day?"

"What else could you expect, beautiful angel?
It is my element; I should not sleep if I had not
drawn my sword, and I should fall ill if three days
were to elapse without my ridding the earth of an
impertinent fellow or a rival."

"O good Heavens!"

"But let us leave that subject and speak of you,
delightful creature. You seem to me fresher and
more beautiful than ever; it is the unfolding of
the bud, it is the opening of the flower, it is the
fruit which — By the way, how are you?"

"Very well. Did you come to give me a music
lesson?"

"Yes, if you will permit me the pleasure. It is
a long time since I had that happiness."

"I hope you're going to teach me something
new."

" By Jove! I'm not at the end of my tether. Besides, were new songs lacking, your beautiful eyes would inspire me to improvise a ballad in sixteen couplets."

Blanche brought her sitar and handed it to Chaudoreille, who raised his eyes to Heaven and heaved a big sigh as he took it.

"Are you going to be ill, Monsieur Chaudoreille?" questioned the young girl, astonished at this moaning.

" No, I am not ill; however, I feel rather uneasy," answered Chaudoreille, venturing to try the effect of the glances and smiles which he had studied before the glass.

"You seem to have difficulty in breathing," responded Blanche; "perhaps your supper last night did not agree with you."

" Pardon me; I swear to you it did not trouble me in the least. I have a horror of indigestion. Out upon it! I never put myself in the way of having it."

"Sing to me the air you are going to teach me; that will make you feel better."

"She is innocence itself," said Chaudoreille to himself while tuning the sitar; "she doesn't understand what makes me sigh. Despite that, however, I can see that she's glad to see me. Patience; before long her heart will awaken, and I shall be its conqueror."

Blanche took up her work again; Chaudoreille

seated himself near her, and after a quarter of an hour's tuning of the sitar, coughed, expectorated, blew his nose, turned around on his chair, arranged his cape, pursed his mouth, passed his tongue over his lips, and at last commenced in a shrill voice, which pierced the ears, an ancient ditty which Blanche had heard a hundred times before.

"I know that, my dear master," said she, interrupting Chaudoreille in the middle of a point d'orgue, which he seemed willing to prolong indefinitely; "that's one of the three you have already taught me."

"Do you think so?"

"Wait; I'll sing it for you."

Blanche took the instrument, and, gracefully accompanying herself, sang, in a melodious voice which gave a charm to the old ballad.

"That's very well, indeed," said Chaudoreille; "you sing the passages precisely in my manner; I seem to hear myself."

"Teach me another, then," said the young girl, returning the instrument to him; and Chaudoreille intoned a virelay on the great feats of Pepin the Short.

"I know that, too," said Blanche, stopping him.

"In that case I will sing you a charming villanelle."

"Mercy! that will be the third of those you have taught me. Don't you know any others?"

" Pardon me, but as a cursed dog ran off with
my ruff while I was being shaved, I cannot venture a new song while my throat is naked; it
would embarrass the middle notes. Nevertheless,
the villanelle is always a novelty, since I ever sing
it with variations."

" Well, I'll listen," said Blanche, glancing towards the street. Chaudoreille heaved another
sigh, and when he had taken a position which
seemed to him more favorable for displaying his
graces, he commenced the villanelle, which he
sang to Blanche every time that he gave her a
lesson: —

> I have lost my turtle-dove,
>   And her flight I must pursue, —
> Is she not the one I love ?
>
> You regret your own fond dove,
>   As the loss of mine I rue ;
> I have lost my turtle-dove.

At this moment some perambulating singers
came into the street. They stationed themselves
in front of the barber's house and, accompanying
themselves on their mandolins, sang some Italian
songs. Blanche listened eagerly; this music, so
different from that which she heard from her master of the sitar, stirred her pulses deliciously, and
approaching the window she cried, —

" Oh, how pretty that is ! "

" Yes, undoubtedly it's pretty," said Chaudoreille, who believed the young girl to be speaking

of the villanelle; "but it's necessary to acquire
the same expression that I have given it. Notice
it well, 'I have lost my turtle-dove,' — the accent tremulous with grief; raise the eyes to the
ceiling, beat time with the left foot. 'And her
flight I must pursue,' — a distracted air, and always the same accompaniment with the thumb
and index finger. 'Is she not the one I love?' —
a soft, flute-like sound, and make a movement of
surprise while sustaining the falsetto. 'You regret
your own fond dove, —' that demands much expression. 'You regret,' — an exquisitely performed
shake, — 'your own fond dove,' — inflate the sound
and ascend still."

"Ah, I should be contented if I could only hear
such music often," said Blanche, who had paid no
attention to what Chaudoreille was saying, and had
listened only to the Italians.

"I should much like to give you a lesson every
day, lovely damsel; but my occupations overwhelm
me — and then, Master Touquet does not often
permit me the pleasure of seeing you; when far
from you I sing without ceasing, —

You regret your own fond dove."

"It's a barcarolle — is it not, monsieur?"

"No, my dear girl; that's called a villanelle,
the favorite song of our ancient troubadours, and
of shepherds who bemoaned their shepherdesses."

"What a pity that I don't know Italian!"

"What do you require Italian for,—in order to say,

> Is she not the one I love?"

"Be quiet, be quiet; they're singing in French now," said Blanche, pressing close to the window-panes, and signing with her hand to Chaudoreille not to stir.

"What's that you're saying?" cried the sitar master, rising in surprise,—"for me to be quiet! Does that noise out there disturb you too much? To the devil with the street singers who prevent you from hearing me! I hardly know how to restrain myself from going to drive them away with a few blows from my good blade Rolande!"

"If I only dared open my window for a few moments," sighed Blanche. "But no, I must not, for M. Touquet has firmly forbidden me to do so. What a pretty, pretty air! Ah, I shall easily remember that,

> I love to eternity
> My darling is all to me ;

that's the refrain."

"No, divine Blanche, you are mistaken ; these are the words,—

> I have lost my turtle-dove,
> And her flight I must pursue, —
> Is she not the one I love?"

The singers departed. Blanche then left the casement, and, on turning, saw Chaudoreille with his neck elongated, the better to execute a note. She could not restrain a desire to laugh, which was evoked by the face of the chevalier; and the latter remained with his mouth open, not knowing how to take the young girl's laughter, when Marguerite entered the room.

"It's burned at last," said the old woman as she came in.

"What is burned," cried Chaudoreille, — "the roast?"

"Ah, yes, indeed; it's a book of witchcraft, of magic. It was very hard to get it to burn, those books are so accustomed to fire."

"What is that you say, Marguerite? You have books of magic, — you who are afraid of everything? Do you wish to enter into communication with the spirits of the other world?"

"Ah, God keep me from it, Monsieur Chaudoreille. But I'll tell you how that book came into my hands, where it didn't stay long, for it seemed to me that that cursed conjuring-book burned my fingers. My master wished me to change my room —because—but I oughtn't to tell you that."

"Try to remember what you wished to tell me."

"Well, it seems I must quit the room I've occupied, to go into one in which no one has set foot during the eight years I have been in the house; and, to judge by the look of it, no one had visited it for a long time before. It's so dark, so dismal;

the window-panes, which are two inches thick with dust, hardly allow the daylight to penetrate into the room."

"I had an idea — God forgive me — that she was going to recount to me all the spiders' webs she had found there. What do you think of it, my charming pupil?"

Blanche did not answer, for she had paid no attention to what Marguerite said; she was committing to memory the sweet refrain which had appeared so pretty to her, and was repeating in a low voice, —

"I love to eternity; "

and Chaudoreille, seeing her steeped in reverie, would not disturb her, fully persuaded that the young girl could not defend her heart against the charms of the villanelle.

"It's not a question of spiders," resumed the old servant, rather ill-humoredly; "if I had not seen that which — but at the bottom of a closet Mademoiselle Blanche found a diabolical book; it was the conjuring-book of a sorcerer named Odoard. Have you ever heard tell of a sorcerer by that name?"

"No, not that I remember. If you were to ask me about a brave man, a man of spirit, a rake of honor, most certainly I should have known him; but a sorcerer! What the devil do you think I should have to do with him? These people don't fight."

" Monsieur Chaudoreille, — you who are so brave, — you must render me a service."

" What is it ? " inquired Chaudoreille, paying more attention to Marguerite's words.

" Just now, after having burned the conjuring-book of that Odoard, surnamed the great Tier of Tags, I made another inspection of my room, sprinkling holy water everywhere, as you may well suppose."

" And what followed ? "

" At the end of the alcove I perceived a little door, — one would never have supposed there was a door there ; but, though old, I have good eyes, and, while pushing the bed, which made the wain-scot creak, I saw the door."

" To the point, I beg of you," resumed Chau-doreille, whose eyes betrayed the uneasiness he tried in vain to dissemble.

" Well, now, I confess to you, monsieur, that I didn't dare open that door. It was no doubt the door of a closet; but that alcove is so gloomy, so dark. Finally, I'll be very much obliged if you'll come up with me and go first into whatever place we find there. I daren't ask M. Touquet, for he'd scoff at me."

" And he would be right, by jingo ! Why, Mar-guerite, at your age, not to have more courage than that ! "

" What can you expect ? I'm afraid there may be a goblin in that closet, who will jump in my face when I open the door, which has perhaps been closed for many years; for I've never seen M. Touquet enter the room."

" Don't goblins pass through keyholes? Come, Marguerite, I blush for your cowardice."

" No one can say that sorcerers are rare in Paris. Haven't they established a Chamber at the Arsenal expressly to judge them?"

" That's true, I confess; but I don't see what makes you imagine there are any in this house?"

"Ah, Monsieur Chaudoreille, if I was to tell you all I have seen and heard — and at night the noises which — "

" What have you seen, dear nurse?" inquired Blanche, whose reverie had flown, and who had heard the last words of the old woman.

" Nothing—nothing—mademoiselle;" and the old servant added, addressing the chevalier in a low tone, " My master doesn't like me to talk of it, and he'll send me away if he learns — "

" That's enough; I don't wish to hear anything further," said Chaudoreille, rising and taking his hat. "And since Touquet has forbidden you to tell these idle stories, I beg you not to deafen my ears with them."

" But you'll come upstairs with me and look in the closet — won't you, monsieur?"

" Ah, mon Dieu! I hear ten o'clock striking; I should be in the city now; I didn't receive ten crowns for listening to your old stories; I must run. Au revoir, my interesting pupil. I am delighted that my last variations gave you pleasure. I hope before long to give you another lesson. With a master like me, you should be a virtuoso."

While saying these words Chaudoreille drew himself up, placed his left hand on his hip, arranged his right arm as though he were about to take his weapon; but, instead of drawing Rolande from the scabbard, he carried his hand to his hat and bowed respectfully to Blanche; then, passing quickly by Marguerite, who tried vainly to restrain him, he opened the door and went downstairs humming, —

> You regret your own fond dove,
> As the loss of mine I rue.

CHAPTER VI

THE LOVERS. THE GOSSIPS

THE barber Touquet's shop was as usual filled
with a motley crowd of people of all classes.
There were gathered students, shopkeepers, pages,
poets, bachelors, adventurers, and even young
noblemen; for the fashion of the time permitted
these amiable libertines to mingle sometimes with
persons in the lower classes of society, whether
they sought new sensations in listening to a language which for them had all the fascinating charm
of novelty, or whether it was for the purpose of
playing tricks on the persons with whom they
thus mixed.

Master Touquet's shop was large, and more-
over furnished with benches, which latter conve-
niences were an almost unheard-of luxury in a
time when people took their diversions standing,
and when no one was seated even at the play.
The barber by this means extended his custom;
he attended to everything, answered everybody,
and did more himself than ten hairdressers of
today. His hand, which was skilful, nimble and
accurate with scissors or razor, had earned him the
reputation of being one of the best barbers in

Paris, and drew to his shop many fops, because in the middle class one held it an honor to be able to say, while caressing one's chin, " I've been shaved by Touquet." But those whom he had served sometimes remained for a long time in conversation with the persons who were awaiting their turn, the greater part of these idlers desiring to chat for a moment on the news of the day and the adventures of the night. Towards ten o'clock in the morning there was always a numerous gathering at Master Touquet's shop.

There one saw all kinds of toilets ; but then, as today, rich garments did not always betoken rank or fortune in those who wore them. The taste for luxury was becoming general, because consideration was accorded only to those who had splendid equipages and magnificent clothing. An appearance of wealth and power obtained all the honors ; true merit without distinction, without renown, remained forgotten and in poverty. And one assuredly sees the same thing today.

Access to court was easy. For a parvenu to introduce himself there, often nothing more was necessary than a costume similar to those worn by courtiers, — the hat adorned by a feather, a doublet and mantle of satin or velvet, the sword at the belt, the whole enlivened by trimmings of gold or silver braid. Each sought to procure for himself the most splendid personal appearance, and many ruined themselves in order to appear wealthy.

An attempt was, however, made to arrest this tendency to luxurious habits, which could not hide the poverty of the time. By an edict of the month of November of the year 1633, it was forbidden to all subjects to wear on their shirts, cuffs, head-dresses, or on other linen, all openwork, embroideries of gold or silver thread, braids, laces or cut points, manufactured either within or without the realm.

In the following year a second edict appeared, which prohibited the employment, in habiliments, of any kind of cloth of gold or silver, real or imitation, and decreed that the richest garments should be of velvet, satin or taffetas, without other ornament than two bands of silk embroidery; it also forbade that the liveries of pages, lackeys and coachmen should be made of any other than woollen stuffs. But these laws were soon infringed; men will always have the desire to appear more than they are, and women to hide what they are.

Among the different personages assembled in the barber's shop there was one who chatted with nobody and seemed to take not the slightest interest in the relation of the scandalous adventures of the night. This was a young man who appeared about nineteen years of age or a little over, endowed with a physiognomy by no means cheerful; for one ordinarily applies that term to those round, fresh faces, red and plump, which breathe health and gayety. He had beautiful eyes, but was pale;

noble features, but rather a melancholy expression ;
finally, he had what one calls an interesting face,
and this sort are in general more fortunate in love
than those of cheerful physiognomy. The young
man's costume was very simple ; neither ornament
nor embroidery adorned his gray coat, buttoned just
to the knee and cut like our frock coat of today ;
his belt was black ; no ribbons floated from his
knees and his arms ; he neither had a sword nor
laces, nor plumes on the broad brim of his hat.

He had been for a very long time in the barber's
shop. On entering, his eyes had appeared to search
for something other than the master of the place ;
he had thrown glances towards the back shop, and
still continued to do so. Several times already his
turn had come and Touquet had said to him, —

"Whenever you wish, seigneur bachelor."

The young man's simple costume was, in fact,
that which was ordinarily worn by law students in
Paris ; but to each invitation of the barber the
bachelor only answered, " I am not pressed for
time," and another took his place.

After a time the loiterers and gossips departed
and the young man found himself alone with Touquet, to whom his conduct began to appear singular.

"Now you can no longer yield your turn to
anybody," said the barber, offering a chair to the
stranger. " In truth I cannot shave you ; you have
not enough on your chin ; but without doubt you

came for something, and I am at your service, monsieur."

"Yes," said the young man with an embarrassed air, turning his eyes towards the back shop, "I should like — my hair is too long, and — "

"Seat yourself here, seigneur bachelor; you will find that I am skilful; my hand is as well accustomed to the scissors as to the razor."

The young man decided at last to intrust his head to the barber, but as soon as the latter paused for a moment he profited by it to turn and look into the back shop.

"Are you looking for anything, monsieur?" said Touquet, whom this trick did not escape.

"No — no. I was only looking to see if you were alone here."

"Yes, monsieur; you see I have no need of anybody to help me in order to satisfy my customers."

"Indeed, someone told me you were extremely skilful."

"And monsieur has had time to judge of my talent, he has been nearly two hours in my shop."

"I had nothing pressing to do; and then, I wished to obtain some information of you. Tell me, my friend, who occupies the first story of this house."

"I do, monsieur," said Touquet, after a moment's hesitation.

The young man seemed vexed then that he had asked the question.

" May I learn, monsieur, how that interests you?" resumed Touquet, looking at the unknown attentively.

"Ah, it is that I am looking for a lodging — in this quarter. One chamber would suffice me. Do you not take lodgers, and could you give me a room if this house belongs to you?"

" This house does belong to me ; in fact, monsieur, I cannot grant your request. For a long time I have let no lodgings, and I have no room in the house, which is not very large."

" What! you cannot let me a single chamber, a closet even? I repeat to you, I wish to have one in this neighborhood ; I often have business in the Louvre. I will pay you anything that you ask."

"Anything?" said the barber, glancing ironically at the young man's simple garments. " You are getting on, perhaps, a little, monsieur student. All the same, your desires cannot be gratified, and I advise you to renounce your plans."

Touquet dwelt on this last phrase, and the young man's face reddened a little ; but the barber had finished his ministrations, and the former had no way of prolonging his stay with a man who did not appear to wish to continue the conversation, and to whom he feared he had said too much. The bachelor rose, paid, and at last left the shop, but not without looking up at the windows of the house.

" That's a lover," said Touquet, as soon as the

young man had taken his departure. "Yes, his
uneasiness, his looks, his questions — oh, I understand it all. I have served too many lovers
ever to be deceived about that. Curse it! this is
just what I feared. What vexations I foresee!
What anxieties are about to assail me! He must
have seen Blanche, but where? when? how? She
never leaves the house without me, and that very
rarely; however, this young man is in love with
her, I'll bet a hundred pieces of gold. Halloo
there, Marguerite! Marguerite!"

The old servant had heard her master's loud
voice; she mentally invoked her patron saint and
went down to the shop.

"How long is it since Blanche went out without my knowing it?" said the barber suddenly.

"Went out? Mademoiselle Blanche?" said
Marguerite, looking at her master in surprise.

"Yes, — went out with you. Why don't you
answer?"

"Blessed Holy Virgin! that hasn't happened
for two years; then Mademoiselle Blanche was
still a child, and you sometimes allowed her to go
with me to take a turn in the big Pré-aux-Clercs.
But since that time the poor little thing has not
been out, I believe, except twice with you, and
that was at night, and Mademoiselle Blanche had
a very thick veil."

"I didn't ask you if she had been out with
me. And has any young man been here in my

absence who has asked you about her, or who has sought to be introduced to her?"

"Indeed, I would have given him a warm reception. Monsieur doesn't know me. Except the Chevalier Chaudoreille, mademoiselle has seen no one; as to the latter, he came this morning to give her a music lesson."

"Oh, Chaudoreille isn't dangerous; but if some student, some young page, should come in my absence and seek to see Blanche, remember to send such heedless fellows away promptly."

"Yes, monsieur, yes. Oh, you may be easy. Besides, hasn't the beautiful child always about her a precious talisman which will preserve her from all danger? I defy ten gallants to turn her head so long as she carries it, and I will see that she does not leave it off."

"Watch, rather, that she does not open her window; that will be better. If that should happen, I should be obliged to give her the little room which opens on the court."

"Ah, monsieur, Mademoiselle Blanche would die there of weariness; there one can barely see the light, and the poor little thing does not go out, and could only work during the daytime with a candle."

"Unless she opens her window, it will be a long time before she occupies it," said Touquet in a low voice, making a sign to the servant to leave him, which the latter did, saying, —

"What a misfortune not to have faith in talismans! If monsieur believed in them, he would not deprive that poor little thing of every amusement."

The barber had not been mistaken in judging that the young man, who had had so much difficulty in tearing himself away from the shop, was a lover.

The Italian's song had so captivated Blanche's ears that the young girl had stood close to her casement, and had not budged from it during the time that her music master had made his variations on the villanelle. At the same moment Urbain was passing, and he had stopped to listen to the music, and while listening his glance was carried to Blanche's window. At first he had seen nothing but some very small panes; but at last, through these panes, his eyes could distinguish a face so pretty, eyes so blue and so full of the pleasure that Blanche was experiencing, that the young man had remained motionless, his looks fixed upon that window, near which the charming apparition remained. When the music ceased the pretty face disappeared, and the young man had said to himself, —

"I was not in error; there is an angel, a divinity, in that house."

And as that angel, that divinity, lived in the modest house of a barber, the bachelor had believed he should penetrate into the third heaven

in entering Master Touquet's shop; but he returned to ideas more terrestrial on seeing nothing
but men who had come to be shaved, who had
about them nothing divine, despite all the es-
sences with which their chins were besmeared.
Urbain had glanced towards the back shop, hoping to perceive the pretty figure of the first floor,
and had prolonged as much as possible his stay in
the barber's shop. We have witnessed the result
of his conversation with the barber.

The young man departed, very much out of
sorts; he perceived that he had made a blunder
in questioning the barber, who was probably his
adored one's father; for the young men of that
time were inflamed with love as quickly as those
of today. He felt that before going into the shop
he should have obtained some information in the
neighborhood, and he decided to finish as he
should have begun. In all times the bakers have
had very correct ideas about their neighbors, because the neighbors are all obliged to go or to send
to the baker's. Urbain went into a shop at a little
distance, and while paying for some rolls entered
into conversation with the woman who was behind
the counter, — a conversation in which all the servants who arrived at that moment took part.

"Do you know a barber in this street?"

"A barber? Yes, my good monsieur; down
there at the corner of the Rue Saint-Honoré, —
Master Touquet. Has monsieur some business

with him? Oh, he's a very skilful man at his trade,
and has made lots of money, by shaving beards,
or in some other way. What that is I won't pretend to tell you. That's so — isn't it, Madame
Ledoux?"

"It is true," said Madame Ledoux, resting a
basket of vegetables on the counter, "that Touquet has not always enjoyed an excellent reputation. I have lived in the neighborhood for eight
years and, thank God, I know everything that has
passed here, — all that everybody has done here,
and all that everybody is still doing; and that
reminds me that yesterday evening I saw Madame
Grippart come home at ten o'clock with a young
man, who left her in front of the grocer's shop
after having held her hand in his for more than
two hours, while that poor Grippart was peacefully slumbering, for he goes to bed at nine o'clock.
That doesn't trouble him; he well deserves it,
for he went about everywhere saying that his wife
had a strong breath, and those things need not be
said. — But to return to Master Touquet. Oh,
that's a sly blade, a crafty, cunning fellow. I've
known him since he settled in this street; he's
been here nearly fifteen years. He rented the
house which belonged to M. Richard. You know,
my neighbor, the old cloth merchant?"

"The one whose wife had two fat, plump twins
seven months after they were married?"

"Who didn't look at all like their father. It's

the same. Well, this Touquet was then barber,
bathkeeper and lodging-house keeper, and report
says that beside that he helped young men of family in their love affairs. He then kept two shop-
men, and should have made money ; however, he
was for a long time miserably poor, since his shop-
men left him because he did not pay them. Everyone was very much astonished ten years ago when
Touquet kept with him, and began to educate as
his own child, the daughter of a man whom he
did not know, who had come to lodge with him
by chance, and who was killed the same night in
a fight between some worthless fellows and the
officers of the watch. The poor man ! they found
his corpse down there, — Rue Saint-Honoré, before the draper's shop. Do you remember it, Madame Legras ? "

Madame Legras, who had just come into the
baker's shop, began by throwing herself on a chair
and crying, —

" Good-day, ladies ! Good Heavens ! how dear
the fish is today, nobody can look at it."

And Urbain sighed, saying, " The fish will take
us away from the barber " ; but to advance in love
one must often have patience, and in the midst of
all this gossip that which concerned Touquet was
precious to the young bachelor.

" I wished to have an eel to feast my husband,
but it was impossible."

" Is it his birthday ? "

"No; but he took me yesterday for a walk around the Bastile, and one compliment brings on another. I can say with pride that there are few households so united as ours. During the four years that I have been married to my second husband, M. Legras, we have quarrelled only five times; but that was always for some trifling cause. What were you talking about, ladies?"

"Of our neighbor Touquet, about whom this gentleman desired some information."

"Touquet the barber? My word, ladies, you may say whatever you will, but I don't like that man."

"He's a very handsome man, however."

"Yes, of the same height as M. Legras; but there is something hard and false and stern in his appearance."

"Yes, for some time past; formerly he was gayer, more open. Now monsieur never chats; he has grown proud."

"That's not surprising; he has made money."

"Yes, by shaving beards perhaps."

"It's a good deal more likely he has made it by assisting the love affairs of some great nobleman, in procuring and abducting some beauty."

"Come, ladies, don't be so malicious. As for me, you know I haven't a bad tongue. Touquet is very skilful at his trade. I know very well that in order to buy and pay for that house where he now is he must have shaved a good many faces;

but they say now the barber is very steady and economical."

" When the devil is old — "

" Touquet is not old; he's hardly over forty years."

" Adopting that little girl should have brought him good luck."

" That's what I was telling monsieur. Poor little thing ! Nobody knows anything about her, except that she had a father."

" Well, neighbor, somebody found a letter on him having for an address, 'To Monsieur Moranval, gentleman.' "

" Ah, he was a gentleman ? "

" Yes, my dear. Oh, I remember all that as if it were yesterday."

" How fortunate one is in having such a memory ! And what did the letter say ? "

" It seemed that there were only a few lines of which nobody could make much of anything ; someone recommended to this Moranval to take great precautions in the business which brought him to Paris. But what business ? Nobody knows anything about it."

" Did they find nothing else on him ? "

" No ; there is little doubt that the poor man was robbed after being murdered."

" Did they go to Touquet's to inquire what he knew about it ? "

" Touquet answered the officers of justice that

the man had come down to his house the evening
before, and had introduced himself as a gentleman
who was about to remain for some time in Paris;
that he had first asked him to put his little girl to
bed, and that later he had gone out, saying he
should be absent for an hour or so. Touquet
had waited up for him a great part of the night,
and it was not till the next day that he learned
from public rumor that a man had been found
murdered in the Rue Saint-Honoré, a short distance from his house; that, being already uneasy
about his guest, he had gone to see the victim, and
had recognized the man who had arrived at his
place the evening before."

"I hope that's a history. Unfortunately, one
hears only too many similar stories. Ours are really
cut-throat streets, and it is not well, after nine
o'clock, to be out in them. The gentlemen of the
parliament make decrees often enough, but it
doesn't do much good. A little while ago, it seems
a counsellor of the Chamber of Investigation was
similarly murdered. The parliament has just promulgated a new ordinance against these worthless
fellows — haven't they, monsieur?"

"Yes," said Urbain; "the public prosecutor
has just complained of murders, assassinations and
robberies, which take place every day, as many
upon the highways as in the city or the suburbs, by
armed persons who forcibly break into houses, and
that through the negligence of the police officers

who do not properly perform their duty. Parliament yesterday passed a new decree, ordering that vagabonds, men of bad character, and robbers, should vacate the city and the faubourgs of Paris within twenty-four hours."

"Well, you'll see, tonight we shall hear a bigger rumpus than ever."

"And the barber Touquet is not married?" resumed Urbain, who wished to return to the subject of conversation which was interesting to him.

"No, he's a bachelor," said Madame Ledoux.

"And this young girl that lodges with him — "

"She's the little one whom he adopted."

"She had no other protectors?"

"What could you expect, since nobody knew her parents? Touquet has, they say, taken very good care of her; I will do him the justice to say that. He has taken into his house, to wait on the little one, a servant, old Marguerite, a gossip, who is always seeking for preservatives against the wind, the thunder, the sorcerers, or even for talismans to guard her dear Blanche against the snares of the gallants."

"Blanche, then, is the name of the young girl?"

"Yes; that is her name."

"And this old woman is the only one about her?"

"Mercy! isn't that enough? Besides, the little one never goes out, and no one ever sees her even put her nose out of the window."

" Tell me, ladies, don't you think, with me, that
the barber has brought up this pretty child for
himself, and that he would not take so much care
of her unless he was in love with her?''

"Indeed, that might very well be possible. Touquet is still young, and perhaps wishes to marry
her."

" Nonsense ! I don't believe that ; and besides,
they say that the young person is not good-looking. I have heard it said by an ugly little thin
man, with a long sword, who is often at the barber's shop, that the orphan is very ugly."

" Ugly ! " cried Urbain quickly. " That's a
frightful lie ! "

" Ah, monsieur has seen her, then ? " immediately said the gossips, looking at the young man
with a mischievous air.

The latter felt that he had committed an im-
prudence ; but having nothing more to learn from
these dames, he made them a low bow and left the
shop, leaving the gossips to talk among themselves.

" Well, if he hasn't gone, and he didn't tell us
what he wanted with Touquet."

But Urbain had learned enough ; and while
directing his steps toward the Rue Montmartre,
where he dwelt, our lover cogitated thus : —

" She's not the barber's daughter ; he has stood
to her in place of a father, but he has no rights
over her except those accorded to a benefactor by

a grateful heart. She's the daughter of a gentleman, which is much better; my father was a gentleman also, who valiantly fought under King Henry. The old soldiers still remember Captain Dorgeville, and the name which he has transmitted to me is pure and without stain. I am alone in the world; I am my own master. Like her I have no parents, for a year ago death deprived me of my good mother. My fortune is very moderate, — twelve hundred livres income and a little house by the seaside. That is all my father left me; but she has nothing more, and by working I could render her happy. I am about to take my bachelor's degree, but I shall now leave this unfruitful career; science brings fortune too slowly. I don't know, however, if I could please her. Yes, that's the first task with which I should occupy myself. If she loves me, I will ask her hand of the barber. He will wish to assure her happiness; he could not refuse me unless he himself — If these women said rightly he is in love with her. The hard tone with which he answered me this morning, his refusal to lodge me in his house, make me believe it. And that wretch who dared to say that she was ugly! — when object more enchanting never met my eyes. Ah, it wasn't of her he was speaking. If such a thing could happen, I should like to see her, to tell her of the love which she has inspired; and, if I could manage to please her, nothing then could prevent me from becoming her husband."

These were, somebody will say, very foolish plans concerning a young girl whose face one had only perceived through some very dim window-panes; and it was on the possession of this almost ideal object that Urbain already based the happiness of his life. But let us look back on our own lives. We were hardly more reasonable, — happy if between us and the chimeras which enchanted us there was nothing thicker than a pane of glass.

CHAPTER VII

Intrigues Thicken

CHAUDOREILLE now started off at a great pace towards the city. The ten crowns which he felt in his purse, on which he prudently kept his hand while walking, caused him to hold his head even more arrogantly than he usually did. He had placed his little hat over his left eye in such a manner that the old red feather with which it was adorned fell precisely over his right eye, and as he walked mincingly along, at each step that he took the chevalier could thus enjoy the waving of his ridiculous plume.

Never had the Chevalier de Chaudoreille felt so clever, so inordinately satisfied with himself. Blanche's image, so sweet, so beautiful, her delightful manner, which possessed all the innocent witchery of girlhood, was still before his eyes, and as he was never lacking in confidence as to his own merits, he readily persuaded himself that the young beauty could not see him with indifference, and was even a little taken with him. On the other hand, the enterprise with which he was charged by the barber, as the agent of the Marquis de Villebelle, flattered his self-love. He believed himself the friend, the confidant, of the Marquis de Villebelle, although the latter had never spoken to him; but he thought that the adroitness with which he would serve him in his amorous plan would be sooner or later known to the great nobleman and would win his favor. Full of this idea, he hastened to reach the shop of which Touquet had spoken. Before entering, Chaudoreille resumed to himself, —

"One mustn't go in here," said he, "looking like a snob, and turn the shop upside down without buying anything. I must not forget that I am sent by a great personage. They have given me ten crowns on account, as the price of my services, but I can very well spend twenty-four sous."

This determination taken, he opened the door of the shop and entered nimbly; but in wheeling round in order to appear more graceful and to bow at the same time to the right and left, he sent Rolande's scabbard through one of the panes of the glass door, and it broke in a thousand pieces.

Chaudoreille's face lengthened and he felt some confusion, for he calculated that the price of the pane already exceeded the sum he had intended to lay out. Two young persons seated behind the counter burst into laughter, while an old woman placed opposite murmured between her teeth, —

" He must be very awkward."

" I will pay for it," said Chaudoreille at last, heaving a big sigh.

"Indeed I should hope so," responded the shopkeeper; "but has anyone ever seen a man carry a sword bigger than himself?"

At these words the chevalier drew himself up and stood on his tiptoes, and glanced angrily at the old woman.

"It's very astonishing," said he, "that anyone should permit herself such reflections. I carry the weapon that suits me, and if a bearded chin had said the same thing to me, my sword would have immediately taken the measure of his body."

"I didn't intend to say anything to make you angry," replied the shopkeeper, softening; "only it seemed to me that that long sword would embarrass you in walking."

"Embarrass me! That is a different thing," and Chaudoreille turned his back to the shopkeeper to approach the young ladies, saying to himself, —

"I didn't come here to discuss the length of my sword. Let's leave this woman's twaddle."

"What do you wish, monsieur?" said a young, squint-eyed girl, with a flat nose, thick lips and crooked chin, whose dark-red skin seemed covered with a coat of varnish.

Chaudoreille looked at her for some moments, saying to himself, —

"By jingo! she's not very much like the portrait of the little one which they gave me. It's true that love is blind, and that great noblemen like original faces."

But after looking at the person who addressed him, Chaudoreille glanced a little farther and perceived another woman measuring some ribbons. At the first glance the barber's messenger recognized the young girl whose portrait had been drawn for him. She was all Touquet had painted her, though he could not then see the color of her eyes, which were bent on the ribbon. Chaudoreille approached her and, bowing graciously, said to himself, —

"This is our affair. I have an astonishing tact for divining correctly. Other people hesitate for an hour; but I recognize immediately those who have been pointed out to me, and I am never deceived. Here are some delightful ribbons," said Chaudoreille, leaning on the counter, carelessly caressing his chin, and trying to imitate the free manners and impertinent tone of the profligates of the day.

The young girl then raised her eyes to the chevalier; their brightness, their expression, arrested Chaudoreille in the midst of a compliment from which he expected the most happy results.

"By jingo! what a glance! what fire!" said he, taking a step backward, while the damsel continued to look at him.

In order to enchant her he attempted to turn a light pirouette, in which Rolande's scabbard just missed putting out the eye of the cat, which was lying on a neighboring stool. A mocking smile

played on the lips of the young girl, who said,
"What ribbon does monsieur wish?"

"What ribbon? My faith! I don't much know.
Something to match the rest of my costume. It
is to make a knot for Rolande."

"And who is Rolande, monsieur?"

"My sword, beautiful brunette, which I will
pass through the body of him who denies that
you have the most beautiful eyes in the world."

Delighted at his compliment, Chaudoreille said
to himself in an undertone, —

"Take care; we mustn't go too far, or be too
amiable; I must not forget that I did not come
here on my own account. This young girl appears somewhat smitten, from the way she looks at
me. Zounds! if I had a ruff I would with good-
will cheat the Marquis de Villebelle of the little
one. Come, Chaudoreille, hide your charms if you
can; don't dart your glances at this pretty person, and hasten to tell her that she must not occupy herself with you."

While saying this Chaudoreille unrolled and examined twenty different ribbons, approaching them
to the handle of his sword and throwing from
time to time a glance about him, to assure himself that he could speak without being heard by
the other two women in the shop.

This manœuvre did not escape the eyes of the
young girl, who smiled, and seemed to wait for
Chaudoreille to explain himself. Happily for

Chaudoreille, two people came into the shop, and while the old woman and the other damsel were serving them, he opened a conversation in a low tone.

"I did not come here only to buy a ribbon, celestial merchant."

"If you wish anything else, speak, monsieur, and you shall be served."

"Julia, have you not finished with monsieur?" said the old woman impatiently, looking angrily at the long falchion of the chevalier, which, every time he moved, threatened her cat's eyes.

"Monsieur has not decided yet," answered Julia, while Chaudoreille cried with an impertinent air, —

"It seems to me that I should be allowed to choose my own colors. When a man like me comes into a shop, one should, my good woman, keep him there as long as possible; if you wish to have my custom, leave me to chat as much as I please with this beautiful child."

This insolent mode of speech was then so much in fashion, that she remained silent, in place of putting the chevalier out, as would be done now to a coxcomb who behaved like Chaudoreille.

"Oh, by jingo! if one did not keep these little shopkeepers in their place I believe they would permit themselves to make observations to us," said Chaudoreille, approaching for the twentieth time a gold-colored ribbon to his doublet. "This color goes very well with my cloak. What do you think of it, adorable damsel?"

"I think that these ribbons are too fresh to blend with monsieur's clothing, and that that one swears at them."

"I confess that the velvet of my jerkin is a little tarnished, but what could you expect? When a man fights he necessarily attracts dust and powder. Here's a cloak that I've not had more than six weeks, and I'll wager that you would say it had been worn for some months."

"Decide on your ribbon, monsieur," said the young girl, without answering.

"Give me a gold-colored rosette," said Chaudoreille; and he added in a mysterious tone, "I have something very important to communicate to you."

"I doubt it," said Julia.

"Come," said Chaudoreille to himself, "I'll wager that she believes that I'm in love with her and is impatiently awaiting my declaration. I'm incorrigible; I let myself go, and I have turned her head without even perceiving it. Let us hasten to disabuse her. — No, beautiful brunette, you need not doubt it," responded he, lowering his eyes with a coquettish air; "I ought to confess to you that it is not of myself that I seek you, and that I am only the ambassador of Love, when you would have taken me for Love himself."

Julia's hearty laughter prevented Chaudoreille

from continuing, and he did not know at first how to take this excessive gayety; but his self-love always made him place things to his own advantage, and he decided to laugh also, while saying in a low tone to the young girl, —

"Isn't it very funny to behold in me a lover's messenger? — I, who could cheat them all of their conquests. It's a great joke, in truth."

"Come, monsieur ambassador, give me your message," said Julia, looking pityingly at the envoy.

Chaudoreille threw a glance all around him, put a finger on his mouth, examined the persons who were in the shop, pushed from him a stool on which the cat was lying, then leaning toward Julia with the air of a conspirator, he whispered in her ear, —

"A great lord sent me to you. He's a rich and powerful man; he's a personage in favor; he's the gallant who—"

"He's the Marquis de Villebelle," said Julia impatiently. "I've known him for a long time. What does he want with me? What has he bidden you say to me? Come, monsieur, speak."

"It must be that I am very adroit," said Chaudoreille, "when without my speaking she divines everything that I wish to say to her. — Since you know his name," resumed he, again approaching his face to Julia's ear, the latter brusquely pushing him away, "I have no need of telling you. This great nobleman adores you."

"Undoubtedly he did not employ you to express his sentiments."

"No, but he sent me to ask you to meet him. If you do not accord him this favor, he will set fire to the four corners of this street, that he may have the pleasure of saving you, fair Julia, — for it is thus I believe that you are called, which makes me think that you are not French. Have I rightly divined?"

"Has anyone commissioned you to ask that question?" asked Julia, looking at Chaudoreille disdainfully.

The latter bit his lips, put his left hand on his hip, and said in a bass voice, —

"What shall I say to the noble Marquis de Villebelle, of whom I am the intimate confidant, and whom I represent at this moment?"

"Tell him to choose his messengers better," said Julia in a dry tone.

"I was sure of it," said Chaudoreille, taking some steps backward; "she has fallen in love with me; it is my personal attractions that have played me this trick. All this is very disagreeable; I should have disguised myself a little, or at least should not have permitted my eyes to make fresh wounds. There is money to be got here. By jingo! I must not lose sight of that;" and Chaudoreille repeated to Julia, not allowing her, as a matter of prudence, to see more than his profile, —

"What shall I say to the marquis? Where will you walk tomorrow evening?"

The young girl waited for some moments in silence, appearing to reflect deeply; while Chaudoreille fingered his purse, very anxious as to her answer, and saying to himself, —

"In any case, I shall not give them back the ten crowns.

"Tomorrow evening at eight o'clock, on the Pont de la Tournelle," said the young Italian at last; for Julia, in fact, was not French.

"'Tis enough," responded Chaudoreille, continuing to hold himself in such a manner as to show only his profile; "I have nothing more to ask of you; let us part, for fear the sight of me make you change your resolution."

The messenger already had hold of the knob of the door when Julia recalled him.

"You have forgotten to pay for your ribbon, monsieur."

"By Jove! that's true. What the devil has got me? I'm as stupid as possible."

While saying this Chaudoreille drew forth his purse, rattling the ten crowns that it held as loudly as possible, counting and recounting them several times in his hand.

"I don't know if I have any change about me," said he. "Ordinarily I carry nothing but gold, it is so much lighter. How much is it, beautiful merchant?"

"Thirty sous, monsieur."

"Thirty sous for a rosette!" cried Chaudo-reille to himself, making a grimace, and putting the coins back in his purse. "That seems to me a considerable price. You must notice that the ribbon is very narrow."

"For a man who carries nothing but gold," said Julia, "I am astonished that monsieur should bargain over such a trifle."

"I'm not bargaining; but still it seems to me that you might knock something off, and that for twenty-four sous one ought to have a superb rosette. No matter; I'll pay it with a good grace; give me my change."

He presented one of the crowns with a sigh, and while Julia was counting out his change he fastened the gold-colored rosette to Rolande's handle. The effect that the ribbon would produce somewhat mitigated his regrets at paying thirty sous for it. He took the money, and, recalling to himself that they could ask him to pay for something else, he ran to the door, darted into the street and disappeared as quickly as possible.

"And my window-pane," said the old shop-keeper, — "did he pay for my pane?"

"Ah, mon Dieu! no, madame," answered Julia.

"I was sure of it. Run, my good girls, run as fast as you can. That wicked coxcomb, trying to play the spark, with his old threadbare mantle, with his old feather that I wouldn't take to dust

my shelves! He turned everything upside down
here, and just barely missed putting out my cat's
eyes; he was impertinent to me, bargained for two
hours over a rosette, and ran away without paying for the pane. He's some pickpocket, some
cutpurse."

The two damsels opened the shop door and
looked down the street, but could see nothing of
monsieur le chevalier.

"It's my fault, madame," said Julia; "I should
have asked him for the price of the window. I
will pay for it."

"Yes, mademoiselle; that will teach you another time not to listen to the conversation of
these gentlemen who make so much trouble and
haven't a sou in their pockets."

The young Italian did not answer. It is probable that at that moment she was not interested
in the pane of glass or in Chaudoreille.

Night approached. For some hours all had been
silent in the barber's shop; for he, following his
habitual custom, had closed his shutters as soon
as day declined, since he was not in the habit of
receiving strangers and waited on no customers
in the evening. This was the time that Touquet
had chosen for his dinner hour, although people
commonly took this meal much earlier. The barber's dinner, therefore, also passed for a supper.

As soon as Marguerite called from her kitchen,
" We are waiting for you, mademoiselle," Blanche

left her room and quickly went down into the
lower room where the meal was served. Touquet
dined with the young girl. This was the moment
of the day when they were longest together, although the barber always appeared to wish to
abridge the time as much as possible, remaining at
the table only as long as was absolutely necessary
in order to satisfy his appetite, and answering only
in monosyllables to all that Blanche said to him,
so as not to prolong the duration of the repast.

This time the barber was, as usual, seated near
the hearth, waiting for Blanche to come down;
but when she appeared, contrary to his custom,
he raised his eyes to the young girl and seemed
to wish to read hers. Surprised at being thus
regarded by him whose looks had always evaded
her smile, Blanche involuntarily lowered her eyes,
which beamed with truth and innocence, and a
little more color appeared in her cheeks; for the
barber's look was more piercing than usual.

Touquet already seemed reassured. The expression of Blanche's features had dissipated the
uneasiness which he had felt; he placed himself
at the table and made a sign to the lovely girl to
take her accustomed place. The meal seemed as
though it would pass in silence as usual; Marguerite only, while changing the dishes, ventured some
remarks, to which Blanche answered a few words.

But all of a sudden the young girl appeared to
recall an agreeable idea, and cried, —

"My friend, did you hear the music this morning?"

"The music," said Touquet, glancing furtively at Blanche; "yes, I believe I heard it."

"Oh, it was so pretty! They sang in Italian at first; then afterwards in French, — a romance. Wait; I believe I can remember the refrain," and Blanche sang with expression, —

> "I love to eternity,
> My darling is all to me."

The barber knitted his thick eyebrows while listening to Blanche.

"What! you have already learned the romance?" said he in an ironical tone.

"No, not all the romance; the refrain only."

"And that was the first time you had heard it?"

"Yes, monsieur."

"Did you open your window then?"

"No, though I should very much have liked to do so; but I glued myself against the window so as to hear better."

"And to see better, no doubt."

"See! Oh, I like to hear much better," answered Blanche, almost frightened at the barber's glance.

"Are there no curtains at your window?" asked Touquet in a moment.

"Yes, monsieur, there are curtains," answered the young girl timidly.

" Blanche, I've told you that I don't like you
to expose yourself to the oglings of the coxcombs
who pass and repass in the street."

" But, my friend, can anyone see me through
the windows ? "

" Yes ; no doubt of it."

" Oh, well, my friend, if that displeases you, I
won't go to the window again."

Touched by Blanche's sweetness, the barber
assumed a less severe expression, and, rising from
the table, he said, almost kindly, —

" Go back to your room, Blanche ; I will try
soon to render your life less monotonous. Yes, I
feel that you cannot continually remain in such
dull retirement."

" Why, I am all right, my friend ; and if I could
only learn that romance altogether, but M. Chaudoreille only sings me his villanelle, and that is not
amusing."

" I will buy you some others."

" Oh, try to get me the one I heard this morning, —

I love to eternity.

Can you remember it ? "

" Yes, yes ; I will remember it. — But I am
waiting for someone to come ; go upstairs to your
room."

Blanche curtseyed to the barber and gayly went
up to her room, while Touquet said to himself,
following her with his eyes, —

"Come, I was wrong to make myself uneasy; she knows nothing of him."

An hour after this conversation somebody knocked at the barber's door and Marguerite admitted Chaudoreille, who came into the lower room with the important air of a man who is very well pleased with himself.

"You're very late," said Touquet, signing to him to seat himself.

"Why, what the deuce, my dear fellow! Do you think that these affairs are so speedily arranged?"

"I don't believe, however, that you've been all this time in the shop where I sent you."

"No, undoubtedly; but I passed a greater part of the time there. After that it was necessary for me to have some dinner, for you did not invite me to partake of yours, I believe."

"Well, were you successful? Give me an account of your mission."

"I went there. Wait, while I dry my forehead a little."

The barber made a movement of impatience and Chaudoreille passed over his face a little silk handkerchief, which for prudence' sake he never unrolled. After emitting some exclamations of fatigue, during which Touquet impatiently stamped his foot, he commenced his story.

"To go to that place in the city I could take two roads; I don't know but I could take three."

"You wretch! take a dozen if you like, but get there."

"It was necessary for me to get there, and then to return here. I decided on going by the Pont-Neuf, then down the quay into the street. You know, where they sell such good tarts."

"Chaudoreille, you're mocking at me."

"No, I'm not; but it seemed to me I should tell you everything that I did. But you are so petulant. Finally, I took the shortest way. I went into the shop where the young girl works."

"That's good luck."

"I entered with that grace which characterizes me; I bowed first to an old woman who was on the right, and afterwards bowed to two young girls who were on the left. In the middle of the shop I saw nobody but a cat sleeping on a stool."

"No doubt you bowed to the cat also."

"Oh, if you interrupt me I shall get all mixed up. They asked me what I wanted; I answered, dissembling my designs, 'Let me see some ribbons.' They showed me some reds, some blues, some greens, some yellows, some oranges; during this time I examined the two little ones. As nature has endowed me with a penetrating eye, I recognized immediately the one you depicted for me."

"You spoke to her?"

"A moment and you shall see how I conducted the matter. I was sufficiently adroit to get her to serve me. She asked me what color I had decided upon; but I, with careful cunning, did not decide in order that I might prolong the conversation. At last, by a happy chance, some other people came into the shop; then we were less observed."

"And you told her what had brought you there?"

" I decided first for a gold color, and I got her to make a rosette for Rolande. Wait; don't you think this becomes me well?"

So saying, Chaudoreille rose and put his sword near Touquet's face, who pushed the chevalier rather brusquely into his seat, exclaiming, —

"If I didn't restrain myself I should break every bone in your body to teach you not to abuse my patience thus."

"There's no pleasure in conducting an intrigue with you," said Chaudoreille, a little disconcerted at being reseated so heavily; "but if you wish that I should come to the facts, here I am. I made known to her the intentions of the Marquis de Villebelle."

" His intentions? I didn't communicate them to you."

" That is to say, his love, his passion. At last I demanded a meeting for tomorrow evening."

" Well, what then?"

"She hesitated for a long time, reflected for a long time; then I redoubled my eloquence; I pictured the marquis dying of despair if she repulsed his vows."

" Idiot! was that necessary?"

"Yes, certainly; it was highly necessary; the little one was weighing it."

" Did she make any wry faces?"

" No; on the contrary, she gave me the most interesting glances."

" Finally, is she coming?"

" Yes, by jingo! she's coming. Yes; but it took me to decide her."

" Tomorrow evening?"

" Yes, at eight o'clock."

" Where is she to be?"

" On the Pont de la Tournelle."

" That's good."

" As soon as I had got her answer, I attached my rosette."

" Excuse me from the rest; I know enough."

" You must know that in bowing too precipitately I broke a pane, for which they made me pay a crown, and for which I hope I shall be reimbursed. — Ah, that's not all; I know that the lady is named Julia, and also that she is an Italian. You see I did not lose any time. Are you pleased with me?"

" Yes, it's not so bad," said Touquet, with a less gloomy expression, approaching a table on which Marguerite had, according to her usual custom, placed some cups and a pewter pot full of wine. " Stop your eternal chatter; I'm well enough pleased with you. Drink a cup of wine."

"You call exactitude of detail chatter," said Chaudoreille, filling one of the cups up to the brim; "but I was trying to show you that I did not steal the money which you gave me. As for the pane of glass, I had to make that circumstance known to you, for I had only nine crowns remaining. — Ah, I forgot; the gold-colored rosette cost me two crowns, so I've only received seven."

"Two crowns for that miserable knot," said the barber, glancing mockingly at the handle of the sword. "Chaudoreille, you have missed your vocation; you should be a steward; you know how to swell your bills."

"What must I understand by these words, I beg of you?"

"That that rosette did not cost over fifteen sous."

"Yes, for a passer-by, for an unknown, perhaps; but when one represents a great nobleman, shopkeepers fleece him, and I didn't believe that I should haggle. If anyone had asked me three times the price, I should have given it without uttering a word."

"Calm yourself," said Touquet, smiling at the heat with which Chaudoreille tried to prove that he had spent three crowns; "we must reimburse you for your ruff."

"Oh, I'm not uneasy about that, but what shall I do tomorrow? Shall I go to the rendezvous? Shall I carry off the little one?"

"No; that concerns me only. I can trust you
to startle the game for me, but I don't think
proper to let you bring it down."

"You know me very little still, my dear Touquet. I believe that you should render more justice to my adroitness and my valor. If you knew
how many intrigues I have drawn to a successful
end! It's necessary to see me in moments of difficulty. I take precedence over everybody; I would
abduct a Venus under the eyes of Mars, and all
the Vulcans would not make me afraid."

"I don't doubt it, but I don't want to put you
to the proof."

"All the worse for you, for you would see some
very surprising things. No obstacle would stop
me; when I'm excited I'm an Achilles. Wait; I
should just like once, by chance, that you should
find yourself in some danger, that you should have
need of help; then, as quick as lightning, with Rolande in my hand — "

At this moment a noise was heard in the street,
and Touquet, squeezing Chaudoreille's arm exclaimed, —

"Be quiet! be quiet! I hear something."

"What does it matter to us what they are doing
in the street? There are, perhaps, some young
men laughing and amusing themselves. Let them
do it. I tell you, then, that, brandishing my redoubtable sword — "

"Be quiet, then, stupid," resumed the barber,

holding the chevalier's arm still more tightly;
"they are beginning again."

They then distinctly heard the sound of a guitar
which someone was playing near the house.

"Someone who loves music," said Chaudoreille.

"Hush! let us listen," said Touquet, whose
features expressed the most lively anxiety, while
the chevalier murmured in a bass voice, —

"They don't play at all well; they have need
of some of my lessons."

Almost immediately a voice was heard which,
accompanied by the guitar, sang a tender romance,
of which the refrain recalled to the barber the
words which Blanche had quoted to him.

"No more doubt of it," said Touquet, rising
suddenly; "they are singing to her. Ah, reckless
fellow, I'll go and take away from you all desire
to return here."

While saying these words the barber ran to get
his poniard, which hung over the fireplace, while
Chaudoreille changed color and murmured, —

"What the devil is the matter with you? What
are you going to do? and who are you going to do
it to?"

"To an insolent fellow who is in front of this
house. Come, Chaudoreille; follow me. If there
were ten of them, they should have the pleasure
of feeling my poniard. You shall also have the
pleasure of chasing and chastising these black-
guards."

While saying this Touquet ran into the shop and hastened to open the door, being by that means sooner in the street than if he had gone by the passageway. While he precipitately drew the bolts, Chaudoreille rose with a good deal of fury and ran three times round the hall, crying, —

"Where the devil have I laid my sword?"

This feat accomplished, he perceived that Rolande had not left his side, and cried to Touquet, who could not hear him, —

"Stupid that I am! In my hurry I did not see him. I am with you; I have only to draw him from the scabbard. — Come then, Rolande. — It is this cursed knot which holds him. Plague be on the rosette! Touquet, here I am; amuse them a little until I can draw Rolande from the scabbard."

But the barber was already in the street, while Chaudoreille remained at the back of the room, appearing to be making futile efforts to draw his sword, crying all the while, —

"I am with you! Cursed rosette! Without it I should have already killed five or six."

CHAPTER VIII

Conversation by the Fireside

It was really for little Blanche that somebody was singing and accompanying himself on the guitar. Lovers are the most imprudent of mortals. Urbain in loving Blanche was experiencing love for the first time, for he would have scorned to have given the name of love to those momentary caprices of the fancy which are extinguished as soon as gratified; and even at the early date at which we are writing, the young men permitted themselves to have such whims; but when they loved truly that lasted in those good old times, or so they say, much longer than it does to-day, at least among the little shopkeepers. The great have always had their privileges, in love as in everything else.

A first love causes one to commit many imprudences; but the second time that one's heart is assailed by the tender passion, one has a little more experience; and the third time, one knows how to hide his play. It is necessary to become habituated to everything; and if women do not invariably hold to their first love, are not invariably faithful to it, it is only that they may acquire

this habituation, and it would ill become us to
call it a crime in them.

But Urbain disturbed himself very little, as it
will appear; he had unceasingly before his eyes
the face of the enchantress he had perceived at the
window, and he ardently desired to see her when
there should be nothing between them. What he
had heard from the gossips of the neighborhood
had strengthened his hope and perhaps added to
the feeling he already experienced for her, for there
was something romantic in the history of the
young orphan; extraordinary events inflame the
imagination, and that of a lover takes fire very
easily.

But before seeking to surmount the obstacles
which stood in the way of gaining the one he loved
it was first necessary to obtain her love, without
which all his plans could avail him nothing. One
may brave the jealousy of a rival, the watchfulness
of a tutor, anger, vengeance, and the daggers of a
thousand Arguses; but one cannot brave the indifference of the beloved object. Before that obstacle all prospects of happiness vanish. A very
much smitten lover wishes to find a heart which
responds to his own. That brutal love which is
satisfied with the possession of the body, without
caring for that of the soul, could only exist among
the petty tyrants of former times, who plundered
travellers and achieved the conquest of women
at the point of the sword; then, putting their

victims behind them on their horses, as a cus-
tom-house officer possesses himself of contraband
goods, went off to enjoy themselves with their
booty in the depths of their fastness, troubling
themselves very little that the unhappy creatures
responded to their loathsome caresses only with
tears.

Today love is more delicate. Before everything,
one desires to please ; and with his guineas the
great lord wishes to touch the heart as well as the
hand of the pretty dancer; and he succeeds, because dancers generally carry their hearts in their
hands.

While taking his humble meal Urbain said to
himself, —

"How shall I see her? How shall I make
myself known to her? Blanche — what a pretty
name ! and how well it suits her ! But the barber
doesn't seem very tractable ; his house is a veritable fortress. It is necessary, before everything,
that that charming girl should know that I love
her, that I adore her. This morning she listened
to the musicians, and appeared to be greatly
pleased with the last romance they sang. I know
that romance; I'll go this evening and sing it
under her window; perhaps she will show herself; perhaps at night she opens her window to
take the air."

The air was a little nipping, for the season was
severe ; but a lover always believes it is spring-

time. Delighted by the idea Urbain went home
to get his guitar, and waited impatiently, until the
streets should be deserted, to go and serenade a
woman whom he did not know.

This Spanish custom was then much in fashion
in France. There are still some little towns where
it is preserved, and where one may hear between
ten and eleven o'clock sentimental songs accompanied by the guitar ; but in the great capitals it
is only the blind and the organ-grinders who sing
love in the streets.

The hour propitious to lovers having arrived,
Urbain went to the Rue des Bourdonnais ; he had
easily recognized the barber's house, having spe-
cially noted it in the morning ; a feeble light which
shone between the curtains of Blanche's window
seemed to indicate that the young girl was not yet
sleeping, and, without reflecting that the other
dwellers in the house would hear him, Urbain had
sung with the most tender expression he could
put in his voice.

We have seen what followed on this impru-
dence. At the sound of bolts being drawn, the
young man softly departed, and, hiding at the entrance of the Rue des Mauvaises-Paroles, he heard
the threats and the swearing of Touquet.

"He's escaped," said the barber, reëntering the
lower room and angrily throwing his sword on the
table. These words seemed to break the charm
which held Rolande in his scabbard ; and Chau-

doreille, drawing his sword suddenly, and making it flash in the air, ran precipitately into the shop, crying, —

"And now, master singers, I'll let you see something fierce."

"Don't I tell you there's no one there," repeated Touquet, while Chaudoreille appeared to wish to draw the bolts of the door. "I made too much noise; the rascal heard me and ran off."

"Are you quite certain there's nobody there?" said Chaudoreille, still brandishing his sword.

"Yes, quite sure."

"I have a great inclination to go into the street and satisfy myself as to that."

"Do as you please about it; you are your own master."

"No; on reflection, I believe that would be a blunder; they may perhaps come back; it will be better to let them approach without fear; then we can fall suddenly upon them, and give them no quarter."

So saying, the chevalier put Rolande into the scabbard and returned to the lower room, where he seated himself before the fire and again filled his cup with wine, which he swallowed at one draught, to cool — so he said — his anger.

The barber strode up and down; he was strongly agitated, and appeared to have forgotten the presence of Chaudoreille, as he murmured at intervals in a gloomy voice, —

"That which I feared has happened at last! That beautiful bud has been seen, and they will all wish to cull it. They will seek to learn who she is, where she comes from; there will be a thousand remarks, a thousand inquiries, and who knows where that will lead? Bungling fellow that I am! I well had need to guard the child. I believed I had made a master stroke which would disarm all suspicion. I ought to have foreseen that one day she would be sixteen, that she would be charming, and that in order to possess her they would employ all the stratagems which I have often used on behalf of others."

"My dear fellow," said Chaudoreille, carrying to his lips for the third time a goblet filled to the brim, "my honest Touquet, if you don't want to take care of the little one any longer, give her to me, and I'll answer to you for it that no fop shall be allowed to see her face."

"What shall I give you?" said the barber, as if he had only just become aware of Chaudoreille's presence. "What are you talking about? Answer me!"

"Oh, by jingo. you were speaking of the young flower you have sheltered; I heard you very plainly."

"You heard me!" cried Touquet, seizing Chaudoreille by the arm with which he was holding his full cup; "and what did I say? What did you hear? Speak, wretch! Speak, will you?"

"Take care! you're shaking my arm. Here's
my doublet all stained with wine now. What the
deuce! You'll have to give me another."

"What have you heard?" repeated the barber
in a threatening voice, raising his closed fist on
Chaudoreille, while with the other hand he shook
him so briskly by the arm that a great part of the
wine covered the jaws and neck of the chevalier.

"Nothing, nothing, I swear to you," murmured
the latter, lowering his eyes, so as to avoid the
barber's gaze. "I only said to you that this wine
has a fine bouquet, and that if you wished to give
me some bottles to keep I should carefully guard
it from all eyes. I believe that's what I was saying; for, in truth, you've turned me upside down
with your irritable conduct, and I don't know
what I'm saying."

Touquet loosened his hold of Chaudoreille's
arm, as if ashamed of his hasty movements, and,
resuming his calmer tone, seated himself near the
latter.

"There are some things I wish to keep secret
— not that they're of any great importance; and,
for the matter of that, I don't think that you will
ever allow yourself to prate about my affairs; you
are too well aware that my dagger would at once
deprive you of the organ of which you made such
use."

"What the deuce do you suppose I could blab
about you?" said Chaudoreille, drying his face

and his clothing with his little silk handkerchief,
and pinching his lips, as if doubting whether Touquet had not already cut out his tongue. "You
never tell me anything about your business, and
I'm not a man to invent the slightest untruth."

"I've told you what all the world knows, —
that I have sheltered Blanche since she had been
left an orphan at my house, and that I know no
more than anyone else about her father or her
family. She is now grown up and pretty. Lovers
will begin to come; that's what vexes me. They'll
seek to learn everything about this young girl,
and assuredly they won't know more about it than
I am telling you. The one who was singing just
now is known to me; he came into my shop this
morning, and stayed two hours, in the hope that
Blanche would appear. Do you hear me, Chaudoreille?"

"I hear you — if you wish me to," said the
chevalier, continuing to rub his doublet; "for I
don't know if I should or if I should not hear
you. That shall be as you wish."

"I wish you weren't quite so foolish," said the
barber, glancing scornfully at his neighbor.

"No words of double meaning," answered
Chaudoreille; "you know I don't like them. This
cursed wine stains, and for the moment I don't
know where to get another doublet."

"He's a mere child, a scholar, who has not yet
a beard on his chin," said the barber after a mo-

ment's silence, which was only interrupted by the
rubbing of the handkerchief on the spots impreg-
nated by wine. "He shows the small experience
he has had in love intrigues by coming to sing
before my door — in order to let me know who
was there. The poor boy has much need of a lesson."

"He certainly is not first-rate at the guitar."

"I don't believe that he can be known to
Blanche. No — but that romance he was singing, — it's precisely the same as the one she mentioned to me, —

> My darling is all to me."

"That doesn't equal —

> Thou hast lost thy fond dove too.

Zounds! what a difference in the melody!"

"No, Blanche is candor itself; she would not
have spoken to me of that romance had she known
the young man. Why the devil haven't you taught
her something else besides that old rubbish of
Louis the Twelfth's time? If you had taught her
to sing something pretty she would not have been
enraptured at the first romance sung by wandering
minstrels."

"What do you say? Are you talking to me?"
said Chaudoreille, raising his head.

"Of course I am, since you call yourself a professor of singing."

"My dear Touquet, listen well to what I am going to say: I don't tease you about your method of shaving beards, and don't you meddle with my way of teaching music. Each one to his own trade. You know the proverb. I teach my pupils nothing but masterpieces, and I'm not going to cram their heads with the little gurglings of those miserable clowns who travel from Naples here singing the same roulade."

"It's vexatious, then, that the young girls prefer these roulades to your masterpieces. You gave Blanche a music lesson this morning, and she tells me that you have wearied her with your villanelle."

"Had anyone but you told me that?" cried Chaudoreille, rising in vexation. "I should have attributed it to jealousy. But it's getting late; it's been a tiring day, and I must go to rest. If, however, you wish me to remain here for fear the singers should return, I will sacrifice my repose."

"No, no; it's unnecessary," said the barber, smiling. "They won't come back; go to bed."

"You have no need of my services tomorrow evening, then?"

"No — however, if you like to be walking on the Pont de la Tournelle at the hour agreed on, you could at any rate serve as a spy for us."

"Sufficient," said Chaudoreille, pulling his hat over his eyes; "you can count on me in life and in death; I shall be at the rendezvous at the exact hour, and Rolande shall be sharp. Good-by!"

So saying the chevalier passed through the passageway into the alley and opened the door of the house. He thrust his head out into the street, and, after glancing cautiously to the right and left, went on his way like a stag who hears the sound of the chase.

CHAPTER IX

The Closet.   The Abduction

As everything coheres, everything is connected in this lower world, there is no chance; but there are many rebounds which transmit from one to another events, effects, for which we bless or curse fate, — as they are fortunate or unfortunate, — instead of tracing them to their original causes, from which, in truth, we are sometimes removed so far as to have no cognizance of them.

Thus it came to pass that our young Urbain had blessed chance on perceiving that the light was still burning in Blanche's room; but if the young girl had not gone to rest it was not by chance, but because Marguerite could not decide to go up to bed in her new room before knowing where the little door in the back of her alcove led.

Now if the garrulous old maidservant had not confessed to her master that she had witnessed his nightly vigils, the latter would not have made her change her lodging; and the fear which induced him to do so was due to other causes still more remote; thus, by a series of events, Marguerite's gossip had led to Blanche's hearing Urbain's sweet and

tender voice sing the romance which had so enchanted her in the morning.

"Yes, mademoiselle," said the old woman, some
moments before the young lover began to sing,
" I know I should die of fright if I should have
to sleep alone in that horrid room, formerly inhabited by a magician, without knowing where that
little door leads to — perhaps into that Odoard's
laboratory. Who knows whether he isn't still
there? These sorcerers are sometimes shut up by
themselves for half a century, searching for secrets
which will enable them to give human kind into
the hands of the devil. I am sure that M. Touquet, who is very indifferent in regard to everything pertaining to sorcerers, has not once been
into that room. Let me pass the night in your
room, my child; tomorrow, when it's daylight,
we'll go together and open that door, since the
Chevalier Chaudoreille wasn't polite enough to do
so. I can pass the night in this easy chair; I shall
be much better here than upstairs, and I can tell
you some interesting stories before you go to
sleep."

Blanche could not refuse Marguerite what she
asked as a favor; the old woman was relating her
third story of sorcery, and the young girl, who
felt that her eyes were growing heavy, was about
to go to bed, when the sounds of a guitar were
heard.

Blanche listened, and made a sign to Marguerite

to be silent, and soon recognized with delight the air which she was desirous of learning. There is something sweeter, more seductive, in music thus heard in the middle of the night; it finds its way more quickly to the heart. Urbain's voice was flexible and melodious. Blanche, transported, remained motionless, as though she feared by a single movement to lose a sound, while Marguerite, gaping with astonishment, looked at the engaging child without appearing greatly enchanted with the music. But Marguerite was more than sixty years old, and music had not the same effect upon her as upon Blanche; the sounds reached no farther than her ears, while they vibrated deliciously in the depths of the heart of sixteen.

Very soon, however, the noise which they heard in the street put an end to Blanche's happiness; she recognized the barber's voice, and the threats which he pronounced made her tremble, as well as Marguerite, who cried immediately, —

"Go to bed! go to bed quickly, my child, and extinguish the light; if M. Touquet sees that we are still awake, if he should find me in here — O holy blessed Virgin! I shall be lost."

"But why is he so angry?" said Blanche. "Is singing in the streets in the evenings forbidden? I was so pleased to hear that romance. What harm was the young man doing? — for it was a young man who was singing — was it not, dear nurse? It was not the voice of an old man, and, oh, how well he sang! I have never heard such a pretty voice; it had a singular effect on me; it made my heart beat with pleasure — didn't it yours, Marguerite?"

Marguerite, whose heart was beating only with fear, contented herself with repeating, "Go to bed quickly, put out the lamp, and above all don't say tomorrow that you heard the singing; that would prove that you were not yet asleep, and M. Touquet wishes everyone to go to sleep as soon as they go to bed."

Since it was necessary to yield to the insistence of the old servant, Blanche went to bed, but she did not go to sleep; the young singer's voice still seemed to ring in her ears, and on hearing the least sound in the street she imagined that it was the musician again. As to Marguerite, after putting out the lamp, she extended herself in an armchair near the fire and fell asleep, murmuring a prayer to drive away evil spirits.

The morning after this night, so fertile with events, Blanche arose early. She was pensive, pre-occupied, still dreaming of the young singer's voice; she felt new desires, and sighed as she glanced toward the street. Marguerite ran to her work, saying to Blanche, —

"When monsieur is most busily engaged with his customers, we'll go up together into my room; but, my child, above all don't say anything about the music."

Blanche promised her, saying, "Why should he be angry because somebody came to sing such a pretty air under our windows?"

The barber said nothing to the young girl about the adventure of the night; he contented himself with observing Blanche, and the lovely child, remembering the threats which she had overheard him utter against the singer, had no desire to chat; she hastened to return to her chamber, where Marguerite was not long in coming to rejoin her.

"Now is the time," said the old servant; "monsieur has a good many people to shave. Come, my child; come up with me, and above all don't be frightened; I have taken every precaution necessary to drive away the goblins."

"Frightened!" said Blanche, because she saw that Marguerite was trembling. "No, dear nurse, no; I assure you that I'm not thinking of your secret door at all."

Thus saying, Blanche darted lightly up the stairs, while Marguerite followed her more slowly, saying, "Happy age when one has no fear of magicians, because one does not understand all their wickedness, — it is true that she has a talisman."

When they reached the room, Blanche entered quickly, while the old woman made a genuflexion and invoked her patron saint, after which she decided also to go into her new room, throwing anxious glances about her. Blanche had run into the alcove and already drawn the bed into the middle of the room.

"Wait a moment; don't be so imprudent," cried Marguerite to her. "Is it necessary to do things so quickly?"

"But, dear nurse, the sooner we open that door, the sooner you'll be reassured."

"Reassured! that's what I wish. Have you your talisman, my darling?"

"Of course I have. Didn't you sew it yourself inside my corsets?"

"That's true."

"I don't see the door you were talking about."

"It is so well encased in the woodwork."

"Ah, here it is!"

"Wait a moment, mademoiselle, while I throw some holy water before it."

"But there's no key; how can we open it?"

"Well, we must try. I have several keys that I have picked up while cleaning the house, perhaps one of those will open it."

Marguerite advanced tremblingly towards the end of the alcove. She drew from her pocket half a dozen rusty keys of different sizes, and was about to try one of them, but her hand shook and she could not find the keyhole. Blanche seized one key and tried it unsuccessfully, then a second; but at the third the young girl uttered a cry of joy, for the key turned, and Marguerite crossed herself, murmuring, —

"O my God, the door is opening!"

In fact, the door yielded to Blanche's effort and opened, creaking and groaning on its hinges, and the two women beheld a square closet; but, as it received no light except from the little door that opened into it, and as that door led into a dark alcove, one may conceive that there was little daylight there. Blanche remained on the doorsill and Marguerite recoiled a few steps, saying, —

"See now, my child; I was right in thinking that that door led somewhere. Oh, this is as dark as a cave."

"Let us go in here, nurse."

"But not without a light, I hope. Wait; I will go and light my lamp. I don't know that it is prudent of us to enter this closet."

"But, Marguerite, you see very well that there is nobody here."

"I can see nothing except darkness. Wait; take the lamp, and you go first, my darling; you have your talisman; nothing will happen to you."

Blanche entered first; she seemed more curious than alarmed, while the old woman could scarcely persuade herself to follow. The closet was six feet square, and held nothing but two big empty chests placed on the floor, which time had covered with dust and spiders' webs.

"Well now, my dear nurse," said Blanche, smiling, "where are the sorcerers? I don't see anything frightful here."

"In fact," answered Marguerite, glancing all about her; "there's nothing but four walls, no other door, and these two chests are empty. I'm sure that no one has disturbed this place for half a century. No matter; I swear to you that I shall not come back here again. I don't know why I feel so uneasy here. How the floor creaks under our feet!"

"It's because no one has walked here for a long time; this house is old."

"Come, my dear child, let us leave this closet; I shall shut the door and double-lock it, and I shan't open it again while I stay in this room."

Thus saying, Marguerite pushed Blanche before her, then closed the little door and double-locked it, murmuring between her teeth,

"Alas! if some sorcerer should wish to open the door that lock would not resist him; but every night I shall cross my shovel and tongs before it."

This visit terminated, Blanche went down, humming to herself the romance of the evening before, and Marguerite returned to her work.

The barber had ordered dinner early; and at six o'clock in the evening he left the house, repeating to Marguerite:

"Redouble your watchfulness, do not allow any man to go near Blanche without my permission, and inform me if you hear anyone singing in the street."

The old woman promised to obey. Touquet

wrapped his mantle about him and left to execute the marquis' plan. As he was accustomed to
conduct similar intrigues, he knew where to procure everything that was necessary ; and at a quarter to eight he was on the Pont de la Tournelle,
while about a hundred feet from him two men
awaited his orders near a travelling-chaise drawn
by two horses.

For a long time Chaudoreille had been walking
on the bridge. Fearing to miss the rendezvous,
given for eight o'clock, he had arrived at six; bury-
ing his head between his shoulders and hiding his
chin under his little mantle, he tried to give himself
the air of a conspirator. With his left hand on
Rolande's handle and the other holding his mantle, he walked sometimes slowly and sometimes
with a precipitant step ; and every time that anyone passed him he did not fail to murmur, in such
a manner as to be heard, —

"How late she is in coming ! What can keep
her ? I am burning ! I am bursting ! I shall die
with impatience."

As soon as he saw Touquet he ran to him and
pulled the edge of his mantle ; then, looking to see
if anybody was passing, he said to him in a mysterious tone, —

" Here I am."

" Well, hang it, I see you ! " said the barber,
shrugging his shoulders ; " but I'd much rather see
the little one."

"She hasn't appeared yet, I can answer for that. I've looked in every woman's face."

"It's not eight o'clock; let us wait."

"Be easy; I'll go and put myself in ambuscade and examine all the feminine visages."

"Take care they don't slap you; that would draw a crowd, and wouldn't please me."

"Slap me! They're more likely to kiss me, I should say; but I'll make a grimace, so as not to tempt them."

And Chaudoreille, drawing his hat down over his eyes, departed, taking as long steps as his little legs would permit.

In about three minutes Chaudoreille returned to say to the barber, —

"There's a woman who has just come along by the Pont Marie, and who is going to pass over this bridge."

"Indeed! Is she the one we are waiting for? You ought to know, if you've peered into her face."

"No; I wasn't able to do that this time, because she was giving her arm to a man, and he would have been frightened."

"If she's with a man it's not our young girl; one doesn't bring witnesses to a lovers' meeting."

"That's correct," said Chaudoreille, and he started off again.

Some minutes later he returned to Touquet, crying, —

" Here's another one who is coming along this way; but this one is alone, I am sure of that."

" Is it our beauty ? "

" No, it is not she."

"You idiot! what did you come and tell me for?"

" So that you should not make a mistake; I thought it was my duty to avert that."

" Chaudoreille, do me the pleasure of remaining still. I know very well how to recognize her whom I came to meet without your help; although I haven't yet seen her, I am certain that I shan't make a mistake; but, hang it! if she doesn't come to this meeting, I shall send you to drink the water under the bridge, to teach you to do your errands better."

Chaudoreille had not heard the barber's last words; he was already far away, but he returned precipitately, looking scared.

" What is it now ? " said Touquet.

" A patrol of the watch, which I can see coming, and which is going to pass by us."

" Well, what of that ? What has the watch to do with us ? It's not forbidden to walk on the bridge, and, even if they should see us abduct a young girl I can answer for it they'll hardly trouble themselves about that."

" Haven't we a rather suspicious look ? "

" You make me ashamed of you."

" I shall pretend to be laughing, to allay their suspicions."

"Wait, perhaps this will give you more courage."

So saying the barber kicked Chaudoreille; but the latter received it singing, contenting himself by rubbing the part attacked while executing his trills, because at that moment the watch was passing them. When the patrol had departed he breathed more freely, and cried, —

"They have taken us for simple troubadours."

"They should have taken you for a fool. A plague on all poltroons! They are good for nothing except to spoil everything."

"I'm not going to get angry at a matter which doesn't concern me; but on great occasions it seems to me that stratagem is often better than valor."

The barber had begun to be impatient, when a young woman came on to the bridge, walking slowly and glancing from time to time about her. Chaudoreille had not perceived her, because he was in ambuscade at the side of the Rue des Deux-Ponts.

Touquet approached the unknown, looked at her and saw that this really was the young girl whom the marquis had depicted; for her part, the damsel looked attentively at the barber, and seemed to wait for him to address her in words.

"Are you not the Signora Julia?" said the barber in a bass voice, approaching the young girl.

"And you the barber Touquet?" answered she, lifting to him her animated black eyes.

The barber was surprised at hearing himself
named by a person to whom he believed himself
unknown, but, after having considered the young
girl anew, he resumed, —

"Since you know me, you should also know
that the Marquis de Villebelle has sent me to you."

"The marquis is rather ungallant," answered
Julia, "in not coming himself to a first meeting."

"These great noblemen are not the masters of
their time; besides, the marquis has no desire to
converse with you about his love on this bridge."

"Preferring, no doubt, his little house of the
Faubourg Saint-Antoine?"

"It seems to me, signora, that you are very well
acquainted with everything that concerns the marquis; after that I have nothing more to tell you,
except that a carriage is waiting a hundred feet
from here."

"Very well, let us go."

"The deuce!" said the barber to himself, offering his arm to Julia, that he might conduct her to
the coach; "here is a young girl who doesn't make
a bit of fuss about allowing herself to be abducted.
But I must confess that there's something in her
voice and manners very decided and piquant,
which astonishes as well as pleases."

They had reached the carriage when Chaudoreille's voice was heard; he ran after the barber,
crying, —

"There's a woman coming by the side of the

Porte de la Tournelle ; it is our little one ; I recognized her walk."

Saying these words, Chaudoreille perceived that the barber was conducting a person to whom he had given his arm.

"How is this? What does this mean? Must I believe my eyes?" cried the chevalier. "That's our beauty, and what the deuce way did she come? No matter; we've got her; that's the essential thing. I will protect your walk."

Chaudoreille then drew his sword, and, giving no ear to the barber, who bade him depart, ran up to the carriage, crying to the two men who were near, —

"My friends, here they are. Be adroit, be courageous. By jingo! she must enter your vehicle, willingly or by force."

Somebody opened the door, and Chaudoreille was a little surprised at seeing the young person trip first into the carriage. He was about to do the same, and seat himself near her, when Touquet, taking him by the breeches, dropped him on all-fours on the pavement, and, following Julia into the carriage, said to the coachman, —

"Go on!"

"What the deuce! he's going to abduct her without me," said Chaudoreille, picking himself up. "No, not by all the devils! It shall not be said that I did not finish this adventure ; besides, they've only given me something on account, and

I should like to be settled with before the marquis gets tired of the little one."

Chaudoreille immediately darted after the carriage; accustomed to running, he caught up with it, mounted behind, and allowed himself to be drawn at a great gallop, taking care to hold tightly to the tassels, which served to support him.

CHAPTER X

The Little House. A New Game

THE carriage bearing the barber and Julia had soon passed the Porte Saint-Antoine, which at that period had not attained the dignity of the Faubourg, but was in a neighborhood where the road is cut by the boulevards, and which served frequently, as did all thinly inhabited districts at the time of which we are writing, for a meeting-place for robbers, vagabonds, pages, lackeys and cut-purses.

The marquis' little house was situated near the Vallée de Fécamp, which today is replaced by a street bearing the same name, and making the continuation of the Rue de la Planchette. Crossing this unlighted place of evil fame in the middle of the night was, at that time, to expose one's self to as much danger as though passing through the forest of Bondy. However, many noblemen had chosen this quarter for the theatre of their gallantries. They possessed small houses there, their ordinary meeting-places in their love intrigues, and often went out incognito, but always well armed.

The carriage stopped before an enclosing wall;

Chaudoreille looked about him on all sides. The house was isolated, and the wall which enclosed the garden appeared unbroken, but Touquet had already alighted from the carriage; he approached a small door which the chevalier had not perceived, and rang a bell. Before any one could come to open it Chaudoreille had left the place which he had occupied, and had offered his hand to Julia to assist her in alighting from the carriage.

The door was immediately opened by a man servant, who appeared holding a lantern in his hand, and, merely glancing at the carriage and at the damsel who was getting out of it, he contented himself with smiling and making a low bow to the barber.

"Your master has warned you that we were coming?" said Touquet to this person in a low voice.

"Yes, monsieur," answered the servant, "I am waiting for you."

Here the barber, upon turning around to introduce Julia to the lackey perceived for the first time the redoubtable Chaudoreille, who stood bolt upright before the door with his sword in his hand, as though he were a sentinel on guard. The barber shrugged his shoulders impatiently, and, after handing Julia in, he unceremoniously dragged the chevalier by his mantle, and made him also pass into the garden, saying,—

"Since you have followed us here, it is necessary that you should do something for us."

"That is my duty, by jingo," responded the chevalier, while Touquet reclosed the garden gate, after having said to the two men who were near the coach, —

"Wait for me."

They followed along a tiled passageway which led to the house. The garden was gloomy. The servant who carried the lantern walked in front, and Chaudoreille, who found himself the last, glanced from time to time anxiously from right to left ; he wished to open the conversation, and had already exclaimed, "This garden appears to be very large," when the barber turned and ordered him to keep silent. To indemnify himself for this forced silence, Chaudoreille, who was still holding Rolande naked in his hand, struck every tree that he met.

They arrived at the house and entered a vestibule, at the end of which was a staircase, while to the right and the left doors led to the apartments on the ground floor.

Julia, who had followed her conductors without speaking, appeared to examine attentively everything that presented itself to her. Chaudoreille, finding himself near the man with the lantern, uttered a cry of surprise, saying, —

"Why, what the deuce ! I can't be mistaken. It is Marcel, one of my old friends. Don't you

know me? I am Chaudoreille; we spent six
months in prison together, but it was for a mere
trifle. I left it as white as snow."

"Be silent, idiots," cried the barber; "you can
make your greetings a little later. Where is madame's apartment?"

"On the first floor," answered Marcel, putting
his hand in Chaudoreille's, who shook it as if he
had found his best friend.

"Lead us," said Touquet, "and you remain
here."

The latter part of this order was addressed to
the chevalier and it did not afford him much
pleasure; but he was forced to obey. However,
when Chaudoreille perceived that there was no
light in the vestibule where they left him, and
where he found himself in the most complete ob-
scurity, he ascended several steps of the stairs,
crying in a quivering voice,—

"Don't leave me alone here. The night is chilly
and I am afraid of taking cold."

Marcel led Julia and the barber and, after making them pass through several rooms, lighted only
by his lantern, opened a door, saying,—

"Here is the room in which madame can rest
herself."

Julia could not restrain an exclamation of surprise, and the barber himself was lost in admiration. The room which they had entered was
lighted by a lustre hung from the ceiling, and the

light of many wax candles permitted one to admire
the luxury with which this place was decorated.
Delightful paintings of seductive and voluptuous
figures ornamented the wainscot. The furniture
was upholstered in light blue, where silk and silver were blended with art. There were Venetian
glasses, Persian carpets, candelabras in which per-
fumes were burning, while natural flowers were
disposed elsewhere, in pyramids, in crystal vases.
The whole combination tended to make a sojourn
in this place a delight, for here was united everything that would intoxicate the senses and inspire
pleasure.

Julia and the barber had entered the lighted
room; Marcel remained respectfully at the door
and seemed to wait some orders.

"This place is delightful," said Julia; "but I
do not see the marquis."

"You will see him soon, madame," answered
Touquet; "in an hour he will be here. While
awaiting him you can ask for everything that is
agreeable to you. Your desires will be accomplished immediately. This bell communicates
with the floor below. Is not that so, Marcel?"

"Yes, monsieur, and if madame would like to
take something, I have prepared a collation in the
little neighboring room."

Marcel indicated a door hidden by a mirror.
The barber pushed it and they saw a second room,
smaller but equally well lighted, and decorated

with as much magnificence, only the furniture and the hangings were of poppy-colored velvet, ornamented with fringes of gold, while light blue and silver were the only colors in the first.

"He did not deceive me," said Touquet to himself, glancing into the second room, "when he said, that he had made an enchanting bower of this house. What luxury! What magnificence! How much money he must have spent to do all this! And yet he is not happy."

Julia had thrown herself on a lounge and appeared thoughtful. The barber bowed to her, and, making a sign to Marcel, left the apartment with him.

Marcel was a bachelor of twenty-eight or thirty years, short, fat and cheerful; obedient and exact as an Oriental, but endowed with very little genius and incapable of conducting the merest intrigue. The marquis, to whom more adroit, more active, more enterprising people were necessary, but who appreciated Marcel's faithfulness, had found, in order to keep him, no better means of employing him than to make him the keeper of this house. There his functions were limited to a passive obedience to the orders which he received; but he was a stranger to all the intrigues of which this abode was the theatre, and ignored sometimes the correct name of the person who during a short period was reigning sovereign in the little house. This troubled him little, and his indifference was a guarantee of his discretion, a quality which in his employ was very necessary.

"You know Chaudoreille?" said the barber to Marcel, following him into the passageway which led to the staircase.

"Yes, monsieur," answered the valet, "I knew him formerly in a rather unfortunate affair, since I had to pass six months in prison, and God knows if I was guilty. It is in the neighborhood of seven years ago, and I was not then in the marquis' service. I was drinking in an inn, and Chaudoreille was there also; he was playing at piquet with two other cavaliers, and they invited me to make one of their party. I accepted the invitation. I played and I lost. He took my place, put down some crowns for me, saying that we should be partners, and played with surprising good fortune. I was delighted to see him win, but our adversaries pretended that he cheated. Then they disputed, and in place of paying us wanted to fight us so badly that they made a great noise. The sergeants of the watch arrived with their archers and led us to prison, — Chaudoreille and me. That was how we made acquaintance; but since that time I have lost the taste for playing. I wouldn't touch a card now."

"All the better for you. I advise you to keep that resolution."

The barber and Marcel then went down the stairs which led into the vestibule, when cries of

"Thief!" "Beware!" "Murder!" came to their
ears. The cries came from the garden, and Touquet recognized the chevalier's voice.

"What the devil is he at now?" said the barber, hurrying his steps, while Marcel followed him,
repeating, —

"Thieves! That is singular. However, the
doors are close shut, and the walls of the garden
are ten feet high."

Tired of being without light in the vestibule,
Chaudoreille had returned into the garden, where,
since the moon was nearly hidden by clouds, one
could see but a little way from him. The chevalier was singing a virelay which he accompanied
by striking Rolande against the branches, then
barren of foliage. All of a sudden, at the entrance
to some shrubbery, a large white face appeared
opposite Chaudoreille, who stopped and cried, in
a faltering voice, —

"Who goes there?"

Nobody answered him, and he judged it prudent in place of repeating his question to regain
the house. In his alarm he mistook the way, and
at a turn in the alley perceived before him another
personage, who held a club in his hand, with which
he seemed disposed to strike him. It was then
that Chaudoreille, who felt his strength for flight
fail him, made the garden echo with his cries.
Guided by his voice, the barber and Marcel were
soon near him.

"What is the matter? Wherefore this noise?" said Touquet.

"Don't you see that wretch who is waiting for me down there to slay me, while his accomplice is hidden in another bush?"

The barber turned to look in the direction which Chaudoreille designated with his hand. Marcel did likewise, holding the lantern before him. Soon the latter burst into a shout of laughter, and the barber cried, —

"I was sure that this clown would commit some foolishness."

"Why foolishness? Zounds! Why did not these people answer me when I cried to them, 'Who goes there?'"

"That would be very difficult for them," said Marcel. "The one that you perceive over there is Hercules killing the Lernean hydra, and the other is probably Mercury or Mars. Perhaps it was even a Venus which frightened you."

"Frightened me? Oh, no. By jingo, I wasn't frightened; but they should warn people when they have an Olympus in their garden. In any case, if it is Mercury he can flatter himself that he has received five or six strokes from the flat of this sword, and they weren't given by a dead hand."

"And if this young girl heard your cries, wretch," said the barber directing his steps towards the little door.

" I do not think she could," said Marcel, " the room she occupies looks out on the other side of the garden."

The barber then opened the door by which they had entered.

"Remain with Marcel," said he to Chaudoreille. "The marquis will soon be here. If he has any orders for me you will come and communicate them to me immediately, but before monseigneur you must be mute. If the least word escapes you before him, if you commit a single awkwardness, remember I shall take your punishment upon myself."

So saying, Touquet sprang into the carriage, which left immediately. Chaudoreille was pleased to remain, thinking that he would now see the marquis and could find a way to prove his intelligence to him. He took Marcel's arm, remembering that the latter had a very sweet disposition and was easily led, and felicitated himself on the chance which had led to their meeting. The barber alighted when some steps distant from his house. He paid the people, sent away the carriage and hastened to enter, for the marquis would be there towards ten o'clock and it was not far from that now. Marguerite opened the door to her master, who addressed a few ordinary questions to her on the subject of Blanche. The old servant swore to her master that no man had spoken to the young girl. Touquet sent Marguerite away. He wished

to wait for the marquis alone. Ten o'clock had
sounded some time ago and the barber, who
awaited congratulations and a new recompense,
was beginning to be astonished at the lack of
haste on the part of the marquis when, at last,
somebody knocked at the street door and the
great nobleman entered the barber's house.

"Hang it, my poor Touquet, I barely missed
forgetting our rendezvous," said the marquis,
throwing himself on a seat.

"What, monseigneur, you forget a love affair?
That astonishes me, I confess."

"You should, however, be able to understand
it better than another. Why should not one end
by tiring of that which he does every day? I am
utterly blasé in regard to these things. I had, God
forgive me, totally forgotten the little one. I was at
the Hôtel de Bourgogne with Chavagnac, Mon-
theil and some other of my friends. Turlupin,
Gauthier-Garguille and Gros-Guillaume very much
diverted us. The rascals are full of jokes; they
are quite the fashion. Everybody is running to
see them. They have created a furore, above all,
since they represented a comical scene at the cardinal's palace, and since Richelieu has permitted
them to play at the Hôtel de Bourgogne, despite
the protests of the comedians. On leaving there
we went into an inn; we were in the mood for
laughter; we fought with some little shopkeepers
who disputed the possession of a table with us.

They shouted like the devil; the sergeants of the watch came, but we mentioned our names in a low tone and the king's archers helped us to put the rabble out of the place. We remained masters of the field of battle; it couldn't end otherwise. I never laughed so much. Chavagnac actually wished to eat an omelette off the face of a fat draper; the poor devil made some horrible grimaces in his fright; it was really very comical; he escaped by swallowing twelve glasses of brandy one after the other; afterwards we made him roll from the first story to the groundfloor. Finally, my dear fellow, you can conceive that with all this the little nut-brown maid went entirely out of my head, but just then somebody mentioned a master knave; I thought of you and that recalled our rendezvous. Well, now, to come to the point, where do we stand?"

"Monseigneur, I have fulfilled your desires, and for the past hour the young girl has been at your little house."

"You don't say so! What! Is the affair really terminated thus quickly. It doesn't seem as though mademoiselle had made many scruples."

"I must confess, monsieur, that she got into the carriage with a very good grace."

"A little resistance would have pleased me better; it's cruel that one can have immediately all that one desires. These young girls are so impressed when one speaks to them of a great noble-

man. I'm almost sorry I have entangled myself
with this one, for the devil carry me away if I'm
in love with her the least bit in the world. For
very little I'd have you take her back to the place
you took her from. What d'you say, Touquet;
that would be droll, wouldn't it?"

The barber, piqued at the little pleasure evinced
by the marquis at his successful abduction of the
young girl, answered coldly, —

"I see that monseigneur has almost entirely forgotten the one who charmed him two days ago;
if he could remember her he would not show so
much indifference in her possession."

"What, is she really so beautiful? Do you
think she is capable of engaging my affection for
any length of time?"

"I don't know, monsieur, whether she will have
that good fortune; but I have seen many courtesans in the highest vogue who did not equal that
young Italian."

"Is she an Italian?"

"Yes, monseigneur."

"All the better; that alters the case a little."

"Her name is Julia; her face, while not regularly beautiful, has a nameless something that is
very piquant and seductive; and there is in her
voice, in her manner, in everything about her,
something that denotes force and originality. In
short, she is not a languorous beauty, such as one
most often sees."

"Do you know, you pique my curiosity; come, tomorrow, we'll admire all this."

"Tomorrow! What monsieur, and the young girl is awaiting you with impatience?"

"We must let her sigh until then; I have promised to rejoin my friends and finish the night with them. With people of honor one does not break his word; the beautiful Julia must be patient."

"I also left one of my men with Marcel, in case monsieur le marquis should have any further orders to send me. I hope he'll be useful, since Marcel can't leave the house."

"Oh, very well, your man can wait; one can give him a few pistoles more. By the way, I must pay you. Wait! Here's some gold I won at lansquenet this morning. But time's passing, I wager those rascals are getting impatient; I must run and rejoin them. We shall have a delightful night; we are in just the vein for diversion. We'll make some notches in the good citizens of Paris, we'll flog the watch, we'll stop chair porters, and I won't answer for it that we don't steal some mantles on the Pont-Neuf."

The marquis hastily departed and the barber closed his door, saying, —

"After all, he may do as he pleases now, since I have been paid."

While this interview was taking place in the Rue des Bourdonnaise, the young girl whom they

had left in the luxurious boudoir, arose from the
lounge as soon as those who brought her had departed. She approached a mirror which reflected
the whole figure ; one glance sufficed to distract
and give her occupation. Julia arranged her hair,
passing her fingers through it and re-formed its
ringlets ; she examined herself, she smiled ; Julia
was a coquette; so to some extent is every woman,
they say. To judge whether she be more or less
so it is only necessary to count the minutes that
she passes before her mirror; ordinarily she is not
the prettiest who there looks at herself longest.

At last Julia appeared satisfied with herself; she
left the mirror and ran about the boudoir and into
the neighboring room, admiring everything which
she had pretended to view with indifference as long
as anyone could see her. She stopped before an
alabaster clock which bore a little love. The hand
pointed nearly to eleven o'clock. Julia sighed and
frowned, and threw herself into an easy chair, murmuring, —

"He does not come."

While the young girl sighingly regarded the
clock, Chaudoreille asked Marcel to lead him to
the dining-room, saying that he was dying of hunger and that since the morning he had been running in the service of monsieur le marquis. Marcel hastened to offer his guest a good supper, to
which the chevalier did full honor. While eating,
Chaudoreille recounted his exploits to his old

friend, and as Marcel listened to everything in good faith, our Gascon, delighted at finding some-one who had faith in his prowess, had already killed fifteen rivals and delivered eight victims of tyranny, before he had begun a second helping.

"Old fellow," said Marcel, opening his eyes wide, and helping himself to drink, "it seems to me that you have a hot head."

"Hot? By jingo, say boiling; say volcanic. It is not my fault, but I can't be moderate. I am a rake of honor, a real devil; that is the word."

"But why did you call for help against the statues in the garden?"

"Listen, my dear Marcel: At first I could not see that they were statues, and when one is brave one believes that one sees robbers everywhere; you don't understand that, because you are cool-blooded, and, besides that, you can very well understand that I could not allow myself to kill any-body in the Marquis de Villebelle's house without having asked permission."

"Hush, no one names the marquis here."

"Ah, I understand. That is correct. It is neces-sary to have some mystery. Hang it! This is the abode of love incognito. Say, Marcel, have you been living long in this house?"

"Nearly five years."

"You must have seen some beauties."

"I have seen nothing, for here it is necessary to see and not to see."

"I understand very well. What the deuce do you take me for, a caitiff? That is all right. You have a golden place. The marquis is generous, is he not?"

"Yes."

"You earn at least twenty pistoles a year."

"Double that."

"Fortunate rascal. When I say rascal, you are the most perfectly honest man that I know. I even believe that you are the only one that I know. Good old Marcel! I am very much pleased to have met you again. I have looked for you all over, in the gambling houses and in the gambling hells even."

"Oh, I have not played for a long time."

"Nonsense, you are joking."

"No, since our adventure I have lost my taste for playing. To go to prison when one is innocent is very disagreeable."

"Oh, well, old fellow, there are a good many thieves who don't go and that makes the balance correct. As for me, I confess that I still play. It amuses me. Besides, it is the pleasure of a great nobleman, and there is nothing more noble than to play and lose right down to your boots."

"Since I am only a valet I have no need of following that fashion."

"You are wrong. It is always necessary to follow the great. You played a very strong game of piquet."

"Me? Oh, on the contrary, I am a very weak player."

"Pure modesty. Hang it! I wish I could take a lesson from you. We have had our supper. While waiting for your master to come, let us play a game to pass the time."

"That will be very difficult, for we have no cards here. When by chance I have found some upstairs which have been left by my master and his friends I have burned or sold them."

"That is very awkward; and I, who have nearly always a pack in my pocket, necessarily left mine at home."

"Wait, Chaudoreille! taste this liqueur. That will be much better than playing."

Thus saying, Marcel filled two glasses with crême de vanille and placed one before his comrade.

"Yes, I am very fond of liqueur," said Chaudoreille. "This has an exquisite perfume. We could have drunk and played at the same time."

"But I tell you that I have not any cards."

"You have some dice, at least."

"No more than I have cards."

"Mercy! Some dominoes?"

"Nothing to play with, I tell you."

"Devil stifle you! How shall we pass the time without playing? Oh, what a delightful idea! I have thought of a very agreeable little game which you will easily understand. You have before you

a full glass of liqueur and I have the same. They
are of equal size ; I will play you a crown on the
first fly."

"What fly?" said Marcel.

"Listen now. There are a good many flies in
this room, and he whose glass is first visited by one
of them will win a crown from the other. Is it
agreed?"

"That is a droll game, but I like it well enough."

"In that case let's shake hands on it. That
settled, attend to our play."

Chaudoreille no longer budged. With his eyes
fixed attentively on his own glass and that of his
adversary, he waited impatiently for a fly to come
and taste the sweet liqueur. Neither of them made
a movement, for fear of frightening the winged
insects. They had already remained motionless
for five minutes before their glasses when Marcel
sneezed.

"The devil confound you?" cried Chaudoreille. "You drove away the most beautiful fly
which was approaching my glass. She was just
going in."

"Is it my fault if I feel a desire to sneeze?"

"It is a trick, my dear fellow, and, in all con-
science, you should lose the game.

"You are joking, no doubt."

"Well I will pass over the sneeze, but if you
begin again that will count. Wait! The flies are
coming."

They observed silence anew. From time to time Chaudoreille looked into the air and seemed to implore the flies to come and taste his liqueur. At last, after some minutes of waiting, a fly sipped from Marcel's glass.

"I have won," cried the latter.

"One moment," said Chaudoreille, spitefully stamping his foot. "Leave me to judge of this affair."

"It seems to me that there is nothing equivocal about it. The fly is still in my glass."

"But I am anxious to know if it is really a fly. I am not going to lose a crown for a pig in a poke."

Chaudoreille arose and advanced his head, that he might look more closely into the glass which was before Marcel, but no sooner had he by this movement approached his host than he cried, carrying his hand to his nose, —

"The game is off. There is nothing more to be done."

"This is to say," cried Marcel, in his turn rising from the table.

"I repeat, the game is off."

"And why?"

"Why, by jingo, because your breath is strong enough to make flies fall in their flight. After that you see the game is not equal."

"Chaudoreille, I will take the thing as a joke, and I don't care about winning your money, but

I flatter myself that I have a breath at least as fresh as yours."

"Take the thing as a joke?" said the chevalier, putting his hand on the handle of his sword. "Do you wish to vex me? By jingo, if I had known."

"Come, come, calm yourself."

"Do you think I will suffer such injuries. By Rolande, I don't know how to hold myself."

"Will you soon be done?"

"By George! If I believed that you wish to molest me, as if I care about a crown; if I had lost a hundred I should have paid you just the same."

"That is all right. Leave all that."

The more Marcel tried to calm his comrade, the more he lost his temper and shouted, for he believed that Marcel was afraid of him and he wished to profit by his bullying; he even went so far as to draw his sword and run about the room, rolling his little eyes around him as if he would split everything in two. Marcel grew impatient, and seeing that all of his entreaties were vain decided to take a broom handle from behind the door. Putting himself on the defensive, he waited for his enemy to come and attack him, but this action suddenly calmed Chaudoreille's fury. At sight of Marcel on guard with his broom, he stopped and struck his forehead as one who has suddenly received an enlightening idea.

"Great God!" he cried, "What was I going

to do? It was in the house of the noble Marquis de Villebelle that I allowed myself to be carried away by anger? Oh, my courage, how much trouble you give me. All is forgotten, Marcel. Come to my arms. I will forgive you."

Marcel, always a good fellow, threw aside his broom and shook hands with Chaudoreille. They returned to the table, but they played no more, and while in the room on the first floor somebody was sighing and looking at the hand of the clock, in the lower room the two comrades ended by putting themselves to sleep while sampling the fine wines and liqueurs of the marquis.

CHAPTER XI

THE PONT-NEUF. TABARIN

THE ill-success of his serenade had not daunted the young Urbain ; when one is really very much in love one does not lose courage for a trifle. Our lover returned to his dwelling cursing the jealous barber, for he did not doubt that jealousy was at the root of Touquet's exceedingly watchful care of the young girl ; and though he was but little dismayed at the barber's threats, Urbain swore, notwithstanding them, to become known to Blanche, and to do everything in his power to make her love him. The act of swearing is in itself extremely easy of accomplishment — what oaths have been taken and broken within a half century only ; but we are now speaking merely of the oaths of love, which are lighter, necessarily, than some others, and to break them is considered a pardonable offence. Urbain, who had sworn that he would see Blanche, was, however, greatly troubled to invent a way of doing so ; but in love one always swears first and reflects afterwards, and in business it must be confessed there are a good many people who follow the very same course.

On the day after the night on which he had
sung, Urbain was walking in the neighborhood
of the barber's, but he dared not enter the house,
which he ogled sighingly, nor even, for fear of
being noticed by Touquet, could he pass by the
shop. It was from afar that he examined the windows; nobody could be seen at them. She seemed
to be condemned to an eternal seclusion. He
waited until Marguerite should leave the house.
At last she opened the door of the alley; she was
going to get some provisions.

Urbain did not lose sight of the old servant,
but he did not dare to go into the shops with
her. How could he get into conversation? One
is not apt at intrigue at nineteen years of age. At
last, at the moment when Marguerite was passing
by him, Urbain tremblingly accosted her, —

"Madame, I should very much like —".

"I'm not a dame — I'm not married."

"Mademoiselle if I dared — "

"If you dared what?"

"To ask you —"

"Well, why don't you speak?"

"Some news of Mademoiselle Blanche."

"Mademoiselle Blanche! Oh that's what you
are up to, my young dandy? Go along, go your
own way; you're addressing the wrong person.
If you want to talk about that dear child, speak
to my master; he'll answer you, I warrant, and in
the best manner."

So saying, Marguerite left Urbain and went in, murmuring, —

"Monsieur is right, it is necessary to redouble our watchfulness that such a pretty girl may not be besieged by these worthless fellows."

"They're all bound to make me despair," said Urbain, disheartened by the unkind welcome accorded him by the old woman, "but, despite all their precautions, I shall see her, I shall speak to her." And the better to dream of at least seeing her Urbain departed from the house that held Blanche; he walked by chance and soon arrived on the Pont-Neuf.

The Pont-Neuf was then a meeting place for strangers, for schemers, for idlers, for pickpockets, and people who had newly disembarked. It was the most crowded thoroughfare of the capital; unceasingly encumbered with groups of curious people who stopped before the quacks, who were selling their universal panaceas and playing farces, mountebanks, thimbleriggers, pedlers of songs, of ironmongery, of books, of jujubes, it offered to the observer a diverting and extremely animated scene.

Tabarin, who became famous by the scenes which he played in public, and from whom our great Molière has not disdained to borrow some buffooneries, was then established on the Pont-Neuf, towards the Place Dauphine. He had succeeded the famous Signor Hieronimo who, in the

Cour du Palais, sold an ointment to cure burns, after burning himself publicly on the hands and curing the wounds with his balm, while Galinette-la-Galine attracted the passers by his parades.

In addition to Tabarin's show there were still other theatres on the Pont-Neuf. Maitre Gonin, a skilful juggler, had established himself there, and charmed all Paris by his dexterity; while a little farther off Briochee had his marionette show.

Tabarin, the simple clown of an ointment seller, played the innocent, and put a thousand ridiculous questions to his master who, dressed as a doctor, answered his facetious interrogations by calling him big ass, fat pig, etc., and this spectacle drew the crowd. One saw there not only the people but personages from the first classes of society.

Urbain, who was walking along, dreaming of his love, that is to say without noticing anything before him, elbowing everybody who approached him, was pushed by the crowd before the theatre of the fashionable buffoon. The young bachelor heard shouts of laughter from all sides; he saw noblemen, young girls, workmen, and workwomen who, with their noses in the air, listened with delight to a man who was dressed in a clown's cap, smock frock, and large pantaloons, and whose face was covered by a mask; this man was Tabarin. His master, in a doctor's habit, his head covered

with a basque cap, his chin adorned with a long
beard, held some bottles of ointment or balm in
his hands. Urbain mechanically looked and listened with the others; in order to judge of that
which gave so much pleasure to the idlers of that
century, let us, also, listen for a moment.

TABARIN. — What people have you found to
be the most courteous in the world ?

THE MASTER. — I've been in Italy, I have
visited Spain, and traversed a great part of Ger-
many, but nowhere have I remarked so much
courtesy as one sees in France. You observe that
the French, kiss, caress, wish each other well, and
take off the hat.

TABARIN. — Do you call taking off the hat an
act of courtesy ? I shouldn't care much about
such caresses.

THE MASTER. — The custom of taking off the
hat as a mark of friendship is ancient, Tabarin,
and bears witness to the honor, the respect, and
the friendliness which one should feel for those
whom he salutes.

TABARIN. — So you judge all courtesy to con-
sist in taking off the hat? Would you like to
know who are the most courteous people in the
world?

THE MASTER. — Who Tabarin ?

TABARIN. — They are the tireurs de laine of
Paris ; for they are not content with taking off

the hat only, but more often take off the cloak also.[1]

This sally was received with the applause and laughter of the assembled crowd, among whom might undoubtedly be found some tireurs de laine, who plied their trade while laughing still louder than their neighbors.

Urbain did not share the general hilarity; however, he lent his ear to a new scene which the buffoon was playing. Tabarin, seeking to introduce himself to the presence of his Isabelle, whom Cascandre kept from sight as an old duenna, found no better expedient than to disguise himself as a woman, and under this costume to seek a tête-à-tête with his mistress. The harlequin mask which Tabarin wore under his feminine costume lent a thousand absurdities which evoked anew the gayety of the crowd and in which decency was not always scrupulously observed; but the public of the Pont-Neuf was not easily abashed, and the women of good standing who viewed this spectacle contented themselves with spreading their fans before their eyes and crying, —

"What unbecoming, scandalous actions; they should at least forbid these gestures."

Urbain, watching the grotesque disguise of the buffoon, conceived a plan. Why should he not use the same means to introduce himself into the

---

[1] General collection of the Œuvres et Facéties de Tabarin, Paris, 1725.

barber's house? Was it not Love himself who
taught him this strategy by making him a witness
of this scene of Tabarin's at the moment when he
was racking his brain to find out a way of approaching Blanche.

Whether it were Love, Destiny, or a chance
which had led our lover, he was none the less delighted with his idea, and, giving a thousand
thanks to Tabarin, he thought of nothing but
putting it into execution. Immediately, pushing
from right to left, he retired from the crowd. Urbain elbowed a grisette, twisted an old woman's
cloak, crushed the foot of a little woman who, supported on the arm of a young student, had slipped
among the crowd; but, insensible to the injuries
which he inflicted, he continued to make his way
and, finding himself free at last, ran to his dwelling
without stopping to take breath.

Arrived there the young bachelor opened the
drawer of a little walnut-wood secretary and
counted his money, for in every affair it is necessary to have recourse to this cursed money in
order to abolish obstacles and arrive more quickly
at the end which one has in view. His treasury
held only sixteen livres tournois, which is very
little and would not, in our day, introduce one
into the boudoir of a Lais; but when beauty is
accompanied by innocence access is much easier.

Besides Urbain would not take the costume of
a grand lady. On the contrary he wished to dis-

guise himself as a peasant; his awkwardness in that costume would be less noticeable. He looked at himself in his little glass. No beard, no whiskers, not the smallest hair on his chin. Urbain jumped for joy; although some days previously he had sighed to have mustaches, to-day he wished to change into a girl. He was delighted also at not being very tall, and exclaimed to himself, while looking at his feet and hands which were small, —

"How fortunate it is that I'm not a strong, robust, fine man!"

He had only to bestir himself to get the necessary clothing. Urbain took his crown and went to a second-hand clothier, where he asked for a dress for a servant from the country, who, he said, was about his height. They showed him all that constituted the feminine costume, petticoat, corset, apron, cap, neckerchief, shoes; they made him pay three times their value, but our young man was delighted.

These little arrangements having taken some time, Urbain went to dinner. Then, at the close of day, he returned home with his little parcel under his arm, as pleased as Jason carrying the Golden Fleece, as Pluto ravishing Proserpine, as Apollo tearing off the skin of the Python, as Hercules bearing off the Golden Apples from the garden of the Hesperides, or as Paris abducting the wife of Menelas, — and certainly all of those men should have been very well pleased.

Arrived in his chamber our lover rubbed his flint, for at that time nothing was known of sulphur matches. Having procured a light he immediately proceeded to change his state, keeping of his masculine costume only the garment which he judged to be very necessary in order not to freeze under his feminine skirt. Urbain put on the skirt, then the corset, which he endeavored to lace, but he did it very badly ; he crew one string instead of another, he ripped and pulled, he pricked himself. The poor boy was in despair, he looked at himself in his little glass and saw well that all was not right; he never should come to the end. What could he do? Only a woman knows all the mysteries of the feminine toilet. It was necessary, then, to beg some woman to come to his aid, and he recalled that on the story below him lodged an old bachelor whose servant, polite and intelligent, always made him a graceful curtsey. Immediately Urbain, holding as well as he could the skirt and the corset, ran down stairs as quickly as possible and rang his neighbor's bell. The servant opened the door, and burst into a shout of laughter on seeing this person, half man, half woman ; but no matter how he's dressed a pretty boy of nineteen is always interesting, and Urbain's voice was very touching as he said to the maid, —

"Ah, mademoiselle, I'm very much in doubt. I wish to dress myself as a woman, and I shall never come to the end. Would you be so amiable as to help me for a moment?"

"Very willingly" answered the big girl and, without allowing him to beg further, she followed Urbain to his room, where she laughed still more on seeing how he had put on the costume.

"Are you going to a ball?" said she to him.

"Yes, and I wish to be so well disguised that nobody could recognize me."

"All right; wait, I'll dress you, and I promise you you'll look well."

Immediately she commenced undoing all that Urbain had done. Then she examined the garments.

"They're not very elegant," she said.

"They are all I desire, I wish to be very simply dressed."

"But it's necessary to put another skirt on underneath, that one there isn't enough; you haven't hips like us. We must make some for you. And that cap is horrid! I wouldn't go out in it. I'll go and get you one of mine, and everything else that you need. Oh, I'll make you genteel."

And the young servant, without listening to Urbain's thanks, ran to her room, whence she soon returned carrying all that was necessary to turn a young man into a passable looking girl. The new cap was tried, it suited perfectly. Urbain was delighted; he did not know how to testify

his gratitude to the young girl. The latter had
not finished his headdress, there were some bows
to be made and some hair which must be pushed
back. She pinned his kerchief closely about his
neck, stopped, looked at him, and exclaimed, —

"Truly that does very well! Such a white
skin, such a sweet air; anyone would be deceived
in him, that's sure. Wait a moment, till I make
a false bust."

"Is it really necessary?"

"Is it necessary — why, what a question!"

"But I'm stifling in this corset."

"Well, so do we stifle in them, but that's
nothing; it's necessary to suffer a little if one
wants to be genteel. Wait, now, I'll pull your
waist in, then I'll make you some hips, and then,
ah, yes, that's all that's necessary. It's by those
things that one distinguishes the sex."

The young servant kept finding something
more to do for Urbain, and the latter, in order to
be well disguised, allowed her to do as she pleased
with the best grace in the world, repeating every
moment, —

"How good you are, mademoiselle, how can I
ever prove my gratitude?"

Urbain's toilet had lasted more than two hours,
at the end of which time the young girl left him,
saying, —

"There, that's done, you don't look a bit like
a man now; there's not the least thing to make

them doubt that you're a girl. At this hour **you** can go out. Hold your eyes down, look from the side, take small steps, balance yourself straight from the hips, pinch your mouth, throw your nose up a little high, and you won't go to the end of the street without making a conquest. Good-by, monsieur, when you have need don't hesitate to call me if you please."

The young servant departed, and Urbain, after having studied his walk for a little while, decided at last to venture into the streets of Paris in his new costume.

CHAPTER XII

A Nocturnal Adventure

THE bachelor in cap and crinoline felt sufficiently ill at his ease in the streets of Paris. Although he was protected by the darkness of the
night, for there were few who carried lanterns,
every time anyone passed near him Urbain was
afraid that he had been recognized, and fully expected to be taken by the sergeants of the watch,
who would doubtless demand the motive of his
disguising himself, and fleece him to the extent of
a heavy fine or even perhaps lock him up, if he
continued to walk in the guise of a woman in the
good city of Paris, where it was only by distrib-
uting money in handfuls that one was allowed to
pass for what he was not; and, as Urbain had not
a crown about him, because when disguising one's
self as a woman one does not remember everything, even to the putting of money in his pocket,
the young lover felt it necessary to avoid the
police; at all events, he did not fear robbers;
that was much, then, and may still prove something of a consolation to those who have nothing
to lose today.

Little by little Urbain grew more assured; he

began to feel accustomed to his costume, and certain compliments addressed to him in passing proved to him that people were entirely deceived as to his sex. Urbain was careful not to respond to the gallantries offered him by a few cavaliers, but contented himself by walking faster, escaping with muddied skirts since he did not yet know very well how to hold them up and they greatly embarrassed him in jumping the streams of dirty water. At length he reached the Rue des Bourdonnaise; and then for the first time he reflected that it was very late to try to introduce himself into the barber's house. There was no likelihood of Marguerite's venturing out at this hour; his disguise would therefore not serve him till the next day. His assumption of feminine raiment had been useless so far; but does a lover make such reflections? Besides, as Urbain had to habituate himself to wearing women's clothes, he was not displeased at making his first essay at night. While thus thinking he rambled past the barber's house, ogling Blanche's windows, and sending her a thousand sighs which she could not hear because she was asleep, and which probably she would not have heard any better had she been awake.

Wholly engrossed in the pleasure of sighing under his lady love's casements, Urbain forgot that while it is natural to see a young man waiting and sighing in the street at night, a solitary woman doing the like evokes many conjectures. All

of a sudden the young lover was recalled from his
ecstacy by some unknown person who pinched
him very hard on the knee, and said to him, in a
hoarse, rasping voice,—

"It seems to me, little mother, that the one
you're waiting for is something late ; if you'll only
accept my arm we can go and taste some very fair
white wine at the merchant's down yonder.   I'm
a good customer of his, and he has some comfortable private rooms."

Urbain turned sharply round and perceived at
his side a big, jolly fellow, in the garb of a chair
porter, who was offering his arm and smiling
almost to his ears.   Without answering, and little
pleased by this adventure, the young man began
to run, soon leaving his gallant in the lurch.   But
his troubles were not to end there; some two
hundred steps farther on, he was stopped anew
by some pages who essayed to kiss him ; he disengaged himself from them as speedily as possible, and resumed his course.   Later he was in
turn accosted by some students, some lackeys, and
some soldiers, several of them pursuing him.
Urbain, that he might the better escape them, redoubled his agility, and, in order to run faster,
gathered his skirts up about his knees ; but the
higher he pulled them, the greater ardor these
gentlemen evinced in following him.

"Hang it," said Urbain, while running, "I
didn't disguise myself as a woman to be pinched

by all the pages and lackeys of this city. Men are the devil incorporate; I perceive now that it's more agreeable to wear breeches than petticoats, but tomorrow I shall obtain entrance to Blanche's dwelling. Come, courage — they'll leave me alone perhaps."

And Urbain jumped over the puddles, wound among the streets, perspiring and suffocating in his corset, and under the false bosom with which the young servant had stuffed his chest. Turning down the streets at random as he came to them, in order to escape his pursuers, he did not know himself in what neighborhood he was.

At last, not hearing anyone behind him, he stopped to take breath and recognize the place in which he stood. He had passed the bridges and had reached the great Pré-aux-Clercs, in which they had commenced to build houses and open streets; as they had done in the little Pré-aux-Clercs, which towards the end of the reign of Henri the Fourth was entirely covered with houses and gardens.

"Good; here's the new street they call Rue de Verneuil," said Urbain to himself; "and this is the Chemin-aux-Vaches where they've built the Rue Saint-Dominique; I recognize it. But I'll rest for a minute or two, I'm too far from home to return there immediately — I can't walk any farther. Let's get my breath at least. This neighborhood's deserted, and, as night is far advanced, let's hope I shall make no more conquests." Urbain hoisted

his skirts and seated himself on a stone. At the
expiration of half an hour, feeling rested, he rose
and took the way to his lodgings. He walked
quietly along congratulating himself that he should
meet no one else when suddenly, in passing by the
Rue de Bourbon, he saw four men who were leaving it and who, on sight of him, barred the way.

"Who goes there? So late — and the game is
still rising?"

"Upon my honor a charming meeting, it's a
little country wench."

"Better still. I'm very fond of peasants."

"What the devil, marquis ! a peasant who walks
about Paris in the middle of the night. That's an
innocence which seems to me tremendously ad-
venturous."

"Come, chevalier, your thoughts are always
evil. I'll wager the poor child came to Paris for
nothing but to sell her eggs."

"Let her have come for what she will, she
sha'n't return without the impress of my mustaches on her pretty lips."

Urbain realized by the language and manners
of these gentlemen that they were profligates of the
higher classes. Unable to make his escape, for he
was surrounded on every side, he tried to relieve
himself of them by saying in a falsetto voice, —

"Gentlemen, leave me, I beg of you; I am not
what you believe."

But his prayers were unheeded ; they pushed

him, they surrounded him. Urbain, rendered impatient by these manners, saw no means of regaining his liberty save making himself known, and he cried in his natural voice,—

"Leave me, gentlemen, I repeat to you, you are addressing the wrong person."

These words, pronounced by the young bachelor in a manner which left no doubt as to his sex, produced the effect of a head of Medusa on the four young noblemen: they remained motionless for a moment, then they all burst into a shout of laughter, crying: "It's a man. What a unique adventure."

"Yes, gentlemen, it is a man," answered Urbain. "I hope now that you will allow me to continue on my way."

"As for me, I will no longer oppose you," said one of the strangers.

"Come, Villebelle," resumed another, "let the boy go. You can see very well he's not a girl. I believe, deuce take it, that the wine we've drunk didn't allow the marquis to see our mistake. Isn't that so, chevalier?"

"Yes, yes, indeed, gentlemen," answered the Marquis de Villebelle; for it was that nobleman himself, who, as he had said to the barber, made merry with his friends by seeking spicy adventures in the streets of the capital. With a head excited by wines and liqueurs, the marquis, always the leader in the follies and extravagances committed in these escapades, had pressed Urbain most closely, and on the latter making himself known had continued to hold the young bachelor.

"A moment, my boy," said he, stopping Urbain. "We know you're not a girl, that's all very well; but, by all the devils! in this disguise you must necessarily have had some very comical adventures; recount them to us, 't will amuse us, and afterwards you shall be free to go your way."

"Yes, yes," repeated the others; "he must tell us why he's dressed up like a woman."

"I must really tell this adventure at the cardinal's little levée tomorrow morning.

"And I must tell it to Marion Delorme. I'll, have Bois-Robert put it into verse for the court."

"Colletel shall turn it into a comedy. Come, speak on."

"Yet, once more, gentlemen, allow me to go on my way; by what right do you interrogate me? I have nothing to say to you, and I wish to depart."

Saying these words, he endeavored to repulse the marquis anew, but the latter barred the way and drew his sword, crying, —

"Upon my honor, this little goodman is very fractious. It's really too droll. You shall speak or we will make you jump under our swords like a spaniel."

"Insolent fellow," exclaimed Urbain, furiously; "had I a weapon you had not dared to use such language to me, or I should already have chastised you."

"Truly? Oh, hang it. I should like to see how you handle a sword. Come, chevalier, lend him yours."

"What, Villebelle, you wish it?"

"Yes, undoubtedly, a duel with a peasant — that will be a joke."

"Come, gentlemen, make a circle."

So saying, the marquis took a sword from one of his companions and presented it to Urbain.

"Hold," said he, "here's a weapon, defend yourself. Guard yourself, girl-boy, and let us see if you are as brave as you're stubborn."

Urbain seized the sword with ardor and immediately attacked the marquis. Though embarrassed by his petticoats and corset he pressed impetuously on his adversary, who, while parrying his strokes, exclaimed at every moment, —

"Well done; very well done, 'pon my honor! Do you see that, gentlemen? — and that parry — and that thrust. Deuce take it, if he goes on in this way I must use all my skill to —"

A stroke of his adversary's sword, which crossed his forearm, cut short the marquis' words; his sword dropped from his hand, his friends surrounded and supported him, while Urbain himself offered his help.

"It's nothing — a mere nothing," said the marquis; "good-by, my friend, you're a brave fellow,

and I'm pleased to have made your acquaintance;
although I don't know with whom I've fought
this duel. As to you, if some day you find yourself in any embarrassment, if you have a bad business or need a protector, come to my hotel, ask
for the Marquis de Villebelle and you will always
find me ready to oblige you."

CHAPTER XIII

THE TÊTE-À-TÊTE

DAWN had followed this night so fruitful in events, during which sleep had not touched Julia's eyes; uneasy, impatient, twenty times had she arisen from her sofa to go to the door and listen, in the belief that she could at last distinguish some sound, some disturbance which indicated the approach of the marquis. But though she had heard every hour strike during this to her apparently endless night, the seductive Villebelle had not yet arrived.

The brow of the young Italian was clouded; her eyes, always vivacious and lustrous, under her change of feeling were now animated by a gloomy fire which boded ill for those who had caused it; Julia's breast was oppressed, sighs escaped her lips and she walked aimlessly and angrily about the apartment, the elegance of which no longer delighted her; she passed the mirrors without even looking at herself in them. Her vanity was most painfully mortified and humiliated, she felt insulted by the indifference of this marquis who had led her to compromise herself thus, and now failed to keep his appointment, whose conduct, in fact, was inexcusable. What woman would pardon such neglect?

To allow herself to be abducted with a good grace, and to be forced to spend the entire night following in solitude. Love will excuse many things, but self-love excuses nothing.

As soon as daylight paled the light of the candles, Julia opened the door of the boudoir and, crossing several rooms, ventured into the corridor.

" I don't believe that I can escape," she said, smiling bitterly; "they have taken too many precautions to keep me; but monsieur le marquis and his worthy agent no doubt imagine me to be in a state of ecstatic happiness at the mere fact of having been brought to this house. Patience! One day perhaps they will know me better."

Julia went downstairs. Although it was in the depth of winter the morning was beautiful; the young Italian left by the peristyle and plunged into the gardens, where she walked up and down the long pathways and gave herself up to her thoughts.

Day had surprised Marcel and his guest sleeping near the table where they had supped. Marcel awoke first, recalled his ideas, and could not conceive why his master had not returned in the night. However, the door-bell hung in the room where they had slept, and the marquis was a man who was able to make himself heard.

Marcel pushed Chaudoreille, who opened his

little eyes and gazed about him in astonishment, murmuring, —

"By jingo! I am not at home in the Rue Brise-miche nor in the gambling den on the Rue Vide-Gousset. Where the devil have I passed the night? My purse — where is my purse? I had eight crowns in it."

Chaudoreille quickly seized his purse and counted his money, and Marcel said to him, —

"Come, wake up, why don't you? and remember where you are. Do you think me capable of robbing you?"

"Good-for-nothing that I am! that good fellow Marcel — I remember everything now. Forgive me, my friend; but at the first moment I thought I was at a tavern where I sleep sometimes. What the devil! it's broad daylight."

"Yes, and monsieur le marquis did not come in during the night; I can't understand why."

"It is rather singular, and that poor little thing whom we took so much trouble to bring here, what has she done with herself since yesterday?"

"She's slept the same as we have."

"Ah, my dear Marcel, it's easily seen that you have not studied the sex. Sleep! — a woman who is waiting her vanquisher for the first time? She would sooner keep awake all night than go to sleep."

"But when the vanquisher doesn't come, it's necessary for her to do something."

"Never! never I tell you. Wait, here's an example: I had once arranged a meeting with a baroness on the borders of the Seine, near the Tour de Nesle; that also was in winter, and it was horribly cold. Unforeseen events — a duel — prevented my meeting my beauty. I was wounded, and spent eight days in bed. On the ninth, as I passed the neighborhood indicated, by chance, whom should I see there?"

"Your baroness?"

"Exactly. But, the poor woman, she had been frozen for four days, and that because she would not leave the place of rendezvous."

"Our dame has a good fire and everything that she can desire; she won't freeze while awaiting my master."

"What do you say, Marcel; shall I go upstairs and chat pleasantly with her to distract her mind a little?"

"No, indeed, that would be displeasing to monsieur le marquis."

"Well, you're right; I suppose he might take offence at it."

"Don't you think you had much better go and find the person who brought her here, and tell him that monsieur has not come?"

"No, my dear Marcel; Touquet told me to wait here for the marquis' orders, and I must follow his instructions. If he does not come for a fortnight, it's all the same to me; I shall not leave

this.   You have a good cellar and plenty of provisions of all kinds, and I find it very comfortable
here; only, I must go out and get some cards for
the coming night, and I'll teach you some tricks
which you don't understand."

"All right, I'll go and get our breakfast ready;
then I'll go and inquire whether the young lady
wants anything."

"That will do; meanwhile I'll take a turn in
the garden and make the acquaintance of your
Hercules."

Chaudoreille arranged his mantle, put on his
new ruff, which he had bought by chance, which
pleased him greatly because it came up to his ears.
He brushed up his hat, curled his hair anew, and
went into the garden whistling, —

> Viens Aurore,
> Je t' implore ;

a song which good King Henri had brought into
fashion. He paused with an air of defiance before
the statues, and made a grimace at those which
had frightened him the evening before.

At the end of the pathway he perceived Julia,
seated in a thicket which, as yet, was devoid of
foliage. The young girl was deep in thought, and
had not heard him approach. Chaudoreille reflected, uncertain whether he should approach her
or whether he should pass on his way. He concluded to do the first, and drew near her, holding

his left hand on his hip, and, throwing his body back, already beginning to smile. Julia raised her luminous eyes ; but, on recognizing Chaudoreille, a look of humor flashed over her features, and she said sharply, —

" What do you want with me ? "

Chaudoreille paused, arrested in the middle of his smile, and could not find words to answer her.

" Why were you coming to me ? " resumed Julia ; " is the marquis here, or his confidant, the barber Touquet ? "

" No, beautiful lady, I am at present alone with you and Marcel in the house. I have passed the night in watching over your safety, believing that the marquis would arrive."

" Who is this Marcel ? the servant who opened the door to us, I suppose."

" Precisely ! "

" He has served the marquis for a long time in this house ? "

" No, I believe he has only been here four or five years."

" And you, when did you come here ? "

" I came yesterday for the first time."

Julia was silent and Chaudoreille resumed after a moment, —

" Are you acquainted with my intimate friend, the barber Touquet ? "

" What does that matter to you," asked the young Italian, glancing scornfully at Chaudoreille.

" It's nothing to me, certainly — but, since you named him — he's a very worthy fellow, certainly, and I am honored in being his friend."

" That reflects credit on you," said Julia, smiling ironically.

"Yes, most assuredly," resumed Chaudoreille, who had interpreted Julia's smile to his own advantage, " we have seen fire together. He is brave, I'll give him justice for that; he always conducts himself honorably."

" Always? And has he sometimes spoken to you of his parents ? — of his father ? "

" My faith, no; I don't believe he was born from the higher classes. In that matter I am infinitely before him; the Chaudoreilles are of very pure blood and have a stock which goes back to Noah. Under Charles the Bald one of my ancestors had himself shaved — "

" What does it matter what your ancestors did ? I was talking about the barber's family."

" That's all right; but my friend Touquet has spoken very little to me about them. I believe he is from Lorraine and he has told me that he left his country very early and came very young to Paris, for it is only there that talent has a chance of success ; also Touquet has made money, and me, thank God, I am — "

Here Chaudoreille's eyes wandered over his doublet, which was stained in many places, and he covered it with his mantle, resuming, —

" I should be very rich if I had not ruined myself for women."

Julia, who had paid little attention to this last
phrase, said to herself, —

" He ought to be rich if he has helped the marquis in all his follies."

" He is not married," resumed Chaudoreille,
" although he could now find a good match. His
house on the Rue des Bourdonnais is a very
pretty property. Perhaps it's because of the little
one that he doesn't marry; perhaps he is going
to marry her, I shouldn't be surprised."

" What little one," inquired Julia, curiously.

" The young girl whom he has adopted and
who is now sixteen years old."

" The barber Touquet has adopted a child ? "

" Why, yes, of course he has. Why, if you
know him, how is it that you are ignorant of
that ? That's certainly the best act of his life."

" Touquet has done a good action," said Julia,
smiling ironically; " I could not have imagined
that, and is this young girl pretty ? "

" Hang it ! is she pretty ? Well, I believe you !
She is one — but no," said Chaudoreille, correct-
ing himself as if struck by a sudden remembrance,
" she is not handsome at all; on the contrary,
she is ugly, one might even say that she is disagreeable."

" One minute you say she is pretty and the
next you say she is very ugly; you don't seem

to know what you are saying, Monsieur Chaudoreille."

"One can easily lose his wits when near you,
beautiful damsel ; but, by that sword, I swear to
you — "

The bell at the garden gate was heard, Chaudoreille stopped ; presuming that it was the marquis
and that it would perhaps be dangerous for him to
be surprised in a tête-à-tête with Julia, he escaped
by the first pathway and ran to rejoin Marcel,
while the young Italian listened anxiously and her
cheeks assumed a more vivid color.

Marcel opened the door, but it was not the
marquis, it was Touquet, who came alone.

"Your master fought a duel last night," said
he to Marcel, " he was wounded, but very slightly,
it seems. I have come to speak to the young
girl. She is perhaps anxious to know what all this
means. Where is she now ? "

"In the garden," said Chaudoreille, " but I
assure you she is not at all lonely here. It is true
that I have chatted with her — "

"And who gave you permission to do so ?
You're very bold to converse with a woman on
whom a marquis has laid his eyes."

"Yes, I confess that I am very bold — but I
believe you say that monseigneur fought a duel ;
do you know with whom he fought ? "

"Idiot ! Is that our business ? Do you suppose I asked him ? "

"It's true, it's not our business, but — "

"You have nothing more to do here, get out."

"Do you wish me to take myself off?"

"Yes, and immediately."

"Without being presented to monseigneur, that is very awkward; but at least — it seems to me that if they have no more need of me they ought to settle with me."

"Wait! here are ten more crowns; it's more than you are worth, a hundred times."

"Very well, but the rosette and the broken pane of glass —"

"Hang it, stupid! you're not satisfied?"

"It's all right, it's all right, I'm very well pleased. I mustn't grumble," added Chaudoreille to himself, "he might happen to remember the shaves that I owe him."

"Go at once," said the barber, angrily, pointing with his finger to the garden gate. The Gascon hastily thrust the sum which he had received into his purse, and placed the latter carefully in his belt, murmuring, —

"Ten and eight, that's eighteen. By jingo, that will make them stare at the gambling place in the Rue Vide-Gousset and at the bank of the Rue Coupe-Gorge." Then he shook Marcel's hand, and wrapping himself in his mantle left by the middle gate, which was hardly wide enough for him since he possessed eighteen crowns.

The barber hastened to acquit himself of the commission with which his master had charged him, that he might return promptly to his house and be there on the arrival of his customers. He walked hurriedly through the garden, and soon met Julia, who felt her hope vanish when she perceived him.

"Madame," said Touquet, bowing to the young girl, "the marquis' conduct doubtless seems to you rather extraordinary, but you will excuse him when you learn that he fought a duel last night in the grand Pré-aux-Clercs and was wounded."

"He is wounded," said Julia, with emotion, "and dangerously?"

"No, madame, it is a very little thing, an arm only. Monsieur le marquis made this event known to me at break of day and ordered me to come and tell you. He hoped to be very soon recovered, and able within four or five days to come and excuse himself; but, if you are wearied in this place, you are free to return to your shop. I will go and warn you when —"

"No," said Julia, interrupting him brusquely; "do you imagine I can return to the dwelling I have left? I will wait for the marquis."

"You are the mistress, and they have orders to satisfy your slightest wishes."

The barber bowed to Julia, and having given Marcel the marquis' orders, left the little house and returned to his home.

Five days had elapsed since the young Italian had entered the luxurious apartments; there she had found a harpsichord, a sitar, books, some pencils, some sketches, and a wardrobe furnished with everything that could add a charm to beauty. Marcel, always obedient and discreet, brought her everything that she desired, without permitting himself the slightest question; nor did Julia address him, except to ask him for what she thought necessary to distract her, for the most magnificent dwelling does not forbid weariness.

It was late on the evening of the sixth day; Julia was attired with coquetry, in the hope that the marquis would come, but her hope was vanishing. She lay down upon the sofa, where her reverie had yielded to a light slumber, when the door of the room opened softly, and the Marquis de Villebelle appeared at the entrance of the apartment. "She's not half bad," said he, looking at Julia, who was lying carelessly on the sofa; then he advanced towards her; the noise awoke the young Italian, and, opening her eyes, she perceived the great nobleman, whose rich and elegant costume increased the grace of his bearing. He seated himself, smiling, at her side. Julia was about to rise.

"Don't move," said the marquis, "you are very well as you are. I reproach myself with having disturbed your slumber."

"Monseigneur, I had about given you up,"

said Julia, seeking to restrain the uneasiness which she felt at the sight of the marquis. " I have been here for six days, alone in this place."

"Yes, you must have found it very tiresome I can imagine ; but, ma belle, my messenger must have told you that it was not my fault. My arm is not cured yet, but I could not longer resist the desire to see this amiable child who for love of me was willing to live in solitude."

" For love of you, seigneur," said Julia, turning her eyes aside so as not to meet those of the marquis, which were fixed amorously upon her ; "and who has made you believe that I am in love with you, if you please ? "

" Ah, upon my honor, that is divine. Were you awaiting another here, then, my angel ? "

" I was waiting, monsieur, to learn from you what motive you had in inducing me to leave my dwelling."

" Delightful by all the devils — delightful. She does not know why they brought her here. Did nobody tell you, little strategist ? "

" It was from you alone that I wished to hear it, seigneur."

" That is correct. Love is ill made by an ambassador ; the little god does not love pages and valets. He wishes to do his work himself. Come, a kiss first, and we shall understand each other better afterwards."

Julia disengaged herself from the marquis' arms,

which he had wound about her, and withdrawing
from him she cried, —

"Please, sir, cease these liberties which offend
me!"

"Which offend her!" said the marquis, bursting into laughter, while a vivid color sprang to
Julia's cheek. "Come now, what do you mean by
that? Are we playing a comedy? You wish to
make me pay for the weariness of six days' waiting. Once more, sweetheart, it was not my fault;
a duel at the moment when I was least thinking of
it. I must tell you all about that for it was very
droll. I was returning with four of my friends;
we were a little tipsy and were trying to dispute
with everybody. We broke windows, we beat the
watch, we tore off the good shopkeepers' wigs;
what can you expect? one must pass the time and
show these gentlemen of the parliament that one
does not regard one's self as being comprised in
their edicts, which forbid vagabonds, pages and
lackeys to make a noise at night in the streets of
Paris. Finally, we met a girl, which girl was a boy;
he would not tell us why he was disguised, and
became angry at our joking; one of the others
lent him a sword and we fought. For a youngster,
zooks how he went on! it was a pleasure to fight
with him. In short, he gave me this cut, which I
still feel, and which prevents me from using my
arm; so, sweetheart, I beg of you don't be too
cruel, for I am not in a state to lead an assault."

And the marquis again approached Julia, wishing to enfold her in his arms ; but she disengaged herself and seated herself farther off, while the former extended himself on the sofa and looked at her smiling, while whistling a hunting tune.

The breast of the young girl rose more frequently ; she turned her head and carried one of her hands to her eyes.

"What is the matter?" said the marquis, after some minutes. "Are you crying, by chance? Truly, little one, I can't imagine why. They told me that you came here with a very good grace; after which I naturally feel surprised at the severity which you are affecting now; be easy, I will be very virtuous — since you wish it."

So saying, Villebelle seated himself near Julia and took one of her hands, which he pressed between his own. The young Italian raised her eyes to the marquis; there was in the features of the latter something so noble, so seductive, that it was very easy for him to obtain pardon for his audacity; accustomed to triumph, he had trespassed through habit and not through fatuity, and Julia's resistance astonished, but did not anger him.

"Why are you crying?" said he to her.

"I believed that you loved me, and you despise me."

"I despise you? No, beautiful girl; I love you, — as well as I can love; and my love will last, — as long as it will; can you ask better?"

"I wish for love; a constant and sincere love."

"Ha! ha! a constant love; sweetheart, you are exacting. Can we promise that, we others? and in good faith, when the great ladies of the court cannot come by it, to a grisette; should she hope to hold the Marquis de Villebelle?"

"Very well," said Julia, rising proudly and walking towards the door, "the grisette will not yield to the caprice of the great nobleman."

"Upon my honor, she is going, I believe," said the marquis, rushing to retain Julia and gently leading her to the sofa. "Come, no more ill-humor. Is it to quarrel that we are here? Time flies rapidly and carries with it, at every moment, a spark of the enkindling fires of love. One doesn't wait for pleasure to be extinguished before tasting of it. I love you. I adore you, you little wretch; but what do you offer me as the reward of so much ardor?"

"A heart that knows how to love you in a manner in which you have not been loved before today, a heart whose only happiness will be to beat for you, which will not have one thought to which you will be a stranger, nor one desire disconnected from you!"

While saying these words Julia's eyes were animated and she fixed them on the marquis, seeking no longer to hide the passion with which he had inspired her.

"What magnificent eyes," said Villebelle, after

a moment, "but a little too exalted in their expression. You are Italian, that is easily seen, the
burning skies under which you were born do not
allow you to treat love as we French treat it,
lightly, jokingly; which is, after all, the best way;
the others are too sad."

"Say, rather, that we know how to love truly
— while you, seigneur, give the name of love to
the most fleeting fancy, your heart being entirely
a stranger to the real passion."

"Wait, my dear girl! All your discourses on
the metaphysics of love are less convincing to me
than one kiss from those lovely lips, and why
should you keep up such a show of resistance?
Is it generous to profit by my being wounded?"

"Have you always been generous, monseigneur?" said Julia, repulsing the marquis; "and
in this place, even, have you nothing to reprove
yourself withal?"

"Why, how's this, little girl, do you wish me
to follow a course of morals?" said Villebelle,
laughing. "It seems to me you are abusing my
patience a little. 'Pon my honor those lovely eyes
are made to express pleasure rather than wisdom. And sermons from your mouth! a little
grisette who wishes to play Lucretia here. Come,
sweetheart, leave such twaddling talk. Was it from
Tabarin or from Briochée that you learned those
sentences?"

Julia rose, her eyes scintillating, her cheeks a

vivid scarlet, and looking angrily at the marquis cried, —

"And you, seigneur, where did you learn to murder a father in order to abduct his daughter?"

Villebelle remained as if stunned for a moment; his look fixed on Julia, who, dismayed herself at the change wrought in the whole appearance of the marquis, awaited with fear what he should say to her.

The marquis rose, and murmured in a changed voice, —

"What made you think I had ever committed such a terrible crime? Speak, answer, I command you."

"Seigneur," said the young Italian, "I have heard the story of the abduction of the beautiful Estrelle, old Delmar's daughter, but the barber Touquet was then your agent, and I don't doubt that it was he who wanted you to arm yourself against an old man who was defending his daughter."

"You have heard some one speak of an adventure which has been forgotten for seventeen years and you are barely twenty. You have not told me all — have you known Estrelle? Is she still living? Speak, pray speak, and count on my gratitude if you assist me to recover that unfortunate woman."

"You loved her well, did you not?" said Julia, gazing tenderly at the marquis.

"Yes, yes, I loved her — I should love her still. Pray tell me, is she still living? Answer me."

"I know no more than you, seigneur, I swear to you. I have never met the woman who bore that name, and chance made the adventure known to me. On seeing you and on finding myself in this house, to which Estrelle was brought, the remembrance of these events was presented to my thoughts; forgive me for having recalled them to you — you were then very young; I know, also that old Delmar did not die of his wounds. As to his daughter, I repeat to you I know no more of her than you do. But you had outraged me in comparing me to those women whom you can purchase every day with your riches, while I only desire your love. I am Italian and I revenged myself!"

The marquis did not answer, he walked slowly up and down the room, from time to time sighing and glancing around him; but he did not appear to perceive that Julia was there.

"Yes, I passed a month with her here," said the marquis, looking around the boudoir, "this abode was not what it is today. I have embellished it, changed it, in order to drive away the remembrance of her; but never since have I experienced such entrancing moments as those spent near Estrelle."

A long silence succeeded these words; then the

marquis took his hat and cloak and slightly inclined his head to Julia, as he said, in a low
voice, —

"I shall see you again tomorrow."

Then he hurriedly quitted the little house in a
very different frame of mind from that in which
he had entered it.

CHAPTER XIV

URSULE AND THE SORCERER OF VERBERIE

FOR some few days after his nocturnal adventure of the duel Urbain refrained from wearing his feminine costume. He was not at all anxious to make any further conquests and to thus expose himself to adventures which were hardly likely to always result to his advantage; the young bachelor felt that before he again disguised himself as a girl he should make sure that his stratagem would bring him nearer to obtaining an interview with Blanche.

He began to watch Marguerite again, prowling incessantly around the barber's house, and obtaining all the information he could get as to the character of the old servant; and he promised himself that he would avail himself to the utmost of her credulity and superstition. His plan being carefully considered and arranged, an old messenger, commissioned by him, accosted Marguerite and asked her if she knew of a place for a young peasant, a very pleasant and virtuous girl, who had lately come to Paris and found herself without employment. The kindly old serving woman at once gave two addresses where she said they would perhaps take the young girl, and continued on her way.

The next day while going, according to custom, to buy provisions, Marguerite was stopped by a country woman, very modest in demeanor, but with an awkward air, who curtseyed to her and thanked her with lowered eyes.

" What are you thanking me for, my child ? " said Marguerite, " I do not know you."

" Because you interested yourself in me yesterday and tried to find me a place."

" Oh, are you the one they recommended to me ? "

" Yes, mademoiselle."

" Did they engage you ? "

" No, mademoiselle."

" I am sorry for it, for you seem to me very pleasing, very honest. Where do you come from?"

" From Verberie, mademoiselle."

" Why did you come to Paris?"

" I have lost both my parents and I thought I should find work more easily in a great city."

" Yes, but great cities are dangerous places for virtuous young maids such as you appear to be. They should have told you that, my child."

" Yes, they did, mademoiselle! but I am not afraid of anything."

" Why, you must believe yourself very wary, very strong, to think you can escape the snares they'll set for you."

"Indeed it's not that, mademoiselle, but it is that — I daren't say — it's a mystery, a secret."

Secret and mystery had the same effect upon the old maid as love and marriage have upon a young maid — they aroused all her feelings. Marguerite's little eyes beamed and she cried, —

"What, my child! you have a secret? I am not curious, but you interest me ; I should like to be useful to you, but it's necessary that I should know everything that concerns you. What is this mystery that you dare not mention?"

"Mademoiselle, I did not wish to confide in anyone in Paris, for somebody told me there were pickpockets who would steal my treasure."

"You possess a treasure?"

"Oh, yes, mademoiselle ; but one with which I could still die of hunger."

"Why, indeed, what does that matter, my child, hasn't every young girl a treasure without price — her innocence, her virtue — and those who guard it the best are not always the richest. When I see shameless women, who live in luxury and abundance, riding in gilded carriages, it makes me feel ill. But about your secret, my child ; would you refuse to confide in me?"

"No, indeed, mademoiselle, you appear so respectable, so good, that I cannot refuse you."

Marguerite half smiled and tapped the country woman on the arm, for praise is a flower whose perfume is grateful at any age.

"Out with it then," she said. "What is it?"

"Mademoiselle, I'll tell you with much pleasure; but it's a long story, and I must go into a good many houses this morning. If you would let me tell it to you this evening at your house, that would be better, for I dare not say all that in the street; some one might hear me and take me for a sorcerer, and I'm very much afraid of the Chambre Ardente. God knows, however, mademoiselle, that I understand nothing of magic, and I'm more afraid of the devil than I am of men."

"Oh," said Marguerite, whose curiosity had reached an unbearable point, "this mystery of yours is of itself extraordinary?"

"Yes, mademoiselle."

"Indeed! Well, this is very embarrassing; to receive you in the house is difficult. Where do you live, my child?"

Urbain hesitated for a moment, then replied:—

"Near thé Porte Saint-Antoine."

"Oh, good heavens — that's more than a league from here. I could never get there; my master's a very strict man and doesn't wish that anyone should have visitors."

Marguerite reflected for some moments, then her curiosity carried the day.

"Well," said she at last, "come this evening at seven o'clock; it'll be dark; but look well at that house over there — that alleyway."

"Oh, I shall recognize it."

"Don't knock; keep near the door. I'll let you in, and show you up to my room. At that hour my master doesn't ordinarily need my services, and he never leaves the lower room."

"That's enough, mademoiselle, I'll be there at seven precisely."

"What is your name?"

"Ursule Ledoux."

"Above all, Ursule, don't gossip with anybody about this. It's no crime to receive you, but my master's a little ridiculous and might find it wrong. Besides, my child, one must be discreet in everything. You'll tell me your secret this evening, Ursule?"

"Yes, mademoiselle."

"At seven o'clock, the house over there."

Urbain departed, delighted by the success of his stratagem, breathing with difficulty, partly from the hope of seeing Blanche and partly because his corset impeded his respiration; and Marguerite reached her dwelling, saying, —

"This young girl looks as sweet as she looks honest, and there's no harm in receiving her for a moment — it'll amuse my poor little Blanche a little; she's been rather sad for some days and seems more lonely than usual; and we shall know the secret which — mon Dieu, if seven o'clock would only come soon."

Marguerite hastened to find Blanche. Since

the night of the serenade the lovely child had
been even more dreamy than before; she sang
nothing but the refrain of her dear romance, and
the villanelles, the virelays, the old songs amused
her no longer. Marguerite drew near to her and
said mysteriously, in a low tone, —

" This evening we shall have a visitor."

" A visitor," said Blanche. " Oh, M. Chaudoreille I suppose."

"No, indeed, a very pleasing, very honest young
country girl whom you don't know. A poor child
who possesses a treasure and who is looking for a
place as cook; she wishes to remain virtuous, and
for that reason has come to Paris; she is afraid of
the devil, but of nothing else."

" But dear nurse, I don't understand."

" Hush! hush! keep still! This evening she
will come, and we shall hear her story; there is a
question of a very curious mystery, but be silent;
it is not necessary that M. Touquet should know
anything about that for he might forbid this poor
Ursule from coming to chat with us, and that
would displease me very much because she will
amuse you a little, my child."

" Oh, be easy, dear nurse, I shall say nothing,"
cried Blanche, and she jumped about her room for
joy because the announcement of this visit was for
her an extraordinary event. The least thing new
is a great pleasure for those who pass their lives
deprived of all gayety. It is thus that a storm or

even a shower will distract and occupy a poor prisoner; that a bottle of wine will make a feast for a man of small means habituated to drinking nothing but water; that the sound of a Barbary organ appears delightful to the country people; that a ticket for the play crowns the wishes of the poor workwoman of ten sous a day; that a little muslin dress makes an honest grisette happy; and that Sunday is awaited with impatience by those who work all the week; while for many people fêtes, the theatre, music, diamonds, cannot rejoice their hearts. After all, should not the poor be happier than the rich?

At last seven sounded from Saint Eustache's clock. The barber had long since sent Blanche and Marguerite to shut themselves into their rooms. The old servant went softly downstairs, trying to make as little noise as possible with her heels, and shielding the light of her lamp with her hand. She opened the street door and saw the country girl, who had been waiting for a quarter of an hour.

"That's well," said Marguerite, "you are here; but hush! don't speak, don't make any noise; let me lead you."

Urbain nodded his head and entered the alley-way, while Marguerite softly closed the door. Then our lover was at the height of his joy. It seemed to him that he breathed a purer air in the house of the one he loved. He believed himself in the abode of highest bliss while going up the little crooked staircase ; and the black and crumbling walls that surrounded him had more charm for his eyes than the marbles or the sculptures of the Louvre.

"You are going to see my mistress," said Marguerite, " I have warned her, but fear nothing, she is as amiable as she is good ; you can speak without danger before her, she is discretion itself, — besides, she never sees anybody, and never goes out. My master wishes to shield her against the enterprises of these dandies, of these worthless fellows who seek to cajole the poor girls. It is true that my little Blanche is very pretty ; she would turn the heads of all our noblemen, you are going to see her, and you can judge for yourself; here we are at her room. Come in, come, don't tremble so ; how childish you are."

Urbain was trembling, in fact, and his heart beat so hard that he was obliged to support himself for a moment against the wall. During this time Marguerite opened the door and said to Blanche, —

" Here she is."

Blanche rose and came to meet the young girl whom her nurse had brought, smiling pleasantly at her. Urbain raised his eyes, saw Blanche, and his emotion increased. He had only been able through the panes of the casement to perceive her features very imperfectly, and the charming object which now met his gaze was a hundred times more beautiful than the image which his memory and his imagination had created. He remained for a moment stunned, motionless, not daring to take a step, doubting still whether he could believe his happiness, and looking with delight at the lovely girl, who smiled at him and took him by the hand, saying to him,—

"Won't you come in? Come in and sit down and warm yourself. Why, you're not afraid of me, are you?"

"This is the girl I told you about," announced Marguerite, "but she is a little timid, though she will soon lose that; may she always preserve her modesty in Paris."

Blanche's soft hand slipped into that of the young bachelor and she led him to the fireplace. On feeling the pretty fingers imprinted on his own, Urbain scarcely breathed, and murmured in a feeble voice, —

"How good you are, mademoiselle?"

"She has a very pretty voice," cried Blanche, immediately. "Don't you think so, Marguerite? A voice which I seem to have heard before; it is very singular, I can't recall where I've heard it."

"You are mistaken, my child," said Marguerite, "for myself I think that Ursule's voice is a little rough. But remember that we have not much time to keep her here and she is going to tell us a certain thing."

"One moment," said Blanche, "let her rest for

a minute, she looks tired.   Do you need anything ? "

" No, I thank you," said Urbain, raising his
eyes on the amiable child, and immediately abas-
ing them, for he feared that she would read in them
all the love which consumed him and it seemed to
him that the moment was very ill-chosen to make
it known ; besides, he was so happy near Blanche
that he wished to prolong the time, and, thanks to
his disguise, he could see the sweet girl practise her
graces, her amiability, and learn her character much
better than if he had appeared to her in his true
form.   Before a lover the frankest girl is always
timid, embarrassed, reserved, while with a person
of her own sex she expresses without constraint
the feelings which she experiences.

" And so you are looking for a place ? " said
Blanche, seating herself near Urbain.

" Yes, mademoiselle."

" Have you been long in Paris ? "

" A fortnight, mademoiselle."

" And your parents ? "

" I have none, mademoiselle.   I am an orphan."

" Poor girl ! that's like me, I am an orphan
also, and if M. Touquet had not taken care of me
I too should have had to go to work to earn my
living."

" You, mademoiselle," said Urbain ardently,
but he restrained himself and finished in a low
voice, " that would have been very unfortunate."

" My dear Blanche," said Marguerite, "it was
not that you might tell her your history, but that
she might acquaint us with the secret she is keeping that she came here. Now, Ursule, speak my
child ! "

Urbain sighed ; he would much rather have listened to Blanche than have talked to Marguerite ; but it was necessary to satisfy the old maid,
he needed her ; and it was by exciting her curiosity
that he hoped often to see Blanche. He commenced his recital, disguising his voice, and while
he spoke the beautiful child fixed her eyes on him,
a favor which he owed to his costume, but which
often made him lose the thread of his discourse.

" You have doubtless heard tell of Jeanne Harviliers, so famous a century ago for her witcheries
and sorceries."

" No, never," said Marguerite, drawing her
chair nearer and stretching her neck, because the
word sorcery had already produced its electrical
effect upon the old servant. " Tell us the history
of this sorcery, my child, and try not to omit a
single fact."

" Jeanne Harviliers was born at Verberie in the
year 1528. Her mother, they say, was a wicked
woman, who dedicated her child to the devil as
soon as she came into the world.

" When Jeanne was twelve years old the devil
presented himself to her in the guise of a black
man, armed and booted."

"Dear nurse," said Blanche, "can the devil then take any form he pleases?"

"Yes, of course, I've told you so a hundred times; he changes as he wishes."

"You've always said, dear nurse, that he shows himself as a black cat."

"A cat or a man, what does it matter?"

"I was only afraid of cats before, now I shall be afraid of men also."

"Come, mademoiselle, if you interrupt this young girl like that we shall never know her story. Go on, my child!"

Urbain glanced quickly at Blanche and resumed his narration.

"The black man told Jeanne that if she would give herself to him he would teach her a thousand secrets by which she could work good or evil to people according to her will. Jeanne Harviliers yielded to the proposition of the devil, and pronounced the formula which he dictated; she soon became a famous magician, riding to the witches' sabbaths on a broomstick.

"Jeanne practised her art near Verberie, but, being accused of sorcery, she was for some time obliged to hide herself. She had a neighbor who disclosed her whereabouts, and Jeanne asked the devil to give her a charm, that she might revenge herself. He gave her a powder, telling her to place it in a road where her enemy was about to pass, and it would give the latter a malady of

which she would die. Jeanne did as the devil
had told her, and placed the charm; but another
person passed first over the road, and it was she
who was the victim. Jeanne, distressed at seeing
the sick woman, confessed to her that she had
caused her misfortune and promised to cure her,
but she could not do as she wished for she was
then arrested and thrown into prison. They questioned her; she confessed that she was a sorcerer,
and was condemned to be burned alive. She was
executed on the last day of April in the year
1578."

"How is that? She was a sorcerer and she let
them burn her?" said Blanche with astonishment.

"Yes, mademoiselle."

"How funny that is, and what use was it to
her to be a sorcerer then?"

"Blanche you are far too young to argue like
that," said Marguerite.

"And the devil, did they burn him also?"

"No, mademoiselle, they could not do that."

"That's a pity, for then we should not need
to be afraid of him. Perhaps the devil has been
burned now."

"The demon will always exist, my child!"

"You've told me, dear nurse, that St. Michael
fought with him and vanquished him."

"Yes, of course he vanquished him, but that is
as if he had done nothing. Now, Ursule, go on;
for I do not yet see in all that you have told us

anything relating to yourself, since this Jeanne was burned close on sixty years ago."

"I am coming to it, mademoiselle," said Urbain, recalling his ideas, which Blanche's beautiful eyes had turned to other things than sorcery. "Since the time of Jeanne Harviliers, they talk of nothing in Verberie and its neighborhood except the witches' sabbaths which were held at the Pont-aux-Reine on the highway to Compèigne, in the wood of Ajeux; and where noises were heard of horsemen riding in squads, witches going to their sabbaths, and wizards of all kinds. The good inhabitants of the country, wishing to put themselves on their guard against these emissaries of the devil, went to Charlemagne's chapel, which is now known as the church of Saint-Pierre, and asked the good religious to give them something which would guarantee them against sorceries of all kinds."

"A very good idea, truly," said Marguerite, "they could not have acted more wisely, and what did they give them, my child?"

"The good fathers gave them a robe which had been worn by a pious hermit, who during his life had always made the demons flee from any place where he came. A tiny morsel of that robe was sufficient to ward off all danger from the one who carried it. You may imagine how anxious everybody was to have a piece of it."

"Oh, I can well believe it. If I had been there

there's nothing I wouldn't have given to obtain a piece."

"Well but dear nurse," said Blanche, "is it like mine."

"Hush! let Ursule finish, my child!"

"Finally, mademoiselle, one of my ancestors, who lived then had the good fortune to get a morsel of the pious hermit's robe. She left it to her daughter after her, who left it to my mother, from whom I have it; and that is how this talisman came to me and it is that which makes me afraid of nothing in Paris, and with which I dare risk myself alone in the streets at night."

"Oh, how singular!" cried Blanche, "that's like me; I also have a talisman which preserves me from all danger, however, they won't even let me look out of the window. That's because my protector, the barber, does not believe in talismans."

"He's very wrong, mademoiselle," said Urbain.

"Yes, assuredly he is," said Marguerite, "but, my dear child, have you yours on you now?"

"Yes, mademoiselle. Oh, I always carry it."

"Let us see this precious relic. Only to touch it will do one good."

Urbain felt in his apron pocket and drew forth a small paper folded with great care; he opened it and took out a sample of his breeches which he presented to the old servant, pinching his lips to keep a serious face. Marguerite who had put on

her glasses took the little scrap of cloth respectfully, and kissed it three times, crying, —

"That's it, oh, how good that is! that emits an
odor all about it, an odor of sanctity."

"Do you think so, dear nurse," said Blanche,
who was looking at the little sample of cloth in
surprise, " I should never have thought that a little
rag like that could have any power."

"A rag! O my dear Blanche, speak more respectfully of this relic."

"My talisman is much prettier than that. It's
a little piece of parchment. Wait, here it is."
Saying these words Blanche opened her kerchief,
and signed to Urbain to look in her corset, half
disclosing her virgin neck as she spoke, in order
that the supposed Ursule might better perceive
her talisman.

"Ah, how charming!" exclaimed Urbain involuntarily.

"Is it not," said Blanche, smiling; "it's much
prettier than that scrap of cloth."

Urbain had no strength with which to answer,
he remained motionless, his eyes still fixed on
the place where the lovely child hid her talisman,
while Marguerite, contemplating the fragment of
smallclothes, kissed it anew, repeating, —

"The worth of that has been well proven, which
makes it all the more precious."

Blanche fastened her kerchief, and Urbain, still
moved by what he had seen, sighed deeply.

"What is the matter with you," said the young girl, looking with interest at her whom she believed to be a simple country girl. "You seem grieved."

"Alas, mademoiselle! I was remembering that I was alone and without resources in this city, that I have no parents, no friends."

"Poor girl! Well, we will be your friends. Yes, I feel that I love you already, Ursule."

"Can it be mademoiselle? Ah! if it were only true!"

"Why do you say if it were true? I never say what is untrue; but what I feel I say at once. Isn't that natural? And do you think that you can love me also?"

"Can I love you," said Urbain, warmly; then remembering that Marguerite was there, he resumed less forcibly, but with an accent that came from his heart, —

"Yes, yes, mademoiselle, and all my life."

"Oh, it is so nice to have a friend of one's own age," said Blanche, shaking the bachelor's hand. "At least I shall have some one with whom I can laugh and chat. Marguerite likes to talk very well, but she never laughs and then she never talks of anything but magic and the devil. We shall find other things to talk about, shan't we, Ursule?"

"Yes, mademoiselle."

"I know very little about anything; always

alone in my room, never going out, though I have a great desire to do so ; my protector never comes to chat with me ; I receive visits from one man only."

" From a man ? " said Urbain, anxiously.

" Yes, my music master. Formerly he made me laugh, now he wearies me, for he always sings the same thing to me."

Urbain breathed more freely, and resumed, —

" You sing, mademoiselle ? "

" A little," said Blanche, " and do you sing, Ursule ? "

"Sometimes."

" That's better still. You shall teach me the songs of your country and I will teach you the ones that I know."

" You will let me come to see you again, then, mademoiselle ? "

" Certainly, every evening, if you can. Remember that I am very lonely by myself, in place of which I shall amuse myself with you. She can come to see us every evening, Marguerite, can't she? M. Touquet won't be angry, will he ? "

Marguerite during this conversation had remained in meditation and in ecstasy before Ursule's talisman. She would have given all the world to possess it in her new room, where she had much trouble in going to sleep, but the name of her master drew her from these reflections and she cried, —

"What are you saying about M. Touquet; that he knows we are receiving this young girl without his permission? Oh, no, indeed!"

"But, dear nurse, that's why it is necessary to ask him."

"Ah, mademoiselle," said Urbain, "he will refuse it, and I shall be deprived of the pleasure of seeing you."

"In that case we will say nothing; but if he would take you into his service?"

"Monsieur does not wish to have anybody else in the house. What could Ursule do here?"

"It's a pity, for Ursule must find a place to earn her living; how very disagreeable it is to have a talisman which preserves you from all danger and allows you to die of hunger. It's exactly like mine."

"Oh, I still have time to wait. I have a prospect of something before me," said Urbain, "and my expenses are so very little."

"Had your ancestors ever any occasion to prove the virtue of this talisman?" said Marguerite."

"Yes, mademoiselle, many circumstances prove that, and, above all, my mother had a very strange adventure."

"An adventure," said the old woman, drawing her chair to the hearth. At this moment the church clock struck nine. "O heavens! nine o'clock," said Marguerite, "it is very late; you

must go, my child. If my master perceives that
we have not gone to bed he'll want to know the
reason; come, it's necessary to part."

"And that adventure which she is going to tell
us," said Blanche.

"That will be for tomorrow, if you will permit
it," said Urbain.

"Oh, yes, tomorrow. Can she not come tomorrow, dear nurse."

"So be it," said Marguerite, who was also curious to hear it. "But remember to be prudent,
Ursule, that nobody may know."

"Oh, I'll answer to you for my silence, mademoiselle."

"That's well. Wait, here is your talisman.
Take care not to lose it. Good heavens! how
happy I should be if I had a similar one."

Urbain received the little scrap of cloth, dropping a curtsey and putting it in his pocket, while
Marguerite took a lamp to lead him.

"You are going alone," said Blanche, "perhaps a long distance."

"To the Porte Saint-Antoine."

"O heavens! and are you not afraid to be in
the street so late?"

"Has she not her talisman?" said Marguerite.

"Ah, that is true; I shan't think about it any
more. Good-by, Ursule, you'll come back tomorrow, will you not?"

The lovely child held out her hand to Urbain,

who was about to carry it to his lips, but remembering that he was a woman he was obliged to content himself with pressing it tenderly and followed Marguerite, after glancing sweetly at Blanche. The old woman reconducted him with the same precaution she had taken in introducing him, and closed the street door softly, saying to him, —

"Good-by till tomorrow, and be sure to take good care of your talisman."

CHAPTER XV

LOVE AND INNOCENCE. A SHOWER OF RAIN AND THE TALISMAN

URBAIN reëntered his old dwelling in a state of rapture and intoxication difficult of description. The sight of Blanche, the sound of her sweet voice, her charm, her youthful candor, her touching grace and simplicity, had increased his love; what he had seen of the beautiful girl, had immeasurably exceeded the expectations he had formed of her, from the slight glimpse he had obtained of her on the previous occasion, heightened though it was by a lover's imagination; and when he now reflected that he should see her again on the morrow, — on many morrows, perhaps — that he should hear her and speak to her again, that her soft hand would again rest without fear in his, he could hardly contain himself.

And yet he could not but feel what a pity it was that he could not confess to the lovely child his real identity and the feeling with which she had inspired him, at first sight. For Urbain was painfully conscious that he must not hurry the disclosure of his secret for fear of alarming the timid girl, and that he should first seek to win Blanche's confi-

fidence; in his feminine costume that would be
very easy, she had already said that she loved
him. It is true that the confession of this sentiment was made to Ursule, but, in fact, it was
Urbain who had inspired her with it.

During the day the bachelor resumed his masculine garments, and as soon as night returned he
attired himself in his feminine costume, in which
he had already begun to acquire more ease of
manner; besides, the young servant was always
ready to help the youth when he wished to disguise himself, she was very obliging to him, and
did not neglect to give him lessons. Urbain profited by them, because a young man understands
better how to tear a kerchief than to put it on, and
a youth who is foolishly in love has many grave
distractions, so that the help of the young servant
was very necessary to him. Urbain was very
prompt at his rendezvous, and Marguerite introduced him with the same ceremonial as on the
evening before. Blanche gave him a most amiable
welcome. She went to meet him, and as he was
making her a modest curtsey the artless child
kissed him on each cheek. Urbain was overwhelmed and in the ardor of his joy, had not the
voice of Marguerite recalled him to himself, he
would have pressed Blanche to his heart, and
would have returned a hundredfold the kisses he
had received. But the old woman, always eager to
hear a story of extraordinary adventures, particu-

larly when it related to a talisman, pushed Urbain
to the side of the hearth, and said, —

"Come, children, don't waste time with idle
ceremony; you know how quickly it passes when
one is relating interesting things. Let us sit down
and Ursule will tell us the adventure which her
mother experienced."

Urbain, still much moved by Blanche's kiss, began a story which he had composed in the morning,
and which delighted Marguerite, because it proved
the marvellous powers of the talisman. The story
finished, the old woman asked to be allowed to
look at the relic; she was persuaded that after
having touched it the evening before she ran less
danger during the night in her room. Blanche
then chatted with Urbain and sang to him in a low
tone one of the songs which she knew. The ingenuous child had only known the pretended Ursule since the evening before, but she already regarded her as a sister, called her "my dear," and
related to her all that concerned herself; for
Blanche, brought up in retirement, had not learned
to hide her feelings or to feign those which she did
not experience; her heart was pure and her words
were only the expression of what she felt.

Blanche did not fail to sing to Urbain her favorite refrain, and the latter trembled with pleasure
on seeing that, despite the precautions of the barber, his accents were graven on Blanche's memory,
who said to him, —

"The first time that I heard you speak, it seemed to me that I still heard the voice which had sung at night under my window. That was a very pretty voice, and yours, Ursule, resembles it a little. What a pity that you don't know the romance that they were singing."

"I do know it," said Urbain; "at least I think I know it, for I have often heard it sung, and that makes me remember it."

"How fortunate! Sing it to me, Ursule, I beg."

"But if M. Touquet —"

"Oh, he is in his room; besides, you can sing very low. Wait! Just as I expected, Marguerite is asleep; now she won't be able to scold us."

In fact her deep contemplation of the little scrap of Urbain's smallclothes had put the old servant to sleep. Urbain was almost alone with her he adored. His heart palpitated with joy, long sighs issued from his breast, and he was obliged to turn away his eyes that they might not meet Blanche's adorable gaze.

"Well, now," said the amiable girl, pouting a little, which rendered her still more seductive, "aren't you going to sing to me? That would be very naughty, for it would give me a great deal of pleasure to hear that song. I should like to learn it myself. I beg of you, Ursule; you see Marguerite is asleep; come, don't refuse me."

"I refuse you anything? Of course I'll sing for you, mademoiselle."

" Oh, you are very obliging, and I will kiss you
with a good heart."

Urbain needed not the temptation of so sweet
a recompense. However, he wished immediately
to deserve it. He sang, and Blanche listened with
rapture; the young man, yielding to the emotion
of his heart, sang with much expression and feeling, but his voice no longer resembled that of a
woman, and any other than the ingenuous Blanche
would have perceived the change; but the latter
was far from suspecting the truth, and with her
head turned towards Urbain, remained motionless,
her eyes fixed on him and seeming to fear lest
she should lose a word, while she exclaimed from
time to time, —

" Mon Dieu, that is it ! that's the same thing !
That affects me just as it did the other night. Ah,
Ursule, sing again."

However, the songs ceased, for Urbain had not
forgotten the promised recompense. For some
moments Blanche remained motionless, seeming
to be listening still ; at last she aroused herself
from her ecstasies, saying, —

" It's very singular what a strange effect that
romance has upon me."

" Is it disagreeable ? "

" Oh, no ; if it were I should not want to be
always hearing it, and still it makes me feel rather
sad ; it makes me sigh ; but all the same, Ursule,
you will teach it to me, will you not ? "

"Yes, mademoiselle; but you promised me —"

"To kiss you. Oh, I'll do that willingly."

Without further asking, Blanche imprinted her cherry lips on Urbain's burning cheek. This time the latter was about to return her kiss, and had already taken the young girl in his arms when Marguerite, in sneezing, just missed falling into the fire, and awoke herself with a start, crying, —

"Dear good patron saint, save me; I see the black man and the sorcerer of Verberie."

"Where is he, dear nurse?" said Blanche, leaving Urbain, who was vexed that he had not sooner finished his singing.

"Where?" said Marguerite, rubbing her eyes; "where is what? What did I say?"

"You said you saw the sorcerer."

"Ah, that is because I was thinking of him, apparently. Come, Ursule, it is time for you to go, my child."

"That's a pity, I was going to tell you of an adventure which happened to my aunt which was even more marvellous than the others."

"Oh, that's delightful; that will be for tomorrow," said Blanche. "That will suit you, dear nurse, won't it? You see my good friend suspects nothing; besides, if he should see Ursule and be angry, well, I'll take all the blame on myself and I can pacify him."

"Come, then, tomorrow night, and we will learn all about your aunt's adventures."

"Yes, Mademoiselle Marguerite, but will you have the goodness to give me back my talisman."

"Yes, my dear child, that's right. O my God! what have I done with it? Has Satan tricked me out of it? I was holding it just this minute."

"Wait, dear nurse, here it is," pointing to the hearth, "you have let it fall in the cinders."

"Faith, so I did," answered the old woman, picking up the little scrap of cloth. "Oh, my goodness! it's a little scorched."

"Oh, that's all right, mademoiselle," said Urbain, "that won't have taken away any of its virtue."

"No, assuredly not, my dear child, and if it had been burned its ashes would have retained the same properties."

Urbain took his talisman, said "good-by" to Blanche, repeating to her, "I shall see you, to-morrow," and left the barber's house.

Several days rolled away and every evening the young bachelor had the good fortune to see Blanche. He was incessantly inventing new stories to pique Marguerite's curiosity, and the old woman regularly opened the door of the alley at seven o'clock. The fictitious Ursule's presence had become necessary to Blanche and Marguerite. The latter experienced great pleasure in hearing her relate the doings of the magicians, and the young girl in learning her cherished romance; but Marguerite did not always go to sleep, and

even when she was awake Blanche wished Urbain
to sing; the latter obeyed her, but in order to prevent the old woman from suspecting him he was
careful to disguise his voice, and Blanche exclaimed with vexation, —

"That's not at all good! You don't sing so
prettily as usual today, and it doesn't give me the
same pleasure."

While Urbain was elated with the happiness of
seeing Blanche, and drinking from her eyes the
sweetest sentiment; while the young girl was giving herself, without restraint, to the pleasure which
Ursule's society afforded her, and in confiding to
the latter her slightest thoughts; and while old
Marguerite, her head filled with frightful stories
and miraculous deeds done by the sorcerer of Verberie, was securing herself against the snares of
Satan by rubbing between her fingers every evening the little scrap of the bachelor's breeches, —
what was passing in the little house of the Vallée
Fécamp? was the brilliant Julia still there? and
was the Marquis de Villebelle taking the trouble
to feign a little love in order to subdue the young
Italian.

The barber, having received the price of his
services, disquieted himself very little as to what
was passing in the small house. Chaudoreille, who
never left the gambling-houses while he had money
in his pocket, had not appeared at the barber's for
a month, but at the end of that time he appeared

at his friend's towards the middle of the day. The Gascon's face was longer then usual. His ruff, all in rags, had been stained in several places, and the feather on his hat had been replaced by the gold-colored rosette which formerly decorated Rolande's handle. Chaudoreille's piteous face made the barber smile.

"Where do you come from," said he, "and what have you been doing since I saw you last?"

"I've been very unfortunate," said Chaudoreille, heaving a big sigh, and drawing from his belt the old silk purse, which he shook without producing a single sou. "You see, my friend, I'm reduced to zero."

"How's that? do you mean to say that nothing remains to you of the sum I gave you."

"Not a penny, my dear fellow. I've been robbed in a shameful manner."

"That is to say, you have been gambling."

"Yes, that's true; I've played, but with robbers. They have tricked me in an infamous fashion. If, at least, they had been amiable about it, one knows well that among people accustomed to play there are a thousand little ways in which one can make fortune favorable, but to despoil a friend, a comrade — it's horrible! I'll never play again in my life. Say now, don't you want me to go to the little house to see my dear friend Marcel?"

"On the contrary, I forbid you to do so.

Without the marquis' order nobody should allow
himself to go there."

" That's vexatious, and how did the adventure
end ? "

" What does that matter to you ? For the matter of that I have not seen the marquis again,
but from the moment I ceased to be employed the
intrigue was nothing to me ; besides, it will end
like all the others. It is a caprice which will last
for some days and will be succeeded by another."

" That's correct ; but the little one appeared to
me to have some strength of mind. She said some
very peculiar things to me ; she asked me, among
other things, if I knew your parents."

" My parents," said the barber, with visible
emotion, " that's singular."

" Yes, very singular. I told her you were from
Lorraine and that that was all I knew about you."

" My parents," repeated Touquet, striding about
the room. " I am almost certain that I have none.
My poor father is undoubtedly dead. Oh, I was
a very worthless fellow in my youth ! Precocious
in my passions, a taste for play and a thirst for
gold caused me to commit a thousand excesses."

" Yes, the follies of youth. I know all about
that. As for me at six years old I was flogged for
having stolen a leg of mutton out of the dripping-
pan. At ten for having, in a fit of abstraction,
taken my grandmother's purse to go and play at
little quoits ; at twelve years old I took a rabbit

off the spit and put in its place my old aunt's cat;
but in my ardor to hide my larceny I forgot to
skin the cat, which was roasted with its hair on.
Happily my father was short-sighted, and he
thought it was a little wild boar; at fifteen
years—"

"What does it matter what you did?" cried
the barber, impatiently. "Did the young woman
say anything else about me?"

"No, but if you like, I'll go and draw it from
her, adroitly."

"Idiot! you forget that she is the marquis' mistress? When her reign is ended I shall see her,
and I shall know." The barber said nothing further and would not answer Chaudoreille, and the
latter, after having uselessly repeated several times
that he had been fasting since the evening before,
on perceiving that Touquet paid him no attention left the shop in an ill-humor, murmuring between his teeth, —

"People who become rich are always niggardly
and stingy. That's a fault that I shall never
have."

Some hours after this conversation, the barber,
returning to his customers, met near the Louvre
the brilliant Villebelle, who, wrapped in his mantle,
seemed to be still in high feather.

"I have succeeded, my dear fellow," said he,
drawing Touquet under a portico, where no one
could hear them. "Julia has given herself to me;

but truly the conquest was more difficult than I had thought. The young girl is passionate, romantic; she wishes to be loved, and I have made her believe that I love her. In fact her singular character, her pride, united with her tenderness, her strange conduct, and her speeches, nearly enthralled me. She spoke to me about Estrelle. I don't know how she knew that adventure."

"The young girl knows everything, evidently," said the barber to himself.

"For the rest," resumed the marquis, "she doesn't seem to love you much, my dear Touquet; you are in her black books. She says that you are a master knave."

"What, monseigneur?"

"She refuses my presents; she wishes nothing but my love, it's truly superb. Despite that, I am living with her; I did not care for her to remain in the little house, that would have embarrassed me. I believe upon my honor that I love her a little. But I see two very pretty women going into the jewelry shop down there. I must go there in order to see them nearer." While saying these words the marquis departed hastily, and the barber returned home, thinking of Julia and vexed that he had not learned from the marquis where he had lodged his young Italian.

Chaudoreille had left Touquet's house in a very bad humor. An empty stomach is usually accompanied by a melancholy spirit. The Gascon chevalier while making philosophical reflections on the egotism of man, the caprice of fortune and the manner in which one could win at piquet while slipping the aces to the bottom of the pack, arrived at the Saint Germain fair. Beside the different spectacles assembled in this place to attract idlers, strangers and young gentlemen came there to play different games of cards, of dice, ninepins and skittles.

Chaudoreille walked among the groups formed around these games and looked with a hungry eye at the pastry exposed before the booths. He stopped near the eating places trying to breathe at least the odor of the cooking, but such delights have no power to fill an empty stomach.

" By jingo! " said Chaudoreille all of a sudden, pulling his hat down over his eyes and pulling his ruff up about his neck. " It shall not be said that I did not dine. A man of genius always has re-resources, and his wit should furnish him that which his purse refuses."

Immediately the chevalier, walking with a determined step, threaded the crowd and turned towards the neighborhood where some young provincials were playing skittles and drinking white wine. Chaudoreille looked at them out of the corner of his eye then, seizing his moment, he crossed the place where they were playing, in such a manner as to receive a blow upon the legs from a ball which one of the players was rolling.

"Look out! look out!" cried the young man
who had hurled the ball; but Chaudoreille pretended not to hear and stopped only when he was
struck. He made a horrible grimace on receiving
the blow, and fell, murmuring, —

"Zounds! my dinner will cost me dearly."

The two players came up to him and picked
him up, offering their excuses although they were
not in the wrong. But Chaudoreille was so pale
and appeared to suffer so deeply and made such
pitiful contortions that the two young men were
much moved; first they offered him a glass of
wine to restore him. The wounded man accepted
and drank three glasses, one after the other; he
could not yet walk and they proposed to him to
go into the wine merchant's, who would give him
something to eat. He did not allow them to repeat the invitation; the two provincials ordered
dinner and invited Chaudoreille to be of their
party. Our man was therefore installed at a table
with them, ate and drank for four, gave them some
lessons in skittles, and perceiving that they were
novices of an obliging humor, and not quarrel-
some, he rose at the conclusion of the dessert and
demanded a pistole from them to indemnify him
for the stroke of the ball which they had given
him.

The young men looked at him in surprise, perceiving that they had been duped and that they
had entered into conversation with a gentleman of

very little delicacy. Chaudoreille held himself very upright, his left hand on his hip and his right hand caressing the handle of his sword, rolling his eyes like the damned, while passing the end of his tongue over his mustaches. The poor provincials, not caring to have a duel with a man who appeared to have decided to split everyone in two if they did not satisfy him, hastened to present the sum demanded by their amiable guest. The latter received it with a gracious smile, then, with the tone of a man delighted with himself, he bowed to them, saying, —

"Good-by, my young friends, try to remember the strokes which I have taught you."

While saying these words the chevalier quickly departed, no longer remembering the blow which he had received. With a full stomach and a pistole in his belt, Chaudoreille was very well pleased with his day's work. The white wine which he had drunk had aroused his enterprise and inclined him to undertake some adventures. He felt especially carried towards love, but if it is the custom of Bacchus to render one enterprising, the odor of wine and the speech of a tipsy man are not auxiliaries favorable to love. It had been dark for some time when Chaudoreille left the fair, ogling all the women whom he met and murmuring between his teeth, —

"By jingo! I must make a conquest this evening. I am beginning to get tired of my portress,

who is forty-five years old and has one leg shorter
than the other ; it is true that she overwhelms me
with kindnesses. She bleaches my linen and re-
pairs my ruff; but what does a little infidelity
by the way matter, my Venus will know nothing
about it."

Chaudoreille had reached the Rue Montmartre
when he saw a woman pass by him, dressed like a
country woman. She was alone; the chevalier ogled
her and turned back to follow her. The carriage
of the dame had something very decided about
it, which was pleasing to Chaudoreille; but she
walked with such long steps that he was obliged
to run to follow her. On reaching her side the
gallant tried to enter into conversation with her by
making one of those pretty propositions in use
among those gentlemen who make love in the
streets, and seek their conquests by lantern light.
She did not answer Chaudoreille, but walked
faster. Our man was not at all abashed; he continued to trot by her side doing the amiable, put-
ing his feet in the streams, which he did not see,
and splashing his beauty while whispering sweet
nothings. However, the person whom he was following had reached the Rue Saint-Honoré, a short
distance from the Rue des Bourdonnais. Chaudoreille, receiving no answer, and seeing that nothing
was to be gained by his compliments, decided to
attempt strong measures. He approached the
country woman and pinched her sharply, and

received in return a slap in the face, so well applied that it sent him up against a stone post four feet away.

Urbain was going according to his custom to visit Blanche, when on the way he made the conquest of Chaudoreille. After disengaging himself in so heroic a manner the young bachelor ran up to the barber's house, entering the passageway, where some one came immediately to open to him, and reached Blanche, still much agitated by the adventure.

"What is the matter with you, my dear Ursule?" said Blanche. "You seem excited."

"Just now in the street two men fighting frightened me."

"Poor child, but didn't you have your talisman?"

"Oh, yes, but in spite of that I was afraid."

"I can well believe it," said Blanche, "to see men fighting must be very unpleasant. Come, sit down, my dear friend."

Blanche's sweet words soon made Urbain forget his adventure. According to his promise, it was necessary that he should recount something singular which had happened to one of his cousins. He had promised to recite it the evening before, and Marguerite was in a hurry to hear it. The old servant needed distraction; she had had a frightful dream in the night and in the morning when she awakened she had seen a bat against her window, all of which was very disquieting, and since the morning she had not been easy.

Urbain commenced his story. He was interrupted by the rain, which fell in torrents, and which the wind blew violently against the panes.

"What horrible weather!" said Blanche.

"Yes," said Marguerite, drawing closer to the fire at each gust of wind, "this night will be difficult to pass. I do not know, but it seems to me that something extraordinary is going to happen; that bat that I saw — and in my dream all those people were riding to the sabbath on broomsticks. That surely indicates something."

"Certainly," said Urbain, and the old woman, to reassure herself, rubbed the talisman between her hands.

Urbain's story had lasted for a long time. Marguerite, however, had said nothing, as she was not anxious to go upstairs to bed. Blanche, who never saw Ursule leave without regret, had taken care not to observe that it was getting late and the young bachelor was not the one who would first think of breaking up the party. However, the clock struck, and they counted eleven strokes.

"O heavens! eleven o'clock," cried Blanche.

"O my God!" said Marguerite, trembling, "in an hour it will be midnight."

"But, dear nurse, Ursule cannot go so late and besides by the time she gets there — Wait! do you hear the rain, it is falling in torrents. How can she go to the Porte Saint-Antoine in such weather as this? It's impossible."

"It is certain," said Urbain, "that the roads are very bad. There are no lanterns and often one puts one's foot in holes that one does not see."

"Poor Ursule, her talisman will not prevent her from being drenched, will it?"

"It is true it doesn't guarantee one against the effect of rain," responded Urbain, sighing.

"What is to be done?" said Marguerite.

"It's very easy, my dear nurse, Ursule can sleep with me, and tomorrow, as soon as day breaks, she can go without making a noise. Will you, Ursule?"

Urbain was for some moments unable to answer, for these words of Blanche, "She can sleep with me," had so disturbed his whole being that he did not know what he was doing. At last he murmured in a changed voice, —

"If you think well of it, mademoiselle, I think well of it also."

"Most certainly I wish it, do I not dear nurse? We could not let her go out at this time of night. Why don't you answer?"

Marguerite saw no harm in the country woman's sleeping with Blanche, but rather hoped to gain an advantage thereby in keeping all night the precious relic; and, as her mind had been struck with the idea that some misfortune was going to happen to her, the possession of the little scrap of cloth seemed to her like a benefaction of Providence.

"It's true," said she, at last, "that the weather is frightful, and if Ursule will not forget to go away before daybreak — "

"Oh, yes, dear nurse, and if she is asleep I promise you I will wake her."

"Very well, then I'm willing that she should remain."

"Oh, how delightful," said Blanche, "we shall sleep together, Ursule. I have never slept with anyone. How we shall chat and laugh."

"No, indeed, no, indeed," said Marguerite; "on the contrary you must go to sleep without making any noise that monsieur could hear."

"Very well, we will go to sleep, dear nurse," responded the amiable child, and she added in Urbain's ear, "We will talk very low."

"Well, in that case I will go to bed," said the old servant hesitating to return that which she held in her hand. "My dear Ursule," she said at last, "you have nothing to fear here. If you would permit me to keep your talisman for this night only, because I sleep in a room that is not safe and I can't get that bat out of my head."

"Oh, keep it, Mademoiselle Marguerite," said Urbain, "may it do you much pleasure."

"Yes, keep it, dear nurse," said Blanche, "besides we have mine, that will be enough for us, will it not, Ursule?"

" But — yes, I believe so, mademoiselle."

Marguerite, delighted to possess a safeguard for the whole night, lighted her lamp and turned towards the door, saying, —

" Good night, my children, good night. Mercy, what a gust of wind. Ursule, you must go tomorrow before daybreak."

" Yes, mademoiselle."

" Go to bed as quickly as possible, and extinguish your light, that no one may suspect anything."

" Be easy, dear nurse," said Blanche, "we'll soon put it out."

Marguerite took her lamp and left the room. Blanche closed the door after her.

" Shut your door tight," said the old woman.

" Yes, dear nurse," answered the young girl, and she drew the bolt.

CHAPTER XVI

How Will It End

WHEN one loves ardently, and when one sees that moment approach which heralds the consummation of his dearest wishes, when one is for the first time entirely alone with the beloved of his heart, one experiences an uneasiness, an agitation which one cannot quell, and which one cannot reasonably account for; it is almost as though one feared that one's being would be unable to support the realization of this exquisite happiness, as though one doubted whether hopes so sweet, and which have hitherto been so unattainable, can ever be realized.

It is, above all, when one loves with the candor and good faith of early youth that one yields himself tremblingly to the first interview which sounds a knell to all the cherished past. Why, at the very moment of happiness, should one sigh and fear? Poor mortals, it seems that accustomed to sorrow, we shall always be astonished at being happy. In truth, this astonishment passes with age and experience ; then these delightful rendezvous do not cause us the same emotion ; we regard them only as distractions, and laugh at the uneasiness, the

embarrassment, which accompanied our first inter-
course with the ladies. Ungrateful that we are,
we mock at the source of our happiness, at those
sweet sensations which time has dissipated, with
all the other illusions of our youth, after the manner of the fox in the fable.

"How awkward we were at eighteen years of
age," we say; "how embarrassed and constrained
in a tête-à-tête, trembling like a leaf as we went to
the rendezvous; what a difference now, we go to
them singing, we reach that which we desire more
quickly, we are a hundred times more pleasing."
Yes, but our hair is becoming grizzly, our figure
has become rotund, and some rather deep lines
are imprinted at the corners of our eyes.

If the approach of long-desired happiness causes
in love an inexplicable trouble, what should be
the state of one who, all of a sudden, without having had even the slightest hope, finds himself in a
position where he may obtain the greatest heights.
Such was Urbain's situation; he loved Blanche
with the delirium, the intoxication, which one experiences at nineteen for his first love, and he
found himself at eleven o'clock at night alone with
the object of his tenderness in a little chamber,
separated from all neighbors, with the lovely child
drawing the bolt and beginning to undress herself
to go to bed. What lover at such a moment could
preserve his reason? Poor Blanche, I tremble for
thee! In truth thou hast a talisman, but I have

no great faith in its power; above all, if you allow yourself to remain with Urbain in the situation in which he is placed. The young bachelor tremblingly paused, sighing and saying not a word he remained standing in a corner of the room, while Blanche prepared the bed, coming and going, jumping and laughing, and finally began to undress herself.

"O heavens!" said Urbain to himself, trembling, coloring, and lowering his eyes, but raising them from time to time to look at Blanche. "O my God! what must I do. This is not the moment to declare myself, to make known to her who I am, to implore her pardon, and to confess my love to her; but, yes, it is indeed the moment. However, if that confession should frighten her, if her cries should bring somebody here, or if she should drive me from the room. That will be such a pity when I can, by deceiving her a little longer, share her bed, and — oh, no! that would be very ill done! But how pretty she is! great God, how charming! Ah, I will not look at her." And the rascal looked at her all the time, slyly, it is true, but the more he looked at her the more he felt his resolution imperilled; for each moment Blanche took off some part of her costume, already only a little petticoat covered her seductive form, and the straight corset which had imprisoned her pretty figure was laid upon the bed.

Blanche stopped; however, it was time. She

looked at Urbain, who was still standing there, motionless and silent.

"Come, Ursule, why don't you undress yourself?" said the young girl, approaching the bachelor.

"Because, mademoiselle, I do not know why, I'm afraid."

"What? you're afraid? Are you afraid with me, Ursule?"

"Afraid, mademoiselle? Yes, I feel that I am very much afraid."

"Why, that's just like Marguerite, and I, who am much younger, am a great deal braver. It is true that the wind blows very hard, but it won't carry us away from here. How she trembles! Why Ursule, how can you go every evening alone as far as the Porte Saint-Antoine and yet you tremble with me in my chamber."

"Ah, that's very different."

"Is it because Marguerite has carried off your talisman? But we still have mine. Wait, do you see when I take off my corsets I fasten it here, inside my chemise, for dear nurse says that it is necessary above all to have it during the night, and that it is when they are in bed that the sorcerers come to torment young girls. Is that true, Ursule? Do they sometimes try to torment you in the night?"

"Yes — no, mademoiselle." Urbain did not know what he was saying, for his eyes, despite

himself, turned towards the perfidious talisman
which seemed to be there, like the serpent on the
tree of the knowledge of good and evil, to make
him succumb to temptation.

"You are shivering with cold, Ursule, we shall
be much better in bed ; we shall be warmer. Do
you want me to help you undress ? How you are
sighing. Is it because you are in some trouble ?
You must tell me all about it. It is so pleasant
to have some friend, to be able to tell her all that
one thinks. Let's see ; first, we'll take off this cap
which hides all your face. I am sure that mine will
become you better, let us try it. But sit down
first ; you're so big, my dear Ursule, that I can't
reach your head."

The young bachelor allowed himself to be led
to a chair. He seated himself, and the lovely child,
standing before him, began to loosen the pins
which held his cap and his big brown curls. Urbain allowed Blanche to take off his headdress.
He had decided to make himself known, besides
sooner or later she must know the truth, and in
order not to frighten her it was better that the
metamorphosis should be gently made. The last
pin was taken out, Blanche lifted the cap and the
young man's brown curls escaped on all sides and
fell on his forehead and on his neck. The young
girl uttered an exclamation and stopped. Urbain,
fearing already that she was about to fly, lightly
surrounded her waist with his two arms.

"How funny that is," said Blanche, at last, looking at Urbain with astonishment. "Your hair isn't done at all like that of all the women I ever saw. Is it the fashion to wear it like that in Verberie?"

"Yes, mademoiselle."

"Do you know, Ursule, that the more I look at you the more you look like a man to me."

"Somebody told me that before, mademoiselle."

"But it's really astonishing. Your hair is dressed exactly like that of the men I see passing in the street."

"Do you dislike it so?"

"No — however — it produces a very singular effect on me."

"If I were a man would you be angry?"

"Mercy, yes, I believe I should, for then you couldn't be my friend any more. I couldn't love you as a sister."

"But Blanche, if I were a man I should be your lover. A most tender, a most faithful lover. I could love you to distraction, and love is much stronger than friendship. Then, if you will share my affection, could there exist a mortal happier than I? Dear Blanche, if I could only possess your heart. Is there anything more precious on earth? To obtain it, I would give the last drop of my blood."

While speaking Urbain, engrossed by his love, no longer sought to disguise his voice. His arms still surrounded Blanche and the young girl, greatly moved, dropped on the knees of the young bachelor, saying in a feeble voice, —

" Mon Dieu, Ursule, don't say such things to me. They make me uneasy. I don't know what's the matter with me. I feel that I wish to cry. What use is it to tell such falsehoods, to speak of love and of loving? Ursule, somebody has told me that it is very wrong to talk about those things. O heavens ! since you haven't your cap on, I dare not look at you."

" Blanche ! dear Blanche ! "

" Well now, you're still pretending to be a man, and it frightens me. Come, Ursule, be a woman again, I beg of you."

" No, Blanche, I will not deceive you further. It is a man — it's — the most tender lover who is near you."

By a sudden movement Blanche rose and escaped to the other end of the room ; Urbain did not seek to restrain her, but fell on his knees and held out his hands towards her, seeming to await her forgiveness, while the young girl looked at him with eyes which expressed more surprise than fear.

" What ? are you really a man ? " said the amiable child, after a moment.

" Yes, mademoiselle."

" Are you quite sure of it ? "

" Oh, yes."

"O good heavens! don't come near me, I beg of you."

"Ah, don't tremble so, I am at your feet, the most submissive of lovers."

"Of lovers! I don't know what a lover is."

"It was that I might be successful in seeing you, that I might make known to you all the love that I feel for you, that I have dared to take this disguise. Without that how should I have managed to see you when they keep you in prison in this room?"

"I never go out of it. I should not listen to you perhaps. How did you come to love me?"

"It was through the window that I first saw you. Some singers were standing under the casement. You seemed to listen to them with great pleasure. That night I returned and sang under your window the romance which you like so much."

"That was you?" cried Blanche, joyfully; and already forgetting her first fear she looked at Urbain with more assurance. Her pure and innocent mind could not conceive all the danger of her situation. A more experienced young girl would have cried and have shown much anger, but Blanche, whose soul was a stranger to all dissimulation evinced the same confidence in the young bachelor as she did in Ursule, because she had no other thought which could make her blush. "Why! was that you?" she repeated.

" It isn't astonishing that I found such a resemblance in your voice, but it wasn't good of you, monsieur, to lie to us like that. I was quite sure that you were Ursule and I loved you like a dear friend, and can I continue to love you like that now ? "

" And what should prevent you, if I have not displeased you ? "

" Oh, no ! you haven't displeased me. I even think that you look better without a cap, but it's not allowable to love a man."

" Why not, when that man wishes to become your husband ? "

" Marguerite says that all men are deceivers and then, O heavens ! the devil also takes the form of a man, and presented himself thus to the sorcerer of Verberie. O mon Dieu, if you should be the devil ! "

" O Blanche, what a thought ! "

" But no, you look too sweet — you're not all black, and you haven't any claws."

" My name is Urbain Dorgeville. My parents were honest and respected. I am an orphan. I haven't much fortune, but when one loves truly is it necessary to have much in order to be happy ? Dear Blanche, will you forgive me ? "

" He calls me his dear Blanche, how funny that is ! And if I don't forgive you, what will happen ? "

" You will reduce me to despair and nothing will remain for me but to die."

"Oh, I don't wish that you should die," cried the amiable child, "and I will forgive you, for I should be very vexed if I caused you any grief."

"Can it be," said Urbain, rising and running towards Blanche. The young girl made a movement of fear, then, recovering herself, she smiled, and signed to Urbain to seat himself near her. The happy bachelor placed his chair close up to that of Blanche and very gently took one of her hands, which the ingenuous child allowed him to retain.

"You forgive me for loving you, then?" said he, looking at her tenderly.

"Of course, I'm obliged to, since you say that it will make you die if I forbid you to."

"And you, also, will love me?"

"Oh, I don't know. I loved Ursule very much, however, but you — it wouldn't be the same thing, would it?"

"It would be much sweeter."

"Do you think so?"

"I am sure of it, by what I experience at this moment."

"You are very happy now, then?"

"Yes, very happy; for you are no longer afraid of me, are you?"

"No, I am not afraid of you, but why do you hold my hand like that?"

"I should like to press it always, to hold it incessantly against my heart."

"And is that yet another proof of love?"

"Yes, Blanche, but if it displeases you I will not keep this dear hand."

"Oh, that doesn't displease me, but yours is burning. It makes mine warm. And why are you trembling? Is it love that makes you like that?"

"Yes, it burns me, it consumes me."

"Oh, it must be very unpleasant to love like that."

The young bachelor, to solace, no doubt, the malady which devoured him, carried Blanche's hand to his lips and covered it with kisses. The young girl allowed him to do so, although the passionate glances of her lover were beginning to produce a strange feeling of uneasiness in her heart. Her breast rose more frequently, she sighed, and said in a faint voice, —

"Urbain — Ursule; mon Dieu, I don't know what's the matter with me, but I am afraid I've caught your malady. Wait! see how I am trembling now! Oh, my talisman, my talisman!"

Poor Blanche, what will you do? While promising to himself to respect the virtue of the young girl, Urbain yielded to the ardor which inflamed him, and pressed Blanche tightly in his arms, begging her not to tremble; Blanche, astonished, did not repulse him, for excessive innocence has also its dangers, but at this moment somebody knocked violently at the door of the room and the barber's stern voice uttered these words, —

"Open the door, Blanche! I command you to open the door!"

The young bachelor seemed petrified, and Blanche remained motionless in Urbain's arms, which still enfolded her.

THE BARBER OF PARIS

VOLUME II

CONTENTS
VOLUME II

CONTENTS

CHAPTER I

WHO COULD HAVE EXPECTED IT

THE slap in the face which had been so vigorously applied to the impertinent Chevalier Chaudoreille by Urbain in his character of a good-
looking young woman, though richly deserved,
had been so unexpected, had so thoroughly
stunned the poor little specimen of humanity
that he had remained for some moments supported by the stone post against which he had
been flung by the force of the blow, entirely unconscious as to his whereabouts.

But as his wits returned to their normal capacity, and he fully realized the indignity to which
he had been subjected in being overcome by a
blow from a woman, at a moment, too, when he
thought his success certain, the little fellow drew
himself up with fierce determination, and, as he
rubbed his still tingling and burning cheek, he
exclaimed,—

"Oh, hang it all! Is it likely I will submit to
such treatment. I shall know how to revenge
myself, young Amazon, little as you may think
so at the present moment. Never shall it be
said that Venus withdrew from the transports of

Mars; that slap in the face shall prove costly to her virtue."

Immediately he followed on the steps of his Venus, who was dashing along, jumping over the streams which came in her way. Chaudoreille's sharp little eyes recognized the person whom he was pursuing just at the moment when Urbain reached the barber's house and entered the alleyway, shutting the door immediately after him.

Chaudoreille knew Touquet's house so well that his distance from the pretended country woman could not prevent him from recognizing her place of retreat, and it was with extreme surprise that our poursuivant d'amour perceived that his beauty had taken refuge in the house of his friend, Touquet. He approached the alley, presuming that she might inadvertently have left the door open, but it was closed; besides, the person he had followed had not hesitated for an instant in the choice of a hiding-place, all of which seemed to indicate that the barber's house had been her destination. This incident gave rise to many conjectures on Chaudoreille's part, awakening his lively curiosity; he decided not to leave the house until the departure of the one whom he had seen enter, and walked up and down from the Rue des Mauvaises-Paroles to the Rue Saint-Honoré.

Time passed and Chaudoreille vainly watched, with his eyes directed to the house, noticing that there was still a light in Blanche's room. Soon the rain began to fall and the wind blew violently; but the chevalier, though inadequately protected by a penthouse, under which he had taken refuge, did not dream of leaving the place, and wrapped himself as well as he could in his little cloak, saying, —

"She must come out sooner or later. What the deuce! can she be Touquet's mistress? Oh, hang it! I must seek the clue to this enigma. The light is still burning in my beautiful scholar's room. Hem! I have certain suspicions. That devil of a slap in the face was given to me with so much force that it makes me believe that my Venus may perhaps have a beard. Patience, she will either come out or I shall go in!"

Poor lovers! While you were enjoying so much the pleasure of being together, while you were beginning to understand each other and to exchange loving glances, in which Blanche no longer showed any timidity, you had no suspicion that at a short distance from you a cursed man had his eyes directed to your window and proposed to disturb your happiness; and all because the success of his shuffling, the white wine, and Urbain's fictitious charms had mounted to Chaudoreille's head.

Eleven o'clock had long since struck. We know what had taken place upstairs; now let us see what had taken place below.

Chaudoreille, unable longer to contain himself,

decided to knock at the barber's door. The lovers had not heard him, because at that moment Urbain was kissing Blanche's soft little hand, and in so agreeable an occupation one is not liable to notice what takes place in the street. Marguerite was snoring in a manner which did not indicate fear; in truth, she had gone to sleep with the precious talisman at her side.

But the barber was not asleep; whether it was because of the storm or the wind, or from some other cause, Master Touquet, who rarely slept peacefully in his bed at night, had not yet gone up to his room, and was pacing slowly in his back shop, ever gloomy and preoccupied, and murmuring at intervals, —

"Cursed night! Why do these shadows incessantly disturb my rest? As soon as daylight disappears my torments recommence. I have gold — yes, I have gold, but I no longer enjoy my natural rest. I shall sell this house; I shall go far from here, very far. I shall return to my country, my father, if he is still living. He will be very much astonished at the change in my fortune. He cursed me when I left the country — but I will ask him to forgive me; yes, he will surely forgive my early faults when he sees that I am rich and respected. I shall not tell him all; no, I shall not tell him how I acquired this fortune."

A bitter smile flickered on the barber's pale

lips and he returned to his reflections, from which he was drawn by the knocking at the door.

Touquet started with fright, but immediately appearing ashamed of himself, took his lamp and went quickly towards the door. He did not expect anyone so late, but supposed that the Marquis de Villebelle, finding himself in that neighborhood, was perhaps seeking him in regard to some new love intrigue.

As he drew near the door he recognized Chaudoreille's voice, calling, —

"Open the door, Touquet. Open the door. Don't be afraid, it's me, but it is absolutely necessary that I should speak to you."

The barber opened the door; and Chaudoreille, whose soaked garments were glued to his lean figure, which appeared even more attenuated than usual, being all shrivelled up under his cloak, came into the alley huddled together, as if he were afraid that his head would hit the little lattice-work over the door.

"What the devil has brought you here at this hour?" said the barber, shutting his door, while the Gascon looked towards the end of the alley as though he were trying to see someone. Finally, he put his finger on his mouth and said in a low voice, —

"Are you alone just now?"

"Yes, certainly."

"You have no visitors?"

"Why, no, nobody, I tell you."

"Then it is urgent that I should speak with you."

The barber returned into the lower room, and Chaudoreille followed him, walking on his tiptoes and turning to the right and left, as though he were looking for someone.

"Come, what have you got to say?" said Touquet. "What means this visit, so near midnight? Did you think that I should be inclined to sleep you? Go. There are still gambling dens open in Paris where you can find a bed, but my house shall not serve as a shelter for nighthawks."

Chaudoreille, without appearing in the least disconcerted, listened to Touquet, shaking his hat meanwhile, and wringing his mantle; he smiled with a mischievous air as he listened to the barber's last words, and answered, —

"Your house! By jingo, you make a good deal of fuss about your house. We shall see presently whether you receive any suspicious persons."

"What do you mean by that?" cried Touquet, angrily.

"Hush! Don't make so much noise, I beg of you. Don't wake the cat up, she is asleep."

"Chaudoreille, I'm losing patience. Say what you want, or I'll be the death of you."

"Well, what the deuce! I came to do you a service, and it seems to me that that shouldn't make you angry. Listen now, but I beg of you don't lose your temper, for that will make me break the thread of my discourse."

The barber restrained himself as well as he could, and Chaudoreille, after passing his cuff over the edge of his hat to give it a lustre, commenced his story in a low voice, —

" I was going this morning to Saint-Germain's fair and found myself without money, something which very often happens with me. I had eaten nothing since yesterday."

" You have eaten and drunk since, I'll answer for it."

" Yes, certainly, thanks to my genius. I was making some rather sad reflections on the instability of my luck at piquet, the treacherous chances of lansquenet and the lack of solidity in gambling — "

" I should like to make you reflect at this minute on the strength of a good stick."

" Hush, don't interrupt me. I perceived at the fair two young men, youths, you know ; some of those faces which seem to say, 'Who will come and do me?' those faces without mischief which are a veritable good fortune for men of parts. The poor little fellows were playing at skittles."

" Come to the point. You are abusing my patience."

" This all leads up to the matter which regards you. I approached the innocents and showed them a new stroke which they did not know, I'll

answer for it. In short, we dined together, and
I only took a pistole from them for the lesson,
which was very reasonable, but if they had refused
me I would have spitted them both like sparrows.
Don't stamp your foot, I'm nearing the end. I
was returning gayly, according to my habit, when
I met a country woman in the street who seemed
to me agreeable, although I saw little of her.
Her carriage was free and unconstrained, she
was big and strong; I was very much taken by
her. I caught up to her and I said some charming things to her. Would you believe it? not a
word in response; I repeated them, still no answer; I approached her and pinched her, and, my
dear fellow, I received a most vigorous slap in
the face."

"Well, hang it! she did well. Finish your
chatter if you don't wish to receive a second."

"Stunned for an instant, I soon recovered my
wits. I pursued the traitress. I saw her enter —
where do you suppose? — your house."

"She came into my house? It is impossible;
you are deceived."

"No, by all the devils! I know your dwelling
well enough. She came in by the alleyway and
shut the door immediately."

"What time was it then?"

"About seven o'clock. And I can answer for
it that she didn't come out, for I haven't stirred
from the front of the house."

"What, wretch, that woman has been so long in my house, and you only now come to tell me?"

"What do you expect? I didn't know what to do; between you and I, I thought the dame came to see you, but seeing that there was still a light in my scholar's room, I thought — "

"A light in Blanche's room?"

"Why, yes, by jingo! There's one there at this moment, from which I concluded — "

The barber hastily arose, lit a second lamp, took his sword and directed his steps towards the staircase at the back, saying to Chaudoreille, —

"Remain here and wait for me."

"Why, don't you want me to come with you?"

"Remain, here, I tell you, but if you have deceived me, tremble; your chastisement shall be proportioned to my anger."

"May the devil fly away with him," said Chaudoreille, ensconcing himself in a corner of the room. "I came to render him a service and he's going to flog me if he doesn't find the guilty person. That slap in the face may be followed by something still more cruel."

Touquet ran rapidly up the stairs to Blanche's room; he knocked, and ordered the young girl to open the door; we have seen the effect which these unexpected words produced on the young couple within the chamber.

Urbain remained motionless, his arms still embracing the young girl, who was only half dressed. In a second all the suspicions which the situation would give rise to, in the mind of the person who had discovered them, flashed across him. Blanche, still innocent and pure, though her virtue had been endangered, Blanche would be adjudged guilty, and he was the cause of it. How could he prevent it? All these thoughts, rapid as lightning, transpired during the time which elapsed before the barber knocked for the second time, and loudly reiterated in a threatening voice the order which he had given. Urbain glanced at the chimney, seeing only that way of escaping from sight. He was about to run to it when Blanche stopped him. She had already recovered from her first fright, and said to him, with a calmness which astonished him, —

"Where are you going?"

"To hide myself."

"No, no, it is unnecessary for you to hide. Why not tell the whole truth?"

"O Blanche, if anyone finds me with you — at night?"

"Well, what of it? We have done nothing wrong. It is much better to confess everything at once than to lie about it," and the lovely child ran to the door, drew the bolt and opened to the barber. The latter darted into the room. His first looks were bent on Urbain, who was standing by the hearth. Touquet only looked at him for a moment, for he had instantly recognized the young bachelor, and drawing his sword he rushed upon him, crying,—

"Scoundrel! You shall pay with your life for your temerity."

Urbain remained motionless, appearing to brave Touquet's fury, but seeing the homicidal weapon flash, Blanche cried out, and, quick as the barber, ran and placed herself before Urbain, whom she covered with her body; then, lifting her hands towards Touquet, she cried with an accent which came from her heart, —

"O monsieur, he has done nothing wrong."

The barber's weapon nearly grazed Blanche's bosom, but the young girl's accents were so touching, her sweet features wore an expression so noble, that the barber himself could not resist her. His anger seemed vanquished. He dropped his sword, and said in a less gloomy voice, —

"This man has outraged you, and you don't wish me to avenge you? 'You ask me to pardon him? Very well, I shall not strike."

"What?" said Blanche, surprised. "What, monsieur, is it because of me that you were about to hurt Urbain? Oh, you would have been very wrong. You say he has outraged me; but, no, monsieur, I swear to you he has not. He has told me that he loves me very much, that he will love me all his life, but there is nothing outrageous in that, for when you knocked at the door I believe

I was just going to tell him that I loved him also. You see that I am just as guilty as he is, and that it is necessary for you to punish both of us."

Blanche's words had an accent of truth which it was impossible to mistake. The barber glanced in astonishment at her and at Urbain, who saw that he then believed, despite appearances, that Blanche still retained her purity. However, the disorder which reigned in the apartment, the singular costume of the young girl and of Urbain, which was divided between that of the two sexes, all appeared to confuse Touquet's ideas.

"Listen to us," said Blanche to him, "you shall know the whole truth. Urbain, to be sure, is a little to blame, for he has come to see us every evening for nearly a fortnight, but he came as a young girl. At first I was angry with him also, but finally I have forgiven him. Urbain has such a sweet expression, and then, I already loved Ursule very much, and that made me love him also. He said that he wished to be my lover, my husband, that he could not live without me, and that it would depend upon you to make us happy forever. Ah, you will be good, will you not, my dear friend? You have already done much for me. Give me Urbain for my husband, and I promise you that I will never ask anything of you again."

The barber, while listening to Blanche, muttered to himself, —

"For nearly a fortnight he has been coming here every evening, it is by a great chance that I discovered him today, and yet I believed that I could easily guard a young girl and brave the enterprises of lovers."

"Monsieur," said Urbain, who up to that moment had kept silent, "I confess all the wrong I have done, and love alone must be my excuse; but I adored Blanche, whom I had seen through the panes of that window, and you would not permit any man to approach her. I tried once to begin an acquaintance with you, but the manner in which you received me left me no hope. I then consulted nothing but my love. Thanks to this disguise I deceived old Marguerite, who consented to introduce me here. I saw Blanche, and could I renounce the hope of possessing her? She was deceived as well as her nurse. Under the name of Ursule I had the good fortune to gain her confidence and, by some interesting stories, to amuse old Marguerite. I rejoiced in my happiness without daring to make myself known. Today, on account of the storm, the rain, which fell so violently, the advanced hour, she invited me to remain."

"Yes," said Blanche, with an angelic smile, "He was going to sleep with me. I myself begged him to do so."

The barber knit his brows and glanced angrily at the young man. Urbain instantly threw himself at his feet, crying, —

"I have respected her virtue, her innocence. O monsieur, can I not touch you with my love. Yes, I adore Blanche, give me her hand or deprive me of a life which without her would be insupportable."

"Hear us, my friend," said Blanche. "He will absolutely die if I am not his wife, and if he should die I feel that I should die of grief, too."

The barber appeared to listen to Urbain without being in the least moved by his prayers, when the young bachelor added, —

"I know, monsieur, all that you have done for Blanche. Her father was assassinated, she remained an orphan without any support. She owes everything to you."

"What?" said Touquet, who had paid more attention to Urbain's last words, "you know — "

"Yes, monsieur, I learned all that concerns her whom I adore. She did not know her parents and possessed no fortune, but it is she alone whom I ask of you. You have done well for her. Give me Blanche; she is sufficient for my happiness. I also am an orphan; my family was honest and respectable, but I have no relations left. My name is Urbain Dorgeville; I have an income of twelve hundred livres; that is very little, but I possess besides a little house in the country, on the borders of the Loire, there I shall go to live with Blanche. Far from the tumult of the city, which we shall not regret, nor its pleasures; and far from society, which we do not wish to know, we shall there pass our days in peace and love and happiness."

The barber appeared to reflect deeply. He rose, and strolled about the room with bowed head. Hope and fear were depicted in the looks of the two lovers, who waited with impatience his answer. Finally, he paused, and said to Urbain,—

"You are an orphan? Entirely master of your own actions?"

"Yes, monsieur."

"There is nobody to object to your marrying an orphan without means, and whose family is unknown?"

"Nobody, I repeat to you, can oppose my wishes."

"You will never seek, yourself, to obtain any information in regard to Blanche's family, which, besides, would prove entirely fruitless."

"Why, what does it matter to me who were her parents. She is a treasure in herself."

"And you will go to live with her far from Paris—far from everyone?"

"Yes, for I shall make it my care to be all-sufficient to her happiness."

"O heavens, Urbain," said Blanche, "You know very well that I never left this room, where I saw no one but Marguerite. If I were to live with you in the country do you suppose that I should wish for anything else?"

"Dear Blanche, unite with me then in obtaining the consent of your protector."

The two young people bent on the barber entreating looks. The latter did not notice them and appeared entirely wrapped in his reflections; at last, all of a sudden, he stopped before Urbain, and said, in a curt tone, —

"Blanche is yours."

"Can it be?" cried the young bachelor, in a delirium of happiness. "Blanche, do you hear? He consents to our union."

"Oh, my dear friend, how much I thank you."

And the two lovers fell on their knees before Touquet, their eyes bathed with tears of pleasure and gratitude.

"What are you doing?" said the barber, who seemed ashamed to see the young couple at his feet. "Get up, I beg of you."

"You have made us happy," said Urbain, "and you will not even receive our thanks."

"No, no, I wish for nothing but silence and discretion."

"Aren't you glad now that you didn't injure Urbain? He meant no harm in disguising himself as a girl. It was he who sang so beautifully under my window. Oh, how happy I am! He can sing with me all the time now. He will teach me that pretty ballad and some others, too. Will you not, Urbain, teach me many things? Oh, how happy we shall be."

The barber had some trouble in calming Urbain's transports and Blanche's naïve joy. Finally he succeeded in making them listen.

"Until the time of your union," said he, " I repeat to you, I shall exact the greatest discretion. Urbain you must promise me not to speak of your marriage, and not to bring any of your acquaintances here."

" I swear to you, monsieur, that I will do as you wish; besides, I don't know anybody. I have no intimate friends."

" That is better still, you will have less to regret in leaving the city. Make all your preparations for departure, and procure all the necessary documents for your marriage. As to Blanche, I will give you the letter found on her father; that is all which concerns that matter. When you have made all the necessary arrangements, you can marry Blanche — but in the evening without any stir, with nothing that can draw people to the church to see the ceremony; I dislike idlers and curious people. Afterwards you will immediately start for the country; and you will not return to this city, where your modest means would not permit you to live happily."

"Yes, I agree to all, monsieur."

" Are you coming with us, my friend?"

" No, that is not necessary. Later on, perhaps."

" And Marguerite, can we take her with us?"

" Yes."

"How nice that will be!"

"Up to the day of your departure Urbain can come here, but in the evening only, and not in disguise."

"He will come as a boy. I am very curious to see him like that."

"You understand; it is very late. It is necessary for you to retire. Urbain, I repeat to you, maintain the greatest silence about all this. Hasten your preparations, and Blanche will soon be yours."

Urbain renewed his promises and his thanks to the barber, and took Blanche's hand and covered it with kisses. The young people could hardly believe in their happiness, and the future that was opening before them still seemed a dream of their imagination, but Touquet hurried them.

"I shall see you tomorrow," said Urbain.

"Tomorrow," repeated Blanche, "and not in woman's clothes. Do you hear? I wish to grow accustomed to seeing you as a man."

"Yes, dear Blanche, yes. No more pretence now."

The barber cut their adieux short and led away the young man, and Blanche closed her door, sighing and murmuring still, —

"Tomorrow."

Touquet guided Urbain, holding the lamp in his hand, and walking rapidly towards the staircase; but hardly had he taken ten steps in the passage when his foot caught in something. He lowered his lamp and perceived a little shapeless heap which moved and appeared to want to glide along the wall. The barber ran at this object and, quickly lifting the mantle which covered it, perceived Chaudoreille, with his body on all fours in such a way as not to take more room than a big cat.

"What are you doing there, clown?" cried Touquet, putting his lamp against Chaudoreille's face.

"Me? Nothing. I am picking up a pin."

"Go down to the room. I have told you before that I don't like curious people," and to prove this to him beyond a possibility of doubt the barber kicked the chevalier vigorously, and the latter, not having had time to straighten himself, received the kick in three parts of his body. Touquet did not stop to do more, but led the bachelor to the street door, and opening it for him said, —

"Go, and remember all that you have promised."

Urbain was about to renew his protestations of gratitude, but the barber put an end to them by telling him to go immediately to his dwelling, and closing the door upon him.

Touquet returned into the lower room where he found Chaudoreille, who had resumed his natural size and was promenading with the air of a conqueror, evidently awaiting the thanks of the barber.

"Well, now, by jingo!" cried he impatiently, seeing that the latter said nothing to him. "You have found the magpie in the nest. I haven't dim sight. And that slap in the face, zounds! I recognized a masculine hand. I am never deceived. Well, we have, according to what I see, shown the gallant to the door. As to the little one, hang it! With her sanctimonious air, who would have expected it?"

"Be silent!" cried the barber, advancing towards Chaudoreille with a threatening gesture. "Do not outrage Blanche. That the young girl is still pure is as true as that you are a liar and a coward."

"A coward! By jingo, if Rolande could only speak!"

"Yes, I confess that I found someone there, but that someone was not alone with Blanche."

"That is singular. I didn't hear old Marguerite's voice."

"You were listening, then, wretch."

"No, it was by chance that some sounds reached my ears; some one called out. I thought that somebody had need of help and, following my natural ardor, I went towards the neighborhood from whence the noise came."

"Well, what did you hear? Speak, I tell you!"

"Oh, nothing, some words. It seemed to me that you were promising to unite the two lovers. At least I believe that's what I caught. However, if I had not thought that you were keeping the little one for yourself I would have demanded her hand of you long ago. It seems to me that I deserve the preference over that little masker, who if it had not been for his petticoat would have paid dearly for the slap on the face he gave me."

"You become Blanche's husband!" said the barber, glancing scornfully at the little man. "Listen, Chaudoreille, it suits me to give Blanche to this young man; he will make her happy."

"As to that you are the master, but—"

"But, if you say a word about what you have seen and heard tonight I shall draw down upon you the most terrible vengeance. Do you understand me?"

"Yes, I understand you. By jingo, marry the little one with whom you please. I don't care a fig for the pair of them. However, if there is to be a wedding, I hope—"

"No, there will be neither a wedding nor a repast—"

"That will be gay!"

"But, if you are discreet, I promise you two pieces of gold when everything is finished and Blanche has left this house."

"Agreed. That will suit me, it is as if I held them now; you might as well pay me in advance."

"I prefer, however, not to pay you until afterwards. But the night is drawing to a close; go home, Chaudoreille, and remember your promise."

"Yes, yes, that's settled. Is there any news of the seductive marquis and the young Italian?"

"I believe that fire is already extinguished. But that doesn't astonish me; a fortnight, three weeks, is the measure of the constancy of our great noblemen."

"And after that's ended it's probable that there will be one intrigue after another to conduct. If so remember me, my dear Touquet."

"Very good, go to your bed!"

"In fact, it's about time. I'll go back to the Rue Brise-Miche; fortunately my portress has a liking for me, or else I should run a great risk of sleeping in the street. However, if you wish, I could wait for day here, on a chair."

"No, no, it's necessary for you to go; I need some rest, also, and it seems to me that I shall get little of it this night."

Chaudoreille enveloped himself as well as he could in his mantle and went towards the door, making a grimace. The barber closed it on him and went to his room, saying, —

"I have done well; she will go away, no one will hear tell of her again, and everything regarding her will soon be forgotten."

CHAPTER II

HAPPY MOMENTS

MARGUERITE alone had slept during the night which had wrought so great a change in the barber's household; greatly cheered and calmed by the possession of Ursule's talisman she slept more soundly than she had ever done in her new room. As for Blanche one may well suppose that she did not close her eyes for a moment. The amiable child, still bewildered by all the events which had taken place, had hardly had time to pass from the fear of love to the fear of happiness; she was too innocent, too childlike to have dreamed of love as yet, her poor heart hardly yet realized its own state, though one sentiment stronger than all others dominated its thoughts. She tossed continually on her couch, repeating to herself,—

"He's a boy, and it was he who sang so beautifully. Mercy, who could have expected it? He was so pleasing as a girl; however, I believe he will be still better as a boy. Oh, I wish it was evening now. He said that he loved me — how strange that is — do I also love him? I believe I do. However, I must ask Marguerite what love is, she ought to know that. Poor Marguerite, how surprised she'll be when she learns that he was not a girl. Oh, I wish it was day now."

The day so much desired appeared at length. Blanche had been up for a long time; impatient at not hearing the old nurse come down, she could not resist going up to Marguerite's room. She knocked at the door, exclaiming, —

"Wake up, dear nurse! it's very late. I have a thousand things to tell you. Get up, I beg of you — you have slept long enough."

Marguerite, who never had to be awakened, because she always rose sufficiently early, rubbed her eyes, believing that the house was on fire, sought to recall her ideas, to recover the talisman which had been entrusted to her and which had been lost among the bedclothes, while invoking her patron saint, and muttering, —

"Where has it gone to? I've looked for it — has the devil taken it away from me during the night? Wait now — ah, I shan't find it again. I thought I felt something. It must have been the devil who took it maliciously!"

Finally Marguerite found the little scrap of Urbain's breeches, and recalling all that had taken place on the evening before, she hastened to open the door to Blanche, and said, —

"Has Ursule gone? It's necessary to hasten her away, my child."

"Oh, yes, she's gone; that is to say, he's gone. But don't be afraid, my good friend is willing that he should come — he wishes him to marry me; he's no longer angry. He's coming here this evening as a boy; you will see how nice he is; and when we are married, we shall go into the country and you shall come with us. Oh, how happy I shall be! Come, Marguerite, laugh too; you see it's no longer necessary to have any fear."

Marguerite had no desire to laugh, she would rather have wept, for she understood nothing that Blanche was saying; she opened her eyes as widely as possible and exclaimed, —

"O good God, my dear child, is your head turned this morning? Can that Ursule be a sorcerer? Don't jump like that, I beg of you."

Blanche recommenced her narrative and at last made Marguerite understand that Ursule was a boy. The old woman cried, affrightedly, —

"My God! a boy, and he slept with you?"

"Oh, no, dear nurse, because Monsieur Touquet came in just at the moment when — mercy! I don't know what we were doing at that moment — oh, yes, I believe he was kissing me."

"Holy Virgin! it was a goblin disguised as a girl."

"No, dear nurse, he's called Urbain, he's an orphan like me; but his family was very respectable, and he's going to marry me."

"To marry you?"

"Yes, certainly. You won't oppose it when my protector has given his consent, will you?"

"What, M. Touquet has consented to it?"

"Yes, yes, I tell you. It's finished. Everything is arranged."

The good old woman hardly believed that her ears did not deceive her, but the arrival of her master put an end to her doubts.

The barber looked very stern as he approached Marguerite, and the old woman trembled, for she felt that she was in fault.

"Marguerite," he said, "I could punish you for having betrayed my confidence, for having, despite my orders, introduced someone into the house. You will tell me, like Blanche, that you have been deceived — and I would wish to think so, besides, as I have forgiven it, it is needless to dwell on what is past. The young man will be Blanche's husband; he will make her happy. You will go with them when they leave this house. I have but one command to lay upon you, and that is to keep this incident from all your gossips in this neighborhood. If you commit the least indiscretion, I'll send you away and you will prevent this marriage from taking place."

"Oh, dear nurse, don't say anything about it," cried Blanche.

"No, mademoiselle; no, monsieur," responded Marguerite, still trembling, "I swear to you that — "

"That's enough," said the barber. "You love Blanche, and her happiness depends upon your discretion. Urbain will come in the evenings only, until the day he takes away his bride."

The barber departed after thus speaking, leaving Marguerite still dumbfounded by all that she had heard.

" How is this ? " said she, following Blanche to her room; " M. Touquet consented to this at once ? "

" Yes, dear nurse."

" I'm not to be sent away."

" That surprises me, also ; I was so afraid he would refuse Urbain."

" Urbain — Urbain — but you don't know him, my child ! "

" Why, yes, I do, dear nurse, since he is Ursule."

" I understand that very well ; but Ursule has deceived us."

" It was that he might see me that Urbain disguised himself; it was love that made him do it, dear nurse."

" Love, indeed ! but you cannot yet love him, my child."

" Oh, dear nurse, I believe I shall love him very quickly. Urbain was teaching me how to love yesterday, when my protector knocked at the door."

" Jesu, Maria ! What, my child, in place of calling for help when you saw it was a man ? "

" I desired to do so at first, but if you only

knew! Urbain was not at all alarming, on the contrary; and then he threw himself at my feet and begged my pardon with such a sweet air, with eyes so — O Marguerite, what should I have forgiven him for."

"Good heavens! And your talisman, my girl, did you not have recourse to that?"

"Oh, forgive me, dear nurse, I even showed it several times to Urbain."

"And it didn't cause him to fly?"

"On the contrary, dear nurse, he drew still nearer."

"Come, decidedly everything is upside down. It must be that boy is a magician to work such changes in this house. I shall no longer have any faith in his little relic."

Blanche and the old woman awaited the evening with impatience; Marguerite curious to know the young man who had wrought such prodigies in her master's house, and the young girl ardently desiring to see again him who had caused her to sigh and to experience an entirely new feeling. But Blanche's desires were mingled with that timidity, that bashfulness, which accompany a first love. As the hour of Urbain's arrival approached she felt more restless and dreamy, and already this unknown sentiment inspired her with a secret desire to please; she rose, looked at herself in the mirror, and arranged a lock of hair, then she said to Marguerite, —

"Dear nurse, do I look all right? Do you
think he will love me as much tonight as he did
yesterday?"

"Dear child," cried the old servant, "if he is
capable of changing would he be worthy of you?
When one loves truly, my dear, 'tis for life."

"Oh, that is much better, dear nurse; I should
like to love like that. You will see that there's
nothing about Urbain to frighten one, and I am
sure I shall love him also."

The young bachelor desired with no less impatience than Blanche the moment when he could
return to the barber's house. Since the evening
before Urbain had entirely lost his head, and his
happiness had been so sudden, so unforeseen, that
it had completely unbalanced him for the time.
He had returned to his lodging in the night,
dancing, singing and running in the street. In his
intoxication he had lost his skirt and his kerchief;
but he had no further need of his disguise, and
without troubling himself to pick up those por-
tions of his costume he had arrived at home
partly undressed, but so happy that he would not
have changed his lot for the fortune, the favor or
the power of the cardinal; and in that he was
right, the joys which love brings are not, as is
the case with grandeur and power, mingled with
anxieties and cares.

The next day Urbain would have liked to tell
his happiness to all the world, but he remembered

that one of the first conditions of his marriage with Blanche was that he should keep the matter entirely secret; he contented himself, therefore, with looking at everybody who passed with an air of satisfaction and triumph which indicated a mind impervious to the strokes of fortune.

In the evening his neighbor came, as usual, to propose to help him in disguising himself; but Urbain thanked her; he had no further need of her services and the good-natured girl seemed vexed that the masqueradings were ended.

Urbain wished to please as a man still more than he had wished to do so as a country woman; he put on his collar and his hat with more care than he ordinarily took. He looked to see that his hair did not fall in disorder over his forehead, and sighed as he said, —

"If I should not succeed in pleasing her!" However, the remembrance of the evening before gave him courage, and he took his way to the barber's house. He trembled as he knocked at the door, although the fear of being sent away did not present itself to his mind. The sound of the knocker went to Blanche's heart, and she jumped from her chair, exclaiming, —

"It's he!" and was about to run to the street door when Marguerite stopped her, saying, —

"How now, my child, what are you going to do? It would not be decent for you to go and open the door for this young man."

" Do you think so, nurse. Very well ; go then, Marguerite ; go quickly."

Marguerite hurried as fast as she could, she was anxious to see the young man. She opened the door to Urbain and looked at him attentively ; his gentle and diffident appearance made a favorable impression on the old woman.

" It's singular — he appears to be more embarrassed as a boy than as a girl. Come in, come in, my handsome young spark ; come in. Now we shall see if you've any more stories to relate of the adventures of your aunts and cousins."

" Yes, my good Marguerite," said Urbain, " I shall continue to tell them to you if they give you pleasure."

" He wishes to please me," said Marguerite to herself. " Yes, Blanche was right, the young man is very charming."

The embarrassment of these two young lovers was a very singular thing, inasmuch as they had in their first interview spoken so freely of their love, and were already engaged and certain of being married. Blanche, who had at first wished to run to the door, now dared not raise her eyes, and, on hearing Urbain's step, remained motionless on her chair. The latter, on entering this room where he had been every evening for a fortnight, experienced an uneasiness, a new embarrassment, and paused near the door, holding his hat in his hand, and glancing timidly at Blanche.

"Well," said Marguerite, "here's one who dares go no farther at present. Come, master boy, when you were a girl you didn't thus remain standing motionless and mute at the door; and my poor Blanche, who is afraid to raise her eyes and is trembling like a leaf. My darling, it isn't necessary to blush like that when one has done nothing wrong. You see, I am obliged to encourage you."

However, Urbain gently approached Blanche, bent his knees to the floor and murmured, —

"If you no longer feel friendly to me, if this costume has made you lose confidence in me — I will resume that of Ursule."

The sweet girl timidly raised her head, and bending on Urbain a look of the tenderest love, she said, blushing deeper than before, —

"Oh, it isn't that. Excuse me, I don't know what is the matter with me."

She turned her head to hide her face in Marguerite's bosom, and said in a low tone to the latter, —

"Dear nurse, is it love that makes me feel so shy?"

"I remember scarcely anything about love now," answered the old woman, shaking her head; "however, yes, I believe in my young days it did evince itself somewhat in that fashion."

Blanche turned to Urbain and said to him, with a charming smile, —

"Don't be angry with me; if I am awkward and embarrassed it is because I love you."

Delighted at the candor of the young girl, Urbain took her hand and pressed it against his heart, then, seating himself near her, he renewed the vows with which love for her inspired him. Confidence was soon reëstablished between them ; when two hearts beat in accord, constraint is soon banished. Blanche resumed her gayety, her ingenuousness, and allowed her lover to read all her feelings, and the latter perceived that he had a treasure of innocence and kindness.

Marguerite joined in the conversation of the young people ; Urbain, by his amiability and the deference he showed for the old servant's advice, entirely won her friendship. The young bachelor praised the situation of his little property, which in the midst of a charming country offered delightful walks and all the pleasures of a rural existence. He promised the old woman to give her a room impervious to every enchantment, and to tell her in the long winter evenings some of the gruesome stories which gave her both fear and pleasure.

While chatting with Marguerite, the tender glances, pressings of the hand and sweet smiles of the two lovers established between them that sympathy of mind which gives the first, and perhaps the sweetest, taste of love.

The time passed rapidly, nine o'clock struck,

the hour which the barber had fixed for Urbain's departure, and they knew they must obey his commands if they wished him to keep his promises.

" Must I leave you already? " said Urbain.

" I'm sorry you must go," answered Blanche, sighing tenderly.

" You will see each other again tomorrow, my children," said Marguerite, "and the day will soon come when you will no longer have to part. Monsieur Dorgeville, have you begun the necessary preparations for your marriage? "

" Mon Dieu!" said Urbain, "I was so unsettled today that I could think of nothing but the happiness that I should enjoy this evening; and I have done nothing yet."

" If you are as heedless every day, your marriage will never take place," said Marguerite.

" Oh, tomorrow I will begin to put matters in train. I am anxious for the time when I shan't have to leave Blanche; but I haven't seen Monsieur Touquet this evening. Ought I not to go and say good evening to him? "

"No, it is needless; my master is unlike other men; he has no use for ceremony. He said to me, very positively, 'The young man will come at seven o'clock; you will conduct him to Blanche's room, where you will remain with them, and at nine o'clock he will go. When I wish to speak with him I will seek him, but it is needless for him to endeavor to see me.' "

"What a singular man!" said Urbain; "but I ought to bless him, for he has made me happy, and I accused him. I had a suspicion that he wished to guard this treasure for himself by hiding her from everyone."

"For himself," cried Blanche, "how could that be possible?"

"Forgive me, dear Blanche, love makes one jealous; I see well that I was unjust."

"Yes, yes," said Marguerite, "but hasten to get your documents drawn and marry this dear child."

The bachelor left at last, but Blanche's looks followed him and he could not doubt his happiness; he possessed the heart of an amiable girl who did not seek to hide from him the sentiments with which he inspired her. The next day Urbain took the preliminary steps to hasten his marriage; he had also to sell the little furniture he possessed, for it was very necessary to obtain some money for the journey; and, in regard to that, the bachelor soon saw that Monsieur Touquet evinced no generosity of disposition. But a lover who is about to marry his sweetheart always believes himself rich enough, and, besides, Blanche having been reared in retirement had no extravagant desires in regard to household expenses, dress or ornaments; she would be economical and simple in her tastes, which qualities are often of more value than the bride's dowry.

Evening again brought Urbain to his sweetheart; on this occasion the embarrassment had disappeared, and they gave themselves up entirely to the pleasure they experienced in seeing each other again. The time they passed together rolled on as rapidly as before, but they consoled themselves by remembering that the day would soon come when they would be united forever. On the fourth evening that Urbain passed with Blanche the door opened, and the barber made his appearance.

He slightly inclined his head to Urbain and said to him, in his ordinary brief tone, —

" Are you making preparations for your marriage ? "

" Yes, monsieur," said Urbain, rising and going up to Touquet, " but you know employers never share one's impatience. However, within six days, or a little later, I should have all my papers. I have seen the priest who is to unite us and have made all my preparations for departure."

" That's well."

The barber made no further remark and left the young people, who were for a moment astonished at his conduct; but after all they were not sorry to be able to give themselves up to the pleasure of lovers' conversation with no other witnesses than old Marguerite, who sometimes went to sleep while Urbain and Blanche were silently pressing each other's hands. The time passes quickly when one is happy, and if the days were long for the two lovers, by way of revenge each evening seemed shorter than the last. The more they saw of each other the closer love drew his meshes about their hearts, which seemed formed for adoration, and now they could not conceive the possibility of an existence apart.

But the day of their wedding approached. Only five days and they would pledge their vows at the altar; then they would leave the great city and in a peaceful retreat would enjoy pure happiness undisturbed by the storm and stress of life. This at least was the future they hoped for.

Chaudoreille, urged by a desire to receive the recompense the barber had promised him, had already presented himself three times at the latter's house, saying, —

"Has the marriage taken place?"

"Not yet," answered Touquet.

Then Chaudoreille departed, muttering, —

"I wish they'd hurry now. What the deuce! I need some money. Why, in twelve days I'd have married a dozen women."

CHAPTER III

A Day with Chaudoreille

CHAUDOREILLE, who had not yet received the two pieces of gold which the barber had promised him found himself in his usual penniless condition as he went one fine morning down the Rue des Petits Carreaux. He was just coming from the Saint-Germain fair, where he had not on this occasion found anybody disposed to receive a lesson in skittles, and he was going towards the Saint-Laurent fair, hoping that fortune would be somewhat more favorable to him in the latter haunt.

Following his custom, Chaudoreille walked with his nose in the air, ogling from one side to the other; his left hand on his hip, and his right hand caressing his mustache. As he approached the boulevards he felt somebody pull gently at his mantle. The pusillanimous fellow started with fright, but on turning his head he perceived an old servant maid, and seeing he had nothing to fear he put his hand on his sword, and cried loudly,—

" By jingo ! I thought it was a man and I was going to demand his reason for touching me.

What do you want with me? Don't pull my
mantle so hard, it's a little decayed."

The old woman put her finger on her mouth,
and with a mysterious air, said, —

" My mistress wishes to speak with you."

" Your mistress," cried Chaudoreille, his features becoming cheerful, for he did not doubt that
he had made a conquest, " oh, that's it, my good
woman, I understand you. But is she young? is
she rich? is she? — Never mind, it's all the same,
lead me to her."

" No, she can't receive you today, but be here
tomorrow at dusk. I will come and look for you
and will introduce you."

" It's enough! I'll be here, I'll not fail, whether
it rains or shines. One word, if you please, messenger of love. Can you not tell me where your
mistress has seen me? "

" In the street, I presume, since she was at her
window. Tomorrow evening, monsieur; I can't
stop any longer."

" Go, Flore! go back to Cytherée," said Chaudoreille, as the old woman went off, then he continued on his way, saying, —

" It's an amorous adventure, I know; — this
mystery and a rendezvous at dusk. She has seen
me through the window. By jingo! I do well to
look my best; a pretty man should always carry
himself as if everybody was looking at him." He
then walked along, looking so much in the air

that he ran against a water-carrier who was advancing quietly with his two buckets full, and threw himself so heavily upon him that one of the buckets escaped from his hand.

"Cursed idiot," cried the Auvergnat. "Wait, take that to teach you to look before you!" Saying these words the water-carrier calmly emptied his other bucket over Chaudoreille. The chevalier was drenched. In his fury he drew Rolande from the scabbard and advanced on the Auvergnat; but the water-carrier, without appearing at all dismayed by the falchion which his adversary flashed as he capered and jumped about like one possessed, took one of his buckets in each hand and tranquilly awaited the expected onset of the doughty knight, shouting in an aggravatingly jeering tone,—

"Come on, you baked apple! come on stupid, that turnspit you term a sword doesn't frighten me in the least."

Chaudoreille put Rolande in his scabbard again and then escaped by the boulevard, crying, "Watch," and followed by all the idlers, and these were not a few, of the neighborhood. The chevalier did not pause in his flight until he was positively sure there was no longer anybody behind him. He was then quite near the Fossés Jaunes, which were excavated in the reign of Charles the Ninth, and which extended from the Porte Saint-Denis nearly to the Porte Saint-Honoré. These had been made to still further enlarge Paris. A new wall was built along the Fossés Jaunes, and also two new gates; one, Rue Montmartre, near the Rue des Jeûneurs, replaced the old Porte Montmartre, demolished in 1633; the other, Rue Saint-Honoré, between the boulevard and the Rue Royale, replaced the one situated between the Rue Richelieu and the Rue Saint-Honoré, which was erected in 1631. On the terrace within this new wall they presently laid out the Rues de Cléry, du Mail, des Fossés-Montmartre, de Victoires, des Petits-Champs, etc. However, in the midst of these new constructions the hill of Saint-Roch still preserved its picturesque form and its windmills.

Chaudoreille was trembling, he was very cold; and he could not change at his house, for a reason that one may easily divine. Fortunately the weather was fine and the sun, while it gave little heat, shone on the promenade, established then along the wall of Paris. The chevalier saw no other means of drying himself than that of running for two or three hours in the sun, and he gave himself immediately to that exercise, looking much less in the air than formerly, and only answering some of his acquaintances, who asked him why he ran so quickly, by these words, —

" It's a wager, don't stop me. I have put up a hundred pistoles that I would sweat some great drops."

The chevalier's garments commenced to have more consistence and he stopped to take breath.

"You have missed your vocation, my friend; you should have been a runner for some prince," said a man, who had stopped with two others, and seemed to take much pleasure in looking at Chaudoreille, while one of his companions, of an extraordinarily stout build, laughed at the top of his voice, and the third making comical gestures and extraordinary grimaces seemed to be trying to copy the features and the figure of the runner.

"What do you say, monsieur," said the son of Gascony to the three individuals, who had stopped before him, "can't one run if he wants to, capededious!"

"Oh, his accent renders him even more comical," said the fat man. "Look at him well, comrade, it's necessary to reproduce that face for us this evening. It will be worth its weight in gold."

"I have it," responded the third. "Hang it! may I stifle if I don't copy it this evening, feature for feature."

"Have you looked at me long enough," said Chaudoreille, ogling them from the back, because he did not feel enough courage to look them in the face. "What do you take me to be?"

"Oh, hang it!" said Turlupin, to himself, for it was he who was walking with his two companions, Gros-Guillaume and Gautier-Garguille. "We

must try to make the little man angry. That can't
fail to amuse us."

Approaching Chaudoreille, who was reflecting
on the grimace he should make, he commenced by
striking Rolande's scabbard with the stick which
he held in his hand, saying, —

"What the devil do you call that, seigneur
chevalier?"

The chevalier became at one moment pale, red,
and yellow.

"These men are desirous of seeking a quarrel
with me," said he to himself, looking around him
to see if he could make his retreat. But already
some passers-by had stopped and formed a circle;
for, having recognized the three comedians who
had been drawing crowds at the Hôtel de Bourgogne, they did not doubt they were going to play
some farce with the personage whom they were
surrounding. The sight of all these people calmed
Chaudoreille's fear a little.

"It is unlikely," said he to himself, "that they
will let these three men kill me without rescuing
me." He then endeavored to put a good face on
the matter. Glancing at the crowd with what he
meant to be a look of assurance, he exclaimed, —

"I don't understand why these gentlemen molest me. I take everybody to witness that I have
not insulted them."

A general laugh was the only answer Chaudoreille received, which had the effect of increasing

his ill-humor; he angrily drew down his little hat
in such a way that the gold-colored rosette almost
touched the tip of his nose, and tried to make his
way through the crowd, but they drew closer to
him on every side, and he found himself face to
face with Turlupin, who put himself on guard
with his stick; Chaudoreille turned another way
and was confronted by Gautier-Garguille, who
had placed his hat precisely in the same manner
as Chaudoreille's, and imitated exactly his piteous
grimaces; finally, Gros-Guillaume barred the chevalier's passage with his enormous corpulence.

Chaudoreille was exasperated, he could bear no
more and he drew Rolande. Turlupin advanced
to the combat with his cane, and the chevalier,
having eyed his adversary's weapon out of the
corner of his eye, put himself on guard, crying,—

"Look to it, guard yourself carefully; I ply
a very strong blade."

At the end of the third bout Turlupin feigned
to be wounded; he fell, uttering a horrible groan,
and making a frightful contortion. Gros-Guillaume
threw himself down beside him, exclaiming,—

"He is dead!"

Chaudoreille was stunned and bewildered; he
still held his sword in his hand and looked at
everyone as if distracted. Gautier-Garguille took
him by the arm and led him away, saying,—

"Save yourself; you have killed the son of the
King of Cochin-China."

Chaudoreille listened no further; he went on his way, left Paris and darted across the fields and the marshes; the three hours he had spent in running in the sun had not strained his legs, he felt no fatigue; fear lent him wings, and he did not stop until he believed that he had escaped the pursuit of which he imagined himself to be the object. It may seem astonishing, perhaps, that the chevalier had not recognized, in the three men who had stopped him on the boulevard, the three comedians whose performances were then in great vogue, and who permitted themselves a thousand licenses that the Parisians authorized, and which delighted even the great noblemen. But when Chaudoreille had any money he passed the greater part of his time in gambling houses, and had been but rarely to the theatre called the Hôtel de Bourgogne; besides, Turlupin and Gautier-Garguille were so adept in the art of changing their physiognomies that it was difficult to recognize them unless one had often witnessed their performances.

The fugitive had stopped to breathe for a moment, he looked timidly about him and recognized the locality; he was at the end of the Faubourg Saint-Antoine, near the Vallée de Fécamp, and he perceived about three hundred paces from him the Marquis de Villebelle's little house.

Chaudoreille had fasted since the evening before, he was overcome with fatigue and believed himself menaced by the greatest dangers. In such circumstances he forgot that the barber had forbidden him to go there and decided to ring at the little house and seek refuge.

Collecting his strength he turned towards the dwelling; he rang the bell, and Marcel opened the door almost immediately.

"What, is it you?" said he in astonishment. "Did the marquis or M. Touquet send you here?"

Before answering, Chaudoreille entered the garden, and closed the door after him.

" But what the devil is the matter with you?" said Marcel. "What are you doing here?—and your face is in such a state, all in a cold sweat; one would believe, on my word, that you'd all the sergeants of Paris at your heels."

" And you wouldn't be mistaken," said Chaudoreille, in a scarcely audible voice.

" Why, what are you saying?"

" That I'm pursued, or at least I shall be. That the greatest danger threatens me."

" My God! What have you done?"

" I've killed the son of the King of Cochin-China."

" The son of Cochin-China?"

" Why, yes, just now, not more than a few minutes ago, against the Fosses-Jaunes — near the Porte Saint-Denis — but it was in honorable combat, a duel with equal weapons; and Rolande laid him at my feet. Heavens, what a cry he uttered as he fell — it still rings in my ears. I slaughtered him like a bullock."

Marcel listened with his habitual good-humor; however, Chaudoreille's story appeared so extraordinary that he could not refrain from exclaiming, —

" But, truly, can all that be possible ? "

" What, by jingo, you question its possibility, — my dear Marcel, it's absolutely true. You know me; you know that I'm a hot-headed fellow, a rake of honor. It's a habit I've formed, and what can you expect. I can't reform myself. But this time, at all events, it was not my fault. I was walking quietly along by the city wall; all of a sudden three men came before me and uttered some jokes which were very much out of place and offended me; I politely asked them to allow me to pass, but they still obstructed my way. I immediately drew my sword, the crowd surrounded us, one of my adversaries put himself on guard. I immediately rushed on him; the combat was terrible. My enemy fought desperately; but soon he fell at my feet, making frightful grimaces, and one of his companions told me I had killed the heir to the throne of Cochin-China."

" And what the devil was the Prince of Cochin-China doing on the boulevards with two idiots who allowed him to fight with you ? "

" Faith, I didn't have time to get any information on that point; he had no doubt come to Paris to take some exercise — the poor fellow. But you can imagine that this adventure will become notorious; they'll send out a description of me; they'll put all the squads in Paris in pursuit of me; my dear Marcel, it's necessary that you should hide me for several days."

" I'm very sorry to say that I can't do it; I thought you'd been sent here by my master with orders for me; since that's not the case you must go, for he has expressly forbidden me to receive anybody here except those that are sent to me. M. de Villebelle will discharge me if, on arriving suddenly with some of his friends, he should find a stranger in the place."

"Zounds! I'm not a stranger, since I've already served your master in his love affairs. My dear Marcel, you don't wish my death."

" No, but I don't wish to lose my place."

" You are alone here? "

" Of course I am; but monseigneur may come when one is least expecting him."

" He won't come today."

" You don't know anything about it."

" I beg your pardon; I know that his presence is commanded at court. I only ask shelter of you until tomorrow — but, Marcel, my life is in your hands."

"Come, your fright is very ill-timed."

"The Cochin-Chinas will be leagued against me."

" Let them league themselves."

" I've eaten nothing since yesterday."

" I'm not to blame for that."

" Marcel, will nothing move you ; do you want
me to throw myself at your feet? Well, behold
me there. You are softening, you yield; I see
tears in your eyes."

" Well, only just till tomorrow; but hang it, if
monseigneur should arrive this evening ? "

" I promise you I'll jump over the wall."

Chaudoreille breathed more freely ; and directed his steps towards the house.

" Oh, delightful purlieus, how has my destiny
changed since I quitted you," said the chevalier,
drawing out his little silk handkerchief to dry his
eyes. But on reaching the dining-room, which
he recognized, his sadness appeared somewhat
lessened. He was the first to seat himself at the
table ; he invited Marcel to go to the cellar, and
did not give him a moment's rest until the supper
was served ; for it was then five o'clock, and in
those days everybody dined at midday.

" I'm not hungry yet," said Marcel, as he
seated himself, " ordinarily I don't sup until eight
o'clock."

" Oh, never mind that, I can eat for both of
us, and it needn't prevent our supping at eight
o'clock ; for I do not wish to make any change
in your usual habits. O my friend, what a day's
work ; if you knew all that had happened to me.

At first it began very well; an amorous rendezvous given to me by a lady who fell in love with
me through seeing me from her window."

" Pshaw ! "

" Give me a wing of that fowl. Yes, my friend,
a passion I inspired while watching the flight of
some swallows — but — I am used to that. Pour
me out something to drink. I'm sure she's a
woman of high rank. She sent to me by one of
her slaves, I think it was a mulatto, or she must
take a devil of a lot of snuff, for her nose was the
color of terra-cotta."

"And when are you to meet ? "

" Tomorrow evening. But at present, can I
think of it ? This unfortunate duel has spoiled
all my plans. They'll perhaps put me in the
Bastile for five or six years."

" Well, you are a fool."

" Oh, do you think that anyone may kill the
Prince of Cochin-China like a little shopkeeper
of the Marais. My situation is alarming. Give
me some pasty, I beg of you."

" Did you satisfy yourself that your man was
dead ? "

" If you had heard the cry he uttered as he fell,
you would not doubt it yourself. It's a cursed
day's work ; that thief of a water-carrier brought
this ill luck upon me ! "

" A water-carrier ? "

" Yes, one with whom I fought this morning."

"Are you always fighting?"

"Well, by jingo, I can't take twenty steps without fighting; the government should give me a pension to remain at home. What, another stroke of ill luck? Good God! it seems to me I hear a great deal of noise outside."

"What does it matter to us, it's only some pages, lackeys, or students who are amusing themselves by fighting; oh, I'm accustomed to all that."

"It's more likely they're coming to arrest me."

"Nothing of the kind, I tell you."

"Well, Marcel, you're very fortunate in not being a man of the sword."

"A stick serves just as well to defend me; but I don't seek a quarrel with anyone."

"You're very right; I envy your gentle urbanity. But I believe I hear nothing more. Give me something to drink. I feel calmer."

"Have you done eating?"

"Yes, I can now wait till supper. Marcel, it was here we wagered on the flies."

"I remember it."

"Will you take part in a game to pass the time?"

"Much obliged; but I didn't like the game."

"Oh, it wasn't that one I was about to propose; but I believe I happen to have some cards in my pocket. Come, a hand at piquet?"

"No, I don't care to play."

"Why, by jingo! it's only to pass a few hours;
we shan't ruin ourselves; I haven't more than two
pieces of gold about me; and when I shall have
lost that, to the devil with me if I continue."

Marcel yielded to Chaudoreille's solicitations,
who immediately set out the table and drew a pack
of cards from his pocket, looking at them tenderly
as he placed them between himself and Marcel,
saying,—

"We'll play for a crown on each side."

"It's too much."

"Pooh! one lost, another gained; it's only between the pair of us."

"Yes, but if one wins all."

"Nonsense, we are equally good players."

"But you haven't laid your money down."

"I've told you I've nothing but gold, I'll
change it when I've lost some hundreds."

They commenced to play. Chaudoreille's face
was animated, his eyes were shining, and seemed
as if they would leave their orbits to look at his
adversary's play.

"These cards are not new," said Marcel, "they
are all stained or marked."

"That's because they've been so much used
apparently. I leave it to you," said Chaudoreille,
looking carefully at the backs of the cards which
were at the bottom of the pack.

"Hang it! you've made me a pretty present;
there, these are the seven and the eight."

Chaudoreille won the first game, then a second and a third, because, thanks to the marks he had made on the back of each card, he knew them as well by their backs as by their faces.

"It's singular," said Marcel, "that I never win anything; you always have the best cards."

"What would you have? It's chance, luck; but it will probably turn."

The luck did not turn and Marcel's crowns passed into Chaudoreille's pocket. The chevalier was scarlet, trembling, and the veins on his forehead were swollen by the ardor of his play, when the bell at the garden gate rang violently.

"Oh, the deuce! there's somebody," said Marcel.

"I am lost!" cried Chaudoreille jumping on his chair, "it is somebody come to arrest me."

He immediately rose and ran around the room, went through the first door he saw and disappeared, without listening to Marcel, who called to him, —

"It's monseigneur; it's M. de Villebelle; keep still and I'll let you out without his seeing you."

But Chaudoreille had disappeared and the bell continued to ring. Marcel was obliged to open the gate without knowing what had become of his guest.

CHAPTER IV

The Little Supper

"And pray why did you make us wait so long, clown?" said the marquis angrily to Marcel, as he entered the garden with three men, two of whom were enveloped in their cloaks, while the third had no hat and nothing to cover his velvet doublet, which was stained in many places with mud; this, however, did not prevent its owner from bursting into shouts of laughter as he looked at himself, as though he still enjoyed some frolic in which he had participated.

"Follow me, my friends," said the marquis.

"Oh, I know the way to your little nest of the Faubourg," said one, "it's not the first time I've come here."

"Nor me."

"That's all very well; as for me, messieurs, I make my first appearance here today and in a brilliant costume I hope. Ha! Ha! What the devil! if anybody should happen to divine that I ought to be present this evening at the petit coucher, 'twould be deuced awkward for me!"

"Come, Marcel, show us a light," said the marquis, pushing the valet before him, while the

latter, anxious and uneasy, was constantly glancing around him.

"You've been sleeping already, rascal, for you
look stupefied."

"Yes, monseigneur, that's true, I have been
asleep."

"He lives the life of a canon here. He does
nothing but eat and sleep."

While speaking they had reached the house.
Happily for Marcel the marquis never went into
the lower room, where the card table was still
standing. They went up into the apartment on
the first floor. Marcel lighted many candles, while
the marquis' friends threw themselves into arm-
chairs, and Villebelle took off his mantle, saying, —

"Come, hasten yourself, and serve us supper
of all that you can get together; there are always
provisions here. You have a poultry yard, a pigeon
house; put some fowls quickly on the spit. We'll
play while waiting for them to be served. Prepare
the card table. Open that drawer, there are some
cards and dice in it. Gentlemen, you will perhaps
have meagre fare. I did not expect the pleasure
of entertaining you this evening, but at least you
shall have some good wine. The cellar is well
furnished and we shall not lack champagne."

"Hang it! that's the principal thing," said a
big, pale young man whose features were regular,
but who was disfigured by the scar of a sword-cut
across his left cheek.

" I, too, am of the vicomte's opinion," said his neighbor, who appeared to be some years older, and whose stoutness and high color contrasted with the physique of the first speaker.

" Champagne before everything."

" Oh, I recognize there that drunkard De Montgéran," said the young man with disordered costume. " As for me I am not displeased when the entertainment consists of wine. But let's play, gentlemen, let's play; it's necessary that I should recoup a hat and a cloak."

" You might even add a doublet; for I don't think that you can present yourself anywhere in that one."

" Those cursed shopkeepers, how they did resist this evening. That's all right, I had flogged three of them."

" Yes, but except for the marquis and I you would have been in a very bad position."

" Well! what the devil brought the quarrel about? for I don't know yet why I fought."

" A trifling thing, a mere bagatelle; because I was carrying off with me a little bookkeeper's wife, the impertinent husband permitted himself to shout! The idiot, I should have sent his wife back at the end of two days. Hang it! I'd no desire to keep her."

" Perhaps that's why he was angry."

" I said a couple of words for him to the superintendent; before long our clerk will be destitute."

"That's as it should be, it's necessary to teach these plebeians manners, who persuade themselves that they only take a wife for themselves."

"In your place I should have asked for a lettre-de-cachet."

"We shall see; that might still be done."

During this conversation Marcel had prepared everything; he went down to the groundfloor and, while making his preparations for supper, called his comrade in a low tone, and looked in every corner of the room, but he had disappeared.

"Where the devil has he hidden himself," said Marcel, who then looked in all the other rooms and went down to the cellar, where he called Chaudoreille again without receiving any answer. "He has apparently escaped into the garden and from there he will have jumped over the walls, as he said he would do. However, that astonishes me, for he would hardly care to leave the house."

The marquis and his companions sat down to play, and while waiting for the supper they cracked several bottles of champagne to put themselves in good spirits ; that is to say, to arouse in them the desire to commit new follies. The most extravagant bets were proposed and accepted, and while playing, drinking, singing, each one related his good fortune, his gallant adventures, drew his mistress' portrait, and passed in review the women of fashion, sparing the honest women no more than the courtesans.

At last Marcel came to announce that supper
was served in a neighboring room and the gentlemen left their play to go to the table. The room
in which the supper was served equalled by its
elegance the other rooms of this delightful retreat;
while it served habitually for banquets, the beauty
and the taste of its frescoes, the statues which
decorated it, the sofas which furnished it, the
lustres which lighted it, recalled the salons of ancient Rome where Horace, Propertius and Tibu-
lus, surrounded by their friends and their competi-
tors, sang of love and the charms of their mis-
tresses while passing amphoræ filled with falernian,
or carrying to their lips cups where sparkled
cæcubum or massicum; and while crowned with
myrtle and acanthus, in order to resemble their
deities, proving only too well that they had all the
weaknesses of mortals.

Sybarites of a later time, the young men assembled at Villebelle's drank deep draughts of the
generous wine with which the table was so amply
provided; the marquis furnishing them an example by his avidity in emptying the flasks. De-
corum and etiquette were banished from the
repast, where liberty often degenerated into license.
The convives had drawn the sofas to the table,
and each one, half lying down like a pasha, held
a glass of champagne which he emptied, shouting
with laughter at the follies of which he heard or
at those which he had himself committed.

The young man who had come without a hat, and who was called the Chevalier de Chavagnac, was seated opposite a beautiful statue representing Psyche, to which he often raised his eyes. All of a sudden he interrupted the fat Montgéran, who was singing, by exclaiming, —

"May the thunder crush me, if this Psyche didn't move!"

"What the devil are you saying now?" asked the marquis.

"I'm saying, I'm saying your Psyche has come to life, or I must be blind."

"Oh, hang it, how delightful it would be if that pretty woman could come and take her place amongst us."

"Gentlemen, it was no doubt Montgéran's voice which worked this miracle. A new Pygmalion, he softens marble."

"You needn't make fun of my voice, gentlemen, it is held in no small estimation. It must rather have been your cynical conversation which made poor Psyche blush. But let me sing instead of listening to De Chavagnac's stupidity, who can't see clearly because he has drunk so much."

"Yes, assuredly, I have been drinking, but I can still see. I've been looking at that statue for a long while, and several times it appeared to me as if it moved."

"Marquis, are there any ghosts in your little house?"

"I have never seen any here, but it would be very amiable of them to come and pay us a visit while we are at table. We would make them hobnob with us."

"Come sing, Montgéran, we will listen to you; but be a trifle less artificial. I prefer the natural method."

"Yes, gentlemen, I will then give you; 'The shepherd in order to admire the charms of his shepherdess took the first' — "

"Now, I shall know what it is," said De Chavagnac, rising precipitately and running towards the statue. As he neared it the Psyche made so lively a movement that she would have fallen from her pedestal on to the floor, if the young man had not received her in his arms, and placed her on the ground. All the convives had their eyes fixed on De Chavagnac, who, after placing the Psyche in safety, reapproached the pedestal, which was about three feet high and one and one half in circumference.

"There is something inside it," cried the young man, who perceived that the pedestal was hollow, and had an opening in the side which was turned towards the wall.

"Someone inside it?" repeated the others, half rising. At the same moment a thin, trembling voice, which seemed to come out of the earth, uttered these words, —

"No violence, gentlemen, I will yield without

resistance," and, in a moment, Chaudoreille's little head peeped from behind the pedestal and showed itself to the gentlemen, who burst into a shout of laughter, exclaiming, —

"What a handsome face!"

However, De Chavagnac, who had remained near the niche of the statue, took Chaudoreille by the mustache and forced him to emerge from his hiding place. Then, having examined the personage whose piteous face rendered him still more comic, he went laughingly to take his place at the table, while the poor devil whom he had dislodged threw himself on his knees before them and without daring to raise his eyes murmured, clasping his hands, —

"Gentlemen if I have killed the Prince of Cochin-China it was against my will and because he had provoked me, but I swear to you that I will not try it again; I will not even carry Rolande, if they exact it of me."

"What the devil is he saying?"

"Do you understand any of it, marquis?"

"My faith, no! He is speaking about the Prince of Cochin-China."

"He's a fool!"

"Hang it! we must amuse ourselves with him."

"One moment; it is necessary that I should learn how this clown penetrated here. Hello! Marcel, Marcel."

While Marcel was coming upstairs Chaudoreille's terror became somewhat lessened. While he had been immured in the pedestal a murmuring sound only penetrated to his ears, and he believed that the room was filled with armed men who were looking for him. Now the words which he caught, the name of the marquis which he heard pronounced, taught him the truth. Reassured that his life was in no danger, he began to glance pleadingly at the persons who surrounded the table, and meeting nothing but laughing faces he entirely recovered his spirits.

Marcel entered and, at the sight of Chaudoreille, remained stunned and confused before his master.

"Who is this man, Marcel?" said the marquis. "Is he a thief? is it he or you whom we ought to hang? Come, speak, clown, and tell us the truth, or you shall be chastised in good fashion."

Marcel, trembling, did not know how to excuse himself for having received someone despite the commands of the marquis, and muttered, —

"Monseigneur, I couldn't help it, I did not wish to, I refused him at first."

"Monseigneur," exclaimed Chaudoreille, rising and standing on his tiptoes, "if you will permit me I will relate to your excellency how all this happened, for I see that Marcel will find it difficult to come to an end."

"The trembler has recovered his speech," said the big Montgéran, who could not take his eyes from Chaudoreille.

"Come, marquis, let him speak."

"Yes, yes, he will make us laugh," cried the others.

"Very well, gentlemen, since you desire it. Come, speak, you little cur; and you, Marcel, remain there to give him the lie if he attempts to deceive us."

Though the sobriquet, little cur, made Chaudoreille knit his brow, permission to speak before noblemen of high rank caused him so much pleasure that he immediately assumed a smiling expression, and commenced his speech, —

"Messeigneurs, your excellencies behold in me Loustic-Goliath de Chaudoreille, Knight of the Round Table; descended on the male side from the famous Milo of Crotona, and on the female side from the celebrated Delilah, who, sacrificing herself for her country, had the courage to cut from Samson, her lover, that which made his strength."

Shouts of laughter here interrupted the orator. "It's delightful! he's charming! He's worth his weight in gold!"

"Hang it!" said Chaudoreille, "I was sure that I only had to speak."

"In fact, descendant of Delilah," said the marquis, "what is your business?"

Chaudoreille appeared embarrassed for the moment, then he exclaimed volubly, —

"Defender and protector of beauty — and of

gambling houses ; understanding how to bear arms and to play at piquet; teaching music, and the way to turn the king or ace at will ; succoring young men of family and girls who have been seduced ; bearer of love letters ; master of the sitar ; duellist and messenger, — and all at a very moderate price."

" But what a treasure we have in this man ! "

" Finally, who led you here ? "

" Your excellencies have heard me speak of my duel this morning. I killed the Prince of Cochin-China near the Porte Saint-Denis."

" The Prince of Cochin-China, and where the devil did you find such a prince as that ? "

" By the side of the Fosses-Jaunes. I was walking quietly along, he came up and assaulted me, and I fought him. Isn't that true, Marcel ? "

" Yes, it's very true that he told me all that, monseigneur. He arrived here wild with fright, and exhausted ; he told me that he was pursued, and though I did not understand all his history of the prince, I saw that he trembled, so I consented to allow him to come in for a moment. We were having supper when you came in, monseigneur, and immediately he fled, seeing and hearing nothing."

" Yes, monseigneur," said Chaudoreille, " I believed that the archers and the sergeants were coming to arrest me, and I hid in the first place that I could see."

"Do you think, clown, that I believe the story you told Marcel in order to get some supper?"

"Monseigneur, I swear to you!"

"Peace!"

"There were witnesses to the duel."

"Silence, I tell you! To come to this house to seek Marcel, you must have known that he lived here. Who taught you the way to this dwelling? Did you know that it belonged to me? and if you knew it belonged to me, who gave you the audacity to present yourself here."

Chaudoreille, who perceived that the marquis was no longer joking, answered with less assurance, —

"Monseigneur, I've already had the honor of visiting here in your lordship's service."

"To serve me, rascal?"

"Yes, monseigneur; I served you indirectly in a certain matter with a young Italian, an elopement on the Pont de Latournelle. It was I whom Touquet charged to keep watch."

"O marquis," said the three guests, smiling, "this is clear enough. The chevalier of the Round Table has ministered to your love."

"I've had that honor, monseigneurs," answered Chaudoreille, bowing, and twisting his mustaches.

"Hang it! I don't remember it," cried the marquis, looking hard at Chaudoreille. "What, Touquet, so clever, so inventive, could he be served by such a marionette. Come, that is not possible."

"Monseigneur," said Chaudoreille, compressing his lips, "if you knew the talents of the one you call marionette, you would, perhaps, speak differently. Touquet himself is only a beginner beside me."

"Oh, as to that, clown, it is necessary that you should justify your boasting or that you should perish beneath the stick. For some days I have been suffering from ennui; I don't find anyone, at the court or in the town, who deserves my homage. My Italian, even, has commenced to tire me. I wish — I don't know — I would give all the world for the capacity of falling truly in love; find me a woman who is capable of inspiring me with this feeling. I will give you twenty-four hours to discover this treasure for me. A hundred pistoles for you if you gratify my wishes, a hundred strokes of the stick if you are not successful."

"That's it! That's it," shouted Villebelle's guests, "if he is successful in what you have given him to do, tell us and we will employ him in turn."

"O capededious," said Chaudoreille to himself, "a hundred pistoles if I render him amorous. Zounds! my fortune will be made. But a hundred blows of the stick if I am not successful. How can I render a man amorous who is tired of everything, and that in twenty-four hours. O my genius inspire me! Ah, if my portress resembled this Psyche."

"Wait, drink that," said Montgéran, presenting Chaudoreille with a large glass full of madeira. "That will help you, perhaps, to find what Villebelle wants."

Chaudoreille emptied the glass at a draught, after humbly bowing to the company; then he struck his forehead sharply, made a leap forward, and exclaimed, —

"I have found her!"

"The wine has already operated," said De Chavagnac.

"Come, speak," cried the marquis, "what have you found?"

"Monseigneur," said Chaudoreille, bowing with respect, "deign to permit me to speak to you without witnesses."

"The clown is right," said the marquis rising from the table. "If he should speak before you each one would wish to assure himself of the truth of his recital, and we should become rivals. Marcel carry a light into the next room. Come, my Chaudoreille, I will give you an audience. Have patience, gentlemen, I shall not be long."

Saying these words, the marquis went into the next room, and Chaudoreille followed him with an air so important and mysterious that it greatly amused the three persons who remained at the table.

When Chaudoreille found himself alone with
the marquis, he examined the doors to see if they
were shut, and stooped to look under the table,
but the marquis pulled him by the ear, saying, —

"What signifies all this ceremony?"

"Monseigneur, it is that I'm about to speak of
something mysterious, a secret, and I don't wish
that anybody should know it. I shall expose myself to great danger in speaking; they will perhaps
want to take my life."

"You'll expose yourself to a great deal more by
not speaking," said the marquis impatiently, seizing the fire shovel.

"I'm about to do so, monseigneur. I wager
you've never seen Touquet's daughter."

"Touquet's daughter. Has he a daughter?"

"Not exactly, monseigneur; she's only a child
that he adopted about ten years ago."

"Touquet adopted a child? Hang it! that surprises me."

"I was very sure, monseigneur, that you were
ignorant of the circumstance."

"There's something mysterious about it."

"Very extraordinary. No one would guard a
girl so closely unless he were keeping her for
himself."

"What is this girl like?"

"She's an angel, monseigneur, divinely beautiful, an enchantress; hardly sixteen years of age,
with the figure of a nymph, and Touquet spreads

it abroad that she is ugly and ill-made, that there is nothing pleasing about her. He has even ordered me to tell it all about. If I have seen young Blanche it's only because the barber, wishing to have her taught music, was obliged to introduce me into her room, which she never leaves."

"This is all very singular," said the marquis, "and you pique my curiosity."

"Good! I shall have a hundred pistoles," said Chaudoreille to himself, "that's much better than the two golden crowns which the barber promised me, to say nothing of the honor of acting as the Marquis of Villebelle's business man."

"And you say it's not because he is in love with her himself that he hides this young girl," resumed the marquis, after a moment.

"No, monseigneur, for a few days from now he is about to marry her."

"To marry her?"

"Yes, monseigneur, to a young man whom the beautiful Blanche did not know, I am sure; for no one ever went near her except your humble servant. I bet that Touquet has sacrificed her, and that the poor little thing hates her future husband."

Here Chaudoreille said what he did not think, but he imagined it more prudent to present the matter in that aspect.

The marquis reflected for some moments, then he said, —

" Tell me quickly all that you know about the adoption of that young girl."

"Yes, monseigneur. About ten years ago, Touquet, who then had not a sou, took lodgers in addition to his business as a barber and bath-keeper. One evening a gentleman went to his house, with a little girl five or six years old, and requested a bed. Touquet received him. The traveller went out the same evening, leaving his little girl with Touquet, and that night he was murdered in the Rue Saint-Honoré near the Barrière des Sergents."

" Were the murderers discovered," said the marquis, looking attentively at Chaudoreille.

"Oh, no, monseigneur," responded the latter, smiling almost imperceptibly, " but — sometime afterwards Touquet was possessed of enough to buy the house which he had rented."

The marquis made a sudden movement, like that of a man who is about to step on a snake. A long silence succeeded, during which Chaudoreille kept his eyes bent on the ground, not daring to seek to read those of the marquis.

" And it is the daughter of that man whom he adopted," said Villebelle, breaking the silence.

" Yes, monseigneur, it is she."

" What was her father's name ? "

" Moranval, at least, so I believe. Nothing was found upon him but an insignificant letter, which gave no information in regard to his family."

" And his daughter is beautiful ? "

" As far as I am competent to judge, monseigneur, and if you should see her — "

" Yes, I shall see her."

" Monseigneur, I have the honor to inform you that Touquet has expressly forbidden me to speak of young Blanche and of her coming marriage. In order to be agreeable to your lordship I have sacrificed myself; but the barber is wicked, very wicked. I beg of you, monseigneur, not to tell him that you learned all this from me."

" Be easy about that."

" In any case I beg to be allowed to claim the protection of monseigneur in regard to my duel with the Prince of Cochin-China, which is not a falsehood as monseigneur appears to believe."

The marquis was reflecting deeply ; finally he rose, saying to Chaudoreille, —

" Follow me, and not a word of all this. In twenty-four hours you will return here, and if you have not deceived me you will receive the recompense which I have promised you."

Chaudoreille bowed nearly to the ground and followed the marquis. They returned to the banquet hall, where his guests awaited with impatience Villebelle's return.

" Well," said De Chavagnac, as he entered, " was it worth the trouble of leaving the table ? "

" I think so," answered the marquis ; " but as to that I shall be better able to tell you after

tomorrow. Chaudoreille, go down with Marcel
and make him give you some supper before you
leave." The latter did not wait for this order to
be repeated. He went down to look for Marcel
and, already assuming a patronizing air, made the
valet serve him with all that he thought best, while
saying to his old friend, —

"I am in great favor with your master, treat me
well and I can say two words for you. Above all
never refuse to play a game of piquet with me, or
I'll cause you to lose favor with monseigneur."

Poor Marcel, who understood nothing of all
this, allowed his intimate friend to beat him at six
games. Finally, day appeared, and Chaudoreille
left the house saying, —

"I shall come back this evening at ten o'clock.
The marquis has made an appointment with me."
Then he ventured into the Faubourg, stopping
whenever he saw from afar two men together, and
with a mysterious air inquiring of some shopkeepers if they had heard anyone speak of the
death of Cochin-China. As nobody understood
what he said, he finally persuaded himself that
his prince was dead, but that nobody knew who
he was, and more tranquil as to the result of the
affair he at length ventured to reënter Paris.

After the secret interview of the marquis and
Chaudoreille, the four profligates returned to their
play ; but the party was no longer gay. Villebelle
was preoccupied and took little part in the con-

versation ; the vicomte was sleepy ; fat Montgéran no longer sang, and Chavagnac was tired of
losing. At six o'clock in the morning these
gentlemen separated, each one returning to his
dwelling in the city and the marquis reëntered
his hotel, reflecting on all that Chaudoreille had
told him.

CHAPTER V

Having Money and Power One May Dare Everything

"Only two days more and I shall be your husband, my Blanche," said Urbain, pressing the young girl's hands in a tender transport.

"Oh, my dearest, how very happy we shall be, when we no longer have to part, even for a few hours," answered Blanche, smiling at her lover, "how much I shall like living in the country! I shall breathe more freely there in the pure air, I am sure, than in this close room. We shall play and run on the grass, shall we not, dear?"

"Yes, and we will work in our own garden."

"How delightful! We shall have flowers then, and I am so passionately fond of them."

"We shall have some cows also, I hope," said Marguerite.

"Oh, yes, dear nurse, and some pigeons, and rabbits and fowls—it will all be so delightful. It seems to me that when I was a very little child I lived in the country, in a house where they had all those things."

"Poor Blanche! and is that all you remember of your infancy?"

"I still remember a lady who was always with me, who often kissed me; no doubt she was my mother."

"Poor woman!" said Marguerite; "perhaps she is still living; and to think that no one knows. But away with sad thoughts!"

"Then you'll not regret Paris, my dear Blanche," said Urbain.

"Would you wish me to regret it, dear, when you are with me?"

"Those dear children!" said the old servant rising from her chair; "it is Providence which has brought them together, for they are made for one another. But it's nine o'clock, Monsieur Urbain, you must go."

"Nine o'clock already! The time is approaching when we need part no more, but the days seem very long now, because I spend them away from you."

"It's the same with me, dear; it seems to me that evening will never come."

"I haven't seen M. Touquet for some days."

"And you'll not see him this evening," said Marguerite; "he received a letter after dinner. It was no doubt some pressing matter of business, for he left immediately and has not yet returned."

"Good-by, then, dear Blanche."

"Good-by, my dear."

"Two days more. It seems a long time to wait."

"You have managed to live through a fort-night," said Marguerite.

"Yes, I don't know why, but these last few days seem to me as if they would be eternal."

Urbain could not tear himself away from Blanche; his heart was oppressed; the eyes of both the young lovers were filled with tears; the young girl extended her hand to her friend and he pressed it to his heart.

"I don't know what's the matter with me," said Blanche, "but your going makes me sadder than usual."

"What childishness!" said Marguerite; "no one would suppose that you were going to meet within two days. Isn't M. Urbain coming to-morrow evening? Come, come, it's time to go to bed."

The lovers again said good-by, sighing deeply, and Urbain finally followed Marguerite, who shut the street door on him and then went up-stairs to Blanche and scolded her for her sadness. But she could not restore her gayety, for the dictates of reason may persuade the mind, but cannot allay the fears of the heart.

Not more than a quarter of an hour after Urbain's departure some one rapped loudly at the street door.

"That's Urbain, no doubt," said Blanche; "he saw that I was sad and has come back to console me."

"That's very improbable," said Marguerite; "it's more likely M. Touquet who has returned. However, I am astonished that he should knock, for I thought he had taken his master key."

"Go and see who it is, dear nurse."

"Yes, yes, mademoiselle; but if it should not be monsieur? It is late — we are alone in the house, and I don't know if I ought to open to any one."

"Do you want me to look out of the window, dear nurse, I shall very soon see if it's Urbain."

"Yes, do so; that seems to me more prudent."

Blanche had already opened the window, and she looked down into the street; the night was dark, but love renders the sight clear, and the young girl soon saw that it was not Urbain.

"Who is there," demanded Marguerite, thrusting out her head.

A deep voice answered, "I come from Master Touquet, he has charged me with a commission to his adopted daughter, Mademoiselle Blanche."

"How very singular," said Marguerite to Blanche. "What! monsieur, who has hidden you from everybody's sight, sends a stranger to us at this hour?"

"But, dear nurse, since he has sent him, it is necessary to open to this gentleman. Perhaps something has happened to my protector."

"Is the man alone, my child?"

"Yes, dear nurse, I see nobody but him."

"Why don't you open the door," cried the man in the street, "my message is urgent."

"Wait one moment, somebody will be there. — Remain here, my child."

Marguerite went down, holding her lamp in her hand. She was not reassured, but opened the door, and a man wrapped in a large cloak, his head covered with a plumed hat, appeared before her.

"You've been very slow, my good woman," said he, smiling, "however, I'll indemnify you for the trouble I have caused you."

While saying these words, he slipped several pieces of gold into Marguerite's hand. The old woman did not know if she ought to accept them, but said to herself, "His manners are not those of a robber."

The stranger quickly entered the alleyway and the old woman as she looked at him said to herself, "This is not the first time that I have seen that figure, and I remember his voice. Yes, I believe that that's the friend my master was waiting for so late some time ago."

Marguerite was not deceived, it was in fact the marquis who had introduced himself into the house, having first sent the barber a letter in which he gave him a rendezvous outside, and ordered him to wait there until ten o'clock in the evening.

"Monsieur has been here before, I believe,"

said Marguerite, reassured on recognizing one whom she believed to be her master's friend.

" Yes, yes, my good mother, I have often been here ; but hasten to lead me to your young mistress. It is absolutely necessary that I should see her."

" Is my master ill ? — has he been involved in some quarrel ? Many accidents happen in this city."

" Don't be uneasy, there's nothing of that kind."

The marquis followed Marguerite, who led him to Blanche's chamber, and opened the door, saying, —

" Mademoiselle, here is a gentleman who brings you a message from M. Touquet."

Blanche took some steps forward to meet the stranger ; the marquis had entered abruptly, but on perceiving the young girl he paused, and for some moments remained motionless, occupied in contemplating her. There was something in the aspect of the marquis which compelled respect, and while at that moment there was nothing severe in his expression, the astonishment and admiration depicted on his features lent additional animation to his naturally proud and noble look. Blanche involuntarily lowered her eyes, for she could not meet the fixed gaze with which the marquis seemed to examine her person, and Marguerite dared not utter a word, because the stranger intimidated her also.

"This is truly beyond all that I could have imagined," said the marquis, as if he were speaking to himself.

"Monsieur," said Blanche, with embarrassment, "my nurse informs me that you have something to say to me, some message from my benefactor; has anything happened to him, monsieur?"

"No, lovely Blanche, no; your benefactor, since you deign to so call him, has run into no danger, but I would brave a thousand if by that means I could make you take the same interest in me."

Blanche glanced timidly at the marquis as if she were waiting for him to explain himself better; the latter, in hastening to lead her to a chair, dropped a corner of his mantle, allowing his rich attire to be seen, and Marguerite said under her breath to the young girl, —

"Mon Dieu, my child, look at those precious stones, that lace, this is at least a great nobleman."

"Oh, yes," answered Blanche, in the same tone, "it is superb, but I like Urbain's costume much better."

Villebelle, who had not taken his eyes from Blanche, remained silent.

"Why did you come here then," said she, seeing that he was contented with looking at her.

"Yes," said Marguerite, who sought to resume her ordinary assurance, "for you must have come for something."

"And I have found more than I had believed possible," said the marquis, smiling. Then, without appearing to notice the embarrassment which his presence caused, he approached Blanche, took her hand, and cried, —

"You in this retreat! you hidden from all eyes!—when you should be the ornament of the world and receive the homage of the whole universe."

"Forgive me, monsieur," said Blanche, "but I don't understand you."

"I don't understand you either," murmured Marguerite, fixing her small eyes on the marquis.

"Better still, adorable girl," responded the marquis to Blanche, without paying the least attention to Marguerite. "They did not deceive me, this is innocence itself, the most perfect ingenuousness united to the most seductive grace and beauty."

"But, monsieur, was that what M. Touquet told you to say to me?"

"No, lovely child, not at all," said the marquis laughing, and still retaining Blanche's hand, which she vainly tried to disengage.

"It's necessary however that you should explain yourself," said Marguerite in a dry tone, "you have been here for a quarter of an hour and you have not yet said why you came. It is very late and we are accustomed to go to bed early."

"Oh, well, old woman, go to your bed; I will remain with this lovely child until the return of Master Touquet."

"Do you think I will leave you alone with my dear Blanche," cried Marguerite, rendered still more suspicious by the word old, "no, monsieur, no, I take better care of her than that. Your laces, your jewelry, and your fine appearance do not inspire me with much confidence. Wait! take back your pieces of gold, I don't wish them, for I begin to believe that your intentions are not good, and Marguerite will never second the plans of a seducer, whether duke or prince, even should he offer her the mines of Peru."

The marquis replied only by shrugging his shoulders without turning towards Marguerite, then he seated himself near Blanche and took off his hat and mantle, establishing himself in the room like one who is not disposed to go.

Blanche was trembling, confused; she looked at Marguerite as if to implore her not to abandon her, and the old woman, whom the conduct of the stranger had filled with new dread, forced herself to appear calm, saying in a voice whose faltering accents betrayed her fright, —

"Be easy, my child, I am here, I will not leave you, and while monsieur does not appear to listen to me it is, above all, necessary that he should tell us what he came here to do."

"I have told you, my good woman, I am waiting for Touquet. I must speak to him this evening; that is very important."

"And just now you said that it was he who had sent you; you were deceiving us, then?"

"Perhaps," said the marquis, laughing.

"Very well, monsieur, if you are really waiting for my master, come into the lower room. I will give you a light, and you will find a fire there."

"No, indeed, my good woman, I like this much better than your lower room; the society of this charming child will make the time seem very short, and surely, adorable Blanche, you will not be cruel enough to refuse to keep me company."

"No, monsieur, if you desire it, if it will amuse you, I must wish it also."

"Yes," said Marguerite, "it seems that it is necessary that we should do monsieur's will, but patience — soon I hope — "

At this moment somebody violently shut the street door. Blanche started joyfully, and Marguerite cried, with a triumphant air, —

"Ah! here is my master! We shall now see whether anyone can establish himself here in spite of us."

The marquis rose without answering, took his mantle, put his hat on his head, kissed Blanche's hand, saying to her, —

"Au revoir, charming girl," then left the room saying to Marguerite, —

"Light me!"

All this had happened so quickly that Blanche, who was greatly astonished, had not time to oppose the action of the marquis, and the old servant followed the great nobleman, saying, —

"O mon Dieu, what a man!"

The barber had entered and was taking off his mantle, when the marquis, followed by Marguerite, appeared in the lower room. At the sight of Villebelle, Touquet started with surprise, saying, —

"What, you here, monseigneur!"

He paused and Marguerite cried, —

"Yes, my dear master, monseigneur has been here for three-quarters of an hour. He presented himself as coming from you, and he installed himself in Mademoiselle Blanche's room."

"In Blanche's room," said the barber, appearing violently agitated.

"Yes, monsieur, in mademoiselle's room —"

"That's enough, my good woman, leave us," said the marquis, in an imperious tone.

"Leave you," answered Marguerite, "oh, it is necessary before all —"

"It is necessary to obey," said the barber, in a gloomy voice. "Go!"

Marguerite was dumbfounded, but she dared not reply and left them, saying, —

"Well, I don't understand all this, this man does as he pleases here, it troubles me."

"Well, dear nurse," said Blanche to the old woman, "and what about the stranger?"

"Oh, I don't know who that man can be, but M. Touquet is as submissive as a child before him. I left them together. This fine gentleman said to me, ' Go ! ' and it was necessary to obey him."

"That's very surprising, dear nurse."

"How did you like that man?"

"Oh, he is not so bad, dear nurse, and if I had not been a little afraid of him, I believe I should have thought him very agreeable."

"Ah, mon Dieu, I was very much frightened; he has something satanic in his looks."

"Oh, dear nurse, you're mistaken, he has a very fine face, features which inspire respect, and which are bland at the same time."

"Fie ! for shame ! my child, to admire such an impertinent man. Oh, if your Urbain could hear you."

"But, dear nurse, I should say the same thing before Urbain. Is it not necessary to tell him all that I think? That could not displease him, for he knows how much I love him."

"Come, my child, it's late, go to bed. I am going, too, good-night."

Marguerite went up to her room, saying to herself, —

"Young girls will always be young girls. The most virtuous of them will allow themselves to be favorably impressed by fine compliments, a handsome face, and rich clothing. These are terrible talismans with the women."

When Marguerite had left the lower room, the barber shut the door. His manner disclosed a violent agitation; however, he awaited the marquis' explanation, and the latter narrowly watched and appeared to enjoy his uneasiness.

' May I know, monseigneur," said Touquet at last, " how it is that you are at my house when you appointed another meeting place ? "

" What, Touquet, don't you understand it ? I made a distant appointment with you in order that I might represent myself as sent by you to this young girl, whom you have hidden from me and whom I ardently desired to see. This is one of the little tricks which you yourself formerly taught me, and which are nearly always successful."

The barber bit his lips, but did not answer.

" Well, to be sure," resumed the marquis, " that you should possess such a treasure, an angel of beauty and grace, and hide her from me, your old master ! From me, when you know my partiality for the sex which has led me to commit so many follies."

" It was precisely because of that partiality, monsieur le marquis, that I hoped to shield Blanche from your notice ; I am interested in that young girl, to whom I stand in the place of her parents. I know the impetuosity of your passions, and I don't think the honor of being your mistress for a fortnight will assure the child's happiness."

" And how long, clown, have you made similar

reflections," said the marquis, looking witheringly
at the barber. "After lending aid in all my intrigues, after leading me to commit actions which,
but for you, I should never have thought of,
should you allow yourself to control my morals
and enact the knight errant of the beauties I deign
to distinguish."

"Monseigneur!"

"Remember that though your hypocrisy and
lies may serve you sometimes, they can never deceive me. It is not from me only that you hide
this young girl, for you hold her a prisoner in her
chamber and do not permit her to go out. It is
not because you are in love with Blanche, since
you are about to give her in marriage; besides,
love is a feeling unknown to you; your heart
knows nothing but a thirst for gold. There is in
all this some mystery which I must discover."

Touquet became pale and trembling, and murmured, lowering his eyes, —

"I swear to you, monsieur le marquis —"

"Make an end of this," said Villebelle, interrupting him. "Listen to me. I love, what do I
say, I adore this young girl whom I have seen
only for a moment; for a very long time I have
not experienced sensations similar to those I felt
in her presence. This is not a passing caprice;
these are not desires to which the heart is a
stranger. No, on seeing Blanche I felt moved,
uneasy, softened. I cannot define all that passed

within me. It seemed to me that I recognized that lovely child—that my love for her had existed for a long time. After that you must divine that it is impossible henceforth to live without her. Blanche must be mine; I am capable of every sacrifice in order to arrive at that end."

"Ah, monsieur, that is what I feared," said Touquet, who appeared to be really grieved at what he heard. "You wish to make Blanche your mistress!"

"I wish to make her happiness; I feel that my love for her will be lifelong."

"That is impossible, monseigneur. Blanche is about to be married to a young man whom she loves. You must see that your love cannot render her happy."

For some moments the marquis walked up and down the room, then he cried passionately,—

"I repeat to you, Blanche must be mine—it must be so. I will leave no means unemployed to attain this end. She cannot yet love her destined husband; she has only known him for a few days."

"Monseigneur, who has informed you as to all this?"

"What does that matter to you? That love is but a passing sentiment and I shall know how to make her forget it by overwhelming her with presents, with jewels, and by seeking to invent new pleasures to make each day delightful to her."

" Monseigneur, Blanche is accustomed to retirement; she is not a coquette; your ornaments, your gifts will have no effect upon her."

" Enough of this," said the marquis, " your objections weary me; I have now some orders to give you. I wish you to give me Blanche, on whom I swear to settle an independent fortune. Such a treasure I feel is worthy of a great price. Wait, here are six thousand crowns in notes and gold. You shall have as much more when you have fulfilled my commands."

The barber eyed with avaricious looks the money which the marquis had spread upon the table; then he turned his eyes away, saying in a gloomy voice, —

" Gold! yes, it is always that which draws me on; but this time — no, I cannot. Remember, monseigneur, that within two days Blanche should be united to her lover."

" Then at once, tonight even, it is necessary that she be given into my hands."

The barber appeared to be weighing the proposition in his mind; from time to time he looked at the money on the table, and, finally, speaking with a great effort, he said, —

" It cannot be, monseigneur, I am extremely grieved to have to disappoint you, but matters are too far advanced."

The marquis drew near Touquet, and grasping him tightly by the arm, said in a low tone, —

" It will, then, be necessary that I beg my uncle,
the grand provost, to cause a new inquiry to be
held in regard to the murder of Blanche's father.
Do you think, scoundrel, that I do not partly
divine the cause which has induced you to keep
this young girl so carefully hidden from everybody's sight? Her beauty would be remarked,
and could not fail to draw a throng of admirers
who would have much to say of Blanche, and in
seeking to learn who she is and what family she
belongs to they would obtain new facts about that
unfortunate traveller who was murdered on the
evening of his arrival in Paris. They would make
reflections on the fortune which came to you, nobody knows how, some time after that event."

" Monseigneur," said the barber, whose face
had become livid, while a convulsive trembling
seized his limbs; "monseigneur, what do you
say? Could you believe it of me?"

" I believe nothing yet, but tomorrow I shall
urge the magistrates to make an effort to pierce
this mystery."

" Monseigneur, you shall have Blanche," said
Touquet dropping into a chair as though he were
perfectly helpless.

The marquis smiled triumphantly and seemed
to forget all but his love. Touquet who had been
thrown into a state of the deepest depression and
consternation, remained for some minutes without
daring to raise his eyes, and unable to resume his

ordinary expression. Finally, he rose and murmured, in a broken voice,—

"Believe me, monsieur le marquis, that it is not the suspicions you have conceived which determine me to obey you—my devotion alone—"

"Enough," said the marquis interrupting him; "not another word about that. I am quite willing to believe that appearances are deceitful. We will occupy ourselves only with my love. I don't wish to lose a single instant in obtaining possession of Blanche, and, since you tell me that in two days she was to have been married, it is necessary that she should leave this house tonight."

"I agree with you," said Touquet, "since she is to go the sooner the better. But how can it be done tonight?"

"I don't recognize you, Touquet; you see nothing but obstacles, as for me, I don't know of any. It is not yet midnight, we have some time remaining. I'll go to my hotel and send Germain, my valet de chambre, to get a carriage—and to go only as far as my little house."

"Monseigneur, you must not take Blanche there; she would not be safe; the place is too near Paris. Urbain Dorgeville, the person she was to marry, will make every effort to discover her. The young man adores her; he is enterprising; you have everything to fear from his despair."

"I fear nobody, and you know it. However, I

think your advice is wise. Blanche is so pretty; I already feel jealous of a glance given by her to another, and a good many giddy fellows know my little house. But wait, wait, I have just what will suit me; amongst all the property that came to me from my mother is a château situated in the neighborhood of Grandvilliers, about twenty-two leagues from here, and far enough from the town and the highway to avoid the notice of travellers."

"Very well, monsieur, that will suit perfectly."

"I have only once visited this château, which is called Sarcus, but although I only made a short stay there, I was greatly struck by the elegance of the beautiful estate. The château, built in 1522, was given to Mademoiselle de Sarcus by Francis the First, and in the neighborhood is noted for the marvellous beauty of its architecture, and especially of its façade, in which the artist excelled all his previous works. That is the place to which I shall take, or rather, to which I shall have Blanche taken. Twenty-eight leagues — two trusty men — she will be at the château in ten hours or so. As for myself, after tomorrow I shall arrange my affairs, and pretending at court that I am obliged to go to England, I shall repair secretly to Sarcus to her whom I never more wish to leave. You see, Touquet, my plan is perfect and no one will suspect that I have abducted the young orphan."

"Yes, monseigneur, no one among your brilliant acquaintances; but how shall we induce

Blanche to go with you quietly and prevent a noise and cries which will attract the attention of the neighbors ? "

"Oh, hang it! it will be necessary to mislead her at first—that's your look out. Is your invention so sterile that you can think of nothing to deceive a mere child. You can make her believe that she is going to rejoin her future husband."

"Wait, monseigneur, I've thought of a way, but Blanche mustn't see you. She would suspect something, and my stratagem would fail."

" I repeat to you she will start alone — a postilion and two well-armed men behind the carriage will answer to me for her safety."

"That is all that is necessary."

" It is midnight. I'll go and settle everything. My valet de chambre shall start before at full speed, that he may give my orders at the château and that he may be there to receive our beautiful girl; at two o'clock in the morning I shall be at your door with a coach; you understand me, at two o'clock."

"Yes, monsieur le marquis," said the barber, " I will not forget the hour."

" Manage so as to have Blanche ready to get into the carriage. I leave it to you. Do not try to evade your promise or my vengeance will be terrible."

"You may rely on me, monseigneur."

The marquis wrapped himself in his mantle and

hastily left the barber's shop. Touquet remained alone for some time, thoughtful and depressed ; at length he rose abruptly.

"What does it matter after all," said he, "whether Blanche be with Urbain or the marquis ? Shall I be foolish enough to sympathize with the love of two children ? In keeping this young girl with me I hoped to avoid all suspicion. But at last I shall be relieved of the burden that oppresses me. Come let's put up this gold; the marquis has promised me as much more — and I would have refused him. No. My destiny must be accomplished ; this metal has always served as its compass. I was only sixteen years old when it caused me to commit actions which drew down upon me my father's curse; arrived in Paris, which I had yearned to know, I soon found myself robbed of everything I possessed by people who were more adroit than myself; I had been deceived and I wished to make others suffer as I had suffered. I gave scope to my talents. Up to that time I had done no great wrong — but this cursed thirst for gold. Ten years have passed and have not effaced from my memory that horrible night — when — since then I have not tasted a moment's peace. I will return to my birthplace and if my father is still alive I will try to obtain his pardon ; perhaps then I may regain quiet of mind. But if he knew how I enriched myself."

The barber again gave himself to his reflections,
Soon Saint-Eustache's clock struck one. Touquet
slowly took the money from the table, and, after
locking it in his room upstairs, he went to Blanche's
chamber and knocked at the door.

The poor little girl was not asleep; she had been
too greatly excited by the events of the evening.
She still seemed to see the stranger seated near
her, holding her hand and looking at her with an
expression that she could not define. She felt oppressed; it seemed to her that she should never
see Urbain more. The marquis' figure appeared
constantly between herself and Urbain, and the
sadness the latter had felt on leaving her heightened her own premonitions. Yielding to this in-
definite anxiety, often harder to bear than a real
sorrow, Blanche could not rest, and the sound of
a knock at her door in the middle of the night
awoke in her fresh terror.

" Who is there ? " she cried, in a faltering voice.

" It is I, Blanche," answered the barber ; " open
the door. I have something of importance to tell
you."

The young girl, who had recognized Touquet's
voice, rose, hastily put on a dressing gown, and
opened the door. The barber held the lamp in
his hand and avoided looking at the young girl,
who, on the contrary, wished to question him and
said, —

" Mercy, my good friend, what has happened?"

These words, " my good friend," uttered in Blanche's sweet voice, always agitated Touquet; he forced himself to hide his feelings.

" Calm yourself, Blanche," he said, " and listen to me; Urbain has had a quarrel tonight — a duel."

" O heavens! He is wounded ! "

" No, no, nothing has happened to him, but it was necessary to his safety that he should leave Paris immediately ; had he not done so they would have arrested him; he therefore left for the country."

" He left without me ? "

" Let me finish ; you should have been married here, in place of which you will be married at his house; but to quiet Urbain's anxiety I had to promise that tonight you should rejoin him."

" Oh, at once, my friend, as soon as you please; but why did he not take me with him ? "

" That was impossible ; Urbain had not an instant to lose; by a lucky chance, one of my friends is sending his valet into the country to find a wife. The carriage will come to take you in an hour. Get ready, therefore. He will charge you nothing and you will find everything down there that you need — do you understand me ? "

" Oh, I shall be ready in a moment, and what about Marguerite ? "

" She can follow you later; I need her to make divers arrangements. In a few days I shall come

to see you. I'll leave you now; make your preparations.   I shall come for you when the carriage
arrives."

The barber departed, and Blanche, who had not
the slightest suspicion that anyone would deceive
her, continued her toilet.

"Poor Urbain," she said to herself, "I was sure
that something would happen to him; and he,
also, had a presentiment. How fortunate that he
was able to escape; but I shall rejoin him and I
shall nevermore leave him."

During this time Touquet had returned to his
room, saying to himself, —

"Everything is going well — the little one will
start without making the least difficulty. But if
Marguerite is not asleep; if she should have heard
some words of my conversation with the marquis
and if she wishes to follow Blanche. It is important that the old woman should know nothing —
it is easy to assure myself she is sleeping, since
she now sleeps in the room occupied by Blanche's
father.   Come, I mustn't be weak.   I'll go up."

The barber took his light, and directed his steps
towards a closet which was at the end of his room.
When he reached it he still hesitated; then, making an effort to command himself, he touched a
button hidden by the hangings, and a small door
opened and discovered a small and very narrow
staircase which led to the floor above.   Touquet
turned his eyes, murmuring, —

"Since that fatal night I have not been in this passage."

He mounted the stairs, his wild eyes seeming to fear that they would meet some frightful object, the hand in which he held the lamp trembling, while with the other he held to the wall to steady his tottering steps.

At the top of the staircase was a door closed by two bolts, which he withdrew with as little noise as possible, and entered the little dark closet at the back of Marguerite's alcove, which the old nurse and Blanche had entered without perceiving the door on the staircase, because it was artistically hidden in the woodwork. The barber placed his lamp on the floor, and put his ear to the door which led into the alcove; he soon heard a prolonged snore, which announced that Marguerite was sleeping soundly; however, he softly opened the door so as to thoroughly assure himself of the fact; then he reëntered the little room and left by the secret door, drew the bolts and went down, saying, —

"There is nothing to fear from her."

Suddenly the barber made a false step, he lowered his lamp and perceived some reddish stains on the staircase. Although it was difficult to distinguish what had produced these stains, Touquet recoiled with horror, his hair stood up on his head, his feet refused to carry him over the steps on which were imprinted the marks which caused his fear; in his agitation he allowed the lamp to fall from his hands; it rolled and was extinguished. The barber was left in the most profound darkness in the secret passage. Showing every sign of the most ungovernable terror, he ran as fast as possible down the stairs, bumping his head against the wall, falling and crawling on the stairs.

"Mercy! mercy!" he cried, in a suffocating voice, "do not pursue me. Is it because I am giving up your daughter that you come anew to torment me? Well, I won't give her to the marquis. No, but leave me. Don't touch me with your bloody hands."

At length he came to the foot of the stairs; he reclosed the door hidden by the hangings and without pausing in his room, where he had no light, he went down into the lower room, which was lit by one lamp and by the fire which still burned on the hearth.

He threw himself upon a seat, and looked wildly about him, gradually becoming more assured; finally, he passed his hand over his brow saying, —

"It was a dream."

At that moment he heard the sound of a carriage, which stopped in front of the house, and having entirely recovered his wits he went to open the street door.

"Here I am," said the marquis, alighting from the travelling carriage. "I have come even sooner than I promised. My valet de chambre is already on the way to Grandvilliers. The postilion is in the saddle, these two efficiently armed men will follow the coach, all is ready ; and Blanche?"

" I will go and get her; she believes that she is going to rejoin her future husband who has been wounded tonight in a duel; she has not the slightest suspicion that there is any trickery, and goes of her own free will."

" That's excellent ! "

" But hide yourself, monseigneur, that she may not perceive you, or all will be lost."

" Fear nothing ; I will ensconce myself in the angle of this doorway — I only wish to see her enter the carriage — tomorrow I shall be at Sarcus, and I shall dry her tears."

" I will go and fetch her."

The barber went up to call Blanche, who had heard the carriage and was ready.

" I am here, my good friend," said she, hastily leaving her room, " I knew the carriage had come."

Touquet walked first, and Blanche followed; her heart was palpitating and, although she thought she was going to rejoin Urbain, this departure in the middle of the night had about it something mysterious, singular, which almost frightened her. When they had reached the lower room the sweet girl glanced around her, saying, —

"What! has not Marguerite come to bid me good-by and kiss me?"

"No, no, we haven't time for that," said Touquet taking her hand and leading her into the passage. When they reached the front door the barber put out his head to assure himself that the marquis was not within sight, then he opened the carriage door.

"Come quickly," said he to Blanche, "get in; don't lose any time."

Blanche darted into the street and stepped into the vehicle; her heart grew heavy as she found herself alone in it in the darkness of the night; but Touquet had already closed the door.

"Good-by, my dear friend," she said to him, "I am going to rejoin Urbain, but I shall never forget you. All you have done for me is graven on my heart by gratitude."

"Go on, go on, postilion," cried the barber, in a voice faltering with the emotions he experienced. At this moment two o'clock struck, the postilion cracked his whip, and the carriage which held Blanche started.

"She is mine!" cried the marquis, and the barber hastily reëntered his dwelling.

CHAPTER VI

The Rendezvous. Strokes of Fortune. The Hôtel de Bourgogne. The Sedan Chair

On taking his departure from the marquis' little house in the Faubourg Saint-Antoine, at daybreak, the Chevalier Chaudoreille did not feel entirely reassured as to the outcome of his duel with Turlupin, whom he believed to be a great personage; and whom, incredible as it may seem, he firmly believed he had slain; however, the idea that he was now the confidential agent of one so powerful as the Marquis de Villebelle, which gave him the right to claim that nobleman's protection if it should be necessary to him, gave him the courage to return to Paris, where he summed up the events of the preceding night and their probable consequences. The marquis had promised him a hundred pistoles if Blanche should happen to please him, and Chaudoreille was confident that he should have that sum; but should Touquet discover that it was through him that the marquis had learned of Blanche's existence, he would have everything to fear from the barber's anger. However, he did not forget his rendezvous for the evening.

Forcing himself to banish all thoughts of the barber, and chinking the crowns which he had won from Marcel, he went into a wine shop, where he passed a great part of the day trying to obtain courage by emptying several bottles of wine. Towards evening he felt more enterprising, and returned to his lodging to iron out his ruff, renovate his complexion, dye his mustache and imperial, dust his shoes, and brush his hat; he then set out for his rendezvous, saying, —

"Though she should possess the grace of a princess, I must not forget that I have to return this evening to the Faubourg Saint-Antoine, in order to receive a hundred pistoles from the marquis. Zounds! for a hundred pistoles I would leave the Sultan's favorite and all the odalisks of the Grand Turk."

The day was waning; for the last half hour Chaudoreille had been strolling in the neighborhood where the old woman had accosted him the evening before, looking up at all the windows, having first carefully assured himself that the water carrier was not to be seen. Finally, the servant who had spoken to him previously issued from a respectable-looking house, and, as she passed near him, said in a whisper, —

"Follow me, but do not appear to be with me."

"Very well, Marton," answered Chaudoreille; and he followed on the heels of the old woman, so as not to lose her from sight.

They entered the house ; the servant mounted the stairs, put her finger on her lips and signed to Chaudoreille to follow her. The chevalier did so, but all of a sudden he seized the old woman's petticoat and stopped her, saying, —

"Is your mistress married?"

"Why?" asked the old woman, looking at him mockingly.

"Why! by jingo! because some husbands have very little patience in an affair of this kind. Hang it! a stroke of the sword is soon given, and I can't throw myself thus into the wolf's den."

"Are you not armed, monsieur? and if any-one should attack you, can you not defend your-self?"

"Yes, I know how to defend myself," said Chaudoreille, going down some stairs, "but I have an infinite respect for the marriage vow, and, taking everything into consideration, I should pre-fer to take myself off."

"Come I tell you, monsieur," said the domes-tic running after him, "my mistress is not mar-ried, and you have nothing to fear."

"Well, by jingo! You should explain your-self, my good woman. My life is too precious for me to expose it with temerity. Come, Lisette, go up! I will follow you, but if you have lied to me, tremble!"

The old woman paused on the second landing ; she opened a door and took Chaudoreille into a pretty dining-room and from thence into a small well-furnished parlor, where she left him, saying, —

"Wait here, I will go and tell madame."

"Do not be long, for I am not fond of waiting," cried he, looking around him anxiously.

Left alone he examined the apartment curiously, saying, —

"It is pretty enough, it is all in very good taste; this is a woman of distinction. Come, Chaudoreille, you're in great luck. Don't act like a novice, but show some self-possession. Everything has come to me at once; fortune — money — love — I am sure that I shall finish by making my way. Oh, the deuce! here's a hole in my doublet! But I must pull my hat up in front, it will hinder me from seeing my princess; I feel in advance that I can adore her. But it's dark and they have left me without a light, that's very singular. My heart beats, this is certainly love."

Here Chaudoreille raised his voice, saying, —

"Besides, if anyone should dare to rub against me, Rolande has an edge and four men could not frighten me."

At this moment the door creaked and opened behind Chaudoreille, who started back against a table, overturning several porcelain cups, as he exclaimed, —

"Who goes there?"

"It's me, monsieur," answered the servant. "I came to conduct you to madame."

"Oh! that's right; but you left me without a light and I mistook you for a rat, of which I have a great horror. I would much rather fight with a lion than see only the tail of one of these little animals, but show me the way, my good woman."

The servant led him through another room and opened a door into a handsome boudoir lighted by many candles; a young woman was seated on a sofa at the end of the room. The old woman retired. Chaudoreille, very uneasy in this tête-à-tête, to which he had looked forward, dared not look at the person with whom he found himself, and racked his imagination to find a compliment suitable for the occasion; but his Phœbus was stubborn, and nothing had occurred to him when he heard these words, —

"Will not Monsieur Chaudoreille speak to his old acquaintances?"

Struck by the voice, the little man raised his eyes and uttered an exclamation of surprise on recognizing Julia, the young Italian, who looked smilingly at him.

"Can it be? Is it indeed you whom I see?" said Chaudoreille.

"And what do you find so extraordinary in that, monsieur le chevalier? Did you think that the marquis would always leave me in his little house?"

"No — undoubtedly not, beautiful lady — I do not know — but I was so far from expecting to see you," and he glanced tenderly at her, saying to himself: "I always thought that she loved me, behold me now the rival of a marquis; it's a tremendously ticklish position."

"Be seated, Monsieur Chaudoreille," said Julia, who appeared for some moments very much amused by the embarrassment and the oglings of the little man. The latter, however, resumed his audacity, and was about to seat himself on the sofa beside Julia, but, by a gesture, the young woman indicated to him a folding chair, and signed to him to seat himself opposite her.

"She's afraid of me," said Chaudoreille, seating himself on the folding chair, "she felt that she could not resist me and wished to defer her defeat. There's no need to hurry matters, my eyes can accomplish the business for me."

"Can you imagine why I sent for you?" said the young woman, looking at him mischievously.

"Why beautiful lady — I flatter myself, I presume there are some things that one divines when one lives in society."

"And I think that you are mistaken," said Julia, assuming a serious tone, "and I will explain myself."

"Mon Dieu," said Chaudoreille to himself, dismayed by Julia's change of tone, "Is she going to kill herself on account of me?"

"I am the marquis' mistress; you are not ignorant of that fact."

"Undoubtedly not, since I myself was the messenger of—"

"Silence! do not interrupt me! If I do not seek to hide my frailty it is because, far from having yielded to interest or ambition, love only has caused my fall, and, in the eyes of a woman, love excuses many faults. Yes, I have loved the marquis for a long time. I had often seen him on the promenades, and in spite of all that I heard said about him, I could not resist the feeling which he inspired. My heart yielded itself to him. Be not astonished that I yielded so readily to your proposition. I flattered myself that the marquis shared the devouring flame which consumed me. I hoped to have enough strength not to show my love until I was certain of his. Alas! I counted too much on myself and it was very easy for him to persuade me that he loved me. Ungrateful man! the love which he swore to me has already given place to indifference, and I!—I feel that I love him more than ever."

In speaking of the marquis, Julia became animated; her glance was fiery and her whole person indicated the violent passion to which she was a prey; Chaudoreille, much surprised at what he had heard, and almost alarmed at Julia's fate, drew his stool farther away as she grew warmer.

"Yes," said the young woman who had appar-

ently forgotten that Chaudoreille was there, and
gave way to all her feelings ; "yes, I shall always
love you, fascinating Villebelle— this burning heart
beats but for you! But I cannot bear your indifference ; and if you should love another then
my fury would know no bounds, and in your
blood and that of my rival, I would revenge my
outrage."

"O my God! she wants me to stab the marquis," said Chaudoreille, and he tried to draw his
chair still farther away, but, as it was now up against
the wall, it was impossible for him to go any further,
and he could only glance towards the door from
the corner of his eye, murmuring, —-

"This is a fine rendezvous! That woman's
possessed of the devil. I like my portress much
better."

Julia had ceased speaking, little by little she
became calmer and resumed her ordinary manner,
and, glancing at Chaudoreille, she could not prevent a smile on seeing him glued against the
tapestry.

"Come nearer! come nearer," she said to him,
"that I may tell you what I desire of you. You
are, you have told me, very intimate with the
barber Touquet?"

"Yes— mada— mademois — signora."

"The barber is a man who habitually serves
the marquis in his gallant intrigues ; and I think
that through him it would be very easy for you to

learn if Villebelle has any new conquest in sight.
Do you understand me?"

"Yes, yes; I understand you perfectly."

"Are you willing to serve me?—to inform me
of all you can learn from the barber in regard to
the marquis? and if you yourself should be employed in some love intrigues to come and impart
to me immediately the plans which they have
formed."

"Yes, certainly. I consent with all my heart.
Zounds!" added he to himself, "if she knew
what I said to her lover yesterday, I shouldn't
get out of here alive."

"What are you trembling for?"

"Oh, it's nothing, it's my nerves; that happens
to me often."

"Wait, take this purse; if you serve me zeal-
ously and faithfully, you will see that Julia is
grateful."

The sight of a well-filled purse somewhat restored Chaudoreille's resolution. He took the
money, bowing nearly to the floor, and cried,—

"From this moment, I am entirely devoted to
you; dispose of my arm, of my sword, of—"

"It is neither a question of your arm nor of
your sword, it is of your eyes and your ears only
that I have need. Be on the watch, make the barber talk, inform yourself of the slightest actions
of the marquis, and come and give me an account
of them. Let nobody have the least suspicion of

you and that is all that is necessary to us. Go! and remember to inform me of the slightest circumstance if it has any connection with my love."

"You shall be obeyed," responded Chaudoreille, bowing humbly. Julia rang, the old woman arrived, and, at her mistress' signal, led the chevalier to the door without saying a word.

Once in the street, Chaudoreille breathed more freely.

"Zounds!" said he, "here I am in intrigues up to my neck; Julia's agent, confidential man of the marquis, confidant of the barber, and, what is even more satisfactory, receiving money from all three of them. That's doing pretty well. Hang it! this purse is well-filled. Tomorrow I will clothe myself entirely anew. I shall get some flesh-colored breeches that will make me look like an angel! But I mustn't forget the most interesting item — the hundred pistoles that the marquis is to give me if Blanche pleases him — and I must go to the little house. O Fortune! you are treating me like a spoilt child, but it must be confessed that your favors are directed to a very adroit fellow."

While making these reflections, Chaudoreille had taken his course toward the Faubourg Saint-Antoine, arriving at the little house at eight o'clock in the evening. He rang nearly as loudly as the marquis, and Marcel on opening the door to him said, —

"You make as much noise as monseigneur."

"Apparently it is because I have a right to do so," responded the Gascon, entering with an impertinent manner; then, striding across the garden, he went immediately into the dining-room and threw himself on a seat, saying, —

"Has my friend, the marquis, been here since yesterday?"

"Your friend, the marquis," answered Marcel, opening his eyes wide.

"Why, yes, caitiff! Or the marquis, my friend, if that pleases you better."

"Nobody has been here."

"And has he sent nothing for me?"

"Nothing."

"I must wait for him then. Serve supper quickly for me, all that you have of the best, some of your oldest wines, some liqueur. Come! go about it, in place of standing and looking at me like a statue."

"But what the devil is the matter with you?"

"Marcel, no reflections, I beg of you, and, if you wish to keep your place, render yourself worthy of my protection."

Marcel contented himself with smiling, then he laid the table and served the supper. Chaudoreille placed himself at table, Marcel did likewise.

"Your conduct is a little familiar," said the chevalier to him; "but, as we are alone, I may as well allow you to seat yourself near me—"

"That's very fortunate."

"On condition that you serve me first, always."

During supper, Chaudoreille chinked his money, counted his crowns, calculated what remained to him, and what he expected to receive. Marcel looked at him with surprise, saying, —

"Have you inherited some money?"

"Yes, I inherit like that very often. Zounds! if the marquis keeps his word with me, I shall be able to keep the pace."

The supper lasted long; Chaudoreille was so much preoccupied by his affairs that he did not dream of playing; however, midnight had struck, he had received no message from the marquis, and the chevalier's hopes began to vanish. He sighed, listened and exclaimed, —

"He doesn't come! If he should not have found her charming that would be very difficult for me. Zounds! in place of a hundred pistoles I should receive a hundred blows of a stick."

As his hope diminished, his impertinence became tempered and he clinked his glass against Marcel's, saying, —

"To your health my dear and true friend, for you are my friend. Don't talk to me about noblemen of the court, no one can put any faith in them; my good Marcel, what a good cook he is and what a pleasure it is to me to drink with him."

"You don't think now that I did so ill in seating myself at the table?"

"What! was I so unlucky as to say that to you?"

"Certainly."

"Me,—could I have said such a stupid thing?"

"Yes, there is no doubt of it."

"I was tipsy then, I'd lost my senses."

"I don't know what you had lost, but you said it."

"Listen, Marcel! when I say such things as that to you, I give you permission to curse me."

"That's all right, we'll speak no more of it."

At that moment the bell of the gate was heard. Chaudoreille uttered an exclamation, half rose, and dropped on his chair again.

"That will be monseigneur," said Marcel, taking a light, and he ran to open the door, leaving his guest divided between fear and hope.

Marcel soon returned; he was alone, but he held a small roll which he placed on the table before Chaudoreille, and presented him with a paper on which somebody had written two lines in pencil, saying, —

"Here is what monseigneur has sent you; read it!"

Chaudoreille could not believe his eyes, he looked in turn at the roll, at the paper, and at Marcel.

"Why don't you read it," said the latter to him.

Finally, he took the paper with a trembling hand, and read: "I have seen her; you have surpassed my hopes and I double the promised recompense."

" O my God, Marcel! he's doubled the hundred pistoles."

" Then that makes two hundred; that is to say, that there is, in that roll, two thousand livres tournois in gold."

" Two thousand livres ! "

" Well, what's the matter with you now ? "

" Marcel, give me a little vinegar, I beg of you. I don't feel very well."

" It seems to me that a present like that should make you feel very well. Wait, drink a drop of brandy, that will put you in good shape."

Chaudoreille, a little restored by the liquor, opened the roll, and the sight of the pieces of gold which it held deprived him for some moments of the faculty of speech.   Finally, he murmured, in a voice faint with emotion, —

" Marcel, all this belongs to me."

" I know it, all right."

" And then, there's this purse still ; and these six crowns which I had left — "

" Yes, from the game of piquet, yesterday."

" And I am rich! Oh, it produces a terrible effect, my poor fellow, to pass all of a sudden from poverty to opulence. Alas! I shall suffocate!"

" Drink a little more. My faith ! if good fortune produces such an effect, I'd rather remain without a sou and breathe freely. "

" O Marcel, you're very stupid, my boy ! "

" I don't know at this moment which is the stupider of us two."

" Two thousand livres ! Who would believe that one could thus hold his fortune in the palm of his hand."

" Hang it ! one should hold it there as long as he can."

" Marcel, do you know of any property for sale in the neighborhood ? "

" No, why do you ask that ? "

" It's very necessary that I should place my funds. What the deuce shall I do with all this ! Come ! after tomorrow, I shall set up my house, but first I shall leave my lodging in the Rue Brise-Miche and I shall take one near the cardinal's palace ; I shall need a jockey. Marcel, will you be my jockey ? No, in fact, you are too big. Ah, if it were not so late, I should visit some of the gambling houses ; but I can't expose myself at night in this neighborhood with so much gold on me. What a figure I can cut in the gambling dens and at faro. I shall place first a louis on the card, I shall win, I shall double my stakes, I shall still win. I shan't take it up, I shall win ten times following, and I shall carry away a heap of gold. How can I spend all that. Oh, what an excellent idea ! I can dine and sup twice every day, that will indemnify me for the times that I have had to fast.

Marcel, whom fortune had not overwhelmed with her favors, went to sleep while Chaudoreille made his plans and counted his pieces of gold, but day dawned without the latter having closed his eyes, for, at the least sound, he started and carried his hand to his treasure, which he had rolled in his belt.

Chaudoreille awoke Marcel and ordered him to go and find a sedan chair; but Marcel would not leave the house, under the pretence that he must obey the marquis' orders. Chaudoreille became very insolent again and shouted and threatened, but seeing that nothing would move Marcel, he took leave, and decided to return on foot to Paris.

The little man felt larger by six inches since he had so much gold in his possession. He hardly looked at the passers-by, his nose seemed to threaten the heavens, and he was astonished that the sentinel on guard at the barrier did not present arms to him.

After breakfasting as copiously as possible he walked to the palace which Richelieu had built, and on which he had lavished all that the luxury and taste of the time afforded to please the eye and to leave to posterity a monument worthy of the one who had erected it.

Chaudoreille went into several shops, but he found nothing fine enough or fresh enough or brilliant enough for him. He ordered a doublet of rose-colored velvet slashed with white satin;

breeches of a similar color; a cherry-colored mantle embroidered with silver and a fringed belt with golden tassels. These articles would take the larger part of his fortune; but as he was certain of breaking the bank at faro, he refused himself nothing, and within two days hoped to be arrayed like the most elegant nobleman of the court.

Having ordered his costume, he went into one of the inns in the city, where he was served with a rich dinner and exquisite wines; and having already perceived that it was not so easy as he had believed to dine twice a day, which would be a very great resource for rich people who do not know what to do with their time, he tried to make his repast last twice as long as usual.

At five o'clock in the evening, he finally got up from the table; his face flushed, his eyes brilliant, his legs a little unsteady, and left the inn. It was still too early to go to the gambling house, where the high players do not put in an appearance until towards nine o'clock, and to pass his time until then Chaudoreille decided to go to the play, which he had not visited for a long time. He therefore took his way towards the Hôtel de Bourgogne, which he preferred to the Théâtre des Italiens, because Turlupin, Gros-Guillaume and Gautier-Garguille, famous for the farces which they had played in their little Théâtre de l'Estrapade had obtained permission from Richelieu to play there.

The theatre of the Hôtel de Bourgogne was situated in the Rue Mauconseil; the entrance was very narrow and the corridors very incommodious; the body of the house was composed of a pit and several tiers of boxes. When the court attended the theatre the courtiers carried theii seats with them. Here were represented, following the privilege granted to comedians in January, 1613, all mysteries, and decent and amusing plays; presently, comedies, rather more elevated in tone than the usual buffooneries, were played there; and also some plays in which mythological divinities figured as characters, the poets of the day mingling the sacred and profane; but the low jokes and puns were what captivated and attracted the public.

Chaudoreille entered the house and slipped into the pit, where everyone was standing, and where the fluctuations of the crowd often carried one from one corner to another. The chevalier found himself behind a very tall man and could not see the stage. In vain he drew himself up and stood on his tiptoes; he could see nothing except the backs and the wigs of his neighbors. He tried to protest, but everybody hushed him, for Gautier-Garguille appeared and was about to speak the prologue which preceded the piece. Listen to the buffoon, that you may have an idea of the style of prologue in use under Louis the Thirteenth.

" Gentlemen and ladies, one thing I ought to
say to you, and that is not to incline your ears to
the symphony of this pastime as manual operators
who do not coöperate with the nonsense; and do
not treat it as a deluding music or voice, rather
for the spoliation and express capture of your
purses than to win praise from your ears; the
field of my invention being so sterile that if it is
not watered by the cordial of your kindness it is
difficult for it to produce flowers worthy to be
offered to you.   Philippot will appear immediately, and he hopes, under the assurance of your
indulgence, to make you laugh and cry both
together, so that finally the moderation of one
feeling shall temper the violence of the other.
Gentlemen and ladies, I shall desire, I shall wish,
I shall will, I shall demand, and I shall require,
desideratively, wishfully, willingly, demandatively,
and requireatively, with my desiderations and my
requireations, etc., to thank you for your kind
presence and attention to a little jovial and jolly
farce which we are about to represent, before
which I wish to make a large, small, wide, narrow, and spacious remonstrance, which will make
you laugh."

While Gautier-Garguille was delivering this
bombastic nonsense, Chaudoreille was being tor-
tured, pressed, pushed on all sides, and struck in
the face by his neighbors' elbows; in addition to
which he suffered much anxiety in regard to the

safety of his purse. The little man had urgently begged them to let him go out, but nobody would listen to him. In his despair, and having immediate need of a little air, he adopted the plan of pulling the wigs of two of his neighbors to hoist himself to their height, but the wigs came off, and the heads of two respectable tradesmen of Paris appeared naked before the assembly. The two spectators who felt their wigs pulled off, cried, —

"Thief! watch!" and Chaudoreille mingled his voice with theirs, crying, "Help." The play was interrupted and at last, Chaudoreille was discovered struggling among the legs of the spectators, and rolling on the floor of the pit with the two wigs, which he had not dropped.

The two bald heads treated him as a thief; he returned the wigs and explained his conduct as well as he could; they put him out of the door of the pit, which was all that he wished. He mounted to the boxes and found a place in front and, from time to time, glanced angrily at the public.

However, the piece was commencing. Turlupin and Gros-Guillaume were on the stage and Chaudoreille rubbed his eyes, saying, —

"Why! by jingo! if I had not killed him, I should believe that that was the Prince of Cochin-China."

Presently Gautier-Garguille reappeared; he had counterfeited the Gascon to a marvel, his costume was exactly the same as that of Chaudoreille and he had copied his manners and grimaces so well that the latter cried, —

"Is it another self, I see? — can I have a double?"

The comedian having seen his model in the box, saluted him and made faces at him; the spectators' eyes were turned on Chaudoreille, they recognized in the little man that they had chased from the pit the one whom Gautier-Garguille had copied, and the shouts of laughter redoubled. The chevalier perceived that they were mocking at him and was furious; he drew his sword and threatened the pit, because when one defies everybody together it is as if one defied nobody. The spectators laughed louder still, and Chaudoreille left his box, swearing that he would never again go to the Hôtel de Bourgogne.

Arrived in the street, where some persons had followed him, he again gave way to his anger, exclaiming that he would punish the buffoon who had dared to copy him, that nobody could mock with impunity at a man like him, and that he would spend, if necessary, a hundred pistoles to avenge himself.

While speaking thus, he drew out his purse, chinked his gold, took it out and put it back in his pockets, and finally exclaimed, —

"Who will go and bring me a sedan chair!"

Two men immediately went to execute this commission. While waiting for them to return,

Chaudoreille promenaded before the theatre, swinging himself in the manner which he judged the most noble, and striking his belt every minute to make his gold pieces chink.

The two men returned presently, they had obtained a chair, and would themselves have the honor of carrying Chaudoreille, or so they said to him on their arrival, exclaiming, —

"Here, master! get in, master, you'll be pleased with us."

Chaudoreille, whom nobody had ever called master, felt much pleased, and was about to bow low to the porters, but he restrained himself and darted into the chair, quivering with delight on the cushion which was at the bottom.

"Where shall we go, master?" said one of them.

"To Rue Bertrand-qui-Dort. You will see a lantern at the door of the house where I stop."

"All right, master!"

They closed the door of the chair, and Chaudoreille felt himself raised, and gently carried through the streets of Paris. It was the first time he had been in a chair. The pleasure which he experienced in being carried made him forget the disagreeable scene of the play. He reflected on his dazzling situation, and on the pleasure which he should taste in playing high, and laid new plans. However it seemed to him that he had been a long time in the chair, and the porters were still walking. Chaudoreille wished to know if he were near his destination. There was a very narrow little window on each side of the seat, but these windows could not be lowered. It was late, one could not see clearly in the streets, and Chaudoreille could distinguish nothing.

"Are we almost there," cried he, leaning towards the front; nobody answered, and they continued to carry him. He began to think the motion of his carriage not quite so pleasant, he tried to open the door in front, the only vent by which one could leave a sedan chair, but that door would not open from the inside.

A cold sweat bathed the little man's brow. He conceived a thousand suspicions, recalled divers adventures in which sedan chairs figured, and was bitterly repenting having taken one when at last he felt that they had stopped. He breathed more freely and prepared to descend, but after being deposited on the ground the chair was stood up on end, in such a manner that when they opened the door it was above Chaudoreille's head.

"How do you think I can get out like that?" cried he, trying to climb.

"Before coming out there is a little ceremony to be observed, master," said the porters, in a jeering tone.

"A ceremony, what is it, my boys?"

"It is to give us all the silver and gold that you have about you. We'll relieve you of that."

" What is that you say ? Scoundrels ! Rascals ! "

" Come, do as we bid you and no noise, or that will be worse for you."

As they gave this order, they flashed the blades of their swords before Chaudoreille's eyes, and he fell back in the bottom of the chair, unable to support himself. The two porters were obliged to draw him from the chair themselves. He glanced around him, but he was in a lonely, narrow road, surrounded by marshes, where nobody would venture so late. The robbers searched him, and despoiled him of all that he possessed, then they escaped with their sedan chair, leaving him lying beside a huge stone, half dead with fright.

CHAPTER VII

Poor Urbain

THE morning after Blanche's hurried and un-expected departure, old Marguerite left her room at her usual time. The good woman had heard nothing ; she had slept soundly, for it was long since the pleasures and the pains of love had caused her to suffer from insomnia. Her first movement on arising was to go to her dear Blanche's room to kiss her, as she was in the habit of doing every morning. She found the door of the room half open ; but Blanche was not there, and the extreme disorder of the apartment, the bed which had been slept in but had not been made, the clothing spread upon the furniture, all indicated that some extraordinary event had taken place. The young girl had never left her room without Marguerite, and the latter called Blanche, and receiving no answer and alarmed at this de-parture from her customary habits, and perhaps by a secret presentiment, went downstairs to see if the young girl was with her master, but the bar-ber was alone in the lower room, and then Mar-guerite said, in a frightened tone,—

" O my God ! where can the dear child be ? "

"What is the matter, Marguerite," said Touquet, who was prepared for this scene.

"Blanche, monsieur, Blanche is not in her room. I have sought her vainly for a long time; someone has taken the dear child away from us."

"Taken her away!" exclaimed the barber, pretending to be struck with astonishment. He immediately went to Blanche's room, followed by the old servant, who went as quickly as her legs would permit. After a search, which Touquet knew would be fruitless, he threw himself on a seat, crying, —

"The wretch has fulfilled his threats!"

"Who do you mean, monsieur!"

"That man you saw here yesterday evening."

"I believe you're right, monsieur, it can be nobody except him."

"He was fascinated with Blanche, he ventured to ask her hand of me. I refused it to him and this is how he has revenged himself."

"But, monsieur, you must know where this man lives. He had the bearing of a great nobleman. You can recover our dear child."

"I have very little hope of it. This wretch assumed a brilliant costume in the hope of seducing Blanche, but he is a schemer without name, without a roof, without position."

"A schemer," said Marguerite, looking at her master in astonishment; "but, monsieur, it seemed to me that he was the same friend that you were waiting for so late some time ago."

The barber was for an instant rendered uneasy
by Marguerite's remark, but soon recovering himself, he resumed, —

"You are mistaken, it was not he; I forbid you
to speak to anybody of that again."

"And Urbain, monsieur, — that poor Urbain
— when he comes here this evening — "

"Urbain will unite his efforts with mine to recover her whom he was about to marry."

The barber went out and Marguerite then gave
free course to her tears. The good woman loved
Blanche with a mother's tenderness. She could
not bear to be deprived of her presence, and impatiently awaited Urbain's arrival; for it seemed
to her that he would know better than anybody
else how to discover and restore her lost darling.

Touquet was absent during a large part of the
day. On his return, Marguerite inquired as to
the success of his search, but he answered her
coldly, —

"I have no hope of finding her." These words
chilled the poor old woman's heart; she could
not understand how anyone could be consoled at
the loss of Blanche.

The hour drew near when Urbain could recompense himself for the day's absence.

"Only one day more," said he, as he approached the barber's house, "and she will be
mine." He hurried, his heart palpitating with
love, but on looking up at Blanche's window he

saw no light, and this slight circumstance astonished him and rendered him uneasy; or rather a secret presentiment warned him of his misfortune, for, in love, presentiments are not chimeras.

Urbain knocked and Marguerite appeared, but the grief depicted on her face, her eyes filled with tears, announced that something had happened.

"Where is Blanche?" cried Urbain, looking fearfully at Marguerite.

The old woman could only sigh deeply, but Urbain was no longer near her, he ran, he flew to the room of his beloved, but that room was deserted, its charming occupant was gone. Marguerite slowly followed the young man.

"In mercy tell me," cried Urbain, "where is she? Hide nothing from me."

"My poor boy, collect all your courage. Last night somebody carried off our dear child."

Urbain remained motionless and overwhelmed, while Marguerite told him all that she knew. He listened without interrupting her, and seemed as if he could hardly yet realize his misfortune, but presently, dropping on Blanche's favorite seat, he yielded to the profoundest despair. The tears rolled down his face; at nineteen years of age one sheds them still in the troubles of life; one has not then that strength of mind which is later acquired in the school of misfortune.

Marguerite tried to calm Urbain by saying to him, —

"You will recover her, that dear child, for you are not capable of forgetting her, and coldly consoling yourself for her loss."

"I forget her?" said Urbain, pressing the hands of the good old woman. "Ah, Marguerite, is not my life bound up in that of Blanche? I shall take no rest until she is with me again."

"That's right, my dear Urbain, to hear you speak thus renders me hopeful; besides, our poor little one has with her a talisman, and that lightens my anxiety a little."

"Tell me all the circumstances again; a man came here, you say?"

"Yes, he said he was sent by my master, and came to speak to Blanche."

"The scoundrel! and what did he say to her?"

"Oh, he merely paid her some compliments. He spoke like a great nobleman, and he had the costume and bearing of one, although M. Touquet pretends that he is a wretch without position and without home."

"He knows him, then?"

"There's no doubt of it. I confess to you that I am afraid, although he did not have a wicked appearance, rather a look of pride, and an imperious tone. I was sorry at having opened the door for him, and Blanche, the poor little thing, trembled. But all this didn't last very long. He heard M. Touquet come in, and immediately the stranger took his mantle, saluted

Blanche, and went down to monsieur. I followed him, but they sent me away, and I know nothing further."

Urbain left Marguerite, he darted from the chamber and, in an instant, he faced the barber, whose cold and gloomy look contrasted with Urbain's excitement.

"Well, monsieur, what have you learned? what have you done to recover my bride," cried he. "Speak! what do you know?"

The barber, rendered rather uneasy by the vivacity of Urbain's questions, answered hesitatingly, —

"I have made a thousand inquiries, I can discover nothing."

"And this scoundrel who came here yesterday, who is he?"

"I hardly know him. He sometimes came into my shop, for what purpose I do not know, and I swear to you that he must have heard of Blanche's beauty, for he had never seen her, and formed the idea of introducing himself to her."

The barber appeared so sincere in pronouncing these words that Urbain repented of having suspected him.

"Forgive me," said he, "for daring to think — but you would not make us unhappy. You have given me Blanche, you have been to her as a father. Oh, you will join with me, will you not, in endeavoring to find her ravishers?"

"Yes," answered Touquet in a low tone, "I shall second you, I promise you."

"And the name of that man, you must know it?"

"I never dreamt of asking him his name. Yesterday, on my showing him immediately that his love for Blanche was a folly, he retired, making many threats to which I paid little attention."

"Who could have given him the information which led him to wish to see her? and how could he get into Blanche's room?"

"A few false keys would be sufficient for that, and in this city, you know, nobody is safe in his own house."

Urbain remained silent for some moments and the barber avoided his looks; finally the bachelor exclaimed, —

"Good-by, monsieur, I am going to seek for her whom you gave me to be my bride."

"May you be successful," answered the barber in a gloomy voice, as Urbain abruptly departed, thinking of nothing but Blanche, but not knowing where to direct his steps.

Urbain went first to the different gates of Paris; there he demanded if during the previous night anyone had seen a young woman pass, and gave a description of her. He was sure that everybody would notice Blanche, and that her charming features would fix themselves upon the memory; but he did not obtain the slightest information, they hardly answered him. His simple costume prevented their putting themselves out to oblige him, for in the good old times, as well as today, it was necessary to scatter gold in order to expedite any business.

" If all these people could know Blanche," said Urbain, " they would not show so much indifference."

Not daring to leave Paris without having some indication as to the way that he should take, Urbain continued to walk as chance led him in the capital, though the inhabitants had for some time retired to rest. Thieves, lovers, and soldiers of the watch, alone showed themselves in the gloomy streets of Paris. The young bachelor traversed many streets without meeting anybody, but he still walked on, saying, —

" Why should I go in, I could not sleep, and what could I do with myself at home?"

However, love and despair do not render one indefatigable. Urbain had been walking since eight o'clock in the evening, and it was now nearly three o'clock in the morning. His legs began to fail him, he felt that it would soon be impossible for him to go any further. He looked around him. The moon, which showed at intervals, allowed him to distinguish the junction of some lonely cross roads into which converged some lanes which led to the marshes. Urbain turned towards a large stone which he perceived some steps from him, for he thought he would there seat himself and wait for day, but as he reached the stone his feet struck against something which he had not perceived, and a voice immediately exclaimed, —

"Oh, by jingo! don't kill me; I haven't a sou now."

CHAPTER VIII

THE CHÂTEAU DE SARCUS

THE carriage which contained the unfortunate
Blanche bowled steadily along for several hours,
and in the excitement occasioned by this novel
journey, the lovely child hardly remembered her
former fears. After living in the most absolute
retirement, shut up for years in a single room except at meal times, it seemed like a dream to find
herself in a carriage in the middle of the night,
and alone journeying into the wide world, she
knew not whither. However, the noise of the
wheels and of the horses' feet, mingled with the
cracking of the postilion's whip, as he sought to
increase the speed of his horses, which were already
going like the wind, and the rocking of the vehicle as it swayed from side to side alarmed her
very much and persuaded her of the reality of her
situation.

"I am going to see Urbain," said the trembling traveller to herself, "I am going to rejoin
him; I should not give way to my fears, we are
going to be so happy. Why, since we are about
to be united forever, should I feel anything but
pleasure at hastening the moment? But then, I

had hoped to travel with Urbain and everything
has turned out so differently. Poor Urbain, it's
not his fault; but why did he fight? Oh, I am
so anxious to be with him!—and Marguerite
didn't even say good-by to me. It seems as
though everybody had abandoned me."

The sweet girl dried the tears which had mois-
tened her eyes, then she looked out of the windows, but the darkness prevented her from seeing
anything; she sighed and sank back in the carriage.

"Where are we? I don't know, but it seems to
me they are going very fast. Well, so much the
better, I shall be the sooner with Urbain."

As soon as day began to break, Blanche, who
kept looking out of the windows, could partly
distinguish trees, fields, and houses. Presently
the mist was entirely dissipated, and the young
traveller admired the glory of the dawn, and the
varied scenes which seemed to fly before her.
Soon the carriage rolled along a road bordered
only by trees and hedges; the branches of some
old trees from time to time brushed the top of
the carriage, and this unexpected sound made the
inexperienced traveller tremble. All of a sudden
the view extended widely; the road was edged
with meadows and rich fields. The laborers were
already going to their work; already the furrows
made by the plough could be seen, and the spade
had newly broken the sweet-smelling earth. The

trees were still bare of foliage, but the tips of the branches were reddened and about to break into bud. Everything announced the return of spring. Farther on they passed through a village, the early rising inhabitants of which could be seen at their doors or their windows, hastening to watch the carriage passing so rapidly. Contentment and health were pictured on the face of each peasant; it was their only ornament, for cleanliness and neatness are not distinguishing traits of the country people, whose children play on the manure heap, pell-mell with the ducks and geese. But nature is not always pleasing, and it is not in the outskirts of Paris that one must seek for the shepherds of Florian, the herdsmen of Bertin, the seductive villagers of our comic operas.

Country scenes always please the pure and simple mind, and Blanche, as she passed the villages and farms, and hamlets, exclaimed, —

" How delightful to live here, to walk, to run in the fields and in the woods! Oh, how happy I shall be with Urbain!"

Indeed, the fields and the woods bore a more smiling aspect than the Rue des Bourdonnais, and the barber's gloomy house.

The carriage did not stop; the postilions had orders to speed straight to the château, though the horses should die at the journey's end. Blanche did not know how far from Paris was Urbain's house and country, besides, she did not remem-

ber ever before being in a carriage, and it seemed
to her that in moving so quickly they must have
gone a very long way. About an hour after midday they passed through the pretty town of Grandvilliers, where a great number of manufactories afforded work and means to the inhabitants; but
they did not stop there, and the carriage, turning
to the right, crossed a wide plain and diverged
towards a building which could be seen at a little
distance, and which was justly called the wonder
of the country side. It was the Château de Sarcus, of which the elegant façade could be discerned
in the distance. Blanche perceived the château,
but she was far from thinking that her journey
would terminate there, though she gazed at that
magnificent dwelling and, as the carriage rolled
nearer, she could easily distinguish the sculptures
and admire the work of artists who had surpassed
themselves in order to merit the approbation of
that gallant monarch, who patronized the arts as
much as he admired beauty.

At last they reached the front of the château,
and the carriage, in place of passing, entered the
confines of this handsome domain.

"Well, now, what is the matter?" said Blanche
trying to open the door. "This is not the place,
this cannot be right; Urbain hasn't a big house
like this — the coachman is mistaken."

However, the carriage stopped in a spacious
courtyard. A servant in rich livery opened the

door, and with a respectful air offered his hand to help Blanche alight.

"Oh, no, I don't wish to get down," said the innocent child, looking at the servant in astonishment, "this is not the place I was coming to; certainly they are mistaken, this is a château, it cannot be Urbain's house; besides, he would have been very prompt to meet me."

"No, madame, they are not mistaken," answered Germain, the marquis's valet, who had arrived two hours before the carriage, in order that he might give instructions to the house porter, and have rooms prepared for Blanche. "Your journey terminates here, and everything is in readiness to receive you."

"Here?" said Blanche, as she lightly stepped from the carriage, and looked around her in surprise, "but where is he?"

"He has not yet arrived, madame," said Germain, who had received strict orders to name nobody and to answer the young girl in conformity with the ideas she had formed in regard to her journey.

"What, he's not here yet? and I believe he started before me. He hasn't come here directly, then? Oh, I understand! fearing lest he be pursued, he has been obliged to hide and to make some detours."

"That's it, I am quite sure," answered the valet, smiling, "and I don't think he can get here before evening."

"Poor Urbain, how tiresome to have to wait until this evening."

"If madame desires to follow me, I will lead her to the apartments which have been hastily prepared for her."

"I'm not madame, my name is Blanche. We are not yet married, but as soon as he arrives I hope to be his wife. Show me the way, monsieur, I will follow you."

The man entered a spacious vestibule and mounted a marble staircase, then he led Blanche through some superb galleries, along one side of which were windows of stained glass, while upon the other the walls were adorned with pictures representing the most pleasing mythological subjects. In viewing all that met her sight, Blanche could not restrain her astonishment. She paused and said to Germain, — in a voice which she tried to render still more touching, —

"Monsieur, I beg of you, tell me the truth, — does this superb dwelling belong to him?"

"Yes, mademoiselle, indeed this château does belong to him."

"Ah, I thought it was a château! and he said he had only a little house, and this one appears to me immense ; he must be very rich to have a château like this, and Urbain sometimes regretted that he had not a large fortune to share with me."

"Perhaps he wished to surprise you, mademoiselle."

"That was wrong of him; rich or poor I should love him just as much. Mon Dieu! how large it is, these galleries, these beautiful rooms, we shall be lost here; and how surprised Marguerite will be. Monsieur, are there cows and rabbits here?"

"There shall be everything here that you desire, mademoiselle."

"Urbain has promised me a beautiful cow, and I should like to milk her and to make butter and cheese, that would be so amusing."

Germain turned away to hide his smiles, because the country taste of the young girl appeared very singular to the servant of the great nobleman, but soon he opened a door saying, —

"This is the apartment which they have prepared for you, mademoiselle; if it does not please you, you will choose any other in the château and they will hasten to execute your orders."

"Oh, I like this above everything," said Blanche, as she entered a richly furnished room, adorned with full-length mirrors, "It is very fine here," said she, examining the hangings, draperies and candelabras which ornamented the apartment. She then passed into a second room, decorated with the same sumptuousness, in which was a bed hung with silk curtains, with silver fringe.

"If he were here," said Blanche, sighing, "all this would please me much better. And these windows, what do they look on?"

Germain hastened to open the windows which were all provided with vast balconies. Blanche advanced, and could not restrain an exclamation of pleasure on perceiving a lake which bathed the walls of that part of the château in which her apartments were situated. The lake extended into the middle of a wide meadow, and finally lost itself in some rocks, where the water fell in a cascade into an immense basin. On the right of the meadows one could see woods and shrubberies, and on the other side the view extended itself, far and wide, over a country dotted with hills which afforded a charming landscape.

"Oh, how charming it is," cried Blanche, "what a beautiful view!"

"Mademoiselle can hardly have an idea of what the view is when the fields are covered with verdure."

"But I should like very much to walk in all these places which I see, to run in those meadows and to go on that lake, whose waters bathe these walls and seem to me so pure."

"That is very easy, mademoiselle, for the park belonging to this château extends as far as you can see. When you wish to visit the gardens, run about the park, or boat on the lake, I will hasten to attend you."

"What! does all that I see belong to Urbain?"

"Yes, mademoiselle, all that pertains to the château."

Each word of Germain augmented Blanche's surprise. She could not conceive that her beloved could have deceived her so far. However, she had not the least suspicion of the treason of which she was the victim. The servant pulled the bell and a young country woman came into the room and awkwardly curtseyed to Blanche, who returned her salutation with good will.

"Mademoiselle, this young girl is at your orders. She will serve you as chambermaid if you are willing to accept her services."

"Oh, I can do everything for myself very well; I do not need anybody, I thank you."

"In any case, Marie will come as soon as you ring. Mademoiselle must need rest after the fatigue of the journey; we will retire."

"Yes, since he will not come until evening I will try to sleep a little. The time will seem shorter."

Germain made a sign to Marie, who after having made two other curtseys, left, followed by the marquis' valet. Left alone in her new apartment, Blanche glanced around her with surprise. All that had happened to her since the evening before seemed like a dream. She paused before the furniture, the mirrors, and murmured, sighing, —

"All this belongs to him, but why this mystery? He feared, perhaps, to be loved only for his fortune. Ah, dear Urbain, it is you only whom I love, and I should very quickly leave this fine château if it were necessary for me to dwell in it without you. But we shall be very happy here together, although it will be rather large for us two."

Fatigued by her journey, Blanche threw herself upon the bed. Soon slumber closed her eyes, she rested tranquilly, believing that she was under Urbain's roof.

It was four o'clock when the young girl awakened. Her first care on rising from the bed was to go and look at a clock on the mantelpiece.

"Evening is still far distant," said she sighing, "and what can I do until then? It seems to me that I'm lost in this fine château. If only Marguerite were here, we could talk about Urbain, that would make the time pass quicker."

In glancing about the chamber she perceived a little door which she had not remarked before; she opened it and found herself in a dressing-room where everything was gathered that could be agreeable to a woman of fashion, but Blanche looked indifferently at a handsome dressing-case furnished with rarely beautiful objects. In her plans for a happy future she had seen only a small farm, a stable, a dovecot, and a garden, and her mind could not become accustomed to replace it by the château. She left the dressing-room and returned to the first room, where she saw a table covered with all that could tempt the appetite.

"How attentive they are," said Blanche, "really

they treat me like a queen. Urbain must have told them to take every care of me."

Blanche rang and Marie answered, but she was followed by Germain, who did not wish to lose sight of the chambermaid before the arrival of his master for fear she might inform Blanche of that which he still wished to conceal.

" Was this table laid for me?" said Blanche.

" Yes, mademoiselle," answered Germain, " I thought you would need some breakfast. Excuse me if I offer you nothing but that, but not being forewarned — "

" Nothing but that! You are laughing, no doubt. There is enough here to suffice ten persons, and at M. Touquet's we never had more than two dishes for our dinner."

Blanche seated herself at the table. Germain remained at some distance, and Marie served her without opening her mouth, but curtseyed to her every time that she handed her a dish. So much ceremony fatigued the young girl, who was accustomed to a simple, frugal life. She soon left the table and evinced a desire to walk in the park. Germain immediately led her through a gallery and several passages to a staircase, at the foot of which was an entrance to the gardens. Blanche breathed more freely in the meadows than under the sculptured ceilings of the château. She left the borders of the lake, crossed a little wood and found herself presently in what was designated as

the English park, of which the paths crossed each
other and formed a thousand detours, but when
Blanche turned she always saw Germain in the
distance, who had never lost sight of her.

"He's no doubt afraid that I shall lose myself," said she, "this is all so vast that it would
be easy to lose one's way."

Blanche returned to the château ; Germain led
her back to her apartments, and then asked at
what hour she wished to dine.

"I would much rather wait and sup with Urbain, for he will come this evening, will he not,
monsieur ? "

"I think so," answered the valet, bowing, and
he departed, leaving her sad and thoughtful, for
these words, "I think so," did not seem positive
enough for her. She stationed herself on one of
the balconies which looked on the lake and there,
her eyes fixed on the horizon, gave herself up to
her thoughts, and invoked the night which should
reunite her with her lover. Soon her eyes could
not distinguish distant objects, a light mist seemed
to rise and obscure the scene ; presently the perspective diminished, the horizon closed in ; finally,
she could see only a few steps before her, and
Blanche left the balcony, saying, —

"Night is here, he will come."

Germain entered the room and lighted several
candles.

"As soon as he arrives," said Blanche to the

man, "do not fail to tell him I am here — that I am waiting for him."

"His first care will be to seek you, mademoiselle," answered the valet smiling, and he departed, inviting Blanche to ring if she should desire anything else.

Had not Urbain's face been incessantly before the mind of the young girl, perhaps she would have experienced some fear on finding herself alone at night in a place which she hardly knew, in the middle of a room which seemed to her immense in comparison with the little room which she had occupied at the barber's, but love is the best remedy against fear, and the young girl, who would not go down into the cellar without trembling, although she had a light in her hand, would willingly go there without a candle were she sure of finding her lover. The clock struck nine.

"He cannot be much later," said Blanche, "provided nothing has stopped him on the way, for M. Touquet told me he would be here before me."

She sighed, and opening a window went on to the balcony to contemplate the reflection of the moon on the tranquil surface of the lake ; she was astonished at the silence which reigned in the château, where everything seemed as still as the moonlit landscape. This profound quietude did not indicate the arrival of Urbain, and at that moment Blanche wished to hear some sound which would at least break the solitude of the night. She tried to console herself by saying, —

"My rooms are probably distant from the entrance to the château; this house is so big I cannot hear what passes in other parts of it."

An hour rolled by, and the uneasiness, the sadness, which had taken possession of the young girl caused her to pass alternately from her room to the balcony. Sometimes she opened the door of her room and ventured into the gallery.

Joy and hope no longer animated her beautiful eyes, and she could hardly restrain her tears. At last she dropped into an immense easy chair and said in a broken voice, —

"What new misfortune could have happened to him?"

Suddenly a loud noise was heard. Blanche rose, listened, and thought she distinguished the sound of carriage wheels, the hoofs of horses, and the barking of dogs. Presently the opening and shutting of doors was heard.

"He is come," cried the young girl, and she was about to pass along the gallery to go and meet her lover, but there was no light, she did not know the way and would become lost in all these immense rooms; it would be much better to wait for him in her own. She still listened. The sound of wheels had ceased, but she occasionally heard steps and voices.

"Somebody surely has arrived," said Blanche.

"It can be nobody but Urbain; but why does he not come to me?"

She ran to the bell and pulled the cord several times. Nobody came. Greatly astonished at this, she was about to take a light and venture into the gallery when hasty steps approached.

"Here he is at last," exclaimed she, running immediately to the door, and remaining motionless with surprise and fear on seeing before her the stranger who, on the preceding night, had visited the barber's house.

The marquis paused on the doorsill. He bowed to Blanche with a look at once tender and respectful. The latter had hardly recovered from her surprise, and looked anxiously into the gallery, saying to the marquis in a touching voice, —

"Is not Urbain with you?"

Blanche's accents were so sweet, her voice expressed so much anxiety of mind, that Villebelle felt profoundly moved, and for the first time, perhaps, experienced some remorse at the pain which he was about to cause the young girl. Blanche repeated her question in a supplicating tone, and the marquis answered, turning away his eyes, —

"I came alone."

"O monsieur, in mercy tell me what has happened to him!" exclaimed Blanche, approaching the marquis and extending her arms towards him in her anxiety.

Villebelle looked at her and in that moment the

various feelings which agitated the charming child,
rendered her still more seductive. Her eyes were
more animated than usual, her lips, half opened,
disclosed two rows of pearls, and her hair falling
in disorder over her forehead, gave a new expression to her angelic face. The marquis felt his remorse vanish at the sight of so many charms.
Habituated, besides, to treat virtue as a chimera
and constancy as a folly, he flattered himself that
he would soon be able to dissipate Blanche's
grief, and now, wishing to undeceive her, he fell
on his knees, saying, —

" Deign to forgive me, lovely girl ; this château
belongs to me. You are not in Urbain's house,
but in the house of a man who adores you and
will use every means to promote your happiness."

Blanche seemed as though she did not comprehend him ; she looked at him affrightedly, repeating, —

" I am not at Urbain's house ? But, monsieur,
where is he then ? "

" I'm not very uneasy about that, and I should
advise him not to come here to seek you."

" But it is with Urbain that I should be, monsieur. They were mistaken in bringing me here,
I said so at the time ; I knew Urbain could not
have such a grand house. You are going to make
them take me away immediately, are you not, monsieur ? "

" No, my dear child, it was I who caused you to be abducted and I will yield you to nobody."

"Abducted?" she cried, "what are you saying? Urbain had fought a duel and had to flee, that is why I started in the middle of the night."

" It was necessary to tell you that, in order that you might leave willingly."

" O my God! could that be so? But, no, it was my protector, it was M. Touquet himself, who put me in the carriage."

" Yes, adorable Blanche, it was your protector, it was the honest Touquet who aided my plans and gave you up to my love."

The frightful truth flashed into her mind, her knees failed her, the color left her cheeks, and without uttering a single cry she was about to fall upon the floor. Happily the marquis received her in his arms, he laid her on the bed and rang the bell violently. Germain immediately appeared.

" Call someone, call for help," said the marquis, greatly agitated, "she has lost consciousness. Is there not a woman here in the château?"

"Pardon me, monseigneur." Germain called Marie, and the stout country girl came running.

"Give all your care to this young girl," said the marquis to the woman, " and do not leave her for an instant. If she is long in coming to her senses, send me word."

" Very well, monseigneur," said Marie, curtseying, and Villebelle left the room with Germain.

The marquis, fatigued by his rapid journey from Paris, threw himself upon a lounge as soon as he reached his apartment, and while Germain relieved him of his travelling dress he inquired as to what Blanche had said and done since her arrival.

" Monseigneur," said Germain, " she believed that she was at the house of M. Urbain, and following your orders I have not undeceived her."

" She appears to love him more than I had believed," said Villebelle, sighing.

" 'Tis but the love of a young girl, monseigneur, a fierce fire, which soon burns itself out."

" May what you say be true, but Blanche bears no resemblance to other women whom I have seen up to this day. There is about her a candor, a frankness, finally, a something, I know not what, which commands respect. I cannot explain to you the feeling with which she inspires me. Her tears sear my heart. I wish to win her love by the attentions which I shall lavish upon her. It will take some time, perhaps; but no matter, I feel capable of restraining my passion, of submitting to everything which she may exact of me. You see, Germain, that I am truly in love, for I no longer recognize self, and near Blanche I feel as timid as a child."

" We must see if that will last, monseigneur."

" Ah, you don't understand what I experience. Germain, you must start tomorrow morning for Paris; I will give you what money is necessary, and you will bring back everything you can find of the prettiest and newest in ornaments, stuffs, and jewels. Spare nothing, that we may find something to please Blanche."

" Rely on me, monseigneur."

" How many servants are in the château ? "

" The old porter, who never leaves his door, believing himself the guardian of a citadel; his daughter Marie, whom monseigneur saw just now, and who is the only woman I found at the château."

" Is she capable of waiting on Blanche ? "

" Oh, yes, monseigneur, she's rather stupid, rather awkward, but very faithful and obedient. Her father answered to me for that; besides, Mademoiselle Blanche seemed to prefer to do without a chambermaid."

" Well, go on."

" The gardener, an old idiot, who knows nothing except plants. As to the country people whom we employ, they never come inside the house. Oh, I forgot, an old cook and cellarman, very drunken, so far as I can see, but he is never permitted to leave his kitchen and, in the absence of his masters, shuts himself up in the cellars."

" That is well, but it is necessary to have some people here who can watch Blanche or else she will doubtless find some way to escape, if, in time, she should form such a plan, and I brought from Paris two lackeys who will acquit themselves perfectly in this employment. Ah, Germain, if I can only make Blanche love me, how happy I shall be ; but I am anxious to have news of her, go down and call Marie, I cannot remain in this anxiety."

Germain went down, but soon returned with the young peasant, who had already left Blanche.

" Well, how is she ? "

" That young lady, monseigneur ? "

" Certainly."

" Oh, she returned to her senses some time ago, monseigneur."

" And what did she say then ? "

" On my word, monseigneur, lots of things that I couldn't understand — Oh, wait, I remember, she asked me if you were master of the château, and as soon as I said ' Yes,' she began to cry."

" She wept ? "

" Oh, yes, monseigneur, she did nothing else, and then she asked me your name."

" What did you answer ? "

" Mercy, I said that you were called monseigneur le marquis."

" She asked you no other questions ? "

" No, monseigneur."

" And why did you leave her ? "

" Monseigneur, it was because she told me she would like me to leave her."

The marquis signed to them to leave him. He did not wish anyone to witness the emotion which

he felt. It gave him satisfaction to know that
Blanche was within his walls, but the sorrow which
she showed disturbed his content. He dared not
go back to her yet, deeming it wiser to allow her
time to recover from the first pangs of her grief.
He threw himself upon his bed, but he could not
sleep. The image of Blanche was incessantly before his eyes, and with her came the remembrance
of the many errors of his youth which he wished
in vain to drive from his mind.

While Villebelle endeavored to account for his
insomnia and agitation by attributing it to love,
Blanche passed in tears that night which she had
awaited with so much impatience. Convinced at
last that she was in the power of the man to whom
the barber had delivered her, she felt all the horror of her situation; but accustomed by Marguerite to put all her confidence in a Supreme Being,
and to have no doubt of His power, she prayed
and besought Heaven to reunite her with Urbain.
Upon her knees, her hands raised toward Heaven,
and her eyes bathed in tears, she passed part of
the night, and morning found her still so occupied.

Marie came to take her orders. Blanche wished
for nothing, she desired nothing but her liberty,
and, in answer to that request, Marie brought her
breakfast. An hour later the marquis entered the
room. Blanche did not see him; she was seated
with her head supported by one of her hands and
appeared absorbed in sorrow.

Villebelle signed to Marie to leave them, and looked for some moments in silence at this young girl who had been, since the evening before, reduced to despair because she was pretty and had had the misfortune to please a rich and powerful man, who thought that she should be only too happy to be the object of his passion. However the change which had taken place in Blanche's features, her eyes reddened and still filled with tears, made a painful impression upon the great nobleman. He would have preferred reproaches rather than this silent grief. He drew nearer, that his victim might perceive his presence.

Blanche raised her eyes and looked at the marquis, showing only a slight uneasiness, and let her head fall again upon her hand. Villebelle had expected complaints and reproaches. Surprised at this silence he took a chair, and seated himself near Blanche, who remained silent and continued to weep.

"Are you so very unhappy then?" said the marquis at last, with emotion; and Blanche answered sobbing, but with the sweet tone which never left her,—

"Yes, monsieur."

"Can you regret the barber's gloomy house where you never had any pleasure?"

"It is not the house that I regret, monsieur."

"Here there is nothing to hinder you from being the most happy woman; all your desires shall be laws here, you shall have the most beautiful ornaments, the richest jewelry."

"I don't wish for them, monsieur."

"You will not always think so, my dear child. Formed to please, to attract homage, one day by your features and your toilets you will eclipse the most seductive ladies of Paris."

"I don't understand you, monsieur."

"Forget the years passed in retirement and commence a new life. This dwelling shall become a place of delight; parties and pleasures shall succeed each other here without interruption as soon as your beautiful eyes repay my efforts with a smile. The barber did not deserve your friendship; the wretch would not have brought you up had it not been for his interest to do so; you may dismiss all thoughts of gratitude from your heart. As to the young man to whom he wished to marry you, he is but a boy, somebody has told me, and will soon forget you."

"Urbain forget me!" cried Blanche, starting convulsively. Then she said in a calmer tone, falling back in her chair, —

"No, monsieur, Urbain will not forget me, for I feel sure I shall love him always, and our hearts had but a single thought."

The marquis rose, greatly annoyed, and walked about the room. In a moment he said, —

"It is, however, useless, mademoiselle, to nourish a sentiment which must henceforth be hopeless, for you shall never more see this Urbain, whom I hate without knowing."

Blanche looked supplicatingly at the marquis, approached him and threw herself on her knees, saying, in a voice broken by sobs, —

"Monsieur, what have I done to you that you should punish me like this? If, unknowingly, I have been guilty of any fault, forgive me, I beg of you, but do not separate me from Urbain."

"Rise, I beseech you," said Villebelle, who yielded in spite of himself to the emotion which he felt. "No, you are not guilty, lovely girl, it is I, I alone; yes, I am a monster to make you shed tears. Ah, why did I ever see you—but you are so pretty!"

"Monsieur, has any one the right to shut up a girl because she is pretty? If you punish me by shutting me up a prisoner in your château, that should be forbidden. Is it permitted to a great nobleman to torment poor people at his will? O my God! and the talisman which Marguerite gave me to preserve me from all danger! O poor Marguerite! if she only knew how unfortunate I am."

"Oh, well," said he, leaning towards Blanche, "since you hate me, since I am only an object of dislike to you — "

"I hate you!" said the innocent child, raising her sweet eyes to his. "Oh, no, monsieur, don't believe that; despite all the grief you have caused me, I don't know how it is, but I feel that I should like to forgive you, I feel that I could even love you."

" You could love me, delightful girl," exclaimed the marquis, intoxicated by these words. "O heavens, she could love me and I was just about to consent — oh, never ; rather would I die than lose you or yield you to another. You have given me a foretaste of so much happiness that the idea of it alone transports me. Blanche, Blanche, I shall do everything to merit the love which you allow me to hope for, but to renounce you — ah, that is henceforth impossible. I must leave you, that I may not see those tears which make me detest my love."

Villebelle left precipitantly. Blanche looked after him in surprise, understanding nothing of the transport which he had shown. She was far from conceiving that she had riveted her chains in confessing to the marquis that she had a feeling of friendship for him. Her pure heart did not know how to feign, and the feeling which she wished to give to the marquis was so different from the love she had for Urbain that she saw no harm in allowing it to appear. But Villebelle did not know how to read this ingenuous heart. He imagined that Blanche was about to respond to his love, and did not doubt but that he should, in time, cause her to forget Urbain.

The day rolled by without the marquis again

approaching Blanche. The latter tried to summon her courage, but could not persuade herself that the marquis had any intention except to keep her prisoner, and she had recourse to her talisman, hoping by means of it to abridge her sojourn in the château. In the afternoon, Blanche asked Marie the way into the park, and the stout peasant hastened to lead her to the entrance, where she left her, making a curtsey. Despite her innocent air, the country girl understood that her lord was in love with the young damsel. Marie had remarked Blanche's red eyes, and heard her deep sighs, and, while leaving her, she said to herself, —

"Zooks ! if monseigneur was in love with me, that would not make me cry ; far otherwise."

Although she was alone in the park, Blanche did not even conceive the idea of seeking to recover her liberty. She did not know the way, and was ignorant as to what place she was in, and how far from Paris. She felt that it would be impossible to leave without again falling into the power of the marquis, and she resigned herself to wait until he should send her to her lover. She did not suppose the marquis capable of keeping her always a prisoner, and did not yet divine all the dangers which surrounded her in the château.

Villebelle, learning that Blanche was in the park, hastened to join her there, and the young girl received him almost smiling, and although her features still wore a plaintive expression, she chatted with him on the objects which surrounded them, and answered him with her accustomed sweetness and grace. This conduct appeared so extraordinary to the marquis that he regarded Blanche with as much astonishment as love. However, far from emboldening him, he felt for her a most profound respect, and dared not speak of his love, and, not understanding the power which the child exerted over him, he remained for some time silent and thoughtful, walking at her side.

The next day Marie carried into Blanche's room the things which Germain had brought from Paris; an infinite quantity of those charming nothings invented so that rich men may more easily spend their money. The stout peasant looked on each object with ecstasy, while Blanche hardly took the trouble to look at them.

The marquis came to see his young captive, and perceived that she had not touched his presents.

" Do you disdain that which I am so happy to offer you ? " said he to Blanche.

" I don't wish for any of those things," answered she, sighing. " I do not need all of these ornaments in order to please Urbain. What would he say if he saw me in them ? "

" Still thinking of Urbain ? Have I not told you, mademoiselle, that you will not see him again ? "

"Yes, but I don't think you're so wicked as you wish to appear. How would it help you always to vex me so?"

"Blanche, have you not confessed that you were not far from loving me?"

"Yes, and I still feel the same. With Urbain and you I should be very happy."

"May I not hope by the ardor of my attentions, my love, that I may cause you to forget a first fancy, and that I alone shall occupy your heart?"

"You don't understand me, monsieur. I love Urbain as my lover, my husband; and you — I should like — I don't know, it seems to me that I could with pleasure call you my brother — or my father."

This confession did not entirely satisfy Villebelle, but he hoped everything from time and the constancy of his attentions.

Towards evening Blanche again went into the park, and as on the previous evening the marquis joined her. He walked near her, feeling his love increase every moment. The marquis could not recognize himself. This libertine, this seducer, who had triumphed over the most rebellious beauties, had become timid and fearful before a child who had no other safeguards than her innocence and her virtue.

Twelve days had passed since Blanche had come to the Château de Sarcus, and had wrought no change in the situation. Every morning the marquis paid her a visit, but when, yielding to the grief which she experienced on being separated from him she loved, the sweet child allowed her tears to flow, the marquis left her abruptly. In the evening they walked together in the park, but often in silence or exchanging only a few words. Blanche dreamed of Urbain, and Villebelle, satisfied in being near her, had not yet conceived guilty designs.

At the end of this time, a message from Paris apprised the marquis that his uncle was very ill, and desired to see him before he died. Villebelle, the sole heir of this relative, who was very rich, was obliged to go to him, and decided, although with regret, to leave Blanche for some days. He took Germain with him, but the men servants whom he left at the château had received their instructions; besides the sad Blanche had no idea of escaping. The marquis judged it better not to forewarn the young girl of his departure; and he left the château more in love than ever, and vowing to hasten his return.

CHAPTER IX

THE MEETING. PROJECTS OF REVENGE

WE left our disconsolate young lover at the moment when he was about to seat himself upon a huge stone, and was arrested in the act of doing so by an exclamation uttered by an unseen man.

The words pronounced by this individual have no doubt already caused the reader to recognize our Chaudoreille, who had remained in the place where the robbers, disguised as chair porters, had left him.

Urbain was startled on hearing himself thus addressed, but being one of those persons who are insensible to fear, he calmly seated himself on the stone, saying,—

" Pardon me, monsieur, I did not see you."

Chaudoreille half rose, looked at Urbain, and began to feel reassured. Besides, what had he to fear now? His money was gone and his costume would not be likely to tempt robbers. Rolande, it is true, was still left him, for the thieves had perceived that in his hands the weapon was not dangerous.

" By jingo ! you woke me up, comrade ; and I was having a delightful dream. I still had the two thousand livres of gold in my pockets, when I awakened to the sad reality. O thousand million mustaches! The thieves, the scoundrels! they have taken everything from me. I've had a fine experience; I don't own so much as an obole. O death! O fury! O despair!"

Chaudoreille again threw himself upon the ground, and pulled two or three hairs from his mustache. Feeling that this would not restore his crowns, he quieted himself, and again looked at Urbain, who was sighing deeply, and appeared to pay no attention to the despair of the despoiled man.

"What the deuce! this is a taciturn fellow," said the Gascon to himself; and then he again addressed Urbain.

"I'll wager that you have been robbed, also, comrade. This town is indeed infested with thieves and bandits; one is safe only in the midst of a patrol, and yet one can't be proud of the watch. It was that cursed theatre brought this misfortune upon me; those wretched comedians at the Hôtel de Bourgogne dared to mock at a gentleman of my race. Ah, Turlupin, my friend, I'll get even with you. Tomorrow I'll lay a complaint before the criminal magistrate, and I'll put you and Gautier-Garguille in a dungeon. But, alas, that won't restore my two hundred pistoles. I'll wager you haven't as much on you, comrade — hey? By jingo, you sigh as though they had despoiled you

of the towers of Notre-Dame. Were you robbed
in a sedan chair ? ”

A deep sigh was Urbain's only response ; then
he murmured to himself, —

“ Alas, I have lost her forever ! ”

“ I was sure he'd lost his purse,” said Chaudoreille, “ or rather, that some one had taken it from
him. Did you lose it in this neighborhood, comrade ? ”

Urbain looked at him in surprise, then he
said, —

“ I don't know where she can be. I have been
running all over Paris since eight o'clock, and I
have learned nothing.”

“ If you only had a lantern, that would help
you — was it very large ? If we recover it full,
comrade, you must share it with me. That's understood.”

Urbain rose and seized Chaudoreille by the
throat, and holding him tightly to the ground, exclaimed, —

“ Wretch ! do you dare to insult my sorrow ?
If I should listen to my anger — ”

“ O mercy ! do not listen to it, I beg of you.
Ugh, I can't bear it any longer. What the devil
sort of man are you ? Did you come from the
Château de Vincennes ? Because I offer to help you
look for your lost purse, you try to strangle me ! ”

“ My purse ? what, you were talking about
money ? ”

"How could I talk about anything else after having had so much of it as I have."

"Excuse me, monsieur, I didn't understand you."

"I'm beginning to see that; but, by jingo, we were nearly choked, that is to say, you choked me. What a grip you have, it's like mine when I hold Rolande. It appears that it's not money you've lost, then?"

"O monsieur, would to heaven it were! I would give all I possess to recover her whom I adore — she who was about to become my wife!"

"Poor simpleton," said Chaudoreille to himself, "it's on account of a woman that he's lamenting thus. He doesn't know what it is to lose two hundred pistoles, without counting the small change. But since he's not been robbed, I'll try to make him useful — if I could replenish my pockets by helping him to find his lass!"

The chevalier rose, and seating himself on a stone near Urbain, said to him, in a feeling voice,—

"Tell me your troubles, young man, I'm the protector of everything in nature that suffers — in consideration of a slight gratuity; but I never charge anything, trusting to the generosity of those whom I oblige."

"What could you do for me, monsieur? I have not the least trace of the abductors, nor of the route they have taken. Oh, I feel that courage has abandoned me."

"What a thing to say, young man! Courage should never leave you. For shame! — in all the phases of life it is courage which makes us equal the gods, who, in truth, should not fear death itself, since they are immortal. But to return to you. If you have money it is always a resource. I shall help you to find your sweetheart; two of my friends are detectives, that is to say, they operate as amateurs for the good of humanity. Tell me in what neighborhood did the little one live?"

"In the Rue des Bourdonnais, with the barber Touquet, who brought her up."

"At the barber's? Rue des Bourdonnais — and your sweetheart is named Blanche?"

"Yes, monsieur, do you know her? Oh, pray tell me."

"One moment, one moment, my young friend. Hang it! this is an event for which I — give us your hand; by jingo, you're very fortunate to have met me."

"What! can you help me to find Blanche?" and Urbain threw himself on Chaudoreille's neck.

"This young man is the one Blanche was going to marry," said the Gascon to himself, as he disengaged himself from Urbain's grasp. "It appears as though the marquis had already carried the little one off; but he has paid me, I have nothing more to hope for from him; so I must turn to the young lover's side. However, I shall be prudent and not let him know who I am, nor what I have done in this intrigue."

Urbain pressed Chaudoreille to explain himself, and the latter answered, in a mysterious tone, —

"I am acquainted with neither Blanche nor the barber, but one of my friends goes often to Touquet's shop. I remember now that he has often spoken to me of your approaching marriage."

"That's singular! M. Touquet advised the greatest secrecy, and he himself — "

"But, you see, some one must have spoken of it, since I know it. But a man of high rank, a great nobleman, was in love with your promised wife."

"A great nobleman! what is his name?"

"I don't know yet, but I shall learn it."

"And you are sure of this?"

"Oh, very sure; and it must be this nobleman who has taken away your sweetheart."

"I entreat you to let me know his name."

"Tomorrow, that is, to say, this evening, I hope to learn it. But be prudent, young man, and do not compromise me. I expose myself to great risk in thus helping you."

"Monsieur, you may count on my gratitude."

"I will count on it, you may be sure."

"And I may expect the information this evening?"

"Yes: be near the Porte Montmartre at nine

o'clock this evening. Take care to bring along
with you all the money you can get together, and
I will tell you all I have learned."

"Enough! Oh, that evening were here — "

"And, while waiting for it, I shall have need
of some crowns to give to the friend of whom I
spoke to you, and my pockets are empty because
I have been robbed so much."

"Here is all that I have upon me, monsieur;
take it, I beg of you."

"Very willingly, my young friend," said Chaudoreille; "but day is dawning; we must part
until this evening, at the Porte Montmartre."

"Oh, I shan't fail to be there, monsieur."

"And don't forget anything I have told you.
Good-by; I'm going to work for you."

Chaudoreille departed, and Urbain, slightly
restored by the hope imparted to him by this
man, went to his dwelling that he might there
wait for evening.

While walking alongside the Pont-Neuf, the
Gascon said to himself, —

"It seems to me that the marquis did the business very quickly. The little one is abducted;
this rascal of a Touquet is in connivance with the
marquis, I am certain. I must be audacious now;
the marquis is incapable of speaking of me; I
must go to Touquet's house without appearing
to know anything, and see what he will say to me;
besides, from prudential motives I shall remain

in the shop, and the first angry movement that I see him make, I will spring out of the door and draw a hundred people around me."

This plan settled, Chaudoreille began by going into the first eating-house which he saw, and, for fear of being again robbed, ate and drank to the extent of all the money which Urbain had given him. It was nearly ten o'clock when he left the table. This was the time when the barber's was always the most crowded, and it was the moment which Chaudoreille chose to go there. Before he went into the shop, he ascertained that Touquet was not alone; then he presented himself, and wished him good morning with a wheedling air. The barber answered in his customary tone. Nothing in his manner indicated that he had any suspicion, and Chaudoreille was reassured. However, when they were alone he did not lose sight of the door, while asking indifferently if there was any news.

"Everything is finished," said the barber, "they are married, they are gone, and I hope I shall hear nothing further."

"Oh, they are married," said Chaudoreille, compressing his lips, "the little one has a husband. Her little lover?"

"Why, of course," answered Touquet, brusquely. "What is there surprising to you in that?"

"Me? By jingo! I'm no more surprised than a fly."

" Wait, here is what I promised you. I intend shortly to sell this house, and to retire from business. I have no further need of your visits; you have no more music lessons to give here, so you need not take the trouble to come again. Good-by, I will make you a present of all the shaves for which you owe me."

" Very much obliged, my dear friend, may I be able to prove all my gratitude to you some day."

So saying, Chaudoreille passed through the doorway, and departed from the barber's house.

" He forbids me to return to his house," said the Gascon. " That's very polite. The rascal is afraid that I shall meet the marquis there. The latter probably ordered him to share with me the gratuity he gave him on receiving the pretty little sweetheart at his hands; but patience! if you are a scoundrel, my dear Touquet, I flatter myself that I am also an adroit enough chap. I have no desire to return into your hornets' nest. Come, Chaudoreille, we must show some genius here, my friend. I must set to work to repair last night's losses and to make my fortune over again. Devil take me, though, if I ever again take a sedan chair. First I'll go to the little house in the Faubourg and learn from Marcel if it was there that the marquis led Blanche; after that I shall come back into Paris and go to our jealous Italian's house; there I shall tell her all about it,

— I shall tell her all about it! She'll go into convulsions over it. Finally, I'll keep the appointment I made with the young lover, and after having made him pay me well, I'll tell him all that I know. After that each one of them may win out of it as they best can. As for me, as soon as my pockets are full, I shall settle myself in a faro house, and I will there dare fortune in the midst of players and bankers. By jingo! what a pleasing prospect."

While laying these plans he took his way towards the Faubourg Saint-Antoine. He arrived all out of breath at the little house, and, while opening to him, Marcel asked him if by chance he had again killed a strange prince.

"Not today," said Chaudoreille, affectionately squeezing his friend's hand, which made the latter presume that his great fortune was already dissipated.

"Have you come for the purpose of buying a house in this neighborhood," said Marcel.

"There's no more question of that; I have been robbed, my friend, completely robbed. I took a sedan chair and the wretches who carried me took me into a den and put a dozen or fifteen men after me. Valor could do nothing against numbers; I think, however, that I killed three or four while defending myself. But let us drop that. Tell me, my dear Marcel, has the marquis brought here a new conquest?"

"I have seen neither monseigneur nor anybody from him."

"Marcel, you're lying."

"I'm telling you the truth. There's no one except me in the house."

"The devil! that upsets my ideas a little. You are very sure that you are not lying to me?"

"Why, hang it! if there had been anybody here I should have sent you away before this."

"Do you know if your master possesses any other little properties on the outskirts of Paris?"

"I know nothing except to follow the orders which he has given me, to eat and to sleep; for the rest I'm neither curious nor a gossip."

"You're very wrong, you'll never push yourself. Good-by, Marcel."

Chaudoreille took his way back to Paris, extremely dissatisfied that he had not discovered where Blanche was. Not wishing to go to Julia's house until he had learned more, he decided to make some inquiries at the marquis' hotel.

The brilliant Villebelle's hotel was worthy of its master, and was situated at a little distance from the Louvre. Chaudoreille slipped into an immense court and bowed low to the porter, while asking if monseigneur was in Paris.

"Monsieur le marquis is in England," said the porter, looking at Chaudoreille from the height of his grandeur, and the latter, seeing that he had no way of entering into conversation with the proud guardian, left the hotel, saying to himself, —

"In England? Does he wish to seduce the little one with plum pudding? My faith! I've done all that I can. Come now, let's go and tell the beautiful Julia all that I know. It's not more than five o'clock, I shall have plenty of time to keep my appointment."

Chaudoreille ran to the young Italian's house, where a servant opened the door.

"Is your mistress in?" said he.

"Yes, monsieur."

"Is she alone?"

"Yes, monsieur."

"Go and inform her that the Chevalier Chaudoreille has something of great importance to communicate to her."

The domestic returned shortly, and immediately took Chaudoreille to her mistress. Julia was walking up and down her room, deeply agitated.

"I was waiting for you," said she to the chevalier, signing to him to be seated.

"You were waiting for me, signora?"

"Yes, for I have not seen the marquis since I spoke to you. Never yet has he been so long without coming and I do not doubt but some new intrigue is the cause of his abandonment of me."

"Alas, signora, you have divined the truth only too well.

"Then I have been betrayed," cried Julia, making a movement of fury, while Chaudoreille went to seat himself at a respectful distance, putting Rolande across his knee.

"What did you expect, signora? Men are — men. The marquis did not know how to appreciate your grace, your charms, your — "

"Hold your tongue, and tell me immediately all that you know."

"She wants me to hold my tongue and yet speak," answered Chaudoreille, rolling his eyes affrightedly.

"The name of my rival? Answer me, wretch."

"It's this way, signora — but I beg you let me tell you that by order — "

"The name of my rival, I tell you," resumed Julia, approaching Chaudoreille furiously. The little man, trembling in all his limbs, muttered, —

"Blanche, an orphan, a young girl whom the barber was caring for."

"The scoundrel! I should have known it."

"Blanche was to have been married today to a young man whom she loved and who adored her. The barber had given his consent. I don't know by what chance monsieur le marquis came to see the young girl, but he must have fallen in love with her and abducted her, for the night before last she disappeared, and I strongly suspect my friend Touquet of having aided monseigneur's plans. At all events, the little one is not at the

Faubourg Saint-Antoine ; I have been there and the marquis is not in Paris, since I come from his hotel, where they told me he was in England."

Chaudoreille told all this without taking breath, fearing that Julia would do him some ill if he did not hasten his story.

" This voyage to England is a falsehood," cried Julia.

" I thought so myself."

" The marquis has taken the young girl to one of his châteaux."

" That is probable."

" But to which one ? That's what we must discover."

" I'm of your opinion, that's what we must discover."

" Perhaps this young girl is still in Paris."

" That might very well be. This city is a gulf, a young girl could be lost here like a piece of six liards."

Julia reflected for some moments, and Chaudoreille remained silent, waiting till she should speak that he might echo her words. The young woman walked up and down the room ; one could perceive by the trembling which had possession of her that it was only by a great effort that she restrained her fury. Finally, she stopped before Chaudoreille, and said to him, —

" You think, then, that this Blanche does not love Villebelle ? "

" I think that, at least, she does not yet love him, since she had never seen him."

" How can you be certain of that? "

" In fact — you are right, I'm not certain of it at all."

" Tell me everything that you know in regard to this young girl, how long she has lived at the barber's and his motive for adopting her."

Chaudoreille told Julia the same story that he had told the marquis, and she listened to him with the greatest attention. When he had finished she fell into deep thought, and Chaudoreille dared not disturb her.

" Touquet is a scoundrel," said Julia, " I have known it for a long time, but I wish now to obtain proofs of his crime, and if, in fact, it is he who has given Blanche to the marquis, he should tremble."

" That's right, crime must be punished," and Chaudoreille added to himself, " If she would only hang him, I should not have to fear him any longer."

" Is that really all that you know? " asked Julia.

" Oh, forgive me, signora; in the ardor of my zeal I forgot to tell you that by the greatest chance, I met Blanche's lover tonight. The poor devil was seated on a stone, and I was seated on the ground; I had been despoiled by bandits, who, by the way, have robbed me of the fruits of three years of economy and privations, which I was carrying to a savings bank. The unfortunate love to talk of their troubles ; we chatted and he told me that he was searching for his future wife. I didn't wish to tell him that I strongly suspected the Marquis de Villebelle of being the abductor of his sweetheart, before seeing you ; but I gave him a rendezvous for this evening at nine o'clock."

"Very good, go to this rendezvous and bring this young man to me."

"You want me to bring him to you, signora ? "

"Yes, bring him to my house ; we will plan together, we will unite our efforts ; he that he may recover his mistress, and I that I may punish the ungrateful man who has abandoned me."

"Indeed, that's very sensible, in acting together, you will hear more and do more. I will go to the rendezvous then, and I will bring young Urbain to you. Ah, by jingo ! I haven't yet taken anything today and I am afraid that I have no money about me."

"Wait, wait, take that," said Julia, "serve me faithfully and do not spare that gold."

"For fidelity I'm a veritable spaniel," said Chaudoreille, putting the purse in his belt. "I will go to an eating-house, I shall have time to eat a little and take a glass of spirits ; then I will go to the Porte Montmartre and bring our lover to you immediately."

Chaudoreille hurriedly left ; when he was in the

street he counted the money that was in the purse
and said to himself, —

"Really, if the young lover gives me as much
more I shall be in possession of a nice capital
again, without counting the small change; for this
Julia is a mine of gold waiting to be explored."

At nine o'clock he was in the neighborhood
which he had indicated to Urbain, but he did not
find the young bachelor there; which surprised
him after the desire which the latter had evinced
to see him again promptly. Chaudoreille walked
up and down, being careful to hold his purse in
his hand and to keep away from chair porters.
However, ten o'clock had struck and Urbain had
not come. The chevalier struck his foot impatiently, muttering,—

"Plague take all lovers! they're always half
fools; this one may have misunderstood me and
is perhaps waiting for me at the Porte Saint Hon-
oré, while I am waiting for him here. If I only
knew his address; this is a nuisance, by all the
devils."

Poor Urbain had understood very well, and in
going into his lodging at daybreak his only desire
had been to see the moment of his appointment
arrive. But who can foresee events. We are but
sorry creatures, and yet we form great plans for
the future.

> Today belongs to us;
> Tomorrow, to nobody.

Today, even, does not always belong to us entirely. Hardly had he reached his room when Urbain felt a shiver run through all his body; attributing this indisposition to the fatigue of the night, he got into bed, hoping that a few hours' rest would restore him to his usual health, but nature had not so ordered; a high fever ensued, and delirium took possession of the young man who, since the evening before, had entirely yielded to despair. The young neighbor who had assisted him in disguising himself, established herself at his bedside to watch; because she had a friendly feeling for Urbain, and because women are always ready to prove their friendship in pain as well as in pleasure.

This was the reason why Chaudoreille waited fruitlessly by the Porte Montmartre. Finally, at half-past ten, deeming it unwise to wait longer, he returned in a very ill-temper to the young Italian's house, who, seeing him alone, exclaimed, —

" Why did you not bring him with you ? "

" By jingo ! because I didn't see him."

" What do you say ? "

" I say, signora, that I have vainly watched for him since nine o'clock; Urbain did not come to the place of meeting."

"How vexatious! and you haven't his address?"

" No, if I'd had it I should have gone to his house. What the deuce could have prevented his coming ? "

" Perhaps he has discovered Blanche's retreat;
no matter, we shall find this young man again.
Chaudoreille, tomorrow at daybreak place yourself
in hiding near the barber's house; watch all his
movements, if he goes out follow him, and should
the marquis go to see him, run and let me know.
For my part, I shall go and watch the Hôtel de
Villebelle; it is more than probable that the marquis will repair there shortly. By watching the
movements of the marquis and the barber we shall
discover where Blanche is hidden, and then I shall
know what I ought to do."

" Your orders shall all be executed," said Chaudoreille, bowing to Julia as he left.

CHAPTER X

The Little Closet Again

A week had elapsed during which Julia had spent almost her whole time in loitering around the Marquis de Villebelle's hotel; she had not gained much by this however, for all that she could be sure of was that Villebelle was not there. Chaudoreille, for his part, had made no better progress; he was very sure that the marquis had not been to the barber's, and the latter kept very closely to his shop, rarely leaving home except to go to his customers' residences. What most surprised Chaudoreille was the fact that since he had watched he had not once seen young Urbain go to the barber's house nor had he encountered him in his prowling about the streets. He was ignorant of the fact of which the reader is well aware, that the young bachelor was still kept in bed by fever, and that the impatience and grief which had caused his illness had greatly retarded his convalescence.

Julia whose proud and haughty spirit could not endure the situation in which she found herself, keenly desired to wreak her vengeance on the lover who had betrayed and abandoned her, and

Villebelle being still absent, she charged Chaudoreille to take her place in the neighborhood of
the hotel, and stationed herself in the Rue des
Bourdonnais; Chaudoreille accepted this change
with great pleasure, delighted to leave the neighborhood of the barber's house.   The young woman did not intend merely to watch Touquet's
dwelling, she wished to introduce herself there, to
talk with Marguerite, to learn from the good old
woman all the details of Blanche's disappearance.
Julia was courageous and enterprising; she was
Italian, and she wished to revenge herself; and
thus possessed three times as much as was necessary to compass her ends.

     She was not afraid of Touquet, but she readily
felt that it was only in his absence that she could
hope to speak to Marguerite, and she formed her
plan in accordance with the information which
she had received in the neighborhood, in regard
to the old servant.   Towards evening, Julia saw
the barber leave his dwelling.   As soon as he had
departed, she went and knocked at the door of
the house.   Marguerite was disconsolate at having no news of her dear Blanche, and what com-
pleted the despair of the good old woman was
that she could hear nothing of Urbain.   When
she uttered the name of Blanche before her master
he ordered her to be silent in a severe tone, and
it was only in solitude that she dared to give way
without constraint to her grief.

"Who is there?" asked Marguerite, following her custom.

"Someone who brings you news of Blanche," answered Julia.

On hearing her dear child's name, Marguerite unhesitatingly opened the door; she had, besides, recognized a woman's voice, and grief had rendered her less fearful than formerly. Julia entered; she was wrapped in a black mantilla, larger than those in use among the Spaniards, and wore a cap of the same hue, from which two black feathers fell gracefully on her left shoulder. This costume, her decided step, and the animation which sparkled in her black eyes, gave to the whole person of the young Italian, a strangely fantastic distinction, but Marguerite did not notice all this, and exclaimed on seeing her, —

"Have you brought me back my dear Blanche?"

"Not yet, but I shall make every effort that you may soon see her again. In order to do this it is necessary that I should talk with you; take me to your room."

"But my master has forbidden me to receive anybody," said Marguerite, who began to regard Julia more attentively.

"Your master has gone out."

"He may come in at any moment."

"I know how to avoid him. You are very much afraid of him, are you not?"

"He's so strict."

"Come, my good Marguerite, don't let the fear you feel for the barber make you forget your dear Blanche. Upon the conversation which we shall have together, upon the information which you will give me, depends perhaps the success of my enterprise."

"Oh, to see my darling girl again, I feel that I would dare everything! Come, madame, follow me."

Marguerite went up to her room, followed by Julia, who closely scrutinized everything that she saw. While the old woman placed her lamp on the table and drew up some chairs, Julia took off her mantle; she wore beneath it a red robe, and in a black belt which surrounded her waist, she had stuck a little stiletto with an ebony handle.

This combination of red and black, which, following the old woman's chronicles, had always been the costume favored by magicians, the weapon which glittered in Julia's belt, all united to inspire Marguerite with a secret terror. She looked uneasily at the young woman and murmured, while offering her a seat, —

"May I know, madame, who you are, and where you have known my poor Blanche?"

"Who I am," answered Julia, smiling bitterly, "has no connection with the motive which brings me here. What does it matter, in fact, who I am, provided that I am willing to help you find the one for whose loss you are grieving, and that I have the power to do so."

"The power," repeated Marguerite, who began to be afraid of a private conversation with one who frequented witches' sabbaths, "Oh, you have the power?"

"As to your dear Blanche, I do not know her, and I have never even seen her."

These words greatly increased Marguerite's terror, but Julia continued without paying any attention to it,—

"Listen to me, good woman, my personal interest leads me to seek Blanche. The one who abducted her was everything to me, I adored him, I would have sacrificed my life for him, and the ungrateful man has forgotten me. Do you understand now, the motive which has caused me to act?"

"Oh, I breathe more freely," said Marguerite, "yes, madame, I understand ; this seigneur who came here is perhaps your husband. Alas ! that does not astonish me, men are truly most unaccountable creatures."

"Tell me all that you know, good Marguerite."

Marguerite told her of the marquis' visit and of all that he had said.

"He had never seen her before that day?"

"Never, I can certify to that."

"And you left the marquis with the barber?"

" The marquis ? was he a marquis then ? Well,
I had my doubts about it."

" Please answer me."

" Yes, madame, my master ordered me to go,
and I left him with this marquis."

" And what followed ? "

" I went to bed, madame, and I think that my
dear Blanche did the same."

" That wretch Touquet was in league with the
marquis.   It was he who delivered up to him that
young girl."

" What do you say, madame ? do you think
that my master ? —"

" Is a scoundrel ! "

" Speak lower, I beg of you ; if he should come
in, if he should hear you.   But you are mistaken,
madame, my master had consented to Blanche's
marriage to Urbain."

" The better to hide his plans."

" Poor Urbain, I never see him ; no doubt he
is still looking for our dear little one."

" Where was Blanche's chamber ?" said Julia,
looking curiously around her.

" On the first floor looking on the street, madame.   Since she came to this house she had occupied no other."

" It was to this house that she came, then, with
her father who was murdered ? "

" Yes, madame."

" Were you then in the barber's service ? "

"No, madame, I didn't come here until three years after."

"Where does your master sleep?"

"Directly underneath this. This is why, if he should come in, I am afraid that he would hear us speak."

"Have you always had this room?"

"No, madame, I formerly had the one above Blanche's, and I liked it much better than this gloomy chamber, which has been unoccupied for a long time, and which I believe was formerly the dwelling of a magician named Odoard."

Julia arose and for some moments walked silently about the room. All of a sudden she exclaimed, —

"Oh, if these walls could only speak!"

"In fact," said Marguerite shaking her head, "I believe that we should learn some terrible things; a tier of tags, a sorcerer."

Julia seemed to be thinking deeply when they heard the street door shut.

"O my God! here is my master, I am lost," cried Marguerite; "he has expressly forbidden me to receive anybody."

"Keep still, he shall not know that I am here. Does he sometimes come up into your room?"

"No, but — good Saint Margaret — if he should discover — "

Julia put a finger on her mouth, as a sign for the old servant to be silent. Presently the barber was heard calling Marguerite; who was trembling so that she did not know how to stand.

"Tell him that you are going down," said Julia.

Marguerite approached the door, then, thinking she heard her master coming upstairs, —

"Here he is — he'll see you," said she to Julia.

"You must hide me."

"Wait, I had forgotten it — quick — quick — in this closet."

Marguerite ran to her alcove, passed behind the bed, opened the little door hidden by the tapestry, and Julia, as quick as lightning, entered the closet. The old servant shut the door on her, took her lamp and hastened to go downstairs. Her master was in the lower room.

"You were very slow in coming down," said the barber, looking at Marguerite.

"Monsieur, at my age one cannot move quickly."

"Has anybody been here during my absence?"

"No, monsieur, nobody."

"Urbain, perhaps?"

"I assure you I haven't seen him."

"Chaudoreille?"

"No, nor him either."

The barber asked for what he needed and then made a sign to Marguerite to retire.

"Is monsieur going to stay up late?" asked she.

"What does that matter to you?" asked Touquet looking sternly at her, "I've already told you that I hate curious people as well as gossips."

"That's true. I'm going to bed, monsieur."

The old woman regained her room, closed the door carefully, and then went to release Julia, who had remained without a light in the little closet.

"Come, madame," said she, "come, you needn't stay in there now."

"A moment," said Julia, taking the lamp from Marguerite's hand, "I should like to examine this place."

"Oh, mercy! you will find nothing curious there. We went into it once, Blanche and I —"

"There is a door here," said Julia holding the light to the wall at the back.

"A door? do you think so? We didn't see it, but then we only remained for a moment and without a light."

Julia tried to open the door which led to the staircase, but she was not successful.

"This door is closed from the other side," said she, "it must communicate with some secret passage."

"What does it matter to you, madame? Come, I beg of you."

"It matters greatly to me. Oh, if I could acquire some proof to undo him."

"Proof of what, madame?"

" It's impossible to force this door."

Julia lowered the lamp and examined the floor to see if she could discover a trap door, while Marguerite remained at the entrance to the alcove to listen if her master should come up.

" What is in this big chest? " said Julia.

" It is empty, as you see. I don't know what use it is here, I shall burn it some day."

Julia stooped and lifted the chest, the better to examine it, then she thought she saw some object on the floor. She carried her light there, and found that it was an old portfolio of brown leather, which seemed to have been hidden beneath the chest, and appeared to have been there for some years, for the dust was thick around it. Julia uttered a joyful cry and seized the portfolio.

" What is it? " said Marguerite, " what have you got there ? "

" Something tells me that in this portfolio I shall find that for which I am looking."

" This portfolio? O my God ! where was it, then ? "

" Silence — come, let us shut this door again."

Julia left the closet, shutting the door, and when she had replaced the lamp on the table, hastened to examine the portfolio and the papers which it held. Meanwhile, Marguerite, still uneasy, remained listening near the door, but while doing so she watched Julia, whose features expressed the most lively agitation. Suddenly a cruel joy flashed in the young Italian's eyes, and she dropped on a seat near the table, exclaiming, —

" I shall be avenged."

" But who can that portfolio belong to ? " said Marguerite.

" To an unfortunate man whom your master murdered."

" Murdered ! ah, madame, what are you saying ? "

" Yes, everything proves it to me. This was the chamber in which he was lodged, because the secret passage would assist the murderer in the perpetration of his crime. The unfortunate man had, no doubt, visited this closet, and, without divining the misfortune which awaited him, had judged it prudent to hide under the chest his portfolio, which contains the proofs of an important secret."

" Ah, you make me shudder, madame."

Julia continued to examine the papers. Joy, surprise, hope, vengeance, were expressed in turn on her face.

" At last his fate is in my hands," exclaimed she, " perfidious man, to have betrayed me; tremble lest I inflict upon you torments more cruel than those you have made me suffer. And you, his odious accomplice, I will see that the marquis knows the monster who has assisted him in his amours."

Tremblingly Marguerite listened to Julia. The

latter put back the papers in the portfolio and carefully hid it in her bosom, then resuming her mantle she prepared to depart.

"And Blanche," said the good old woman, "you have not told me more about Blanche, madame."

"Reassure yourself," answered Julia in a solemn tone, "Blanche's condition will now be changed, you will see her again. Good-by, my good woman, keep the closest silence in regard to the portfolio ; Blanche's fate depends upon it."

"Fear nothing, madame."

"I'm going down without a light; Touquet should be in his room by now."

"If you should meet him ?"

"I will not make the least noise."

"But it is necessary that I should go with you to open the door."

"You need not, I can open it myself."

"There is a secret in opening it. O my God, for a mere nothing I would go with you from this house. All that you've said about my master makes me shudder, and since my dear child is no longer here I find this dwelling very gloomy."

"It's very necessary that you should remain here in order to give me, as well as Urbain, information in regard to all that the barber does. Before long, good Marguerite, you shall be happier, and reunited to your dear Blanche."

"Oh, may all that you say prove true."

"Open your door; I don't hear the least sound on the staircase; let us hasten."

The old woman groped her way down, Julia followed her; they arrived at the foot of the stairs and were about to enter the alleyway when the barber, coming brusquely from the corridor which led to the lower room, met them, bearing a light in his hand. Marguerite uttered a cry of fear; the barber quickly held the light against Julia's face.

"Well, do you recognize me?" she said to him in an imperious tone.

Touquet started with surprise, but forcing himself to restrain his anger, he answered, —

"You, at my house, madame! and what did you come to seek here?"

"Some news of Blanche."

"Of Blanche?"

"Yes, that astonishes you! you did not suppose that I knew this young girl? You believed that the Marquis de Villebelle could yield to his new passion without my knowing the object of it, without my learning that you were still the confidant of his amours."

Touquet's eyes blazed with fury as he said to Julia, —

"Jealousy has disturbed your reason, madame. If your lover has left you is it to me that you should betake yourself? Why should you suppose that the marquis is the abductor of a young girl whom he has never seen?"

"Your falsehoods are useless. I know a great deal more than you think. If you should see the marquis before I do, advise him to hasten to restore Blanche to Urbain. If by your perfidious counsels he should become guilty of — he would be the first to punish you for your crime. As for me, you will see me again; I also have a secret to reveal to you."

Thus speaking, Julia walked towards the door. The barber made a movement as if to stop her, but she turned and her hand still grasped her stiletto. Turning on Touquet a terrible look, she rapidly left his house.

CHAPTER XI

The Storm Brews

Too greatly agitated by what she had learned to retire and compose herself to rest, Julia several times during the night reperused the papers contained in the portfolio which she had found at the barber's, and she busied herself in forming new plans and meditating other projects of vengeance. The sleep she had defied did not once greet her eyelids, and dawn found her seated before a little table on which the portfolio was lying examining again a letter which she had taken from it.

At this moment, however, the bell rang thrice, and Julia hastened to lock the papers into their receptacle, and presently Chaudoreille entered her room.

"Well," was Julia's brusque greeting to the chevalier, "what have you learned?"

"Thanks to my assiduity I am at last enabled to bring you some important news," cried the little Gascon with a self-satisfied air. "For the past forty-eight hours I have not budged from before the marquis' hotel, minutely examining all who came or went."

" Well ? "

" Well, indeed! The marquis has returned."

" He is here ? "

" Yes, signora, at his hotel. I saw him arrive this morning in a travelling carriage."

" Very well, I shall see him, I hope."

" What orders have you to give me now? Where is it necessary for me to go ? I am ready."

" You have not yet seen this young Urbain ? "

" Alas, no, I'm of the opinion that the poor boy is dead from love; he was as thin as a cuckoo. I don't see what could have prevented his coming to our rendezvous."

" Return to the hotel. I tremble lest the marquis should leave without our knowing it, and in order to recover Blanche it is important that I should know the least step that Villebelle takes."

" That's very right. I'll return then to my post."

" Take this gold, but redouble your zeal; hasten; if you are tired, take a chair."

" I, take a sedan chair? I would much rather crawl all the way there. Don't disturb yourself, signora, my legs are always at my service."

Chaudoreille gone, Julia seated herself at her desk and prepared to write, but suddenly, throwing the pen far from her, she rose, exclaiming, —

" It's urgently necessary that I should see him, that I should speak to him; I will go to his hotel."

She immediately rang for her maid, and began to make her toilet. Despite the uneasiness she experienced, her mirror was often consulted, and she neglected nothing that would add to her charm. This important task accomplished, Julia sent for a sedan chair, and was carried to the marquis' dwelling. On entering the immense court of this magnificent hotel, the young Italian could hardly master her agitation.

"What does madame desire?" said the porter.

"To see the Marquis de Villebelle."

"Monseigneur returned from England only this morning, and as yet receives nobody."

"It is absolutely necessary that I should speak to him."

"That is impossible."

"Go, at least, and tell him that the Signora Julia desires to see him immediately."

The porter sent a lackey with this message, who soon returned, and said to Julia, with an impertinent air, —

"Monseigneur cannot receive you, and begs you to leave the hotel."

Julia could not swallow this affront; she looked furiously at the valet and abruptly left. Arrived at home she went to her desk and wrote the following note to the marquis, —

You refuse to see me; it depends, however, upon me to render you the most happy or most unhappy of men. I know that you are Blanche's abductor. Respect that young girl.

Hasten to listen to me ; I still wish to forgive you, but at some
moments I listen to nothing but my fury.

The letter written, she entrusted it to a faithful
man, and awaited his return with the most lively
impatience. The messenger at length came and
brought an answer from the marquis. Julia
seized it, and hastily read the following, —

My little Julia : your sweet note made me laugh a good
deal; I find nothing more pleasing than those women who
threaten us with their fury. The only vengeance which a
woman in your situation can take upon a man is to deceive him,
— and God knows whether you would use this means; but it
is necessary, in order that the charm may work effectually, that
it should be taken while he still loves you, without which it
fails of its object. Your reign is past, my dear friend. You
undoubtedly did not think to captivate the Marquis de Villebelle for long, and I sent you a check on my banker to settle
the account. I do not know who could have told you that I
had abducted a certain Blanche ; once more, what does it
matter to you ? Am I not entitled to abduct ten women if that
pleases me. Believe me, you had better not disquiet yourself
about my actions or give yourself the further trouble of writing
to me, for your letters will be returned to you unopened.
Good-by, hot-head, I wish you a faithful lover, since you hold
so much to fidelity.

Julia remained motionless, the letter was still
in her hands, but she did not see it ; one thought
alone occupied her, the thought of vengeance,
she seemed to give herself up to it with delight.

"You will have it, will you ?" said she, " I will
not hesitate longer."

However, the marquis was very much surprised that the young Italian should know who had abducted Blanche, and as soon as night came he wrapped himself in his cloak and went to the barber's house. Touquet himself opened to the nobleman, for the events of the night before and the fear which she had experienced seemed to have paralyzed old Marguerite, who was unable to leave her room.

"You here, monseigneur?" said the barber, with surprise, "I imagined that you were at your château, all taken up with your new love. Can it be that Blanche is already forgotten?"

"Forgotten? Why, I love her more than ever. But I was forced to come to Paris for some days, though I hope soon to return to Sarcus; each moment that I pass away from Blanche seems to me a century. However, I have not yet succeeded, and the remembrance of her Urbain — but let us come to the motive which has brought me hither. How is it that Julia knows that I have abducted Blanche? how could she have come to know this lovely child whom you kept with so much care?"

"You find me as much surprised as yourself, monseigneur. This young Italian had the audacity to introduce herself into my house yesterday evening; she presented herself, so my old housekeeper tells me, as bringing news of Blanche, but really she came to gather the details of her flight."

"She came also to my hotel; I refused to see her; she wrote to me, she threatened me. My fate is, said she, in her hands. You may imagine that I only laughed at these threats as inspired by the jealousy and spite of a woman. However, there's something very singular to me about it all."

"Wait, monseigneur, I believe I have a glimpse of light. Who informed you yourself that there was a charming young girl in my house?"

"Hang it! you recall it to my recollection. It was an original, a little man whom I found at my house in the Faubourg, hidden under a statue, and who pretended to have helped in the abduction of Julia."

"Chaudoreille?"

"It's that same."

"I should have divined it; there's no doubt of it, it was he who told Julia that you had abducted Blanche. If he should happen to know Urbain, I should not be astonished if he has told him also."

"The little clown! I paid him well enough for everything."

"After having caused the abduction, he does his best to help someone to find Blanche."

"Truly, that is not so very stupid; this is a boy who follows in your footsteps; but if you meet him, I recommend him to you. Give him a good beating."

"Be easy about that, monseigneur."

"For the rest, they may do what they please, they cannot snatch Blanche from my hands. This young girl has more power than all of them put together; one tear from her could, I feel, change all my resolutions. When I see her beautiful eyes turned towards me with a supplicating look, I am often about to sacrifice my love and to restore her to him whom she regrets, in the hope of at least obtaining her friendship."

"O monseigneur, what folly! Why, Blanche is in your power, and you are going —"

"No, no, she must belong to me; henceforth for me to separate from her is impossible. Besides, has she not told me that she is disposed to love me?"

"Come, monseigneur, pull yourself together. They will say that you yield to the threats of this little Julia."

"My uncle is very ill, perhaps he will not last through the night. I shall soon return to Sarcus, then I will not again leave Blanche, I will listen to nothing but my love."

"With women, monseigneur, that causes everything to be forgiven."

Since the barber knew that the marquis suspected where he had obtained his fortune, he believed that it was for his interest to lose sight of Blanche. If Villebelle dreamed of reëntering the path of honor, Touquet could no longer feel easy as to himself.

The marquis regained his hotel. As he had foreseen, his uncle expired during the night, leaving him immense wealth; which would lead one to think that fortune does not show her preference to those who make good use of her favors. But someone answers to that, that fortune does not make happiness; it is, therefore, necessary to console the unhappy a little.

A week sufficed the marquis to settle his affairs. At the end of that time he prepared to return to Blanche, to whom he carried presents of every kind, which were carefully packed in the travelling carriage.

Chaudoreille, who was continually on the watch about the hotel, saw these preparations for departure, and ran to tell Julia.

"Enough," said the young Italian, "I have long been prepared for this, and I have bought two good horses. You shall come with me."

"To the end of the world; I am devoted to you."

"I do not think that we shall have to go very far, we shall have nothing to do but follow the marquis' carriage."

"I understand you."

"You can ride a horse?"

"Perfectly; however, I prefer donkeys, they don't trot so fast."

"Idiot! can one hope to follow a post-chaise on an ass? Make all your preparations."

"They are made. I have my wardrobe upon me; as to my purse, yesterday evening I had some cursed ill-luck while you relieved me at the hotel. I didn't remain in the gambling-house longer than between five and ten minutes, and I had well calculated my play; well, I can say with Francis the First, I have lost everything but honor."

While Chaudoreille rattled on, Julia donned a large cloak, and took all the money which remained to her. Then she sent the Gascon to his post, while she went to get the horses. Towards seven o'clock in the evening the marquis got into his carriage with Germain and started for the Château de Sarcus, not for one moment thinking that Julia and Chaudoreille were following his carriage from afar.

Leaving the travellers to make their way we will return to poor Urbain, who, for a long time past, had languished on his bed, kept there by illness and grief. He was heartbroken at being without strength to go in search of his dear Blanche, and the good girl who gave him every care, incessantly repeated to him, —

"The more you disquiet yourself, the longer you retard your cure."

Someone had told him that a great nobleman was Blanche's abductor, and he was in despair at not having been able to keep his appointment with this man, who would have told him his rival's name. But at last he felt better and could go out, and the first use which he made of his returning strength was to go to the barber's house. It was closed on every side, the shutters had not been taken down from the shop, although the hours of labor had long since begun ; Urbain knocked, but no one opened to him.

"It is useless for you to knock," said a neighbor to him, " the house is empty and is for sale. You must inquire at the agent's, Rue des Mauvaises-Paroles."

"And the barber ?"

" The barber has left it, I tell you, there's nobody there."

" And Marguerite ? "

" She died a week ago."

" Marguerite is dead — is it possible ? "

" Why, what is there so extraordinary in that ? The poor woman wasn't young."

" Where can I find M. Touquet now ? "

" I can't give you any information. That man was a bear, and he spoke to nobody."

Urbain departed, discouraged at this new event. He grieved for the good Marguerite, who had been the witness of his love and his happiness. He had no idea of any way in which he could obtain information as to Blanche's fate. He went to the Porte Montmartre and waited for three hours, in the hope that he who had given him an appointment would come there ; but he waited in vain, and then turned despairingly towards his lodging. The good-natured girl, to whom he made his lament, tried to console him by saying, —

"If it's a nobleman who has abducted your mistress, you must go and ask for her at all the great noblemen's houses."

Suddenly Urbain uttered a joyful exclamation, and a slight smile animated his pale and sorrowful features.

"There still remains one hope," he said.

"And what is that, monsieur?"

"In the midst of all these events I had forgotten that adventure, however, it may yet serve me."

"What adventure; monsieur?"

"Listen to me. You remember that in order to see Blanche I was for some time obliged to disguise myself as a woman."

"Oh, yes, monsieur, I remember very well. Didn't I help to dress you and to put in your pins?"

The girl smiled. Urbain paid no attention and continued, —

"One evening, I think it was the first time that I wore my disguise, having been accosted by several men, I escaped them by traversing many streets and it was very late when I found myself in the Grand Pré-aux-Clercs. I had almost reached my dwelling when I was stopped by four men, whom by their language I recognized as noblemen of the court. I confessed to them that I was a man, hoping by that means to escape them, but one of them wanted me to tell him the motive for my disguise. I refused, he persisted; I got angry, he threatened; in short, one of his companions lent me his sword and we fought, I wounded my adversary, but very slightly, I think. 'My friend,' he said to me then, tendering me his hand, 'you are a brave man and I am very pleased to have made your acquaintance; if you should some day have need of a protector, come to my hotel, ask for the Marquis de Villebelle and you shall find me ready to oblige you.' Those are his exact words."

"The Marquis de Villebelle? Oh, I have sometimes heard my master speak of him. They say that he is a great nobleman, very generous, but a very wild fellow."

"No matter, he offered me his protection, and I shall have recourse to it."

"Mercy, monsieur, you will do well, and who knows whether he's not acquainted with the rascal who has stolen your darling."

"Yes, I hope that the marquis will help me to recover Blanche. These great noblemen tell each other their adventures, their good luck; such a brave man should have some pity on my torture. Why have I not already spoken to him — but his hotel?"

"Oh, he's very well known, monsieur, and it will be very easy for you to find that out."

On the morrow, as soon as it was day, Urbain went out to try and find the one on whom he placed his last hopes. He obtained information as to the marquis' hotel, and he soon arrived there.

"Monsieur le Marquis de Villebelle?" said he entering the court, and timidly addressing the porter.

"This is his hotel, but monsieur le marquis is not in Paris."

"Is not in Paris?" exclaimed Urbain, his heart contracting.

"No, he is travelling."

"Travelling? And will he soon be back?"

"He'll come back when he pleases. Do you think monseigneur needs your permission in order to go travelling?"

"That was not what I wished to say, monsieur, but I am in such haste to see monsieur le marquis, to speak to him."

"You can see him when he comes back, whenever monseigneur is willing to receive you."

The insolent porter returned to his lodge, took his glass and his fork, and resumed a copious breakfast, without paying any further attention to the young student, who remained in the court, heaving big sighs, as he said, —

"He's not in Paris; how unfortunate I am."

Ten minutes later Urbain softly approached the porter's lodge, and said to him in a supplicating tone, —

"Monsieur, can you not tell me where the marquis has gone?"

"What? Are you still there?" answered the porter without turning his head. "Can't you leave me to eat my breakfast in peace? I tell you that monseigneur is travelling. There are some people who are so stubborn; they all say the same thing, 'I wish to see monseigneur,' and they bother my head from morning till night."

Urbain would not be repulsed; he knew the customs of Paris, and took out his purse, in which he had put several crowns, and made it chink in his hand. Then the porter deigned to turn towards him, and said to him, a little more politely, —

"I'm truly sorry, but monseigneur is really absent, and between ourselves, I believe he will be so for a long time."

"O heavens!" said Urbain, "and he is my only hope. Oh, monsieur, if you know where monseigneur is, I entreat you to give me his address."

The young man held out his purse and advanced.

"Come in for a moment," said the porter opening the little door of his lodge; "yes, of course, I know where monseigneur is. It's very necessary that we should know that, in order that we may send him any important letters that may be addressed to him; but it's a secret. However, if you'll promise to be discreet, and to let nobody know that it was I who told you, — "

" I swear to you not to do so."

" Then I'll tell you. Monsieur le marquis is at his Château de Sarcus, situated in the neighborhood of Grandvilliers. Take the road to Beauvais and — "

Urbain did not wait to hear more; he threw his purse on the porter's table, hastily left the hotel, ran to his lodging, took all the money he had left, and the same day set out to seek the marquis at his château.

CHAPTER XII

The Return to the Château

During the absence of the marquis from the Château de Sarcus the unhappy Blanche had passed some sad and monotonous days; she had grown used to seeing and talking with him, and hoped to induce him to allow her to rejoin Urbain; so the day after Villebelle's departure, astonished at not receiving his accustomed visit, she believed that he was disposed to take her back to Paris; but in the evening, not meeting him in the park as usual, Blanche, on her return to her room, asked the maid for some news of her host.

"Monseigneur has gone, he went away yesterday," answered the country girl.

"Gone without me!" exclaimed Blanche, raising to heaven her beautiful eyes, filled with tears and despair; "can it be possible that he wishes to keep me always a prisoner in this château, then?"

"Don't grieve, mademoiselle," said the good-natured girl, "monseigneur said that he would not be long absent."

Blanche made no answer, but returned to her

room, and there passed her days in grief and discouragement. She regretted the absence of the marquis, for the sweet child flattered herself that he would yet yield to her prayers. She had several times seen that her tears caused him emotion, and she still hoped that he would reunite her to Urbain ; but left alone she no longer hoped, and the days rolled slowly by for the young prisoner. However, the return of springtime embellished the earth ; the trees regained their foliage and the grass its verdure, the meadows were dotted with flowers, and the birds came again to the groves to sing the season of love. But, indifferent to the scenes which spread before her eyes, Blanche looked without pleasure on this charming perspective, with which at any other time she would have been delighted. The sorrow with which her heart was filled, threw a gloomy veil over all the objects which surrounded her.

Sometimes while walking in the park, Blanche considered the idea of escaping ; but in what direction could she take her flight ? Besides, the park was surrounded with very high walls, and the doors which led to the country were always scrupulously closed. The young girl was ignorant of the fact that in the absence of the marquis, two men servants watched her every step.

A deep melancholy seized her, the servant, Marie, tried in vain to distract her ; sighs and tears were the only response which she obtained. Ten days had passed when Marie came running **one** morning to tell Blanche her master had arrived.

This news seemed to reanimate the young prisoner, and she waited impatiently for the marquis to come and speak to her. Villebelle, who ardently desired to see his captive, did not tarry in coming to her, and was greatly struck by the changes which had been wrought in her whole person.

"You have forgotten me, then, in this château?" said Blanche sighing.

"I forgotten you?"

"Why did you not take me to Paris, then? Are you going to keep me here long?"

"At least, Blanche, I will not leave you again."

"Let Urbain come to us, and I will not ask you to let me go away again."

The marquis knit his brows and tried to distract Blanche by offering her several pretty trifles which he had brought from Paris; but these presents were no better received than the first, and did not even evoke a smile from the young girl. In the evening Blanche and the marquis again walked in the park. Villebelle, more in love than ever, recalled the barber's counsels and promised himself the conquest of his captive, but when he was near Blanche, he felt all his resolutions vanish. One look from the lovely child put a curb on his desire, though it penetrated to the depth of his heart, and Villebelle said to himself,—

" By what magic does this young girl inspire me with a respect that is stronger than my love ? "

Blanche, rendered confiding by her innocence, was seated at the entrance of a grotto which was surrounded by thick shrubbery. The marquis placed himself beside her. For a long time he remained silent, tenderly watching her. Then he took Blanche in his arms and was about to cull a kiss from her charming mouth, when she turned her supplicating eyes towards him, saying, —

" In pity, monseigneur, let me go."

Without knowing why he did so, he allowed the lovely girl to escape from his arms. He remained alone in the grotto; Blanche, experiencing a novel fear of the marquis, had fled, and the latter, cursing his weakness, returned to the château, vowing that he would no longer tremble before a child.

Julia and her companion had arrived at Sarcus and had seen the marquis enter the château. Chaudoreille had only fallen three times on the way, but he asserted that that was because his horse had been frightened. However, he complained greatly of fatigue, to which his companion appeared insensible, as she scrutinized the château which the marquis had entered, and its high towers illuminated by the sun.

" This is where he went, then," said the young Amazon, guiding her horse close against the walls.

" Yes, signora, there's not the least doubt that he went there, since we have seen him go in," answered Chaudoreille, who had alighted from his horse, where he was not comfortable.

"That's the Château de Sarcus, according to what a peasant told me."

"It is, in faith, a very fine castle. My ancestors had ten or a dozen like that; but they played for one every evening at piquet, and you know that luck is not always favorable. But ugh! how tired I am, this palfrey trotted so hard."

"And within these walls Blanche is shut up."

"That's very probable. By jingo! but we came at a good pace, and at the present time I would defy the best jockey in France,"

"How shall we know on which side this young girl is?"

"I think it's first necessary to know where we can get some breakfast; you must be terribly fatigued, signora."

"I don't feel in the least tired, the hope of vengeance has doubled my strength."

"I have had nothing to double mine; I'm knocked up, exhausted, and I'm as hungry as a hunter."

Julia alighted from her horse and led the animal to Chaudoreille.

"Mount him," she said, "and take the other by the bridle. Go to the village, which you see over there, find an inn, and there wait for me. I wish to examine the château."

"Enough, I'll go and make them get breakfast

ready. Oh, under what title shall we present ourselves? I have been thinking that it would be
better to preserve our incognito in this part of the
country."

"Say what you like."

"I shall say that we are Moors from Spain,
that we have come from Granada to give lessons
in castanets. That will prevent all suspicion, and
our rather dark skins will foster the supposition."

Julia did not listen further to Chaudoreille and
walked towards the château, while the chevalier,
not caring to remount, took both horses by their
bridles and went hobbling along to the village.

Chaudoreille inquired for the best inn. There
was only one in the village and he reached it, leading his two horses after him. The master of the
inn came to meet him, and Chaudoreille, trying
to pull himself up, said to him, —

"I am Malek-al-Chiras of Granada, professor
of castanets in the two Spains, and come to France
with my sister, Salamalech, to dance the bolero before Cardinal Richelieu. We shall perhaps stay
for some time in this village, but we wish to preserve the strictest incognito. Do you understand?"

"I don't understand very well," said the innkeeper, looking stupidly at him.

"In that case, prepare at once an omelette with
bacon, give me a room, and take care of my
horses, which are Arabian."

The innkeeper understood this better, and led his guest to a chamber on the first floor, to which Chaudoreille mounted with pain, so greatly had his long ride on horseback discommoded him.

After resting for some hours he went to the table, and had been there for a long time when Julia came in search of him.

"I awaited you with impatience," said Chaudoreille, while dismembering his third pigeon.

"Well, what have you learned?"

"My faith, I've learned that we shall not have fish for dinner."

"Idiot! I was speaking to you of the marquis."

"It seems to me that as I left you at the château, you should know more than me."

"I have been all around it, but I did not see anybody. You should have asked these peasants what they know of the château."

"They look as stupid as geese. How should these people know anything? By the way, you are my sister and you are called Salamalech."

"Chaudoreille, do you think that I brought you here to listen to your foolishness? Make haste and rest yourself and we will visit the neighborhood of the château; we will see if there is any way of introducing ourselves into the park."

"Begging your pardon, it will be very difficult for me to stir today. I am nailed before this table."

Finding it would be impossible to get her companion on his feet again, Julia left the inn, after
taking a little nourishment, and again went to
prowl around the walls of the château.

" The devil's in that woman," said Chaudoreille
to himself as he got into bed, " she would be worthy to carry Rolande at her side. My good host,
put Rolande there, under my bolster.   That's it,
so that at the first alarm I can get him. Now see
that you shut my door, and when my sister Salamalech returns tell her that I beg of her not to
waken me before tomorrow at midday."

While Chaudoreille slept, Julia made the tour
of the park and noticed a place where the wall was
broken, and where it was possible to introduce
one's self into the interior of the garden ; but not
wishing yet to risk it, she returned to her inn and
tried to obtain some information about the inhabitants of the château.   The peasants knew but
one thing, and that was, that for the present, their
lord was at Sarcus."

" But did not somebody bring a young girl to
the château, some days ago ? " asked Julia.

" When monseigneur is here the house is full of
ladies and gentlemen," answered the host; who believed that the brother and sister had come to play
their castanets before the marquis.

Julia decided to take a little rest, but the next
day at dawn she repaired to Chaudoreille's room.

" Monsieur, your brother, is still sleeping," said

the host whom she met, " and M. Malek-Al-de Granada has forbidden that anyone should wake him before noon."

Julia, without listening to the host, went into the chevalier's room. He was sleeping soundly, and she pulled him rudely by the ear.

" Did I bring you here with me," said she, "that you might sleep ? "

"Oh, by jingo ! how cruel you are, I was in my first slumber."

" Come, get up ! "

" Get up? get up? I respect decency too much to rise before you."

" Get up, I tell you."

" Well, since you will have it so," and Chaudoreille put his two little thin legs out of bed, saying, " It appears that I cannot make her run away."

"You will go to the château, you will enter the first court, under the pretext of admiring the architecture, and you will chat with the porter."

" And if I am recognized ? "

" By whom ? "

" By monseigneur."

" Do you think he amuses himself by walking in the court? He is with his young captive."

" That is presumable."

" We will meet here presently and you will tell me all that you shall have learned. For my part, I am going to find my way into the park."

After a good breakfast, Chaudoreille started, enveloping himself in a mantle or cloak which Julia had given him, and which was so much too large for him that part of it dragged on the ground; but he admired himself very much in it, and felt himself six inches taller.

As he drew near the château, his first care was to look and see if there were a sentinel upon the wall, but perceiving nothing that seemed to indicate that the castle was upon a war footing he decided to advance. On arriving before the principal gate he walked for an hour, far and wide, before knowing if he should go into the château or not. The old porter, smoking his pipe before his door, perceived this little figure, trailing a cloak, and coming and going for a long while in the same circle. Irritated by this conduct, the porter left the château and walked towards Chaudoreille, to ask him what he did there. The latter, seeing a man walk with long steps towards him, imagined that the porter suspected him and was about to arrest him. Immediately he began to run on the sward, but presently his feet became entangled in the train of his cloak and he rolled on the grass. The porter, hearing someone calling in the château, did not continue his walk, and on rising Chaudoreille saw nobody. He then hastened to take the way to the village.

"This is enough of it for today," said he, "another time I shall not be so imprudent, I'll hide in the thickets which are within cannon shot of the castle," and he returned to his inn where, while awaiting dinner, he played at little quoits with his host, and insisted on teaching madame, his wife, to dance the bolero. Julia, hearing the noise, found Chaudoreille in the courtyard of the inn, in the midst of the fowls and manure, making many bows to a little woman of forty years, and beating time with Rolande, saying, —

"In Granada nobody dances except sword in hand. Ah, here is my sister Salamalech, she can make curtseys without touching her heels."

Julia pushed the dancing master into her room, saying to him, —

"What are you doing in that courtyard?"

"What the deuce! I did it the better to preserve our incognito, for prudence' sake."

"What have you learned this morning?"

"Many things. I believe there is a garrison at the château. I saw an armed man come out. As to little Blanche, I have a suspicion that they are keeping her in a subterranean dungeon."

"You're a fool. I've spoken to a young girl who lives at the château; I made her gossip. Blanche is in one of the towers which overlook the lake."

"Then the soldier whom I questioned must have lied to me. I had him, however, with my sword at his throat."

"Nobody has arrived at the château?"

"Oh, nobody, I'm sure of that, I have not lost sight of it."

" This evening I shall introduce myself into the park and I hope — "

"I hope that I'm not to introduce myself there."

"No, you are to watch outside."

" Ah, I'm good at watching outside ; besides, I have the eyes of a cat, I can see clearly at night."

According to his custom the marquis went to visit Blanche on the day after the scene in the grotto, but she experienced a new dread at sight of him. She recalled how passionately he had folded her in his arms, and despite her innocence she felt a degree of fear as she saw him approach and seat himself at her side. The marquis knew women too well not to perceive the change in Blanche's manner. He tried to read the young girl's eyes, he wished to see again the sweet expression which so charmed him, but Blanche kept her eyes downcast, she trembled, and feared to meet those of the marquis. After a shorter visit than usual Villebelle left Blanche, and went to reflect on the means which he should employ to overcome her resistance. He awaited the evening impatiently, he flattered himself that he should be more fortunate in the gardens in making his peace with his young prisoner ; but Blanche listened to a secret voice which told her she was not safe in the park with the marquis, and she did not intend to go there.

It had long been night, and vainly had Ville-belle walked up and down the pathways where the young girl walked every evening. He did not meet her.

" She fears me," said he, " however, she does not hate me, she herself has told me so."

On passing before the grotto where they had sat the evening before, the marquis believed that he saw a shadow flit before him. Persuaded that it was Blanche, he ran to seize her. The person whom he pursued paused, turned, and, by the light of the moon, the marquis recognized Julia.

" You in this neighborhood, and in my park ? " said Villebelle, with the greatest astonishment.

"Yes, monsieur le marquis," said Julia with a bitter smile, " does that astonish you ? Monsieur de Villebelle should, however, understand all the pleasure which I experience in being near him."

" Once more, what are you doing here ? "

" There was a time, monsieur le marquis, when my presence caused you no weariness, when you told me with the most tender vows that you would love me forever. Remember how often it was necessary to repeat those vows in order to make me yours."

The marquis made a gesture of impatience and exclaimed, —

" And is it to tell me this that you introduced yourself at night into my château ? "

" No," said Julia, giving way to all her fury.

"Another motive led me to this place; it was the hope of vengeance. You have laughed at my love, at my grief; I will revel in your sufferings, you shall shed tears of blood when it will be too late."

"This is too much; your threats weary and make me despise you. If you have the power to fulfil them, why are you waiting for your revenge?"

"I am awaiting the presence of an indispensable witness, your worthy confidant, the barber Touquet."

Saying these words Julia glided among the trees, and disappeared before the marquis could stop her. Greatly surprised at this singular meeting, he was careful on reëntering the château to warn Germain; and ordered him to redouble his watchfulness in order that no one might gain access to Blanche.

CHAPTER XIII

The Marquis Visits Blanche at Night

The marquis returned in great agitation to his apartments. He was greatly incensed, but not at all intimidated by Julia's threats, which he attributed to spite and her jealousy. However, despite his lack of consideration for her he had cast off, there was something in the voice of the young Italian which carried conviction, and her eyes appeared to be animated by a barbaric joy when she had fixed them on those of the marquis, and warned him to beware.

Vexed at not having forced Julia to explain herself, Villebelle called his valet, and ordered him to search the park with some of his people, and if he met a woman to bring her immediately to the château. Germain, the gardener, and three men servants hastened to investigate the park and gardens, but they returned to the château without meeting anybody, and the marquis passed the night in reflecting upon the event. The presence of Julia had disturbed his peace; he feared that she would come and bring Blanche news of her lover. At daybreak he wrote to the barber and ordered him to come to the château.

Marguerite was dead; the old servant could not bear the loss of Blanche, and the fury of her master after Julia's visit. The barber, who had for a long time desired to sell his house, was about to go to a lawyer, when a letter was brought to him by a messenger from the marquis.

"He wishes that I should go to Sarcus," said Touquet to himself, after reading the note; "the marquis still has need of me. He has at times, an inclination for virtue which causes me uneasiness, but he pays generously; besides I can refuse him nothing. He has divined a part of my conduct, and if some day he should desire to ruin me as an expiation for all his own follies — for it is often in this manner that great folks repair their errors — but no, the marquis will commit follies as long as he lives; it is above all necessary that he should triumph over Blanche's virtue, for that would insure my safety."

Touquet made the preparations for his departure, and on the next day but one he arrived at the château, and presented himself to the marquis, who was awaiting him in his apartment.

"You see, monseigneur, with what haste I have obeyed your orders," said the barber, bowing.

"That is well; your presence here may be very useful to me. I feel that I need someone who will make me ashamed of my weakness. Would you believe that I am no further advanced in regard to Blanche?"

"I shouldn't believe it unless you told me so, monseigneur."

"It is certain that I should never have dreamed of it myself. She has been for three weeks at the château, and I have hardly dared to kiss her hand. Some days ago we were in the park, and I tried to advance a little further, but she supplicated me to let her go in so touching a voice, it affects me in a manner which I cannot account for, but I was nearly heartbroken at having caused her pain; since that time she has not left her room. When near me, she is fearful, embarrassed, and always in tears."

"All that will end, when you have made her yours, monseigneur."

"Have you seen her lover? This Urbain of whom she talks incessantly, and whom she calls at every moment of the day."

"No, monseigneur, and I presume that young Urbain, more reasonable than Blanche, has already forgotten that little love affair."

"The poor little thing is always thinking of him. If I could persuade her that he no longer loves her, — she would not, however, believe me. But in speaking to you of Blanche I forget the motive which induced me to send for you. You can never divine whom I met the day before yesterday, in the evening, in my park — Julia."

"Julia!" cried the barber, starting with surprise.

"Yes, she had entered these premises. But how could she have discovered that I was here?"

"I can't imagine, monseigneur."

"She had the audacity to threaten me, jealousy and rage shone in her eyes; she also spoke to me of you. I didn't understand all she was saying to me, and she disappeared when I was about to force her to explain further."

"Monseigneur, this young girl has some evil design."

"I think that, also. However, she has not reappeared since, and every evening my people make a general search in the park."

"No matter, Julia will do her utmost to take Blanche away from you."

"How do you think she will do it? You must visit the neighborhood, and if you discover Julia, tell her from me that I forbid her to present herself on these premises. If she still dares to come I can easily obtain a lettre-de-cachet, which will relieve me from her importunities."

"That will be the best thing you can do, monseigneur. Tomorrow I'll begin my researches."

"During the time which you are at the château, avoid passing through the park by the side of the lake, for you might be seen by Blanche, and I don't wish that she shall know you are here; I don't think that the sight of you would give her pleasure, and I desire to keep her from all that might add to her grief."

"I've never seen monseigneur so much in love."

"No, never has any woman inspired me with that which I feel for Blanche."

"I'm going to get some rest. Tomorrow at daybreak I shall take my way; I will search the neighborhood, I will visit the smallest cottages; Julia cannot evade my search, and as soon as I know where she is, I answer for it, monseigneur, that you will not see her again."

The barber was about to go as he said these words, but there was an expression on his face which did not escape the marquis. Villebelle ran to him and stopped him, saying in a severe tone,—

"Touquet, you have misunderstood me. Remember that I do not wish that any harm should come to Julia. That young girl is passionate, headstrong, but her love excuses it. One should always forgive the faults of which one is the first cause. I should, perhaps, have further considered her sensibility; I have treated her with too much disdain. If she will consent to become reasonable, promise her all that she shall ask. Scatter gold, that she may be happy. In addition to that, I wish to speak to her myself, that she may explain to me what she wished to tell in her letter."

"In that case, monseigneur, as soon as I have discovered her retreat, I will hasten to let you know it."

The barber bowed low to the marquis and left the apartment.

" That man is a deep scoundrel," said Villebelle, as he watched Touquet depart. " For a long
time I thought he was only a schemer and a thief;
why should he still be necessary to me? But I
can't charge Germain to speak to Julia. Julia!
I believed for a little while that I loved her. Ah,
what a difference there is between that passionate,
vindictive woman and the sweet and charming
Blanche. Why should Julia love me so passionately, and yet I cannot kindle in the breast of that
timid child a spark of the fire which consumes
me?"

While the marquis was dreaming of Blanche,
who, sad and solitary in her lonely room, passed
her days in praying to Heaven and weeping for
her lover, Julia, after her nocturnal meeting with
Villebelle, sought to gain speech with the young
prisoner. The watchfulness of the marquis' people did not prevent her from gliding through the
park; but though she drew near the lake it was
impossible to reach the tower; they had taken
away all the boats for fear that one of them should
serve as a means of approaching Blanche's windows. As for Chaudoreille, being ordered to watch
all who entered or left the château, he hid himself
in a thick bush, which was about two cannon shots
from the entrance to the castle ; and there, having Rolande bare at one side by way of precaution, and a bottle of wine at the other, he passed
his day with a pack of cards, studying a new man-

ner of turning the king and of re-turning the aces, hiding entirely under his immense mantle at the slightest sound.

The day after his arrival at the château, the barber commenced his search. Not imagining for a moment that Julia would conceal herself at Sarcus, he visited Damerancourt, and Grandvilliers, and returned towards the evening to Sarcus. As he approached the village, he perceived in front of him a little man enveloped in a brown cloak, under which it was difficult to distinguish his body, but a long sword, whose handle protruded from one side of his cloak, betrayed who carried it.

" It's Chaudoreille," said the barber to himself, and he hastened that he might catch up with him. The little man, when he heard someone behind him, was seized with terror, and also tried to walk faster, but the unfortunate cloak entangled his legs at every step, and soon he felt himself pulled by the handle of his sword. He turned and was petrified at seeing the barber Touquet.

" Where are you going, Chevalier Chaudoreille ? " said the barber, in a mocking tone.

" Where am I going? By jingo ! How are you, my good friend ? "

" You clown," said the barber, " I've heard some fine things about you."

" One mustn't believe all that one hears, my dear Touquet."

" And don't you think I ought to believe mon-

sieur le marquis? It was you who told him about
Blanche, despite your vows."

"You know very well that between ourselves
an oath is not binding, and what have you to complain of? I was the means of your obtaining a
large sum of money."

"And do you serve Julia now?"

"Yes, I serve Julia. I will serve you, if you
wish, I will serve anybody; I have always been
very obliging."

"Where is Julia?"

"She wishes to preserve her incognito."

"Answer, wretch, no more lies."

"Ow! leave go of my ear, you are hurting me.
We are lodging in this village at the inn; there is
only one here. Julia passes as my sister, and I for
a Moor of Granada, professor of castanets."

"What are Julia's plans?"

"The devil carry me away if I have any idea
of them. She passes her days and a part of her
nights in prowling about the château, like a fox
watching a chicken. Between ourselves I believe
she's a little cracked."

"And with what design did she bring you
here?"

"Simply to keep her company. She likes my
society very much, I sing villanelles to her."

"Listen to me, I ought to break your back to
punish you for what you've done."

"O my dear Touquet, that was a joke."

"Get along with you, I despise you too much to strike you."

"That's very civil on your part."

"Have you told me the truth?"

"If you doubt it, come with me to the inn. Julia will not be long before she comes in."

"No, I can't go there this evening; but I forbid you to say a word to her about our meeting."

"As soon as you forbid me, it's as if you had cut out my tongue."

"If I don't find Julia tomorrow in the place you have told me of, monsieur le marquis himself will see that you are punished, and this time there will be no quarter given you."

"You may be sure I'll obey you."

"Good-by, I'm going back to the château."

"And I to the village — where I shall not await your visit," said Chaudoreille, in a low tone, gathering his cloak up under his arm that he might walk more quickly.

Touquet returned to the château and sought the marquis. It was night, and Villebelle was seated before a table as sumptuously furnished as was possible at the château; but the marquis, presuming that he should make a long sojourn there, had had his cellars replenished, and if the fare was not so delicate as in Paris, the wines were no less exquisite. The marquis appeared gayer than usual. He had already emptied several bottles, and near

him were several letters which he read while supping.

"What news?" said he, on perceiving the barber.

"My researches have not proved vain, monseigneur, Julia is at the village; she is living at
the inn under an assumed name. I have seen
Chaudoreille, who is now her confidant."

"Ah, the little Gascon. Have you thrashed
him soundly?"

"Not yet, monseigneur, I wished first to get
your orders, and I have not seen Julia."

"You have done well, I will speak to her myself. Tomorrow we will go together to the village; I shall make the heedless girl hear reason,
and we shall know this grand secret which she pretends she has to tell me."

"A secret?"

"Yes, and it's necessary, she says, that you
should be present when she tells it."

"Me? monseigneur."

"Tomorrow she shall be satisfied. Do you see
those letters? All of those were sent to me from
Paris. They are from the great ladies who regret
me; there are reproaches, promises, vows, and a
little of everything. Here, throw all that in the
fire."

"What, monsieur le marquis, even those which
are unopened?"

"Yes, of course; do they not all say the same

thing? Ah, a single smile from Blanche is worth all the sweet nothings of these ladies. Why is she not here, near me?"

"If monseigneur desires it—"

"That she may come with her eyes full of tears? No."

The marquis filled a large glass with wine, which he drank at a draught, when he exclaimed,—

"I'm commencing, however, to fear that I sigh in vain; Blanche is near me, in my château, but I dare not—but to employ violence, I cannot resort to that."

"Without employing violence, monseigneur, are there not a thousand ways? She sleeps undefended—and you have double keys to all the rooms."

"What perfidy!"

"Not greater, monseigneur, than taking her in a carriage, telling her that she was going to join Urbain."

"Be silent, you are a monster; and to listen to your horrible counsels renders me more criminal than yourself."

"It was not I, monseigneur, who counselled you to fall in love with Blanche, but since she is in your power, it seems to me that your scruples are a little tardy."

The marquis remained silent for some moments; then he resumed,—

"This morning she spoke to me less coldly; I

remained several hours with her; she seemed to me less timid. I took her hand, and she left it for a long time in mine."

"What more do you wish for, monseigneur? In secret Blanche loves you; but do you think that so timid a young girl will confess what is passing in her heart? It is not until after she has yielded that she banishes all constraint."

"Blanche loves me, say you? Ah, if it were true. But it is late; go and take some rest. Tomorrow we will go and see Julia."

Touquet bowed to the marquis, and looked stealthily and scrutinizingly at him; then he took a candle, and departed in silence. For a long while the marquis remained at the table, buried in thought, or drinking glass after glass of wine. He seemed to wish to drown in the liquor the thoughts which pursued him. Finally he rang for Germain, and said to him in a gloomy voice, —

"Who has the double keys to the château?"

"The porter should have them, monseigneur."

"Bid him come here, I wish to speak to him."

The old porter hastened to obey his master's orders.

"Are there some double keys for these apartments?" said the marquis.

"Yes, monseigneur, there are even triple keys; 'tis an ancient usage that dates from —"

"Go and get me those of the tower which looks on the lake."

The porter departed, and soon returned with a bunch of keys, saying,—

"If monseigneur wishes I will conduct him through the château,"

"Give me those and go, I do not need your assistance," said the marquis, snatching the keys from his hand.

The old man, stupefied, bowed and departed, without daring to raise his eyes on his master. The marquis dismissed his servants, saying that he had need of rest, and presently the most profound silence reigned in the château and in the grounds pertaining to it.

As for the Marquis de Villebelle, he walked irresolutely about his apartment, holding the bunch of keys in his hand, and meditating deeply. He was apparently still undecided as to what course he should take, and muttered to himself from time to time,—

"No, I cannot make use of these keys — she seemed to give me her confidence and I dare not abuse it; but must she pass her life thus? To be so near her, to have abducted her in vain. What would all the libertines say of me, all the people of fashion, if they knew of my conduct? But if they could see Blanche! Why did that cursed Touquet speak to me of these keys? I should have divined that when he entered this château, that man would advise me to commit some wicked action."

Some moments passed, and at last the marquis took up a candle, and exclaimed, —

"It is settled; I will listen only to the passion which leads me."

He left his room, which was separated from the tower where Blanche was lodged by a long gallery adorned with portraits of the marquis' ancestors. Villebelle walked slowly, pausing often to listen, and trembling for fear he should meet someone; he kept his eyes down, and seemed afraid to look at the portraits of his ancestors, who, for the most part, had honored their country by their bravery and virtue. At this moment something told him he was about to commit an act which was unworthy of the name which they had transmitted to him, and when his eyes met by chance one of those noble faces with which the gallery was hung, he seemed to read in it an expression of indignation and scorn. At last he reached the end of the gallery, and never had it seemed to him so long; he mounted a grand staircase, crossed several rooms, and entered the tower which held the young girl. A violent trembling seized him. Wishing to master his uneasiness, he hastened his walk. All the doors of communication were open, and he soon found Blanche's room. He paused, and looked at the keys which he held in his hand; he still hesitated, but, seeking to deaden himself to the crime which he was about to commit, he tried several keys,

and was soon in Blanche's room. The deepest
silence reigned in this place; the marquis stepped
very softly, taking each step with precaution.
The door of the bedroom was not closed. Villebelle looked in, and by the light of the lamp
placed on the hearth, perceived the young girl
asleep.

"She sleeps," said the marquis; "she thinks
herself safe in this shelter, but her breathing is
oppressed; she seems as though she were going to
speak; if I could but hear her."

He approached the bed. Blanche was dreaming of her lover; softly she breathed Urbain's
name, and extended her arms as if imploring
someone; then she murmured, —

"O dear God! they still keep us apart."

Villebelle felt moved and softened.

"No, she does not love me," said he softly;
"in her sleep she is always thinking of Urbain."

He sighed profoundly, and was about to depart,
when Blanche awakened, opened her eyes, and
called out in terror, —

"O heavens! who is there?"

"It is I, Blanche," answered the marquis in a
halting voice.

"You seigneur? so late in my room? What
do you want with me?"

"Be calm, I beg of you."

"But you are trembling yourself, seigneur,
what has happened?"

"Nothing, nothing; I wished to see you — to speak to you, to look at you once more."

"Ah, don't look at me so, monsieur le marquis, you frighten me."

"Frighten you? Ah, Blanche, is that the feeling with which the most faithful lover should inspire you? Yes, my love is at its height; I can no longer master it; you must make me happy; you must be mine."

The marquis already held Blanche in his arms. The young girl uttered a piercing cry, and gathering her strength, disengaged herself, jumping lightly from her bed, but Villebelle again seized her; he tried to cover her with kisses; he tried to stifle her cries. Blanche threw herself at his feet, extended her arms towards him, supplicatingly, and cried in a heart-breaking voice, —

"Mercy! mercy! if only for today."

These accents penetrated to the depths of the marquis' soul. The sight of Blanche at his feet, of her tears and of her despair, restored him to reason, but fearing that he might no longer be able to master his passion, he precipitately left the young girl, and distractedly fled to his room.

CHAPTER XIV

Urbain's Visit to the Marquis. Chaudoreille's Last Adventure

Blanche remained motionless and silent for a long time in the place where she had implored, and her loveliness and the nameless charm of her innocence had obtained, the pity, the forbearance of a man who had been about to wrong her womanhood. At last a flood of tears relieved her heart. She rose and then looked about her with terror; she listened tremblingly; at the least sound caused by the wind on the lake she shuddered, and imagined she heard the marquis returning. She passed the night in cruel anxiety.

"All is over," she said, weeping; "my hope of happiness is completely shattered. O my well-beloved Urbain, I shall see you no more; they will separate us forever, but I will die rather than cease to be worthy of thee."

The marquis had rested no better than his victim. Divided between love and remorse, regretting at times having yielded to what he called his weakness, and cursing a passion which made Blanche unhappy, he saw day break without having closed his eyes.

Astonished at having received no orders in regard to Julia, Touquet presented himself before the marquis; he remarked the dejection of the latter's features, and sought to divine the cause of it. Villebelle's gloomy and melancholy tone did not indicate that he was happy; he remained silent, and the barber dared not question him. At this moment Germain entered the room, and announced to his master that a young man had presented himself at the château, and begged the favor of speech with him.

"A young man?" said the marquis. "Is he an inhabitant of the neighborhood?"

"No, monseigneur, his dress is that of a young student; he expresses himself well, and appears to have the greatest desire to see you."

"He did not tell you his name?"

"He says that you know him without knowing his name."

"How very singular, can he be a messenger from Julia?" said Villebelle, looking at the barber.

"I don't think so, monsieur le marquis. The description which Germain has given of the stranger is not that of Chaudoreille."

"When they introduce this young man, Touquet, step into the next room; it is possible he wishes to speak to me alone."

The barber departed and Germain returned with Urbain, who, having travelled without stopping, had arrived at Sarcus, and was waiting impatiently at the porter's lodge for the answer which the marquis should send him."

"My master consents to see you. Follow me, monsieur, I will take you to him," said Germain to Urbain; the latter joyfully hastened to follow the valet, who introduced him to the marquis.

Urbain entered the room trembling; approaching with embarrassment the great nobleman, who was seated on a sofa, and who looked curiously at the young man, unable to resist a certain interest which Urbain's refined and distinguished face inspired.

"Deign to excuse, seigneur, the liberty which I take," said the young bachelor, bowing low to the marquis.

"Speak, monsieur, what do you want of me?"

"I come to implore your protection. You gave me permission to have recourse to it. We have already seen each other at Paris, some time ago; I was disguised, I met you at night in the Grand Pré-aux-Clercs, fought a duel —"

"What, my brave fellow, was that you, who were dressed as a girl?"

"Yes, seigneur, I had the misfortune to wound you in the arm."

"And I tell you that that was just, for I was wrong, as I usually am. Hang it! I'm delighted to see you again; give me your hand, you are a brave fellow."

The marquis rose, came towards Urbain and

cordially shook him by the hand. The latter, delighted by this welcome, did not know how to evince his gratitude.

"Seat yourself near me," said Villebelle, "and tell me what has procured me the pleasure of receiving you in my château."

"Monseigneur, you had the goodness to offer me your protection if I were unfortunate, and I come to claim it."

"You do well, my dear fellow; speak without fear. Is it money that you need, I have it at your service; don't spare it, I often enough make a bad use of it, once at least let it serve me in making somebody happy."

"Fortune could not render me happy, for it is love which causes my trouble, monseigneur."

"Oh, you are in love; that's different, I am in love, also; and at this moment it does not make me very happy, either. But come, tell me your love affairs."

"I love, I adore, a charming young girl — ah, monseigneur, there is nobody to be compared to her."

"Perhaps, but go on."

"She did not know her parents, but the man who had brought her up gave me her hand. Only one day and we should have been united, when a wretch introduced himself into the house where she lived and carried off from me the one who was about to become my wife."

" That's very singular," said the marquis, struck by Urbain's recital, " and do you know the name of this ravisher ? "

" No, monsieur le marquis, but after that I learned that it was a great nobleman, a rich and powerful man — Ah, my only hope of discovering this monster lies in you, for you perhaps know the place where he lives. Monseigneur, have pity on my torture, help me to recover her whom they have stolen from me, help me to recover Blanche, and the unfortunate Urbain will owe you more than life."

At the name of Blanche the marquis rose abruptly. Urbain threw himself at his feet, seized one of his hands and looked imploringly at him ; but Villebelle turned his head that the young man might not see the change which had come over his face.

" Get up, get up," said the marquis, seeking to master his emotion ; " I wish to serve you, yes, but I cannot promise to restore to you the one whom you have loved."

" Among the noblemen of the court, there are men who glory in betraying innocence and snatching a young girl from her relations ; seigneur, if you have the least suspicion — sometimes the slightest indication will put one on the track."

The marquis appeared to reflect deeply ; Urbain, who believed that he sought to recall some circumstance which had interested him, waited with most lively anxiety for him to speak.   After a long silence Villebelle said, —

"You are very young, Urbain."

"I am nineteen years old, seigneur."

"This — Blanche is, no doubt, the first woman whom you have loved ? "

"Yes, seigneur, and she will be the last."

"You are mistaken, my friend ; at your age one loves ardently, but it is a flame which quickly evaporates.   It is only to one like me that — bereft of the illusions of youth and wearied with change — a true love is a need of the heart and should be an insurmountable feeling.   Like you, at nineteen years of age, I believed that I should love for life; I deceived myself.   Believe me, you will still be happy."

"Without Blanche ?   That is impossible."

"You have some little fortune ? "

"I have a little country house which my father left me, and twelve hundred livres income."

"With so little, distraction is not easy.   I wish that you could taste some of the pleasures of your age, and in their vortex you would soon forget your first love."

"I thank you, seigneur, but I cannot accept your benefits.   I repeat to you, I can never taste pleasure separated from her I love."

"Well, what I have offered you would facilitate your researches.   Do not refuse me, it is only on that condition that I promise you to second your efforts. Wait for me here, do not leave this room."

So saying, the marquis went into the room where Touquet was waiting.

" Urbain is there," said he, "the young stranger who asked to see me is Blanche's lover."

" I know it, seigneur, I recognized his voice and I listened."

" He comes to beg my help in discovering the abductor of her he loves."

" He could not better address himself."

" I almost felt ready to give him his sweetheart."

" What folly ! "

" But Blanche's image is too deeply graven in my heart.   However, I wish to try and indemnify poor Urbain for the evil which I have caused him ; and the power of gold — "

" It is the remedy for all evils, seigneur."

" Yes, to a venial soul like yours ; you have never known the sweetness of love."

" But it is necessary, seigneur, to get rid of this young man for a long time. What prevents you — by means of false advice — from sending him to England, to Turkey, to the devil even ? "

" In fact, I comprehend."

" Travel will distract him from his love ; you are a generous rival. Some others in your place, profiting by the occasion, would shut this young man up in some dungeon in this château."

"Oh, how horrible! to betray the confidence of this mere boy."

"In place of that you will give him money, so that he can live like a great lord."

"Could I ever pay him for the treasure I have taken from him?"

The marquis opened a desk, took sixty thousand livres in notes, which he placed in a pocketbook and returned to find Urbain. The young bachelor, as he noted the elegance of the interior of the château, said to himself, —

"It is, perhaps, in a similar abode that Blanche is lamenting at this moment."

"In thinking of what you have told me," said Villebelle, "I recall certain circumstances which might, perhaps, put you on the track of her whom you are seeking."

"O monsieur le marquis, deign to tell me."

"The Marquis de Chavagnac has often made people talk about him by abducting beautiful girls; he has suddenly left Paris, and one may presume that it was on some similar adventure."

"Ah, it is he who has stolen Blanche from me."

"Remember well that I do not affirm anything."

"And does anyone know to which of his châteaux he has gone?"

"He is not in France, and, according to what I have learned, has betaken himself to Italy."

"To Italy? Then that is where I must go."

" Take this pocketbook as a mark of my es-
teem, and do not spare that which it holds."

" Seigneur, I do not know if I should."

" Believe my experience; with gold one may
gain the duennas, one may seduce jailers, one may
surmount many obstacles."

" It will be to you, then, that I shall owe my
happiness, my felicity. O seigneur, I do not know
how to express my gratitude to you."

" Go, Urbain, make a tour of Italy, and perhaps you will there find happiness."

The young bachelor still wished to express to
the marquis all his gratitude, but the latter would
not permit him, and again wishing him a pleasant
journey, he rang for Germain, who conducted
Urbain to the door of the château.   Hardly had
the young lover quitted the marquis' apartments,
when Villebelle called Touquet, and ordered him
to follow Urbain at a distance, and not to lose
sight of him until he was certain that the bachelor
had left Sarcus.   Urbain departed, penetrated
with gratitude to the marquis, but while passing
through the great gate, he experienced a sadness
for which he could not account.   He could hardly
leave the château, and turned to cast a last glance
at the antique towers of Sarcus.   Wrapped in
thought, he walked slowly down the first road
which he came to, greatly touched at the welcome
which he had received at the château.   He hoped,
thanks to the benevolence of the marquis, soon

to be in Italy, not doubting that it could be any other than the Seigneur de Chavagnac who had carried Blanche off.

Urbain had already gone some distance from the château, and was about to enter a lane which led to the village, when a shout of, " Take care there ! " made him raise his head, and he saw before him a man on horseback. The rider, however, managed his horse so badly that the animal was standing across the path, having his head resting on a bush, to which he seemed to be attached.

" By jingo ! won't you turn, proud animal; beware lest in place of the spur I bury Rolande's point in your side. Take care there, what the deuce ! My horse is skittish, you frighten him."

The voice and accent of the chevalier immediately struck Urbain; he recognized the man who had made an appointment with him at the Porte Montmartre. Chaudoreille, after his meeting with the barber, had had no thought except to leave the neighborhood of the château, and without making his resolution known to Julia, who would, he was very certain, oppose it, he had waited till the next day, when she had left the inn ; then, taking the bag which contained the effects and money of his companion, he had sold one of their horses and, under the pretext of exploring the neighborhood had started on his way, with the intention of escaping to parts unknown. But the fugitive did not know how to hold his horse, although since his journey to Sarcus he had believed himself one of the best jockeys in France. Continually twitching the bridle of his horse for fear the animal should run away, it had taken him an hour to cover barely half a mile of road. He commenced to fear that he could not depart quickly enough by this mode of travel, when Urbain met him in the little lane, which the horse refused to leave.

Urbain, delighted at seeing the man again who had promised to tell him the name of Blanche's ravisher, uttered a joyful exclamation, and ran towards Chaudoreille. The sudden cry and approach of the young man frightened the horse, which jumped, and sent his rider six feet from him into a thick hedge.

"All the bones in my body are broken," cried Chaudoreille, while falling.

Urbain ran to help him up, and to make his excuses, but the chevalier drew away from him, and while rubbing himself looked at Urbain, who did not cease to repeat, —

"I am Blanche's lover, the young man whom you met that night, and whom you promised to meet at Porte Montmartre."

"My faith, that's true, I recognize you now; but why the deuce did you run at me, and shout so loud? This is the first time that I have been unhorsed."

"Monsieur, oblige me by keeping your promise; tell me the name of Blanche's abductor. I can now recompense you beyond your hopes."

"Hush!" said Chaudoreille, drawing Urbain towards the hedge which hid them from sight of the château; "imprudent young man, don't speak so loud."

"Why not?"

"Silence, I tell you. What! you are at Sarcus, and you don't know the name of your sweetheart's abductor?"

"No, of course not; I came to beg the Marquis de Villebelle's protection, and thanks to him I hope —"

"Oh, for once this is too much! Young man, you interest me. I am about to risk myself for you; but you have promised me a liberal recompense."

"Here, take this gold, these notes, and speak at once."

"Your sweetheart's abductor is no other than the Marquis de Villebelle."

"The marquis?"

"Why yes, by jingo! and your little girl is now at the Château de Sarcus."

"No, that is not possible; you are deceiving me. The marquis has heaped benefits upon me."

"The better to disarm your suspicions. Zounds! how young you still are. I tell you that your Blanche is at the château, and that the barber—"

" Is before you," said a stern voice, which came from the other side of the hedge, and, at the same moment, the foliage parted and Touquet appeared before the astonished Urbain; while Chaudoreille, whose legs failed him at this sudden apparition, fell again into the hedge, muttering, —

" It's the devil."

" This wretch has not told you all, Seigneur Urbain," said the barber. " Under pretext of serving you he has given you some half confidences, but I wish you should know all the obligation under which you lie to him. You were about to wed Blanche, and nothing was opposed to your marriage ; the marquis had never heard of that young girl, whom I had carefully kept from his sight, foreseeing to what excesses he would be carried; but Chaudoreille, in spite of his promises, gave the marquis a most seductive portrait of your sweetheart and told him of your approaching marriage. Finally, it is to him that you owe Blanche's abduction and the loss of your happiness. Answer, clown, is not this the truth ? "

" I cannot deny it," answered the chevalier, half dead with fright, " however, circumstances—"

" Wretch ! " cried Urbain, " you are the cause of all my suffering, defend yourself. The first act of my vengeance shall be your death."

While travelling, Urbain carried a sword; he drew his weapon from the scabbard and advanced towards Chaudoreille, but the words, " by your

death," and the sight of the naked sword put new
strength into the legs of the little man. Abandoning the cloak which impeded his flight, he ran with
all his might, pursued by Urbain, who still threatened him with his sword; while the barber, mount-
ing Chaudoreille's horse, went at full gallop to the
château. The chevalier, who imagined that he
felt the point of Urbain's sword pricking his back,
redoubled his speed; but Urbain, animated by a
desire for vengeance, had very nearly caught up
to him, and was not more than twenty paces behind him when they entered the village. This
flying man, pursued by another with a sword in
his hand, attracted everyone's attention.

"Out of the way! out of the way!" cried Chaudoreille to the crowd, while Urbain shouted,—

"Stop that wretch."

The innkeeper who was at his door said,—

"Why, that's Monsieur Malek-Al-Chiras,
castanet teacher. What can he have done with
his Arabian steed?"

The fugitive entered the first door that he found
open, which was one in the house of an old dowager. Chaudoreille mounted the staircase; arrived
at the first floor he perceived a key in a door, he
entered precipitantly, carefully taking the key with
him and locking it after him. At the same instant, a voice cried, —

"Monsieur, what are you doing here? Nobody
can come in, I am not visible."

It was the dowager, who was dressing at the moment when the chevalier, entered her chamber, desperate. Chaudoreille did not answer, he heard nothing but Urbain's steps.

"Monsieur, I am making my toilet."

"Make anything you please," said he at last, "I shall scarcely worry myself about it."

"Leave this room, monsieur."

"Me, leave the room? By jingo! I'll take very good care not to do that. Do you wish me to go to my death? I'm pursued by a man who absolutely wishes to fight with me."

"Well, then, fight. Can't you defend yourself?"

"I can only defend myself when I am not attacked."

"What use is your sword then, monsieur?"

"That does not matter to you. Ah, zounds! I hear him."

In fact, Urbain had discovered Chaudoreille's retreat. He knocked at the door and ordered him to open.

"Answer that there is nobody here," said Chaudoreille to the dowager, "you will save the life of the most amiable man in Europe."

The old woman answered on the contrary, —

"He is here, but he has locked himself up with me and he has taken the key."

"Oh, well, one can break in the door," said Urbain, "if this wretch refuses to open it."

Chaudoreille looked round in search of a hiding-place, but feared the dowager would betray him. Finally his glance rested on the chimney, and seeing no other means of escape, he ran and climbed into it with the agility of a squirrel. At that moment someone forced the door, and Urbain entered, followed by some of the village people. They did not see Chaudoreille, but the dowager indicated the way by which he had fled. Going down into the court they perceived the chevalier on the roof, creeping along a gutter and endeavoring to reach the neighboring house. The way was dangerous, but the fear of fighting seemed to have blinded Chaudoreille to all other perils. Already his foot touched the next roof, and, using Rolande to feel his way, he turned his head to see if Urbain was behind him; this movement made him lose his equilibrium, he slipped, then disappeared. They ran to the place where he had fallen; the descendant of Delilah had fallen on some cabbages, but not having loosened his hold of Rolande, the long sword had passed through the middle of his body. Thus perished the prudent Chaudoreille, while trying to avoid a combat.

CHAPTER XV

Julia's Story. What Was Contained in the Portfolio

The barber left Urbain in full pursuit of the luckless chevalier and putting his horse at full gallop tore back to the Château de Sarcus, in order that he might immediately apprise the marquis of that which had taken place. He arrived in short order at the château and hastened to present himself to Villebelle, whom he informed of the meeting of Urbain and Chaudoreille and the disclosures that had been made.

"Then this young man is aware that I have grossly deceived him, that I am Blanche's abductor and that she is now at the château?" said the marquis. "He is young and ingenuous, his love for this hapless child is pure and virtuous, he sought to honor her in making her his wife,—how vile and dishonorable must I appear in his eyes!"

"What does the opinion of this beardless boy matter to you, monsieur le marquis? The most important thing you have to think of is how to prevent his coming in contact with Blanche, and that, now, will be rather difficult. Now that he is sure that she is here, he will employ a thousand stratagems to introduce himself into the château —"

"No, this boy shall not rob me of the woman whom I love."

"If he comes, as I am certain he will, to demand satisfaction, it's a sure thing that you cannot refuse to fight him, and that will be the best means of disembarrassing yourself of him. With your cool blood and your skill with the sword, you ought easily to be able to vanquish a man blinded by fury."

"Wretch! do you wish that I should be bathed in the blood of this child? No, I am already guilty enough. But what prevents me from leaving Sarcus, from carrying Blanche to a country where Urbain cannot discover her? Yes, tonight even, we will start. We will go to unknown parts. Go immediately and find Germain. The preparations for our departure must be made in the greatest secrecy, and Blanche must not know of them until the last moment; at midnight we will leave the château. By this means I hope to make all traces of Blanche lost to Urbain forever."

"That is a very good idea, monseigneur, but Julia —"

"I shall trouble myself no more about her now, besides, this step will also relieve me from her importunities. Go, run, and order everything for tonight."

Touquet hastened to execute the marquis' orders; it was already late, and there remained only a short time to Villebelle in which to make his preparations for a voyage which he presumed would be of long duration. The more he reflected, the more he approved of his plan. He imagined that Blanche would find, in travelling in strange countries, distractions which would make her soon forget the persons whom she had left in France, and he flattered himself that he would soon see the consummation of all his wishes.

Eleven o'clock struck. The night was fine; everything was in readiness for their start, some fresh and lively horses were harnessed to a travelling carriage. The marquis was still in his apartment, occupied in finishing some letters to his stewards and some intimate friends in Paris. Near him was the barber, to whom he gave his last instructions; charging him in case he should see Urbain again, to advise that young man to forget a woman whom he could never possess; and to enjoy himself with the large fortune which Villebelle had placed at his disposal.

The barber listened quietly to the marquis; his eyes were fixed on the gold and the bills of exchange spread on the desk by the side of a pair of travelling pistols. A few moments later Villebelle was about to tell Marie to go and call Blanche, when the door of the room opened softly. The marquis, surprised that anyone should dare to come into his room so late, raised his eyes and recognized Julia, wrapped in her black mantle.

" This woman again ! " exclaimed Villebelle, while Touquet turned and remained struck with astonishment on perceiving the Italian.

" Calm yourself, seigneur," said Julia, closing the door of the room, " this visit will be the last that I shall make you."

" How did you come here ? What do you want? Speak, hasten to answer me unless you expect me to punish you for your strange conduct."

" I fear nothing, seigneur, it is very little matter what becomes of me after this. I find you here with your confidant, which is just what I wish. Deign to listen attentively to me.   That which I am about to tell you will, I am sure, change all your resolutions, and your departure will not take place."

Julia's singular tone, and her unexpected appearance at so late an hour, inspired Villebelle with curiosity and a secret terror. He signed to the young Italian to speak. The latter seated herself between the marquis and the barber, who waited impatiently for her explanation, and after looking attentively at them for some time with a peculiar expression, she at length began her story.

" It is first necessary, monsieur le marquis, that you should know that I am the daughter of a man named César Perditor, who passed for a sorcerer in the eyes of ignorant people, and whose reputa-

tion became such that he was obliged to quit Paris
to protect himself from death, or, at least, from a
perpetual prison in the dungeons of the Bastile."

"César! I often heard speak of that famous
sorcerer," said the marquis. "Did he not hold
his conferences in a quarry near Gentilly?"

"Yes, seigneur; and there it was that an old
man came to consult him, an old man whose
daughter you had abducted, and whom you had
wounded with your sword — the unfortunate
Delmar."

"Estrelle's father?"

"Exactly, monseigneur. Old Delmar told his
troubles to my father, and begged him to give
him the means to revenge himself upon you; but
despite all his skill César would have had difficulty in satisfying the old man if, while receiving
the confidences of a great part of the noblemen
and of the women of fashion, he had not learned
where your little house was situated, and to what
neighborhood you had taken the young Estrelle.
He told it to the old man, and the latter rescued
his daughter from your hands."

"What? It was her father who took her from
the shelter where I had placed her?" said the
marquis with surprise, and appearing at every
moment more interested in Julia's tale. "And
what became of her?"

"One moment, seigneur, you will learn all if
you will allow me to continue. Old Delmar had

regained his daughter, but you had dishonored her, and the adventure had caused too much stir to allow them to remain in the city that you lived in. He possessed some fortune; he sold everything, realized his property, recompensed my father for the service he had rendered him, and carried Estrelle to the depths of Lorraine, and there she gave birth to her child."

"Good God! she was a mother! can it be possible that Estrelle made me a father? Ah, Julia, in mercy finish."

Julia seemed to enjoy for some moments the marquis' uneasiness, then she resumed her story.

"It was at this time that my father was obliged to escape from Paris in order to avoid arrest, and the report spread that he had perished in a dungeon of the Bastile; but he had amassed sufficient for his subsistence, and leaving his dangerous occupation, he had no thought but to live in peace. I was then in Italy, my birthplace. My father came to seek me, and brought me to France, the climate of which pleased him. Unable to return to Paris, where he would have been recognized, my father settled in the neighborhood of Nancy; there he again saw old Delmar and his sad daughter, secretly bringing up a child of whom she could only call herself the mother with blushes. Later he became acquainted with a poor farmer who had been reduced to poverty by the misconduct of his son, a wretch who, after committing a crime

in the country where he was born, had fled, carrying away from his parents all that they possessed,
and leaving them in the direst poverty."

" The history of this man can have no connection with Estrelle's child," said the marquis, impatiently; "in pity, Julia, finish what you have
to say to me."

" Pardon me, monsieur le marquis, that is more
important than you think, and it is very interesting to your worthy confidant, who has already
recognized his father in the old farmer of whom I
have spoken."

The barber, who had given great attention to
Julia's last words, immediately exclaimed, —

" Oh, was that my father? I was guilty towards
him I confess; love of gold made me commit
many faults, but I always had the intention of
repairing the wrong I had done, and there is still
time for it."

" No, it is too late," said Julia, casting at the
barber a terrible look.

" Is he dead?"

Julia remained silent. The marquis rose abruptly, exclaiming, —

" Well, then, cruel woman, have you amused
yourself sufficiently with my torture? When are
you going to make an end of this?"

" You are both very impatient," said the young
Italian, smiling bitterly; " but there is little more
to tell you. Old Touquet asked my father

whether he had, in his travels, heard his son spoken of. My father could tell him nothing satisfactory. Soon after we went to dwell in a village near Amiens; it was there that I lived up to the age of fifteen years. Then my father died; and I came to Paris, where I went into a shop as a simple workwoman. My father had left me no property except a manuscript containing the most curious adventures of his life, and the secret history of the persons who had consulted him. This is how I learned, monsieur le marquis, of the abduction of poor Estrelle, and it was in examining these notes of my father that I saw in what manner the barber Touquet had acted toward his parents."

"Is that all that you know?" said the marquis. "Have you learned nothing more in regard to Estrelle and her child?"

"A short time ago I did not know anything further, seigneur, but chance has put me in possession of all that you would know, thanks to a visit which I paid to the barber, for it was at his house that I found the clew to the mystery."

"At my house?" said Touquet, looking at Julia in surprise.

"Yes, at your house, in the closet hidden at the back of the alcove in Marguerite's chamber."

Pale and trembling, the barber muttered, —

"You have been in that closet — but there was nothing there; no, I am very certain of it."

" You are mistaken, for in disturbing, by chance, a chest which stood on the floor, I found this portfolio, which probably had been hidden by the person whom you lodged there, who, not knowing how to dispose of these important papers, had deemed it wise to put them in this secret place during the time that he stayed at your house."

The barber looked with terror on the portfolio which Julia had drawn from beneath her cloak, while the marquis exclaimed, —

" Do these papers come from Blanche's father ?"

" They come, in fact, from the person who brought that young girl to the barber's house. Seigneur, read first that one."

Julia gave a paper to Villebelle, who uttered a cry of surprise as he read, —

" Certificate of the birth of Blanche, daughter of Estrelle Delmar."

" O my God ! " said the marquis, breathing with difficulty, " can it be ? "

" Wait, seigneur, do you know Estrelle's writing ? "

" Yes, that is it, I recognize it."

" Read this note."

The marquis took the letter and eagerly read it, —

I feel that I am about to die, but, at least, my father has forgiven me. He had forbidden me to make Blanche's existence known to her father, and, as long as he lived, I respected his orders ; but he is no more, and I am about to follow him to the tomb. Villebelle, Blanche is your daughter, the fruit of our love. Good-by. Love her more than you have loved her mother. I forgive you.

ESTRELLE DELMAR.

"O Blanche, O my daughter!" exclaimed the marquis, abandoning himself by turns to his joy and his remorse, "I am your father and I have made you unhappy."

"Finish this letter, seigneur," said Julia, "there is something there which concerns your confidant."

The marquis saw some lines added by Estrelle's hand and read,—

I have no relations; my daughter will be presented to you by a worthy friend in whom I have every confidence, and who goes to Paris under a fictitious name to try to obtain some information about a son who has dishonored him. I have confided to him the fortune which I have left Blanche; my daughter needs nothing but her father's friendship, but if he repulses her, the old Touquet will take his place.

"Touquet," cried the marquis, looking at the barber.

The latter appeared thunderstruck. He looked at the letter, a cold sweat stood out on his forehead; he could not utter a word.

"Yes," said Julia, "yes, unhappy wretch, it was your father who came to your house with Blanche, whom he was taking to the marquis; he had taken the name of Moranval, no doubt, that he might be more likely to get news of his son in Paris. Perhaps he even knew in whose house he was taking lodgings. Answer, wretch, how did you treat that traveller?"

"Do not question me," said the barber, walking wildly about the room, "I am a monster. Do not come near me; I have murdered my father!"

"And for ten years you have deprived me of my daughter," cried the marquis, starting from Touquet with horror. "You were about to make me the most guilty of men, your horrible counsels were thrusting me to a crime — wait, wretch, and receive the price of all your misdeeds."

The marquis seized one of the pistols which were on the desk and directed it towards Touquet. The shot sped, and Julia looked coldly on, as the barber fell at her feet.

"That death was too kind for you," said the marquis, "but, thanks to Heaven, I have not committed the last crime. O my dear Blanche, you are my daughter; that was the cause of the secret feeling which pled for you. I will make you happy, and you shall forget my unworthy love; henceforth, it is only a father who presses you in his arms."

The marquis left the room followed by Julia. He did not walk, he flew towards the tower inhabited by Blanche. As he approached, his voice, calling Blanche, woke the echoes. They reached the door of the room, which was locked on the inside; the marquis, who had not taken his keys, knocked and reknocked, calling Blanche and begging her to open. Nobody answered, but presently a sound reached the marquis' ears, which seemed to be caused by the fall of some object in the waters of the lake. Villebelle experienced a sensation which he could not define; he ran and called Germain, obtained his keys and entered Blanche's apartment; it was empty, and everything announced that the young girl had not gone to bed; but one of the windows looking on the lake was open. Led by a secret presentiment, the marquis went on to the balcony. His eyes searched the lake, and he called again, —

"Blanche, my daughter."

Nobody answered, but an object showed at intervals on the surface of the lake, and seemed to move.

"It is she," cried Villebelle, and immediately jumped into the lake. It was indeed the unfortunate Blanche, who, since the scene of the preceding night, expecting at every moment some new attempt on the part of the marquis, had not tasted a moment's rest. She had not gone to bed, fearing to be surprised in her sleep, and watched trembling, believing at the slightest noise, that her abductor was about to appear. Blanche had decided to die rather than cease to be worthy of Urbain. On hearing hasty steps approaching her room, and recognizing Villebelle's voice calling her loudly, a most violent terror had seized her; and not doubting but that he had come to accomplish his infamous purpose, she had thrown herself into the lake, pronouncing Urbain's name.

The marquis swam towards the object which he perceived in the water, but another person who had been in the park, had also thrown himself into the lake. It was Urbain, who, certain that his sweetheart was in the château, had profited by the night to introduce himself into the gardens. The young bachelor had heard Blanche's sweet voice uttering his name, then a sudden sound caused him to look towards the lake and he had flown to the help of the unfortunate girl, with whom he had at length reached the brink; where presently he was joined by the marquis, Julia, and the people of the château, attracted by their master's shouts. Blanche was stretched on the grass, while Urbain on his knees beside her called her loudly, when the marquis came running in the greatest despair and threw himself on the ground, supplicating Heaven to give him back his daughter.

" His daughter ? " cried all those around him.

" Yes," said Villebelle, gazing on Blanche's discolored features with despair, " yes, it is my daughter, my child, whom I have made unhappy, whose death I have caused. Ah, I would have given all my fortune to kiss Estrelle's daughter, to hear her call me father, and by my passions, my vices, I am deprived of my greatest treasure. Oh, my dear Blanche, return to life; before death closes your mouth, tell me, at least, that you will forgive me. But no, I shall not have even that last consolation; she is dead without having once called me father."

The marquis threw himself on the body of his daughter, which Urbain watered with his tears; he took Blanche's hands and held them against his heart, seeking to rewarm them, to reanimate them, but all efforts were vain. Blanche could no longer hear her father's cries, nor the sobs of her lover.

www.ingramcontent.com/pod-product-compliance
Lightning Source LLC
Chambersburg PA
CBHW032255020726
47495CB00001B/112